HUNGARIAN
FOLK MUSIC

ENCORE MUSIC EDITIONS

Reprints of outstanding works on music

HUNGARIAN FOLK MUSIC

BELA BARTÓK

TRANSLATED BY

M. D. CALVOCORESSI

HYPERION PRESS, INC.
Westport, Connecticut

Published in 1931 by Oxford University Press, Oxford
Hyperion reprint edition 1979
Library of Congress Catalog Number 78-62328
ISBN 0-88355-722-3
Printed in the United States of America

Library of Congress Cataloging in Publication Data
Bartók, Béla, 1881-1945.
    Hungarian folk music.

    (Core collection reprints)
    Translation of A magyar népdal.
    Reprint of the 1931 ed. published by Oxford Univer-
sity Press, Oxford.
    Bibliography
    1. Folk music, Hungarian—History and criticism.
2. Folk-songs, Hungarain—History and criticism.
I. Calvocoressi, Michel D., 1877-1944.   II. Title.
ML3593.B1613 1979   781.7'439   78-62328
ISBN 0-88355-722-3

CONTENTS

INTRODUCTION

Folk-music and Peasant music.—Materials of the collection of Hungarian Peasant music.—A systematic arrangement of a bigger collection.—General classification of the Hungarian materials.

THE term 'Peasant music' connotes, broadly speaking, all the tunes which endure among the peasant class of any nation, in a more or less wide area and for a more or less long period, and constitute a spontaneous expression of the musical feeling of that class.

From the point of view of folk-lore, we may define the peasant class as follows: it is that part of the population engaged in producing prime requisites and materials, whose need for expression, physical and mental, is more or less satisfied either with forms of expression corresponding to its own tradition, or with forms which, although originating in a higher (urban) culture, have been instinctively altered so as to suit its own outlook and disposition. The indefinite expression 'more or less' is used with reference to the relativity of the very expression, 'peasant class'. For a similar reason, when defining peasant music, the question of area and period was specified but loosely; for the very definition of peasant music is elastic. It must take into account the fact that the area referred to may vary from the smallest conceivable to a very wide one; it refers to a countless series and number of tune-types, ranging from types that can hardly be considered as peasant music proper, if at all, to types that are peasant music in the narrowest sense of the term. As to the question of the origin of the tunes—viz. whether their authorship is known or they were taken from the music of another class, such as the ruling class—our definition waives it aside as non-essential.

It should be admitted that practically every recent European peasant music known to-day arose under the influence of some kind of 'national' or 'popular' art music.

Under the above term come musical products—chiefly single, unaccompanied melodies—from authors who, being musically educated up to a degree, mix in their work the idiosyncrasies of the style of the peasant music of their country with the commonplaces of the higher types of art music.[1]

Very probably the influence of 'popular' art music upon peasant music exerted itself as follows. Let us start by admitting that among the peasant class of a certain country there exists a certain traditional, more or less primitive musical style. This peasant class is in constant contact with more cultured classes, such as, for instance, the town-dwellers (who may be using the same language or another), and also with the peasantry and perhaps the upper classes of the neighbouring countries. Two opposite tendencies

---

[1] Cases in point are most of the Hungarian tunes used by Liszt in his Hungarian Rhapsodies and by Brahms in his Hungarian Dances.

I

assert themselves among peasants: one is to preserve old traditions (which tend to the preservation of old customs) unaltered, and the other is towards imitation. Instinctively, the peasant looks upon the more favourable circumstances of the upper classes as embodying an ideal condition, almost out of his reach; and he endeavours at least to imitate some of the outward signs of this condition. And when this imitative tendency becomes stronger than the conservative instinct, and when contact between the peasant and the idealized upper classes is frequent enough, the peasant—perhaps unintentionally—gets hold of many cultural products of these classes. But, peasant life being, comparatively speaking, self-contained and secluded, these foreign, borrowed elements undergo a certain transformation, so long as they do not constitute mere sporadic outcrops but take firm root among the peasant class, spread, and endure.[1] If we find these changes in one particular element—or, to talk music, in one particular tune—we see that in proportion as the borrowed tune spreads through the country, a number of variants occur, according to the regions in which it is adopted. But if the borrowed tune or fragment of tune is so thoroughly assimilated that it finally becomes distinctly different from what it originally was, and perhaps by then has absorbed certain of the characteristic traits of the traditional style of the regional peasant music, and if the process results in a certain homogeneity, a new, homogeneous style of peasant music crops up: such is the style of recent Hungarian peasant music. In all likelihood, elements of that kind must have contributed in some measure to the formation not only of the more recent, but even of the oldest known styles of peasant music in any country—Hungary not excluded. But the materials needful to prove this point by comparison are not available in sufficient quantity.

Whether peasants are individually capable of inventing quite new tunes is open to doubt. We have no data to go by. And the way in which the peasant's musical instinct asserts itself encourages no such view. Yet peasants—even individually—are not only capable of altering, but strongly inclined to alter, all the musical elements of which they get hold. Alterations of this kind may be considered as the work of the peasant community as a whole. And how very strong the individual instinct for alteration and variation is can be seen by comparing the so-called individual variants of any one tune. Performance by peasants, exactly as performance by a great artist, includes a good deal that is almost extemporization; for instance, the same person, performing the same tune, will at times introduce minor, surface alterations, which do not affect the essential quality of this tune. Repetitions of a tune will usually include slight rhythmic alterations;

[1] I wish to emphasize that these foreign tunes—e.g. 'popular' art tunes—never become peasant music unless peasants resort to them instinctively. Artificially introduced music, such as the patriotic and other songs taught in schools, do not generally serve the purpose of expressing the peasants' instinctive feeling, as occurs with tunes spontaneously adopted.

at times the pitch (or perhaps even the note itself) will be changed. It is admissible that a few of these unessential alterations will in the course of time become permanent. Then other performers may introduce other changes of similar kind; and the last link in this chain may turn out to be altogether different from the first. It is obvious, indeed, that no essential alteration of a musical element can come from one individual peasant. And there can be no doubt that with peasants who people one geographical unit, living close to one another and speaking the same language, this tendency to alter, in consequence of the affinities between the mental disposition of individuals, works in one way, in the same general direction. It is thus that the birth of a homogeneous musical style becomes possible.

Taken in a narrower sense, the term peasant music connotes the totality of the peasant tunes exemplifying one or several more or less homogeneous styles. So that in this narrower sense, peasant music is the outcome of changes wrought by a natural force whose operation is unconscious; it is impulsively created by a community of men who have had no schooling; it is as much a natural product as are the various forms of animal and vegetable life. For this reason, the individuals of which it consists—the single tunes—are so many examples of high artistic perfection. In their small way, they are as perfect as the grandest masterpieces of musical art. They are, indeed, classical models of the way in which a musical idea can be expressed in all its freshness and shapeliness—in short, in the very best possible way, in the briefest possible form and with the simplest of means. On the other hand, the favourite national or popular art songs of the ruling classes contain, besides a few interesting tunes, so many musical common-places, that their value remains far lesser than that of peasant music in the narrower sense of the term.

When a new musical style arises, or is near arising, among a peasant class, and when in this class the conservative instinct lacks strength, the new style gradually obliterates the older style or styles. This is what has happened among Hungarians. If on the contrary the conservative instinct remains active, older and newer styles coexist. This has happened, after a fashion, among the Slovaks.

At times it is, not a popular art music, but the peasant music of some adjoining country, representing a higher degree of culture, that exercises the influence leading to the birth of a new style. Then we encounter either tunes which differ in nowise from their models—as occurs with the old music of the Máramaros Rumanians, whose tunes are exactly similar to the Dumy tunes of the Ukrainians—or a new, very different style of music, such as the new style of the Máramaros Rumanians, which was obviously very much influenced by that of old Hungarian peasant music. It may also occur that a peasant class comes simultaneously under the influence of the peasant music of two neighbouring countries. A case in point is shown by contemporary Slovakian peasant music, in which traces are to be found of a slighter western (German or Czech) current of influence, and a stronger south-eastern current, which originates in recent Hungarian peasant music.

Investigation of musical folk-lore has two objects:

(1) To constitute as rich a collection as possible of peasant tunes, scientifically classified, and principally of the tunes of neighbouring peasant classes that are in close contact with one another.

(2) To determine, by careful comparison, every one of the musical styles recognizable in the above materials, and so far as possible to trace them to their origin.[1]

Hungary, before her dismemberment, was one of the best fields available for an investigation of this kind. There new styles had cropped up and were cropping up even in our own time; so to speak, right in front of our eyes. And there the older styles endured—at certain spots—in a wonderful state of purity. The greater part of the materials came from the music of the Hungarian, Slovak, and Rumanian peasants. The present book deals with Hungarian peasant music, and aims at determining the various styles that stand forth in it, their historical interconnexion, and their relations with the peasant music of Hungary's neighbours.

The Hungarian-speaking zone extends far beyond the frontiers established by the Trianon Treaty. North of the Czechoslovakian political frontier, its boundary is marked, roughly, by the towns of Nyitra, Ipoliság, Kassa, Munkács, and Ungvár. East of the Rumanian political frontier, it extends over Szatmár and Nagyvárad. In Erdély (Transylvania) are the Székély, a population of at least 300,000, a definite linguistic unit connected with Hungary by countless Hungarian-speaking tracts in the direction of Szatmár and Nagyvárad. There are two Hungarian-speaking tracts outside the previous Hungarian frontier in the Bukovina and Moldavia. In the Bukovina are the Bukovinian Csángó's, a Hungarian-speaking tract comprising five villages; and around Bákó (in Rumanian Bacău) are the several villages of the Moldavian Csángó's. In the Banat, in the Bácska, and in Slavonia (now Yugoslavia) are a number of Hungarian villages. We have a wealth of materials from all these localities except the Moldau region.

The whole of the Hungarian-speaking region may be divided into four parts, each characterized by a different musical dialect: I, the Transdanubian region (south and west of the Danube); II, the Northern region (north of the Danube and of the upper Tisza); III, the Tisza region, or region of

[1] This, however, is, as mentioned before, practically impossible with regard to the musical styles which we consider oldest. We cannot determine evolution processes which took place several centuries ago any more satisfactorily than we can answer the question how organic life first cropped up.

4

the great Alföld; and IV, the region of the Erdély musical dialect (the Bukovina belongs to this region). Henceforth we shall refer to each of these regions by means of the corresponding Roman numerals.

Let it be remarked that differences between the musical dialects referred to are perceptible only in the tunes exemplifying the so-called old style. Therefore the division into dialect-regions is valid only so far as these old tunes are concerned.

The following materials will be used for the comparative investigation. Printed collections:

1. Színi, Károly: *A magyar nép dalai és dallamai* (200 *darab*). Pest. Heckenast Gusztáv; first edition 1865, second edition 1872.
2. Bartalus, István: *Magyar népdalok, egyetemes gyűjtemény*. Band I–VII. Budapest, 1873–1896.
3. Kiss, Áron: *Magyar Gyermekjáték-gyűjtemény*. Budapest, 1891. Hornyánszky Viktor.

Színi's collection contains 136 tunes which may be considered as originating from the peasant class. Considering the fact that he was no qualified musician, the recording is very good indeed.

In the seven big volumes of the Bartalus collection, issued in great pomp and burdened with piano accompaniments, are 411 such genuine peasant tunes, plus 32 borrowed from Színi. The recording is far inferior to Színi's, although Bartalus was a 'qualified' musician.

Kiss's collection of children's games is the best of the three. To record those far simpler tunes was, of course, a much easier matter. Out of the many examples which he gives of this particular category of peasant music, 42 may be regarded as other peasant tunes (not children's games).

The other old collections (Mátray, Füredi, &c.) contain an even smaller proportion of useful materials, and may be left aside.

In short, the best three collections published before 1900 provide in all 589 peasant tunes; or, excluding variants, 476—out of which 301 are variants of tunes appearing in more recent manuscript collections.

The new collections, started at the beginning of this century, contain about 7,800 tunes (including variants). They are:

1,492 phonographed tunes [1,2] collected by Béla Vikár (from 1898 to 1910 or thereabouts).

47 phonographed tunes [1,2] collected by Ákos Garay.

About 2,700 tunes, part of which are phonographed [3] and part noted down, collected by Zoltán Kodály (1904–21).

[1] The phonograms belong to the Ethnographical section of the Hungarian National Museum, in Budapest.

[2] Most of the phonograms were noted down by B. Bartók and a few by Z. Kodály.

[3] A small part of the phonograms belong to the Ethnographical section of the Hungarian National Museum; the greater part belong to the collector.

2,721 tunes, part of which are phonographed[1] and part noted down,
collected by Béla Bartók (1904–18).
307 tunes, mostly phonographed,[1] collected by Antal Molnár (1911–12).
348 tunes collected by Mrs. Zoltán Kodály (1917–20).
260 tunes, some phonographed,[2] collected by László Lajtha (1911–14).

A hundred and fifty tunes from these collections, originating from
dialect-region IV, were printed under the title: *Erdélyi Magyarság. Népdalok. Közzéteszik Bartók Béla és Kodály Zoltán. Kiadja a Népies Irodalmi Társaság. Rózsavölgyi & Co.*, Budapest, 1923. These will be referred
to as Sz.N. (Székely Népdalok).

So great an abundance of materials cannot be properly dealt with unless
some kind of system is adopted. For the purpose of *lexically* classifying the
Hungarian, Slovak, and Rumanian tunes, the best system is that of Professor
Ilmari Krohn, the Finnish folk-lorist,[3] slightly modified.

According to the modified system, all the tunes are reduced to a common

final, the most suitable being 𝄞 . Thence the actual classification takes
place as follows:

1. We divide the tunes according to the number of their lines (a tune-line
is that portion of a tune allotted to one line of the text) into two-line, three-
line, and four-line tunes. Certain repetitions of lines in sequence form,
through which some of the tunes appear to consist of five or even six lines,
are not taken into account. Such are the fifth line of tunes No. 235 and
236, and the first and third lines of tunes Nos. 243–245. Tunes containing
such double lines come into the category of four-line tunes.

2. A further classification is based upon the height of the final note of the
various tune-lines: for two-line tunes, the final note of the first line;
for three-line tunes, firstly the final note marking the chief caesura (which
may be at the end either of the first line or of the second); for four-
line tunes, firstly the final note of the second line (chief caesura), then the
final note of the first line, and lastly that of the third line. The order of
the groups and sub-groups thus obtained is determined by the order of the
said final notes from the lowest upwards—e.g. four-line tunes whose chief

caesura is marked by the note 𝄞 come before those in which it is

marked by the note 𝄞 .

---

[1] Most of these phonograms belong to the Ethnographical section of the Hungarian National
Museum, a few to the collector.

[2] The phonograms are the property of the Ethnographical section of the Hungarian National
Museum.

[3] See *Sammelbände der Internationalen Musikgesellschaft*, iv. 4 (1903).

The final notes will be indicated by figures so as to simplify matters, according to the following table:

Notes																	
Figures	I	II	III	IV	V	VI	VII	1	2	3	4	5	6	7	8	9	10	11

accidentals being added when needful: e.g. ♭3 = 🎼 .

The final note of the chief caesura will be marked ☐, that of the previous melodic line ⊓, that of the following ⊔; which means that ⌐♭3⌐ ⌐5⌐ ⌐4⌐ indicates a four-line tune whose first line ends with 🎼, the second

ending with 🎼 , and the third with 🎼 .[1]

3. Further sub-groups are determined by the number of syllables to a tune-line, the order of these sub-groups following that of the numbers (that is, starting from the smallest). These numbers are indicated by small-fount Arab numerals, separated by commas (e.g. for tune No. 117: 12, 10, 10, 12). Double lines are indicated by two numerals between which is the sign + (e.g. for tune No. 244: 7+7, 6, 7+7, 6). If all lines consist of the same number of syllables (that is, if the melodic strophe is isometric), one figure will of course suffice to determine the strophe (e.g. for tunes 1 to 6: 12; for tunes 7 to 32: 8).

4. Finally, the tunes are grouped according to their compass. The lowest and highest note of a tune are indicated by the corresponding figures, joined by a hyphen (e.g. for tune No. 15: VII-8).
Accordingly:

☐4☐ ☐4☐ ☐1☐, 8, 1–8, indicates a four-line tune whose first and second line

end on 🎼 , the third ending on 🎼 . All lines consist of

8 syllables, the lowest note is 🎼 , the highest 🎼 (see tune

No. 22).

☐2☐ ☐V☐, 7, 10, 10, V-5, indicates a three-line tune, in which the chief caesura

occurs at the end of the first line. The first line ends on 🎼 , the

second on 🎼 ; the first line has seven syllables, the second and

[1] Naturally, the fourth line always ends with 🎼 .

7

third have ten. The lowest note is ♮ , the highest is ♮ (see No. 311).

Thus, all coinciding tunes find place near one another; so do most of the variants.

There is hardly an East European nation in whose peasant music several styles do not coexist—old styles more or less well preserved and newer styles (perhaps in course of formation), besides many borrowed and acclimatized foreign elements which have not led to the constitution of a particular, homogeneous style.

At the time when a certain style is in full bloom, a great number of tunes identical in build crop up; each one shows one or several stereotyped features of a certain kind. Among these we find, in the peasant music of the Hungarian country, the frequent adoption of a fixed formula for ending a pattern (or at least before the chief caesura): for instance, [VII] [VII] 8 is characteristic of certain Rumanian regions; [1] [5] [5] 11 is a stereotype in the new style of Hungarian peasant music. An abundance of very similar tunes supplies the decisive proof that we are confronting a fully mature style, and consequently that we are dealing with peasant music in the narrower sense of the term.[1]

Hungarian tunes are extraordinarily rich in different endings to tune-lines. This alone shows that here we have to deal with several styles. But upon closer examination, certain types are seen to recur so frequently as to stand out from the mass; for instance, tunes marked [1] [5] [?] predominate, and tunes marked [?] [3] [?], 8 are fairly numerous.

The next step is to determine, as far as possible, the relative age of the salient types. To this effect, we start by admitting that the primitive may have come into being earlier than the less primitive. Primitivity or complexity refer:

(a) To the melodic structure (the build of the tunes). The various stages of evolution may well be:

(1) Short tunes consisting of one-bar or two-bar motives or of duplex motives forming periods evolved from these single motives. Such are a

[1] When we have to deal with a very great mass of tunes similar in character, it is sometimes difficult to determine whether one is a variant of another or should be considered as independent. One is led to one of two extremes: either to consider all these tunes as forming one group of variants, or to treat them as independent tunes that differ from one another only in a few of their curves. Moreover, there exist styles which depend chiefly upon the variation extempore, in performance, of one single tune. Cases in point are the Dumy tunes of Ukraine and the identical so-called Hora lungă tunes of the Máramaros Rumanians. Cf. *Beiträge zur ukraïnischen Ethnologie*, vols. xiii, xiv, B., Kolessa: *Melodien der ukraïnischen rezitierenden Gesänge* [*Dumy*], Lemberg, 1910, 1913; *Sammelbände für vergleichende Musikwissenschaft*, vol. iv; B. Bartók: *Volksmusik der Rumänen von Maramures*, München, Drei-Masken-Verlag, 1923.

great number of Russian dance tunes, the Rumanian bagpipe dance tunes, the peasant music of the Arabs.[1]

(2) Three-line or four-line tunes in definite, rounded-off form, but lacking any more definite structural architecture (see examples Nos. 1–72).

(3) Four-line tunes in rounded-off form, and characterized by a perceptible architectural plan (e.g. AABA or ABBA, the letters referring to each tune-line, and lines of identical content being indicated by identical letters).

Naturally, there exist transitional types or types which are modified in a certain direction.

(b) To the rhythm.

The various stages of the evolution of rhythm may be conceived thus:

(1) *Tempo giusto* (strict) rhythm[2] consisting chiefly of equal values. It is likely that the earliest music arose in connexion with rhythmical motions of the human body (work, dancing). No complicated rhythmic pattern could evolve out of these primitive elements.

(2) *Parlando-rubato* rhythm. In proportion as tunes gradually became independent of the body's motions, the dance-like rigour of the original terse rhythm relaxed. The rhythm of the tunes was then bound to adapt itself to the rhythm of the words; and performers were enabled to emphasize and prolong single notes. This stage of evolution is illustrated by the old *parlando-rubato* tunes of the Hungarians (see Nos. 1–6 and 19–24), Slovaks, and Rumanians.

(3) *Tempo giusto* rhythm, evolved out of the *parlando-rubato* method of performance. Many rhythmic patterns originating in this *parlando-rubato* method of performance may have become set quantities even in *parlando-rubato* performance. Supposing that a tune of this kind comes to be performed *tempo giusto* (say, for the purpose of dancing), it will naturally retain the complicated rhythmic patterns created by *rubato* performance. And the *tempo giusto* rhythm marking this third stage of evolution will be far more complex than the original *tempo giusto* rhythm, that which characterized the first stage.

(c) Regarding the structure of separate tune-lines (the number of syllables in the corresponding text-lines), it may be posited that short text-lines, generally speaking, came into being at an earlier stage of evolution than longer text-lines; and symmetrically divided lines (e.g. 8 syllables, whose accentuation marks a division into 4+4) occur at a more primitive stage than asymmetrical (e.g. 8 syllables = 3+3+2). Regarding the structure of the strophes, we may consider tunes consisting of isorhythmic or

[1] Cf. Bartók, *Die Volksmusik der Araben von Biskra und Umgebung* (*Zeitschrift für Musikwissenschaft*, Leipzig, 1920, ii, pp. 489 ff.).
[2] In this book *Tempo giusto* is used always in the sense of 'strict (i.e. *non rubato*)' rhythm never in the ordinary sense.

isometric lines as more primitive than those whose lines are heterorhythmic or heterometric.[1]

(*d*) Tunes whose compass is small may be considered as more primitive than tunes with a bigger compass.[2]

(*e*) Various stages of evolution may be recognizable in the scales of the tunes. An incomplete (e.g. pentatonic) scale is more primitive than a complete, heptatonic scale; and this in turn is more primitive than a scale comprising chromatic degrees.

(*f*) Lastly, it is possible to determine the stage of evolution by examining whether the tunes of a period (considered at the time when a style is in full bloom) may be divided into several categories or not. Probably, only one category of tunes existed at the outset. At a later stage, extraneous influences begin to assert themselves, and lead to the formation of distinct categories of tunes to be used on special opportunities (e.g. marriage songs, death songs, &c.). These extraneous influences would affect, first and foremost, all music-making connected with religious ceremonies. In Eastern Europe, changes of this kind took place as an inevitable consequence of the introduction of Christianity. Afterwards—and much later—dance music came under various foreign influences, probably in conjunction with the introduction of foreign (e.g. urban) dances. The tunes originally used on every occasion, and characterized by their homogeneous style, were at this second stage preserved only in the actual songs in use for the purposes of singing only, not with reference to any special occasion; also, perhaps, in a few of the dance songs.

To-day, this second stage is most clearly observable in Rumania, where besides the primitive style of tunes associated with no special occasions there exist very different, sharply differentiated categories of Christmas songs (Colinde), Marriage, Death, and Dance Songs.

In the primitive stage remains, for instance, the peasant music of the Arabs of the Biskra region. There we observe one style only, to which belong songs associated with no special occasion, dance tunes, and part of the religious music alike.[3]

The third stage of evolution is almost to be considered as a step backwards. The peasantry of many East European countries have in the course of time, and under the influence of urban culture, given up their old customs and the corresponding ceremonies. With the disappearance of these ceremonies, any category of music associated with them became superfluous. Therefore the new style of Hungarian peasant music com-

[1] isorhythmic = in even rhythm, heterorhythmic = in uneven rhythm; isometric = in even metre (even number of syllables), heterometric = in uneven metre (odd number of syllables).

[2] Points (*c*) and (*d*) do not always apply; when trying to determine the relative age of tunes points (*a*) and (*b*) should be considered first.

[3] See p. 9, footnote 1.

prises one category only, whose tunes (all *tempo giusto*) are used for dancing as well as for singing, without reference to any special occasion.

So that we may divide the whole of the available Hungarian peasant music into three main groups:

A. Tunes in the old style.
B. Tunes in the new style.
C. Tunes that belong to neither style, and represent a mixed (heterogeneous) style.

A. THE OLD STYLE OF HUNGARIAN PEASANT MUSIC

THE Rumanian peasants of certain isolated regions (such as the districts of Bihar and Hunyad) remain practically untouched by West European (urban) culture and have preserved to the present day a method of music-making which is, if not altogether primitive, at least very old. The collector coming into such regions feels as if he had stepped right into the Middle Ages. There is absolutely no possibility of revolutionary changes having occurred in the peasant music of these regions through any intrusion of foreign elements: the peasants live in thorough seclusion, out of reach of the questionable blessings of urban culture. Their cultural level is such as to make it certain that for a very long time no kind of musical evolution can have taken place among them. They are, with hardly an exception, illiterate; their decorative art is primitive, unaffected by factory products; they manufacture their own clothing and hardly ever leave their small native homeland.

The treasure of their tunes may easily be divided into the above-mentioned, sharply differentiated categories, among which the most important is, in this instance, that of the non-occasional tunes, of actual songs pure and simple. The question arises whether a similar position did not obtain among neighbouring people in olden times, so long as their cultural level remained equally low.

And in point of fact, we find in the treasure of Hungarian tunes a fairly large number of examples which are analogous to the above-mentioned non-occasional Rumanian tunes from the points of view of both their antiquity and the part they play in peasant life. These are remains, fortunately preserved up to our time, of a style whose colour is antique, and which nowadays is gradually sinking into oblivion.

We also find—in small numbers—tunes associated with special occasions (ceremonies), whose character is likewise antique, and which tend to disappear. We may suppose that in older times Hungarian peasant music consisted solely of these and other similar elements, and comprised categories as sharply differentiated as Rumanian peasant music still comprises to-day. These categories were, in all likelihood, the following:

(*a*) Tunes of actual songs pure and simple, associated with no special occasions (to lyrical or ballad texts), and dance tunes related to these (and sung to texts referring to the dance, generally in a jocular spirit).

(*b*) Marriage songs.

(*c*) Dirges.

(*d*) Harvest songs.

(*e*) 'Match-making' songs.[1]

(*f*) The so-called *Regös* songs and the children's game-songs (rounds) connected with these.[2]

When describing the old style, we shall refer to category (*a*) only, whose content is most definitely characteristic of this style. The marriage and harvest songs, which are of foreign origin, belong to Class *C*; so do most of the 'match-making' songs.[3] We give no description of the Laments, because Zoltán Kodály has dealt with this type thoroughly in his *Magyar Siratok* (Hungarian Dirges) published by Rózsavölgyi & Co., Budapest. The Regös and children's game-songs, which greatly differ in character from all the other peasant tunes, call for special treatment.[4]

TUNES OF SONGS PROPER (i. e. non-occasional) AND OF DANCE SONGS
IN THE OLD STYLE

The old-style *parlando-rubato* tunes associated with no special occasion resemble, in certain outward features, the corresponding *parlando-rubato* tunes of Rumania.

The old-style dance tunes seem to be *parlando-rubato* tunes which have hardened to *tempo giusto*. This point will be dealt with further.

The description of the songs coming under the present heading should be prefaced by a few remarks on the prosody of Hungarian folk-poetry.

As is well known, the main accent of all Hungarian words is on the first syllable. Each line of the text, therefore, begins with an accent. Upbeats and rhythmic progressions are foreign to Hungarian tunes.[5]

But, as Kodály points out in his essay on 'The Pentatonic Scale in Hungarian Peasant Music' (in the periodical, *Zenei Szemle*, i, 1917, Temesvár): 'the "propping-up", by means of an up-beat, of the opening of a tune-line

[1] The text of these songs names a girl and a boy whom the villages know to be, or suspect of being, in love with one another. The commonplaces of the text—viz. jocular allusions to amorous relations—are invariable: only the names of the pair are inserted (see text of examples 9, 85, 152, 175, 199, 230, 249, 256, 262, 265, 267, 298, 300, 308, 311, 314, and 319). Should these songs be sung without any person being named in them (which in actual fact never happens), the names would be replaced by the words 'this boy' and 'this girl'.

[2] On the Regös songs see Julius Sebestyén, *Regösénekek*. Magyar Népköltési Gyűjtemény, iv; Budapest, 1902 (with 28 tunes).

[3] A small proportion of the 'match-making' songs are sung nowadays to tunes in the new style; these therefore belong to Class *B* (No. 83). One (No. 9) was sung to a tune belonging to Class *A*.

[4] Let it be mentioned here that the Hungarian game-songs are altogether similar in character to those of Slovakia and of Western Europe. On the other hand, this type is not to be found in Rumania.

[5] The same applies to the tunes of the Czechs and Slovaks; their language obeys the same law of accentuation, and the structure of their song texts is likewise founded upon the accent. The structure of the lines in Rumanian peasant poems is similar; but this cannot be accounted for by the accentuation laws of the Rumanian language.

13

appears to be a psychological necessity'.[1] Therefore the older method of performance often was to introduce each line of the text with an interjection consisting of one syllable (such as hey, ey, i, ə) or more, sometimes of a hummed consonant (m, ñ, hñ, &c.) which is no integrant part of the text. The note or notes to which these insertions are sung play the part of up-beats, which in turn are no integrant parts of the tune. (We find up-beats of this order in the older Slovakian tunes, and more often in the Rumanian method of performance.) Cases in point are the notes before the third line in example 2, the first and third in example 3, the second and third in example 4, &c.

I. Tunes to text-lines of 8 or 12 syllables.

Rhythm and tune-strophe. The tune-strophe consists of four isometric lines. In the great majority of cases, viz. in about 70 of the tunes,[2] the lines consist of 8 syllables (see Nos. 7–32). There are seven or eight instances in all of tune-strophes whose lines consist of 12 syllables (see Nos. 1–6). Each line of the latter order may be reduced to the rhythmic schema

♪ ♪ ♪ ♪ ♪ ♪ | ♪ ♪ ♪ ♪ ♪ ♪ | ,

and each line of the former to

♪ ♪ ♪ ♪ | ♪ ♪ ♪ ♪ | .

All the twelve-syllable examples are performed *parlando-rubato*; so are most of the eight-syllable.

In *parlando-rubato* performance the quavers of the original schema are often lengthened or shortened, reasonably and at times unreasonably. This method of performance frequently has all the characters of extemporization. In some of the tunes, part of the alterations of values have become permanently fixed and are by now part and parcel of the tune. They are to be considered, perhaps, as hardened forms of *rubato* (see Nos. 7 a, 8).

Such changes affect firstly, in eight-syllable strophes, the last, or last two (sometimes the last four), syllables of the tune-line. Indeed,

> the first and third tune-lines often end in ♪ ♩. or even ♩ ♩ (Nos. 10, 20, 22);

in the endings of the second and especially of the fourth lines an idiomatic musical feature is to be noticed: an ending in ♩ ♪ ♪ ♩ (more rarely ♩ ♩ ♩) or in ♪ ♩. ♫ ♩ | is characteristic of regions I, II, and III (see Nos. 10, 15, 24, 27, 29); in region IV the second line often ends in ♩ ♩ ♩, the fourth almost uniformly in ♪ ♩. or ♩ ♩ (see Nos. 12, 14, 16, 17, 19, &c.).

[1] Cf. Vincent d'Indy's assertion (in his *Traité de Composition*): 'Toute mélodie commence par une anacrouse exprimée ou sous-entendue.'—*Translator's note.*

[2] Henceforth, when figures of this kind are given, no account will be taken of variants. Let it be noted that of widespread tunes often over fifteen or twenty variants occur.

The beginning of the original line-rhythm is less frequently altered; that of the first line hardly ever. Sometimes that of the second and third lines is altered (in No. 31 it is ♩· ♪). Often—and especially in region IV, the first bar of the tune is sung in fairly quick tempo; but with the second and third bars the tempo gradually reverts to the normal (Nos. 4, 22). In regions I, II, and III the original rhythm of the middle part of lines is less frequently altered—a most characteristic rhythm of this region occurs in Nos. 24 and 32; in region IV, on the contrary, alterations are so many and so varied that they can be reduced to no schema.

In the few available twelve-syllable strophes, extension of values usually occurs only at the ending of lines: ♪ ♩· (𝄽) or ♩ ♩ 𝄽 (No. 3), but at times at the end of the first half:

♫♫ ♪ ♩· | ♫♫ ♪ ♩· 𝄽 ‖ or ♫♫ ♩ ♩ | ♫♫ ♩ ♩ 𝄽 ‖

But then—and probably in order to avoid tedious uniformity—this extension will be omitted from the middle of the third (or the fourth) line (No. 2). The first syllable of the first line is never lengthened; that of the third or fourth sometimes is, that of the second less frequently. There are hardly any other extensions in the twelve-syllable strophe. Apart from the above-mentioned alterations, the rhythm of the lines is almost that of a monotonous recitation.

It should be emphasized that the changes of value (as well in the eight- or twelve-syllable *parlando-rubato* tunes as in the six- and eleven-syllable tunes of similar order which will be referred to later) do not depend upon the length, natural or positional, of the syllables sung. This at least is what all investigations and experiments seem to prove. Certain tunes have been phonographed several times, sung by the same singer to the same text— when it occurred that at the same place and upon – ◡ syllables the tune would be sung sometimes ♩· ♪ and sometimes ♪ ♩· Yet one finds many cases of, for instance, a ◡ ◡ group of syllables being given shortened note values. In our own opinion, such attempts towards an adjustment of the tune to the rhythm of the text should be ascribed to the influence of the newer style—a style among whose idiosyncrasies we find the so-called 'adjustable' *tempo giusto* rhythm which will be referred to in due course.

The eight-syllable *parlando-rubato* tunes of region IV, very varied in their rhythm, are mostly very rich in ornaments (not so the twelve-syllable). But neither the ornamentation nor the alterations of rhythm are constant quantities: whenever a tune is repeated—be it by the same singer—they may change, at times quite considerably.

Evidently the old style is dying out. Only the older peasants know the tunes that stand for it; and when they know them, they are reluctant to sing them because the younger generations, the abettors of the new style,

15

deride all that is 'old-fashioned'. Possibly the vacillations of rhythm-forms and ornamentation which we notice came as a first sign of decline. This may be inferred from the fact that in the *parlando-rubato* tunes of the Wallachs, which are as rich in ornaments and may be observed at the full of their vitality, the alterations of rhythm-schemas and the ornamentation are constant enough to ensure, e.g., that when several people sing together, rhythm and ornamentation coincide exactly for every strophe.

Another probable sign of decline is the striking scarcity of ornaments in the old tunes of regions I, II, and III.[1] The Székely of region IV, owing to their geographical position, were naturally better enabled to preserve the old tradition of highly ornamented singing.

Before describing the rhythm of the old dance tunes, it must be pointed out that it is fairly difficult to determine whether every tune which is in *tempo giusto* rhythm, but otherwise similar in character to the *parlando-rubato* tunes in the old style, is a dance tune or not. Not a single trace of the old dances themselves remained at the beginning of this century: so that the question cannot be answered except on the strength of indications contained in the texts. And very few of the *tempo giusto* tunes have texts referring to dancing (so-called 'dance words'),[2] or a text of any kind showing with certainty that the tunes were used solely for the purpose of dancing. So that I shall draw no hard and fast line, but generally describe the rhythm of the *tempo giusto* tunes without raising the question whether they are dance tunes or not. Except in rhythm, they do not differ from the *parlando-rubato* tunes: so that when dealing with scales and structure, I shall make no special reference to them.

Since the structure of the old *tempo giusto* tunes is identical to that of the *parlando-rubato* tunes, we may infer either that the former are the original *tempo giusto* form (in uniform rhythm) of the latter (first stage of the evolution of rhythm, see p. 8) or that they are forms, hardened into *tempo giusto*, of original *parlando-rubato* tunes (third stage of the evolution of rhythm). Unfortunately we have no palpable clue to either effect; so that we must rest content with the mere hypothesis.

As mentioned before, there is no example of old twelve-syllable tunes *tempo giusto*.

Of the eight-syllable tunes, about 23 are in *tempo giusto* rhythm, the following schemata occurring:

[1] Exceptionally (and the few exceptions are provided by very old folk) we encounter among these examples of richer ornamentation (see No. 40).

[2] By 'dance words' we mean texts—consisting for the most part of one strophe only—whose content humorously, jocularly, or ironically refers to the various aspects and consequences of merry-making, and which are either sung to the dance tune or recited in dance rhythm at the time of dancing.

(a) Isorhythmic tune-strophes (tune-lines in similar rhythm).

1. $\frac{2}{4}$ ♩♩♩♩ ┆ ♩♩♩♩ ‖ (even quavers in strict rhythm).—Two examples.

2. $\frac{4}{4}$ ♩ ♩ ♩ ♩ ┆ ♩ ♩ ♩ ♩ ‖ (the same as the first, but the tempo only half as fast).—Two examples.

3. The same, but in so-called 'adjustable' *tempo giusto* (see pp. 28–9).— Eight examples (No. 28, Sz.N. 21, 29).

4. $\frac{2}{4}$ ♩♩♩♩ ┆ ♩ ♩ ┆ ♩ ♩ ‖ —Five examples (Nos. 11, 13).

5. $\frac{2}{4}$ ⎰ ♩ ♩ ┆ ♩ ♩ ┆ ♩♩ ♩ ┆ ♩ ‖ —Two examples (No. 25).
   ossia ⎱ ♩. ♪ ┆

6. $\frac{2}{4}$ ♩♩♩♩ ┆ ♩♩ ♩ ┆ ♩ ‖ —Two examples (Sz.N. 109).

7. $\frac{4}{4}$ ♩♩♩♩ ♪ ♩. ┆ ♩ ♩ ‖ —One example (No. 30).

(β) Heterorhythmic tune-strophes (tune-lines in dissimilar rhythm).

Only two forms of these are known; they are illustrated in examples 9 and 18.

As seen, types (a) 3 and (a) 4 are the most frequent. Rhythm (a) 4 occurs also, in the Slovakian fund, in the tunes borrowed from Hungary. In the same fund, (a) 2, (a) 6, and possibly (a) 5 also occur (in tunes which are not pentatonic in structure).

We shall deal more fully with the 'adjustable' *tempo giusto* rhythm when describing the old heptasyllabic tunes (p. 28).

As regards heterorhythmic forms, we may posit that they originate in the similar rhythm-forms present in far greater number in Class *C*.

Tempo giusto tunes, even in region IV, are very sparely ornamented— often, indeed, not at all.

Scales and compass. The scale of tunes in the old style may be derived from the following semitoneless pentatonic scale:

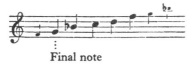

Final note

The importance of pentatony in Hungarian peasantmusic was first acknowledged by Kodály. He dealt with the point at length in his afore-mentioned work,[1] making it clear that three forms of pentatonic scale are preserved in old Hungarian tunes:

(1) The pure pentatonic scale (Nos. 2, 3, 15 [variant 1], 59, 302).

(2) The pentatonic scale in which the second and sixth degree of the

---

[1] See p. 13 *supra*.

diatonic scale occur, but as secondary, ornamental notes only (Nos. 7 *b*, 12, 19, 21, 26, 38, 60, 64, 244).

(3) In certain tunes, whose pentatonic base is recognizable, these second and sixth degrees occur as real notes to which a separate syllable is sung (these notes generally occur on a weak beat, never at the end of a tune-line) (Nos. 1, 4, 6, 10, 16, 17, 18, 29, 32, &c.).

In cases 2 and 3 the second degree will usually be *a'* or *ab'*, the sixth *e"* or *eb"*, so that the original pentatonic scale becomes Dorian, Aeolian, or Phrygian.[1]

Another kind of alteration of the pentatonic scale crops up now and then, which is characteristic of Dialect-region I: it is the sharpening of the 3rd degree, or of both the 3rd and the 7th. At times this sharpening is lesser than a semitone, and the result is a neutral third or sixth[2] (as in examples 15, 74 *a*, 261); at other times it is a full semitone, so that the outcome is a kind of major or mixolydian scale.[3] But even then the pentatonic structure remains so obvious that the origin of all such scales is unmistakable (Nos. 7 *b*, 33 *c*, 40, 56, 74 *b*, 244; No. 9 from Dialect-region III stands alone of its kind). The major-like scale evolved from the pentatonic differs from the true major scale in several respects: one is that its 5th degree lacks the harmonic character of a dominant.

Pentatonic structure also reveals itself in the so-called pentatonic turns of the melodic line. Thus, when parts of a tune revolve around the degrees

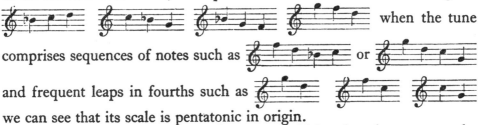

when the tune comprises sequences of notes such as or and frequent leaps in fourths such as we can see that its scale is pentatonic in origin.

When no such feature occurs in a tune which otherwise seems to be ancient, or when the last notes of the tune-lines are the second or sixth degree (namely, the degrees which the pentatonic scale does not comprise), then the tune belongs not to the old style but to Class *C*.

The compass of the tunes may be VII–7, VII–8, VII–9; 1–7, 1–8, 1–9; comparatively rarer are VII–5, 1–5, and 1–b10.

Melodic structure (form). We shall consider melodic structure from two points of view: (1) according to the final notes of the tune-lines; (2) according

---

[1] The fourth possible combination, a scale with *ab'* and *e"*, never occurs.

[2] When peasants perform, it occurs fairly often that certain degrees—chiefly the 3rd and 7th, but now and then the 2nd and 6th too—are intoned unsteadily This may be observed in Rumania as well.

[3] The third or seventh is sometimes raised and lowered in the course of one tune.

to the relative contents of tune-lines (i.e. according to whether the contents of the lines are all different, or whether two or more of them are of similar content).

The most important final note is that of the 2nd line, the chief caesura, which divides the tune into two equivalent parts completing one another: into question and answer, so to speak. In eight-syllable and twelve-syllable tunes in the old style, this note is generally ⌊♭3⌋ (that is, ♭•). This is the case in 30 eight-syllable tunes (Nos. 12–21) and 4 twelve-syllable (Nos. 1–3).

The end note of the first line is usually ⌈5⌉ (twelve examples out of the 34),

    seldom ⌈4⌉ or ⌈7⌉,
    more seldom ⌈♭3⌉, ⌈1⌉, ⌈8⌉, or ⌈VII⌉.

The end note of the 3rd line is usually ⌊♭3⌋ (eleven examples),

    seldom ⌊1⌋,
    more seldom ⌊4⌋, ⌊VII⌋, ⌊7⌋, ⌈5⌉.

The most frequent type of tune (seven examples) is that in which the 1st, 2nd, and 3rd tune-lines end in ⌈5⌉, ⌊♭3⌋ ⌊♭3⌋ respectively (No. 17); so that this should be considered as the prototype of old eight- and twelve-syllable tunes.

Geographical distribution of tunes whose chief caesura is ⌊♭3⌋:

    29 from Dialect-region IV.
    2 from Dialect-regions I, II, III.
    3 from Dialect-regions I–IV.

As can be seen, the end notes of the first and third lines, being the least important supports of the tune, are subject to certain vacillations (even within one group of variants). But it occurs that even the main support of a tune, the chief caesura, which probably at first was invariably ⌊♭3⌋, is in many tunes or groups of variants shifted, for certain reasons, from its original place. Then it generally finds place at ⌈1⌉. We have 17 eight-syllable tunes in which this occurs (Nos. 7–11).

In 4 out of these 17, the end note of the first line is ⌈1⌉;
    less often we find ⌈4⌉, ⌈5⌉, ⌈7⌉, ⌈8⌉, and ⌊♭3⌋.
In 5 the end note of the fourth line is ⌊♭3⌋;
    less often we find ⌊1⌋, ⌊5⌋, ⌊VII⌋, and ⌊4⌋.

Geographical distribution:

    10 from Dialect-regions I, II, III.
    3 from Dialect-region IV.
    4 from Dialect-regions I–IV.

Of tunes whose chief caesura is [5] we have 15 eight-syllable examples (Nos. 24–32) and 1 twelve-syllable (No. 6).

In four of these the end note of the first line is ⌐7¬;
  less often we find ⌐♭3¬, ⌐4¬, ⌐5¬, ⌐8¬, ⌐1¬.
In seven the end note of the fourth line is ⌊♭3⌋;
  less often we find ⌊4⌋, ⌊1⌋, ⌊5⌋, ⌊7⌋, and ⌊VII⌋.
The structure characterized by ⌐7¬ [5] ⌊♭3⌋ is the most frequent (Nos. 29, 30).

Geographical distribution:
  14 from Dialect-regions I, II, III.
  3 from Dialect-region IV.
  3 from Dialect-regions I–IV.

The chief caesura [4] is to be found only in 7 eight-syllable tunes (Nos. 22, 23) and 1 twelve-syllable (No. 4).

  4 of these are from Dialect-region IV.
  1 of these is from Dialect-regions I, II, III.
  3 of these are from Dialect-regions I–IV.

Lastly, we have four tunes whose chief caesura is [VII] ; all four are from Dialect-region IV. These undoubtedly come from the Rumanian fund, in which they are represented in many variants, and in which many other tunes with the same chief caesura are to be found. It is only in the projected book on Rumanian folk-music that it will be possible to deal thoroughly with these tunes.

Although it is a fact that most tunes with the chief caesura [♭3] come from Dialect-region IV—as indeed the greater number of tunes in the old style—we must beware of the false inference that this caesura is characteristic of the said region only. Owing to their geographical position, the Székely preserved the remnants of the old style far better: thence it becomes possible to explain the striking number of such tunes in their region. It is very likely that of old, such tunes were as strongly represented in all other regions inhabited by Hungarians, and that various differentiations in musical dialect cropped up far later, through various displacements of the chief caesura. Indeed, the removal of this chief caesura to [1] is characteristic of Dialect-regions I, II, III (and most especially of district I); and the removal to [5] of Dialect-region III.

It should be added that removals of the chief caesura to another degree (generally the next) occur even within one group of variants; e.g. a ⌐4¬ [♭3] ⌊4⌋, 8, VII–8 tune (No. 15) has variants in which the chief caesura is [1]. In other groups of variants the original [5] is sometimes altered to [♭3] (No. 67); or the reverse may happen (No. 60).[1]

[1] One or two tunes suggest the suspicion that even the most important note, and the note

To a certain extent the melodic line depends upon the position of the cadence-notes. A beginning on the 7th or 8th degree (at times thus: ♪), or, more generally, a note belonging to the higher part of the octave (from ♭3 to 8), is characteristic of the old style. In most tunes whose chief caesura is [♭3], [4] or [5], this high position is maintained in the first, second, and third lines, whereas in the fourth line the melody falls from 5 to 1 (in the [1] tunes of Dialect-regions I, II, and III, the fall naturally occurs at the end of the second line; and it occurs at the end of the first line in [1] tunes. But even then the beginning on the 8th (or 7th) degree remains characteristic of the first line and often of the second line too.

Comparing the contents of all four tune-lines, we obtain the following schemata (see p. 9 for explanation of capital letters):

Schema ABCD occurs in 3 twelve-syllable and 30 eight-syllable tunes (Nos. 14, 15, 20, 23, &c.).

Schema ABBC in 1 twelve-syllable and 18 eight-syllable tunes (Nos. 10, 12, 26, 27, 30).

Of AABC we have 9 instances (Nos. 7, 8, 28).

Of A^5B^5AB 4 (Nos. 21, 24, 32).

    (A^5 is higher by a fifth than A.)

Of ABCB 5 (No. 11; Sz.N. 26).

Of $AABB_v$ 1 (Bartalus, iv, No. 43).

    (B_v = B with a slight deflexion at the end.)

Of AA_vBB_v 2 (Nos. 18, 25).

Of $ABCC_v$ 1 (Kiss, p. 67).

So that there is an enormous preponderance of the non-architectonic structures ABCD and ABBC, the former consisting of lines which differ from one another, and the latter of lines of which only the second and third are similar in contents. A striking fact is that the schemata ABCD, ABBC, A^5B^5AB occur chiefly in *parlando-rubato* tunes, the others almost exclusively in *tempo giusto* tunes. The structure ABCD is frequent in tunes belonging

---

least subject to alterations, the final note, did not remain unaltered. If we lower the final note of No. 5 by a degree (making it ♪) without altering any other of its notes, we have a [5] [4] [♭3] tune, which might well be taken for a variant of No. 4. Perhaps this is the actual origin of the tune. Possibly its original final note was raised by a degree, as occurred with another tune belonging to Class *C*, a [4] [♭3] [♭2] tune in the Phrygian scale. Tune Sz.N. 123 suggests a similar hypothesis. It seems as if its final note had been lowered by one degree. If we raise it by a degree, we have a [4] [♭3] [VII] tune, very closely related to Nos. 17 and 19. For this reason I ascribed these two tunes to the old style—otherwise they should go into Class *C*.

to Class *C*—a fact which may be ascribed to the influence of the old style. On the other hand, in Class *C* the structure ABBC is hardly to be encountered. In the other sub-groups of the old style it is very scarce: so that it may be considered as characteristic of the old, eight-syllable *parlando-rubato* tunes.

A^5B^5AB is a remarkable structure, particularly characteristic of Hungarian peasant music. Here the first and second lines are similar to the third and fourth respectively, but a fifth higher. Hence they are to be figured $\boxed{7}$ $\boxed{5}$ $\boxed{\flat 3}$, $\boxed{8}$ $\boxed{5}$ $\boxed{4}$, or $\boxed{9}$ $\boxed{5}$ $\boxed{5}$, more seldom $\boxed{4}$ $\boxed{5}$ $\boxed{\text{VII}}$. The fifth possible combination, $\boxed{5}$ $\boxed{5}$ $\boxed{1}$, does not occur. (In No. 21 the original $\boxed{5}$ slid down to $\boxed{\flat 3}$ under the influence of the numerous songs of region IV whose chief caesura is $\boxed{\flat 3}$. There are even several instances of the main caesura brought down from the original $\boxed{5}$ to $\boxed{1}$—as in examples 71 *a* and 302.)

Closely connected with A^5B^5AB is the form $A^5A^5{}_vAA_v$. Here the first two lines, being similar except for a difference in the cadence, constitute a period—which the third and fourth lines repeat a fifth lower (Nos. 67, 71 *a*, 74 *a*, 302). For the purpose of simplification, both these forms are given as A^5B^5AB in our statistics. Both occur in all sub-classes, but are comparatively infrequent.[1] In the tunes belonging to Class *C* are to be encountered rhythmically modified (heterometric) forms of structure A^5B^5AB. These appear also in materials from Slovakia, both in tunes originally borrowed from Hungary and in native tunes. But this may be held to be a specifically Hungarian structure, especially in its isometric pentatonic form (see further under Class *C*, pp. 67–8).

In structure AA_vBB_v, AA_v and BB_v form one period each. This structure is very scarce in old-style tunes, but is one of the structures characteristic

---

[1] And this shows in an interesting way that even a rare occurrence may under certain conditions be characteristic. I dare not devote more than a footnote to the bold hypothesis that A^5B^5AB, or perhaps the even simpler $AA^5{}_vAA_v$, may have been the initial structural scheme of Hungarian peasant tunes, out of which the less old and more complicated ABCD may have sprung. One may imagine the process thus: in the beginning there existed only two-line tunes, whose structure was either AA_v or AB. For some reason or other, these developed into four-line tunes, the whole original structure being repeated a fifth lower. This might have originated in the performance of tunes on some two-stringed instrument tuned in fifths, or upon a fairly long flute, whereby the transposition would have been effected mechanically either by passing from one string to the other or by increasing or decreasing the strength of the blowing It is surely remarkable that in most ABCD tunes the AB lines should occupy the higher region of the octave, exactly as A^5B^5 lines do: in other words, that the striking downward tendency of A^5B^5AB tunes should be noticeable also in ABCD tunes. This descending direction is in itself characteristic of old-style tunes, as shown by the descriptions given here of their melodic lines. It is equally remarkable that these tunes sometimes show variations from the structure A^5B^5AB which come nearer to the structure ABCD (Nos. 71 *a* and 71 *b*) and conversely. At times a strongly modified structure A^5B^5AB may be conjectured beneath a structure ABCD (Nos. 27, 29, 30, 54, 57).

In the pentatonic tunes of the Tcheremissians a peculiar structure is to be found, which, however, corresponds in all essentials to this structure A^5B^5AB. See musical examples I–III in the Appendix and the remarks accompanying these.

of the new style of the Máramaros Rumanians. Hence it is legitimate to infer that the one or two known examples of it available in the Székely region penetrated there from Máramaros, so that they actually should belong to Class C. However, example 25 was placed among old-style tunes on account of its almost pure pentatonism.[1]

Although a certain symmetry can be observed in structures A^5B^5AB, AA_vBB_v, and $AABB_v$, they are not really architectonic structures; for the latter structures depend upon architectonic co-ordination which arises only when the first and fourth lines correspond.

Yet it is not impossible that the germs of the architectonic structure of the new style (Class B) are to be sought in the forms A^5B^5AB and even perhaps $ABBC$ of the old style, although one can point to no evolution from the one to the other.

The isometric twelve- and eight-syllable tunes in the pentatonic system which have just been described are the most characteristic examples available of the old style. They are the oldest known materials of Hungarian peasant music, not to be found among any other races—even neighbouring races—except as obvious imports.

Proofs of antiquity are:

The pentatonic system;

The more primitive structure, rounded off but not constituting architectonic form;

Isometry of tune-lines;

And the fact that the tunes played in old Hungarian peasant music a part similar to that played in Rumanian peasant music by eight-syllable *parlando-rubato* tunes.

(Less weighty, yet worthy of mention, is the fact that the texts of these tunes, especially in region IV, show unmistakable signs of antiquity both philologically and by virtue of their subject-matter.)

It is difficult to determine which are the older: the twelve-syllable tunes or the eight-syllable. For although the latter's organization is more primitive, the former have probably retained their pentatonism more nearly intact.

The question of origin is altogether obscure. One thing we can ascertain, and that is, that the tunes did not originate in the peasant music of neighbouring countries. Nothing similar is to be found in the peasant music of the South Slavs, of the Germans, or of the Slovaks (with the exception of a few tunes in *tempo giusto* already mentioned, such as No. 11 *a*). Yet when we start comparison with Rumanian materials, the question becomes rather more difficult; for then we encounter many tunes whose structure

[1] The same structure occurs in example 196, which is placed in Class C, and originated in Máramaros.

is similar to that of Hungarian tunes—there even exist a few tunes which crop up both in the Rumanian corpus and the Hungarian. The point cannot be investigated fully except in the projected book on Rumanian folk-music already mentioned. Here I shall content myself with the following brief indications:

Rumanian peasant music, in the region of old Hungary, determines, from the point of view of musical dialect, two distinct regions, each of which has music so sharply differentiated that we seem to have to deal with the music of two unconnected, and not even adjoining, races. On the other hand, the old Hungarian style remains entirely homogeneous throughout far more distant regions populated by Hungarians up to West Hungary; only slight shades of differentiation occurring in each separate musical dialect of this wide region.[1]

Four or five of old Hungarian [b3] and [5] tunes are sung, in almost exactly the same form, in the Rumanian region that lies in closest propinquity to that of the Székely, and especially among the polyglot population of Mezöség: such are Nos. 16, 21, and 26.[2] And in the same region crop up a few songs, not quite exactly corresponding to these, but similar in structure. But in the Rumanian regions bordering upon the Hungarian Dialect-regions II and III we encounter no offshoots of the old Hungarian style, not even the faintest trace of an influence exercised by this style. And of course there is no reason to assume that the small Rumanian zones in the immediate neighbourhood of the Székely country might have exercised the slightest influence upon the Erdély region and the compact Great Hungarian region (including West Hungary, where music is cognate)—to which end the wide Rumanian ring, characterized by music of an entirely different kind, would have had to be traversed first. Moreover, let us remember that in the old Hungarian peasant music there are six separate formations, viz. twelve-syllable, eight-syllable, and—as will be seen presently—six-, seven-, eleven-, ten-, and nine-syllable tune-lines, which all tally so far as regards essential characteristics: whereas Rumanian peasant music has but one form, the eight-syllable *parlando-rubato*. Hence it is inconceivable that one nation should have taken over this eight-syllable form, and evolved, from the materials thus acquired, so great a diversity of new forms while the original users of this one form failed to extend and vary it.

It is far more likely that the Székely, who for many centuries had stood on a higher cultural level, exercised some influence upon the neighbouring Rumanians.

[1] This consistency of the old Hungarian style, so far as regards essentials, is illustrated by tunes Nos. 16 and 19 (from IV), 20 (from II), and 15 (from I).

[2] No. 16 was taken up by the ruling classes of Rumania, who propagated it; so that it has become known in Erdély and in the Banat. My collection of tunes from Bihar includes many variants of it. (See *Chansons populaires du département Bihar* [Hongrie], Bucarest, 1913, published by the Academia Româna, Nos. 231, 233, 234, 236, 237.)

Apart from these tunes actually taken over, the Rumanian corpus includes tunes which are similar, to a degree, to the Hungarian four-line, eight-syllable tunes.

The main distinctive features are:

(1) In Rumanian tunes of the above order the chief caesura is usually $\boxed{\text{VII}}$; the first and third lines sometimes end with the same note (see Bartók, *Chansons populaires roumaines du département Bihar*, Nos. 81, 95, 98, 106).

(2) Contrary to what happens in Hungarian tunes, the tune, in the first two lines, generally begins with VII or 1 and moves between VII (sometimes 1) and 5 (sometimes 6).

These tunes are also differentiated, in a measure, from the genuine, purely Rumanian tunes by other features common to them and to the Székely tunes, the correlations resulting from contact. The genuine Rumanian tunes, however, are nearer to the Yugoslav tune-types.[1]

When trying to discover the actual origin of the old style, one may ask whether its pentatonism does not come from Asia. My own opinion is that there may be a certain connexion between this pentatonism and that of the Tatars and Tcheremiss. Perhaps even both may have a common origin (see Nos. I–III in the Appendix, and the remarks referring to these examples). Unfortunately the music of the races connected with the Hungarian is little known; and so very few materials are available for the purpose of scientific comparison, that it is not yet possible to solve the question.

II. Tunes to six-syllable text-lines.

As regards *structure* and *scales*, all the foregoing remarks apply, generally speaking, to this sub-class, of which about thirty examples are available (see Nos. 33–43).

$\boxed{\flat3}$ as chief caesura occurs in 11 examples (Nos. 34–36; Sz.N. 62, 67, 77, 79, 85, 101, 102, 111).

$\boxed{1}$	,,	,,	5	,,	(No. 33; Sz.N. 19, 24).
$\boxed{5}$	,,	,,	7	,,	(Nos. 37–42).
$\boxed{4}$	,,	,,	3	,,	(Sz.N. 121).
$\boxed{8}$	,,	,,	1	,,	(No. 43 and Sz.N. 150).
$\boxed{\text{VII}}$	,,	,,	3	,,	(Sz.N. 2, 4, 8).

[1] The Rumanians have a kind of tune, pentatonic in structure, and consisting of 5, 6, or 7 lines (all these tunes variants, such as might result from improvisation, of the same tune) which is characteristic of the district of Szatmár (possibly also of the district of Szilágy) and of the northern part of Maros-Torda. This type of tune, which has become Rumanian but cropped up under Hungarian influences, occurs now and then among the Székely, and may then be considered as taken over from Rumanians.

As regards the final notes of first and third lines, the proportions are practically identical to what we found in the foregoing sub-class.

The facts of geographical distribution also coincide with what is observed with reference to this foregoing sub-class; and the same remarks concerning melodic design and compass apply.

Of structure ABCD we have 22 examples (Nos. 33, 34, 35, 41, 43).

,,	A^5B^5AB	,,	3	,,	(Nos. 40, 42; Sz.N. 77).
,,	ABAC	,,	1 example	(No. 37).
,,	AABB	,,	1	,,	(No. 38).
,,	AABC	,,	1	,,	(Sz.N. 62).
,,	ABBC	,,	1	,,	(No. 36).

Again we note the predominance of structure ABCD (especially in *parlando-rubato* tunes). On the other hand, the scarcity of structure ABBC, so characteristic of the foregoing sub-class, is very striking.

Rhythm. About half the tunes (exactly 17) are in *parlando-rubato* rhythm; the remainder are *tempo giusto*.

The basic rhythm-schema of each line in the *parlando-rubato* tunes is ♩♩♩♩♩♩ ‖.

This basic schema, however, undergoes so many alterations (far more than was the case in the foregoing sub-class) that it is hardly possible to adduce types. In tunes that are performed with less *rubato*, the extension of the final note of each line: ♩♩♩♩ ‖ ♪ ♩. ‖, or only of the second and fourth: ‖: ♩♩♩♩♩♩ ‖ ♩♩♩♩ ‖ ♪ ♩. :‖ is typical. The latter recalls, in a measure, the half of a twelve-syllable line.

In *tempo giusto* tunes we find the following rhythms:

(a) isorhythmic strophes:

1. $\frac{2}{4}$ ♩ ♩ ‖ ♩ ♩ ‖ ♩ ♩ ‖ . . . . in 1 example (No. 37);
   ossia: ♩. ♪

2. $\frac{2}{4}$ ♫♫ ‖ ♩ ♩ ‖ . . . . . ,, 1–2 examples;
   ossia: ♪ ♩.

3. $\frac{2}{4}$ ♫ ♩ ‖ ♫ ♩ ‖ . . . . . ,, 2 examples (No. 38; Sz.N. 121);

4. $\frac{2}{4}$ ♫ ♩ ‖ ♪♩ ♪ ‖ . . . . ,, 2 ,, (No. 35);

5. $\frac{2}{4}$ ♫ ♩ ‖ ♩ ♫ ‖ . . . . . ,, 1 example (No. 39);

6. $\frac{2+3+2}{8}$ ♫ ♪ ‖ ♫ ‖ . . . ,, 1 ,, (No. 34 a);

7. $\frac{2}{4}$ ♩ ♩ ‖ ♫♫ ‖ . . . . . ,, 1 ,,

26

(β) heterorhythmic strophes:

1. $\frac{2}{4}$ ‖: ♫ ♩ | ♫ ♩ | ♫♫ | ♩ ♩ :‖ in 1 example (Sz.N. 8);

2. $\frac{2}{4}$ ‖: ♫♫ | ♩ ♩ :‖ ♫ ♩ | ♫ ♩ | ♫♫ | ♩ ♩ ‖ in 2 examples (Sz.N. 19, 101);

3. $\frac{2+3+3}{8}$ ‖: ♫ ♪♩ | ♪♩ | $\frac{3+2+3}{8}$ ♪♩ | ♫ | ♪♩ :‖ in 1 example (No. 36);

4. $\frac{2}{4}$ ‖: ♩ ♫ | ♫ ♩ | ♩ ♫ | ♩ ♩ | ♩ ♩ ♮ :‖ in 1 example (No. 42);

that is, we have but one or two examples of each scheme: no particular scheme seems to have become widespread in the old style. On the other hand, identical rhythm-forms, especially (α) 1, 2, 3, 5, (β) 1, 2, 4, appear far more often in tunes belonging to Class C; so that we have more reason to believe than we had in the case of *tempo giusto* eight-syllable tunes that these strict rhythm-forms cropped up in the old style under the influence of the tunes belonging to Class C.[1]

Most of these types are plentiful in Slovakian tunes (whether these be taken over from Hungary or aboriginal). Hence one is led to suspect the influence of some alien rhythm; but this does not mean that the tunes which give rise to the suspicion are not Hungarian: it is the rhythm alone which actually points to a possible foreign influence.

There is no single instance of $\frac{2}{4}$ rhythm ♩ ♫ | ♩ ♫ ‖ in Hungarian peasant music. This rhythm, apparently, is repugnant to the Hungarian peasant's musical instinct.[2]

In the sub-class under notice it is the *parlando-rubato* tunes that are most characteristic of the old style. Their structure is usually ABCD, and their frank pentatonism evinces their antiquity. It is impossible to say whether they are as old as the tunes belonging to the previous sub-class, older, or less old. But the point is of no consequence.

III. Tunes to seven-syllable lines.

These tunes played in old Hungarian peasant music a part very different from that played by the tunes described so far.

Their rhythm is always *tempo giusto*. It is possible that originally they were used as dance tunes only. They are much more scarce. We have but 24 examples of them (Nos. 44–54).

[1] One may doubt indeed whether the *tempo giusto* six-syllable tunes should be taken to belong to the old style or to Class C. Exact discrimination is most difficult, and Class A as well as both other classes will be found to contain tunes whose classification must needs remain doubtful. But as such cases are comparatively few, the possibly inaccurate classification will not affect the accuracy of our general conclusions.

[2] This remark applies to Classes A, B, and C. A few exceptions occur in Class C (Nos. 92, 184); but they obviously originate in art tunes.

⟨♭3⟩ as chief caesura occurs in 12 examples (Nos. 48–52; Sz.N. 54, 58, 59, 104).

⟨1⟩   ,,   ,,   7   ,,   (Nos. 44–47).

⟨5⟩   ,,   ,,   4   ,,   (Nos. 53, 54).

⟨VII⟩   ,,   ,,   1 example.

Their geographical distribution is practically similar to that of the previous two sub-classes. The tune-strophes are always isorhythmic, the schemes being:

1. $\frac{2}{4}$ ♩♩♩♩ | ♫ ♩ ‖ in 6 examples (Nos. 44, 51, 53).[1]

2. $\frac{2}{4}$ ♩♩♩♩ | ♪♩ ♪♩ ‖ ,, 2   ,,   (No. 46).

3. $\frac{2}{4}$ ♩♩♩♩ | ♩ ♫♩ ‖ ,, 2   ,,   (No. 49).

4. $\frac{2}{4}$ ♩ ♩ | ♩ ♩ | ♩ ♫ ‖ in 1 example (No. 54),

and finally

5. $\frac{4}{4}$ ♩ ♩ ♩ ♩ | ♩ ♩ ♩ ‖ by way of adjustable *tempo giusto* rhythm in 13 examples (Nos. 45, 47, 48, 50, 52).

Schemes 2, 3, and 4 are variants of the primitive scheme (1). Probably all tunes except the two examples under heading 3 are dance tunes.

Scheme 5: $\frac{4}{4}$ ♩ ♩ ♩ ♩ | ♩ ♩ ♩ ‖ seems to be a rhythmic enlargement of scheme 1. We call it 'variable' or 'adjustable' because a remarkable phenomenon arises in connexion with it, viz. the crotchet pairs ♩ ♩ adjust themselves to the quantity, natural or positional, of the syllables of the text (the same occurs with the $\frac{4}{4}$ rhythm ♩ ♩ ♩ ♩ | ♩ ♩ ♩ ♩ ‖ mentioned under α 3 on p. 17).

The adjustment takes place as follows:

With two long syllables (– –) we have ♩ ♩;

  ,,   one long and one short (– ◡) we have ♩ ♩ or ♩. ♪;

  ,,   one short and one long (◡ –) we have ♪♩. (seldom ♩ ♩);

  ,,   two short (◡ ◡) we have ♪♩.

These general rules—of which the second and third cover two orders of possibility each—are not absolutely binding. There are plenty of instances of rhythms devised 'in defiance of rules'; for instance, in No. 50 the rhythm ♪♩. occurs on the syllables 'vĕkōny' and 'jāj dĕ'. Such exceptions cannot yet be reduced to any kind of principle or system.

The second bar of the ground-scheme changes almost always into ♪♩. ♩. —a conclusive formula whose power is so compelling that it very seldom

---

[1] This primitive rhythmic scheme occurs in the primitive peasant music of many other countries.

28

alters into ♩ ♩ ♩ (and even more seldom into ♩. ♪♩) in accordance with the eventual quantity (– – or – ◡) of the text syllables.[1]

The first bar of the ground-scheme may take any of the following eight forms, of which 6, 7, and 8 are the most frequent:

1. ♩ ♩ ♩ ♩ ‖   2. ♪♩. ♩ ♩ ‖   3. ♩ ♩ ♪♩. ‖   4. ♩. ♪♩ ♩ ‖
(– ◡)(– ◡)   (◡ ◡)(– ◡)   (– ◡)(◡ ◡)   (– ◡)

5. ♩ ♩ ♩. ♪‖   6. ♪♩. ♪♩. ‖   7. ♪♩. ♩. ♪‖   8. ♩. ♪♪♩. ‖
(– ◡)   (◡ ◡)(◡ ◡)   (◡ ◡)   (◡ ◡)

The ninth possible combination ♩. ♪♩. ♪ never occurs. When the syllabic combination – ◡ – ◡ crops up, it is sung to form 4 or 5, as is the case in the fourth bar of No. 86. The avoidance of this ninth combination is probably due to the same psychological law which absolutely excludes the rhythm ♩ ♫♩ | ♩ ♫♩ ‖ from all *tempo giusto* six-syllable examples of Hungarian peasant music. And in point of fact, there is a certain similarity in the halting fall of both these rhythmic schemes which Hungarian peasant music so carefully avoids.

Naturally, the rhythmic combinations change from verse to verse, according to the metric idiosyncrasies of each new verse.[2] Consequently, here we have to deal not with any permanent and absolute rhythm but with an ever-changing rhythm, originating in an extra-musical factor. In Hungarian peasant poems no rule or binding practice determines the succession and alternation of long and short syllables; and the tune-rhythms which these texts suggest, and which are associated with them, are correspondingly free and variable.[3]

The dotted rhythm (♩. ♪ or ♪ ♩.) of these tunes is at times subject to certain alterations. If the tempo is quick, ♪ ♩. and ♪ ♩. become slightly less sharply marked and come near to ♩ ♩ or ♩ ♩ ; conversely, in a slow tempo, the differentiation of the two note-values increases, and we get

[1] In performance the cadence formula ♪♩. ♩ usually changes, as our musical examples show, into ♪♩. ♩ 𝄽 or ♪♩. ♪ 𝄾 𝄽 . Both these forms are rhythmically equivalent to the original form, to which we therefore have kept in all our schemata.

[2] There are very few instances of the 'dotted' rhythm of the first verse continuing to assert itself forcibly, and unchanged, despite changes of metre in the following verses—except as regards the fixed conclusion ♪ ♩. ♩ which often persists.

[3] It may occur that such tunes are performed apart from the text—hummed, or whistled, or played on some instrument; then the tune-rhythm, liberated from the influence of the text-metre, becomes more uniform; and the combination ♩. ♪♪♩. predominates almost throughout.

almost ♫♩ or even ♪♩·· and ♩♫ or even ♩··♪ respectively. And
again, when the tempo is slow, the original even rhythm suggested by
spondaic metre (♩ ♩) may become ♩₃♩ —although, curiously, never ♩ ₃♩.

So that in proportion as the tempo permits it, and according to the
performer's mood, an almost endless series of variants (ranging from ♩ ♩
through ♩₃♩ and ♪ ♩· to ♪♩··) is used. (The resources of current nota-
tion are unequal to the task of setting down all the intermediate stages
between ♩· ♪ and ♪ ♩·· .)

It is this adjustable *tempo giusto* that occurs most often in the sub-class of
the seven-syllable old-style tunes. This rhythm-schema has a particular
significance; for it probably was the starting-point of the evolution of the
eleven-syllable old-style tunes on the one hand, and on the other of the new
tunes belonging to Class *B*.

One may assert with every chance of certainty that the adjustable *tempo
giusto* rhythm constitutes a mode of performance born in Hungary and
manifestly Hungarian. There are many Slovakian tunes which are in
adjustable *tempo giusto* rhythm; but all these should be considered as being
of Hungarian origin or having arisen under Hungarian influences. The
same applies to the new-style tunes of the Máramaros Rumanians, whose
rhythm corresponds to the adjustable *tempo giusto* rhythm of Hungarian
seven- or eight-syllable tunes.[1] Let one proof be adduced: in Hungarian
regions, as is shown by documents dating from the beginning of the nineteenth century, this rhythm existed far earlier and was far more widespread
than among the Slovakians and Moravians, among whom it spread—as
shown by the printed collections of their folk-songs—only towards the end
of the nineteenth century.

From the point of view of the musical contents of each tune-line, the
old seven-syllable tunes fall into the following categories:

ABCD of which there are 13 examples (Nos. 44, 46, 50, 52, 54; Sz.N. 104).
AABC   ,,   ,,   5   ,,   (Nos. 49, 53; Sz.N. 54, 58, 59).
ABBC   ,,   ,,   5   ,,   (Nos. 45, 47, 51; Sz.N. 103).
A⁵BAC   ,,   ,,   1 example (No. 48).

As mentioned before, both these and the tunes forming the second group
of Class *C* (which are in the same rhythm) exercised a great influence on

[1] In Máramaros are to be found, apart from tunes purely and simply borrowed from
Hungary, certain tunes whose rhythm is similar, but which are different in structure and contents from their Hungarian prototypes: viz. this Rumanian music style was born under Hungarian influences, but contains forms which generally differ from the models in which they
originate (see fuller particulars in the afore-mentioned book, *Die Volksmusik der Rumänen von
Maramureş*).

the evolution of the new Rumanian style of Máramaros. The nature and effects of this influence will be dealt with in the projected book on Rumanian folk-music. Let it simply be noted just now that the Rumanians have borrowed certain tunes directly. The Máramaros corpus contains, among others:

No. 28 (*Volksmusik der Rumänen von Maramureş*, No. 128),
  ,, 45 (ibid., No. 45),
  ,, 50 (,,   ,, 104),
  ,, 52 (,,   ,, 107),
Sz.N. 54, 58, 59, and 104 (ibid., Nos. 96, 98, 97, 105).

* * *

After having referred to some of the above rhythm-schemata as highly probable early stages in the evolution of the more complicated rhythm-forms which will be dealt with further, let us again survey these schemata.
The three forms

$$\tfrac{2}{4} \; \text{♪♪♪♪ | ♪♪♪♪ ‖} \; ,$$
$$\tfrac{2}{4} \; \text{♪♪♪♪ | ♫♩ ‖ and}$$
$$\tfrac{2}{4} \; \text{♪♪♪♪ | ♩ ♩ ‖}$$

may be connected with one another: possibly the second derives from the first, the last two quavers (feminine ending) having merged into one crotchet (masculine ending); the third might have evolved from the second by substitution of a crotchet to the third pair of quavers—the 'strong' masculine ending ♫♩ becoming a 'weak' masculine ending ♩ ♩.[1]

So that we have to deal with two original rhythm-groups: one quick, the other slow in pace.

	(α) Quick-pace rhythms	(β) Variable, slow-pace rhythms
with feminine ending:	1. $\tfrac{2}{4}$ ♪♪♪♪ | ♪♪♪♪ ‖	1. $\tfrac{4}{4}$ ♩ ♩ ♩ ♩ | ♩ ♩ ♩ ♩ ‖
with strong masculine ending:	2. $\tfrac{2}{4}$ ♪♪♪♪ | ♫♩ ‖	2. $\tfrac{4}{4}$ ♩ ♩ ♩ ♩ | ♩ ♩ 𝅗𝅥 ‖
with weak masculine ending:	3. $\tfrac{2}{4}$ ♪♪♪♪ | ♩ ♩ ‖	3. $\tfrac{4}{4}$ ♩ ♩ ♩ ♩ | 𝅗𝅥 𝅗𝅥 ‖ [2]

[1] Perhaps the evolution took place in the opposite order.
[2] Rhythm β 3 does not appear in old-style six-syllable tunes, but is common in tunes belonging to Class C—which tunes may have exercised some influence on the further phases of evolution of the old style. These further stages will be considered later.

31

In all likelihood the later old-style rhythm-forms, and also most of the forms of Class *B* (new style), evolved out of (β) 1, 2, and 3.

* * *

The following three sub-classes (tunes sung to eleven-, ten-, and nine-syllable lines) belong, without possible doubt, to a more recent period of the evolution. Indeed, their rhythm-forms may be derived from the above β forms of the foregoing three sub-classes.

IV. Tunes to eleven-syllable text-lines.

Here the simplest, and apparently oldest, rhythm-form is:

Tempo giusto

$\frac{4}{4}$ 𝅘𝅥𝅯𝅘𝅥𝅯𝅘𝅥𝅯𝅘𝅥𝅯 𝅘𝅥𝅯𝅘𝅥𝅯𝅘𝅥𝅯𝅘𝅥𝅯 | 𝅘𝅥𝅮𝅘𝅥. 𝅗𝅥 ‖ ; this formula may be considered as derived straight from the seven-syllable $\frac{4}{4}$ 𝅘𝅥 𝅘𝅥 𝅘𝅥 𝅘𝅥 | 𝅘𝅥𝅮𝅘𝅥. 𝅗𝅥 ‖ adjustable *tempo giusto* formula, of which the variable crotchets in the first bar were changed into their equivalent in quavers. The derivation is proved by examples (Nos. 56, 58) in which the two notes of each pair are similar; e.g.

is probably derived by duplication from

; and

might likewise originate in . This oldest of eleven-syllable rhythms underwent, in the course of time, many changes.

The following schemata occur

(*a*) in isorhythmic strophes:

1. $\frac{4}{4}$ 𝅘𝅥𝅯𝅘𝅥𝅯𝅘𝅥𝅯𝅘𝅥𝅯 𝅘𝅥𝅯𝅘𝅥𝅯𝅘𝅥𝅯𝅘𝅥𝅯 | 𝅘𝅥𝅮𝅘𝅥. 𝅗𝅥 ‖ in most cases (Nos. 58, 60, 61, 65; Sz.N. 6, 99, 106).

2. $\frac{4}{4}$ 𝅘𝅥 𝅘𝅥 𝅘𝅥 𝅘𝅥 | 𝅘𝅥 𝅘𝅥 𝅘𝅥 𝅘𝅥 | 𝅘𝅥𝅮𝅘𝅥. 𝅗𝅥 ‖ in 2–3 cases (No. 62).

3. $\frac{3}{4}$ 𝅘𝅥𝅯𝅘𝅥𝅯 𝅘𝅥 𝅘𝅥 | $\frac{2}{4}$ 𝅘𝅥𝅯𝅘𝅥𝅯𝅘𝅥𝅯𝅘𝅥𝅯 | 𝅘𝅥𝅯𝅘𝅥𝅯 𝅘𝅥 ‖ in one case (No. 67).

(β) in heterorhythmic strophes:

1. $\frac{4}{4}$ ‖: 𝅘𝅥𝅯𝅘𝅥𝅯𝅘𝅥𝅯𝅘𝅥𝅯 𝅘𝅥𝅯𝅘𝅥𝅯𝅘𝅥𝅯𝅘𝅥𝅯 | 𝅘𝅥𝅮𝅘𝅥. 𝅗𝅥 :‖ 𝅘𝅥 𝅘𝅥 𝅘𝅥 𝅘𝅥 | $\frac{2}{4}$ 𝅘𝅥𝅯𝅘𝅥𝅯𝅘𝅥𝅯𝅘𝅥𝅯 | $\frac{4}{4}$ 𝅘𝅥𝅮𝅘𝅥. 𝅗𝅥 | 𝅘𝅥𝅯𝅘𝅥𝅯𝅘𝅥𝅯𝅘𝅥𝅯 𝅘𝅥𝅯𝅘𝅥𝅯𝅘𝅥𝅯𝅘𝅥𝅯 | 𝅘𝅥𝅮𝅘𝅥. 𝅗𝅥 ‖ (common; No. 57; Sz.N. 82).

2. $\frac{4}{4}$ ‖: 𝅘𝅥𝅯𝅘𝅥𝅯𝅘𝅥𝅯𝅘𝅥𝅯 𝅘𝅥𝅯𝅘𝅥𝅯𝅘𝅥𝅯𝅘𝅥𝅯 | 𝅘𝅥𝅮𝅘𝅥. 𝅗𝅥 :‖ 𝅘𝅥 𝅘𝅥 𝅘𝅥 𝅘𝅥 | 𝅘𝅥𝅯𝅘𝅥𝅯𝅘𝅥𝅯𝅘𝅥𝅯 𝅘𝅥𝅯𝅘𝅥𝅯 𝅘𝅥 | 𝅘𝅥𝅯𝅘𝅥𝅯𝅘𝅥𝅯𝅘𝅥𝅯 𝅘𝅥𝅯𝅘𝅥𝅯𝅘𝅥𝅯𝅘𝅥𝅯 | 𝅘𝅥𝅮𝅘𝅥. 𝅗𝅥 ‖ (common; No. 59; Sz.N. 100, 149).

3. $\frac{4}{4}$ ‖: ♩ ♩ ♩ ♩ | ♩ ♩ ♩ ♩ | ♪ ♩. ♩ :‖ ♩ ♩ ♩ ♩ | ♫♫ ♫ ♩ | ♫♫ ♫♫ | ♪ ♩. ♩ ‖ (in one case; Sz.N. 78).

There are also *parlando-rubato* tunes in which the final bars of the first three lines occur mostly as ♫ ♩ ┌. The first bar of each line consists of *parlando* quavers; and the last bar of the fourth line is ♪ ♩. ♩. These tunes are found chiefly in Dialect-regions I, II, and III (Nos. 56, 66).

Form a 2 is a marked step in the further evolution: the change that took place is that the first bar of form a 1 has become twice as slow in pace. Hence was evolved the rhythm of most of the tunes belonging to Class *B* (new style).

The rhythm of the third line in β 1 is also a significant formation, which plays an essential part in the eleven-syllable examples of Class *B*. Again, this rhythm may have been derived from a 1 simply by a reduction of the pace of the first bar's first half.[1] The third line of β 2 arose, in all likelihood, from the third line of β 1, the final formula ♪ ♩. ♩ being shortened into ♫ ♩.

In this sub-class the invariable, not adjustable *tempo giusto* rhythm, a 3, occurs only in Dialect-region I.[2]

Very characteristic of region IV is a noteworthy *rubato* form of the set dance rhythm: the group ♫♫ becomes something like ♫ ♪ ♩, ♫ ♩ ♪, ♪ ♩ ♫ or ♫ ♩ ♩, the group ♫ ♩ becomes ♫ ♩., the group ♪ ♩. becomes ♫ ♩... These quintuplets have no set rhythm. Consequently, in every pair of bars, each bar or portion of a bar will be performed in a variable tempo; but the aggregate time affected to the performance of each pair of bars remains the same for all pairs; in other words, the conditions of *tempo giusto* are maintained so far as regards the large divisions of the tune; but within these large divisions we have small melodic clauses performed *rubato* (this we see in Nos. 61, 64; the mode of performance of Nos. 55 and 63 is far closer to the usual type of *parlando-rubato*).

No. 64 constitutes an exceptional occurrence: a heterometric tune-strophe resulting from the elimination of the final bars of the first and

[1] Yet this formation might also be considered as derived from a 2, the crotchets in the second bar of a 2 being converted into quavers.

[2] Naturally, in all other variable rhythm-forms, the adaptation takes place only so far as the crotchet-pairs are concerned—never the quaver-pairs. Yet it may occur (when the pace of performance is unusually slow) that even the rhythm of the quaver-pairs is altered, ♫ becoming ♪ ♩ or ♩ ♪, and when the tempo is very slow, ♪ ♩. or ♩. ♪, according to the rules given on p. 28. Indeed, when the tempo is exceptionally slow, a similar alteration of the crotchet-pairs may take place even in so-called 'invariable' *tempo giusto* rhythms (see No. 70 and the appended remarks).

second lines ♪♩· ♩ ; this is the one instance of heterometric tune which we are justified in considering as belonging to the old style.[1]

The sub-class of the eleven-syllable tunes comprises about 35 examples, in which the chief caesura is as follows:

$\boxed{\flat 3}$ in 17 cases (Nos. 57–60).

$\boxed{5}$ „ 7 „ (Nos. 65–68).

$\boxed{1}$ „ 5 „ (Nos. 55, 56).

$\boxed{4}$ „ 4 „ (Nos. 61–64).

$\boxed{VII}$ „ 1 case (Sz.N. 6).

$\boxed{7}$ „ „ „ (Sz.N. 149).

The geographical distribution is similar to that of the previous sub-classes.

ABCD   occurs in 21 cases.

AABC   „   5   „   (No. 61).

A^5B^5AB „   4   „   (Nos. 65, 67).[2]

AA_vBB_v „   4   „   (No. 55; Sz.N. 106).

ABCB   „   1 case (Bartalus, vi, No. 45).

V. Tunes to ten-syllable lines.

Eleven examples of these are known (Nos. 69–72 and Sz.N. 115, 117, 137, 141). In two of these the chief caesura is $\boxed{\flat 3}$. Three examples only belong to region IV.

ABCD   occurs in 4 cases (Sz.N. 117).

ABBC   „   3   „   (Nos. 69, 70).

A^5B^5AB „   3   „   (Nos. 71, 72).

AABC   „   1 case (Sz.N. 137).

Their rhythm is *tempo giusto*; but a few have *parlando-rubato* variants. The rhythm-schemata are as follows:

1. $\frac{2}{4}$ ♫♫ | ♫♫ | ♩ ♩ ‖ (No. 71 *a*; Sz.N. 115).

2. $\frac{2}{4}$ ♫♫ | ♫ ♩ | ♩ ♫ ‖ (Nos. 70, 72).

3. $\frac{2}{4}$ ♫♫ | ♫ ♩ | ♪♩ ♪ ‖ (No. 71 *b*; Sz.N. 137, 141).

Ossia: ♪♪ ♪

4. $\frac{2}{4}$ ♫♫ | ♫ ♩ | ♩ ♩ | ♩ ‖

---

[1] The peculiar extensions of the lines in No. 68 are not to be considered as a new formation.
[2] It would be more correct to describe No. 67 as: $A^5A^5_vAA_v$.

The strophes are uniformly isorhythmic, and the rhythm is set, invariable.[1] The origin of these songs is not yet clear.[2]

VI. Tunes to nine-syllable lines.

Only four of these are known :

1. $\boxed{7}$ $\boxed{b3}$ $\lfloor b3 \rfloor$, A⁵A⁵ᵥAAᵥ (No. 73 and Színi No. 158).
2. $\boxed{7}$ $\boxed{b3}$ $\lfloor b3 \rfloor$, A⁵A⁵ᵥAAᵥ, ABCCᵥ, and ABBC (No. 74 a, b, c).
3. $\boxed{5}$ $\boxed{4}$ $\lfloor 5 \rfloor$, ABCD.
4. $\boxed{7}$ $\boxed{5}$ $\lfloor b3 \rfloor$, A⁵B⁵AB (Színi No. 140).

There are also variants with $\boxed{5}$ and with the structure A⁵B⁵AB. It occurs only in region I, often with a major third (No. 74 b).

In 1 and 2 the original $\boxed{5}$ has become $\boxed{b3}$.

The rhythm of 1, 2, and 3 is : $\frac{2}{4}$ ♪♪♪♪ | ♩ ♩ | ♪♪ ♩ ‖

The rhythm of 4 is : $\frac{2}{4}$ ♪♪♪♪ | ♪♪ ♩ | ♪♪ 𝄽 ‖

Their rhythm is set and invariable. Their origin is not yet clear.

Judging by their texts, the eleven-, ten-, and nine-syllable tunes, despite their predominant *tempo giusto* rhythm, were hardly dance tunes (perhaps one or two of the nine-syllable were). As regards their rhythm, they may be considered as a transition towards the tunes belonging to Class *B* (new style). In all other idiosyncrasies they agree so closely with the tunes belonging to sub-classes I–III, that they must be kept in Class *A*.

Another noteworthy ABCD tune-structure must be mentioned. Instances of it occur in every old-style sub-class. In this structure all subsequent lines repeat the first line in a descending sequence. Hence the representative figures will be, mostly, $\boxed{5}$ $\boxed{4}$ $\boxed{b3}$ or $\boxed{4}$ $\boxed{b3}$ $\boxed{2}$. Such are Nos. 4, 5 (possibly 23), and 62.

This structure is frequent, in Class *C*, in tunes whose origin is undoubtedly Western (Nos. 183, 206, 217, 250, or in the tune—well known in association with the text 'Szeretnék szántani'—with a few alterations). Hence it might be inferred that this structure found its way into Class *A* at a late period, in consequence of foreign influences. Nevertheless 4, 23,

[1] When the pace of performance is exceptionally slow, the quaver-pairs adapt themselves to the metre of the text (No. 70).

[2] However, rhythm-schema No. 1 might have derived:

(1) From the $\frac{2}{4}$ ♪♪♪♪ | ♪♪♪♪ | ♪♪ ♩ eleven-syllable type, the strong ending having become a weak ending.

(2) From the $\frac{2}{4}$ ♪♪♪♪ | ♩ ♩ | ♩ ♩ | type (as occurs with the first schema of the nine-syllable sub-class); both crotchets in the second bar, or, as the case may be, the first crotchet only, are replaced by the equivalent in quavers. But there is no proof to support this hypothesis.

and 62 may well be included in Class *A*, because in all other respects they tally in a fair measure with the old-style tunes.[1]

A few twelve-, eight-, and eleven-syllable tunes in Class *A* are to be found (especially in region IV) in mutilated, two-line forms, constituting, so to speak, half-tunes. A case in point is No. 2, of which we find many such variants lacking the first and third lines. With eight- and twelve-syllable tunes it is generally the first and second lines that drop out. Often the full four-line form of half-tunes that are to be encountered is not discoverable. A few isometric *parlando-rubato* twelve- and eight-syllable tunes in Class *C* underwent similar curtailments.

Before summing up the main points that concern the old style, a few words should be said of the relationship between tunes and texts.

An important question is whether each tune is actually bound to a particular text in conjunction with which it constitutes an indiscerptible unit.

So far as concerns the old style, what we see to-day (that is, at the time of recording) is that generally a tune is bound to a particular text (this is especially true in regions I, II, and III, e.g. with regard to ballad-texts: e.g. No. 29 is never used except in conjunction with the poem 'Fehér László'). On the other hand, it must be noted that when the rhythm and ornamentation of old tunes point to a state of decadence, these tunes are hardly likely to represent the original treatment of their text. Indeed, in such cases, various alien influences may have been at work, as can be clearly seen in Rumanian tunes.

Using as term of comparison the presumed original state of Rumanian peasant music, we come to the following inferences:

During the hey-day of a style of peasant music a great number of tunes closely resembling one another (and indeed almost impossible to differentiate) arise, all similar in rhythm and in strophe-structure. That every one of these, differing from the remainder only in a few melodic details, should ever have been closely bound to, and inseparable from, one particular text, is psychologically impossible. Far more probable is the condition of things which we observe nowadays in Rumanian peasant music, viz. that any text, epic or lyric, consisting of eight-syllable lines may be sung to any tune of the eight-syllable type.

We conjecture that a similar condition of things may have obtained in Hungary.[2] The relation between texts and tunes which we may observe nowadays in Dialect-region IV confirms this conjecture in most cases.

---

[1] The structure of these might be more accurately described as A⁵A⁴A³A (No. 217) or A⁴A³A²A (Nos. 183, 206, 250).

[2] Naturally, twelve-syllable texts could only be sung to tunes of the twelve-syllable type, and so forth.

Generally speaking, it is only in such borrowed art-songs in folk-style that tune and text form an inseparable whole. These songs subsist, without undergoing any essential alterations, among the peasant class, but do not contribute to the birth of a coherent style of peasant music (see pp. 1–3).

A second question is how each separate line of the text is placed under each line of the tune.

Most often each tune-line is affected to a new text-line; each verse therefore consists of four different lines. However, in a few songs from region IV an old-fashioned disposition of the text continued to prevail: only two text-lines are affected to the tune, the first being repeated under the second tune-line, and the second under the fourth tune-line (see No. 4): the actual verse consists of two text-lines only.

As in Rumanian peasant music, this state of things should be considered as the primitive state. It may even have occurred (and in Rumanian songs many cases in point are available) that at one time all tunes were sung to one single text-line used four times in succession.

Synopsis.

The oldest-known Hungarian peasant music consists of tunes embodying the so-called old style, which are associated with no particular circumstance or purpose. These tunes consist of four isometric text-lines of twelve, eight, six, seven, eleven, ten, or nine syllables.

The oldest of these are the twelve-, eight-, and six-syllable *parlando-rubato* tunes. Less old are the eight-, six-, and seven-syllable tunes in invariable *tempo giusto* rhythm. Comparatively recent are the eight-, seven-, and eleven-syllable tunes in variable *tempo giusto* rhythm, and all the ten- or nine-syllable tunes.

Characteristic features of all these tunes are:
The pentatonic scale.
The original main caesura $\boxed{\flat 3}$, which is common to all, but in a few instances became, in the course of time, $\boxed{1}$ or $\boxed{5}$.
The non-architectural structures ABCD, ABBC, and A^5B^5AB; the first being characteristic in all cases, the second as regards the *parlando-rubato* eight-syllable tunes, and the third (comparatively rare) again as regards all sub-classes.

The differences in musical dialect are:
In Dialect-region I tunes in *parlando-rubato* rhythm are characterized by a certain rhythm of the line-ending (see p. 14), by a slight raising of the third and seventh, and by the main caesura $\boxed{1}$.
The same rhythm and main caesura, in *parlando-rubato* times, are characteristic of Dialect-region II.

37

The same rhythm in *parlando-rubato* tunes and ⑤ as main caesura are characteristic of region III.

Characteristic of region IV are: another rhythm of the line-ending in *parlando-rubato* rhythms; an emphasized *rubato*, richer ornamentation, and the preservation of the main caesura ♭3 .

These old-style tunes are to be considered as purely Hungarian creations; so far as we know, nothing similar in style and character is to be found in any other country. The *parlando-rubato* eight-syllable tunes exercised a strong influence upon the peasant music of the Rumanian districts adjoining the region of the Székely. The seven- and eight-syllable tunes in adjustable *tempo giusto* rhythm exercised a decisive influence upon the evolution of the newer Rumanian style born in the Máramaros region.

Out of the rhythm of the seven-, eight-, and eleven-syllable tunes in adjustable *tempo giusto* rhythm was evolved the rhythm of most of the tunes representing the new Hungarian musical style (Class *B*).

The corpus of available materials comprises in all the following numbers of tunes:

Twelve-syllable,	about		7
Eight-	,,	,,	70
Six-	,,	,,	30
Seven-	,,	,,	24
Eleven-	,,	,,	35
Ten-	,,	,,	11
Nine-	,,	,,	4
	In all about		181 [1]

[1] These figures do not include the variants, of which there exist, on an average, four or five for every tune. The Színi, Kiss, and Bartalus collections contain in all only 38 old-style tunes (apart from a small number of variants). Of these 38, 30 are variants of tunes included in the manuscript collections. All of them are included in the above statistical table.

B. THE NEW STYLE OF HUNGARIAN PEASANT MUSIC

Melodic structure, Compass, and Scales. The new-style tunes differ most obviously from the old-style tunes through their structure, which is rounded, architectural. The following table shows the comparative frequency of the four structural schemata, of the most usual two chief caesuras ⬚1 and ⬚5, and of the various forms of verse (which consist of lines whose contents range from six syllables to twenty-five).

Main caesura.	Structural plan.	Number of syllables in first and fourth lines (or in all four lines in isorhythmic texts).																		Sum total.
		6	7	8	9	10	11	12	13	14	15	16	17	18	19	21	22	23	25	
⬚1	AABA	—	—	—	—	6	5	6	6	24	22	4	10	11	8	1	3	1	2	109
⬚5	AA⁵BA	8	8	13	4	18	39	9	8	14	17	6	1	4	3	2	—	—	—	154
	AA⁵A⁵A	7	4	16	6	35	31	4	1	5	—	—	—	—	—	—	—	—	—	109
	ABBA	—	—	2	7	67	131	32	13	24	14	3	—	2	—	—	—	—	—	295
		15	12	31	17	126	206	51	28	67	53	13	11	17	11	3	3	1	2	667

(N.B. The first and fourth lines (A–A) may fail to tally exactly, through syllables being added or dropping out. The same may happen with regard to the inner lines (A⁵A⁵ or BB). These occurrences are referred to on pp. 47–8.)

If it be admissible that short lines are older than long lines, the table will show that the oldest architectural forms are AA⁵BA and AA⁵A⁵A, and the most recent is AABA; for the first two occur only associated with texts whose lines are short, and the third in association with long lines only.

There is an intimate connexion between the structural plan and the position of the main caesura. In form AABA this caesura is ⬚1, in all other forms it is ⬚5. In all four forms the final note of the first line is ⌐1; the final note of the third line is most often ⌊5⌋, fairly often ⌊4⌋, ⌊3⌋, ⌊2⌋, ⌊1⌋, less often ⌊6⌋, ⌊7⌋, ⌊8⌋, ⌊9⌋. There is one instance of ⌊V⌋. In other words, the lines A⁵A⁵ or BB are exactly similar except for their final note.

The *compass* may be: 1–8, 1–9, 1–♭10, 1–10, 1–11. It may also happen that in the first or fourth line of major or minor tunes ♯VII is occasionally touched; in Doric or Aeolian tunes the lowest note may be VII (No. 101).

The outer lines (A-lines) of tunes whose structure is AA⁵BA or AA⁵A⁵A usually move between 1–5 (or 1–7 if the third is minor). Very often their first note is 1. But in ABBA or AABA tunes the compass of the A-lines very often is 1–8, and the tunes often begin either with 8 or with the leap of an octave

(an idiosyncrasy inherited from the old style).

In forms ABBA and AA⁵BA, line B moves between 5–8, 5–9, or 5–10. It very

39

seldom extends below 5, except when the final note of the third line is ⌊1⌋, ⌊2⌋, ⌊3⌋ or ⌊4⌋. Certain stereotypes to be encountered in the tune-lines are referred to on pp. 48–9.

Scales. The most usual scales are the Dorian, the Aeolian, and the major. The Mixolydian scale, fairly frequent, occurs (very naturally) only in forms ABBA and AABA. Only two instances of the Phrygian scale are known (Nos. 131, 133). In some tunes the A-lines (or, as the case may be, the A⁵ lines) are in the major scale, whereas the B-lines are in the Mixolydian (No. 142). In the B-line of tunes in the Dorian scale the third may be raised (No. 119).

Tunes in the Dorian or Aeolian scale often show pentatonic turns—relics of the old style (No. 105). Sometimes these turns are to be found, not in all four lines, but only in the A-lines or the B-lines. The characteristic melodic turns are the same as were described when dealing with the old style (p. 18).

In many tunes in which the third is minor—these perhaps were originally Dorian or Aeolian—the influence of the modern melodic minor scale (upwards e f♯, downwards f e♭) is perceptible.

It is likewise to the influence of recent art-music that the presence of chromatic changing-notes simultaneously with diatonic ones should be ascribed (e.g. in Nos. 119 and 142 c♯ next to c♮ by way of changing note).

The main caesura may exceptionally fall on any of the following degrees: ⟨2⟩, ⟨♭3⟩, and very seldom ⟨7⟩, ⟨8⟩, ⟨9⟩.

The structure of tunes in which it is ⟨2⟩ is without exception ABBA, and these tunes are in the major scale. We have 23 such tunes:

2 have outer lines consisting of 9 syllables,
5   ,,   ,,   10 ,, (No. 93 *c*),
16   ,,   ,,   11 ,, (Nos. 96, 108).

The final note of the third line is usually ⌊2⌋, more seldom ⌊V⌋, ⌊VII⌋, ⌊1⌋, ⌊5⌋, very seldom ⌊4⌋, ⌊6⌋.

The compass is v–6 (or ♯VII–6).

If we compare the structure of these with that of the Mixolydian ABBA tunes whose main caesura is ⟨5⟩, the difference proves to be that the tunes with ⟨2⟩ are lower by a fourth than those with ⟨5⟩, yet their final note remains 🎼. Therefore they seem to be 'authentic' variants of (existent or non-existent) Mixolydian tunes whose structure is ABBA ⟨5⟩ and whose conclusion is plagal.[1] In point of fact, there exist variants with the main caesura ⟨5⟩ of tunes with the main caesura ⟨2⟩—such are 93 *b* and

---

[1] The terms 'authentic' and 'plagal' are used as they are with regard to old church modes. The following example will best show what is meant by referring to a change from an authentic form to a plagal or vice versa:

Let us take tune No. 93 *b*, which is Mixolydian and whose structure is ABBA with the main

93 c—but of most tunes with the main caesura [2] no such variants are forthcoming. The origin of the latter is probably similar to that of the former.[1]

N.B. A few of the Mixolydian AABA tunes have authentic variants—e.g. Nos. 144 and 150. (Their authentic form is [1] [1] [V] or [1] [1] [2].)

We have 45 examples of tunes whose main caesura is [♭3] (and exceptionally [♮3], as in No. 87).

The structure ABBA is found in 30 of these. The outer lines are:

$$
\begin{array}{rl}
\text{in} \ \ 1 \ \text{instance} & \text{six-syllable,} \\
,, \ \ 5 \ \text{instances} & \text{eight-syllable,} \\
,, \ \ 2 \ \ \ ,, & \text{nine-syllable,} \\
,, \ \ 11 \ \ \ ,, & \text{ten-syllable,} \\
,, \ \ 22 \ \ \ ,, & \text{eleven-syllable,} \\
,, \ \ 2 \ \ \ ,, & \text{thirteen-syllable,} \\
,, \ \ 3 \ \ \ ,, & \text{fifteen-syllable.}
\end{array}
$$

These are properly accessory forms of the Aeolian and Dorian ABBA forms with [♭3] for the original [5]. There exist variants of tunes Nos. 105 and 107 in which the fifth bar is 𝄞 ♪ ♩ ♭♩ . A similar relation exists between tunes Nos. 88 and 87. But a good many tunes (such as No. 82) have no variant with [5]. These arose, perhaps, by analogy.

Of tunes whose structure is AA³BA or AA³A³A (No. 84) with the main caesura [5]. If the final notes of the first and fourth lines is changed from 𝄞 ♩ to 𝄞 ♩ so that we have 𝄞 ♪ ♩ instead of 𝄞 ♪ ♩ , the outcome will be tune No. 93 c obtained as a variant of 93 b. Then 93 b is the 'plagal' form of the tune, 93 c the 'authentic'. The cadence formula of the first and fourth lines of 93 b is 'plagal', that of the corresponding lines of 93 c is 'authentic'.

The passage from one of these forms to the other is frequent in the corpus of tunes belonging to Class B, and even more frequent in Class C. It constitutes a significant fact, which throws light on the origin of certain unusual scales. For instance, it is not unlikely that the Mixolydian scale, fairly common in Class B, should have accrued from a 'plagalization' of major tunes. Indeed, the group of variants 93 a, 93 b, 93 c does not afford a very satisfactory case in point, for there the original form is very probably 93 a, in which the notes of the triad 𝄞 ♩♩ are the main notes of the tune. In variant b the upper two notes of the triad have slid upwards, and the main notes of the tune are 𝄞 ♩ . In other words, the displacement has transmuted the original minor scale into a Mixolydian. Tune 93 c (a variant in major) was derived by a similar process from 93 b.

[1] A well-known tune with the main caesura [2] belongs to this group; it originates in a popular art-song on the text 'Eresz alatt fészkel a fecske' ([1] [2] [5], 11. V–5). Its authorship is unknown.

41

caesura $\boxed{\flat 3}$ we have 15 instances ($A^3 = 3$ degrees above A). They are cast in the same mould as AA^5BA and AA^5A^5A tunes.

Forms AA^3BA and AA^3A^3A occur far more frequently in the Slovakian corpus (but always in invariable *tempo giusto* rhythm). Hence, tunes of similar structure encountered in Hungarian peasant music may be ascribed to Slovakian influences.

There are very few tunes with the main caesura $\boxed{7}$, $\boxed{8}$, $\boxed{9}$ (No. 109) in which the unusual final note may have cropped up as a substitute for the original $\boxed{5}$. Tune No. 132 constitutes an exception: it may be considered as a plagal form of a major tune with $\boxed{1}\ \boxed{5}\ \boxed{2}$ 15, 15, 13, 15. The change from authentic to plagal raised the original main caesura $\boxed{5}$ a fourth, viz. to $\boxed{8}$. There exists only one tune whose main caesura is $\boxed{\flat 6}$; this tune may be considered as a plagal form of a tune (existent or non-existent) with the main caesura $\boxed{\flat 3}$.

The origin of the architectural forms AA^5BA and AA^5A^5A in Hungarian peasant music is for the time being altogether obscure. A few examples of such forms are to be found in Mátray's collection, printed as early as 1854;[1] and eight tunes in Sušil's collection of Moravian peasant songs [2] printed in 1859 show the same structure.

There is no acceptable proof that this structure is originally Hungarian—for the main reason that we have no collection of Hungarian folk-music dating from the first half of the nineteenth century. However, I feel convinced that it was born in Hungary and was known throughout the country even at the beginning of the nineteenth century.[3]

It is even more difficult to determine whence the impulse came to devise these two types of structure. To indulge in hypotheses would be otiose. Yet I wish to point out—without attempting to draw any conclusion from it—one surprising analogy: the relation which exists in the opening of a fugue-exposition between the subject and the answer on one hand, and the relation between the A-line and the A^5-line of Hungarian new-style peasant tunes. There even exist a few instances in which the transposition by a fifth from the A-line to the A^5-line follows exactly the same law as determines the answer in a fugue (Nos. 110 and 113; Bartalus, i, No. 56).[4]

[1] Mátray Gábor, *Magyar Népdalok Egyetemes Gyűiteménye*, Books I–III, 1852, 1854, 1858. See, e.g., Book II, No. 69.

[2] Fr. Sušil, *Moravské Národní Pisně*, Brno, 1859 (containing 1,890 tunes): Nos. 251 *c*, 291 *a*, 330 *a*, 390 *a*, 549, 709 *e*, 795 *a*, 774 *d*—in all of these the tune-lines are short (6–10 syllables).

[3] In the course of recent investigations (even at the very beginning of the present century) AA^5BA and AA^5A^5A tunes were collected from singers sixty or seventy years old. These elderly people would declare that they had received the tradition of these tunes from their grandparents, &c. But, naturally, such statements are of no scientific value.

[4] It is uncertain whether, from the point of view of evolution, there is any connexion between the old-style A^5B^5AB forms and the new-style AA^5BA forms. But I wish to point out that we have a few instances of German folk-tunes in AA^5BA form; e.g. Erk-Böhme, *Deutscher Liederhort* (Breitkopf & Härtel, 1893), vol. i, p. 280.

Possibly structure ABBA originated in the apparently older AA⁵BA structure, whose A⁵-line may have become similar to the B-line. This is quite possible, considering that, broadly speaking, the position of A⁵ and that of B are practically the same.[1] This structure was current in the middle of the nineteenth century, and probably far earlier—although the earliest printed instance (Bartalus, ii, No. 173) appeared in 1875 only. Tune No. 90, in ABBA structure, was known to many old people at the beginning of the present century: hence it is natural to infer that the structure was common property at least fifty years ago.

This structure is undoubtedly a purely Hungarian product; it was transplanted into Slovakian and Moravian folk-tunes towards the end of the nineteenth century, under Hungarian influences.

Structure AABA corresponds exactly to the binary song-form of art-music. One can well understand its important part in the new style; for it had long been usual in Hungarian peasant music—in tunes belonging to Class *C*. Moreover, the old-style structure AABC may be conceived as a transition between the old ABCD forms and the new AABA style.

Rhythm and strophe-structure. It has already been shown that the tunes consist of four lines.

The rhythm of the lines, rich in changes, can always be brought back to one of the *tempo giusto* rhythmic forms of the old style—chiefly to the adjustable forms.

Again, two kinds of *tempo giusto* rhythms are represented: the adjustable (more frequent) and the invariable. Let us again put down the seven *tempo giusto* rhythmic schemata which have been the starting-points of further evolution.

With feminine ending:

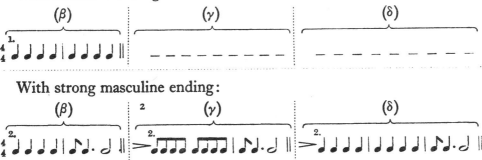

With strong masculine ending:

---

[1] Perhaps this structure might also be compared with structure ABBC, which is most characteristic of the old style. In this case we should admit that, in the course of time, the c-line of a few tunes became similar to the A-line. It is a change of this kind that we notice in No. 74 *c*.

[2] ⟩ means: derived from the previous schema.

With weak masculine ending:

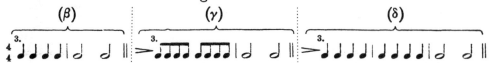

At β we see the three forms referred to on p. 31; at γ, the first stage of further evolution; and at δ, the second stage.

Note. β1 can occur only in B-lines (inner lines). The feminine ending appears to have been found unsatisfactory at the end of a tune.

The later stages may have been reached as follows:

(a) by expansion (thus did δ2 and δ3 arise from γ2 and γ3):

1. (No. 110);

2. (No. 101);

both probably arising from γ2 by partial expansion.[1]

Note. Both may also have arisen from δ2 by contraction, as shown below under (b).

(b) By contraction:

1. (from β2);

2. (No. 107, 3rd line) (from δ2).[2]

(c) By pairs of quavers replacing crotchets (e.g. γ2, γ3 from the original β2, β3):

1. (No. 79) (from β3);

2. (No. 117) (from δ3 and δ2);

3. (from a1);

4. (No. 131) (from δ3 and δ2);

the cadence coming out of (3rd line of No. 93 b, c).

(d) By a minim replacing two crotchets, or a crotchet two quavers:

(No. 93) (from γ2).

(e) By repetition of single rhythmic clauses (bars):

1. (Nos. 128 and 133) (from γ2 and γ3);

2. (from δ2).

[1] Form a1 is already known from the old style (see p. 32, form β1).
[2] b2 is also known from the old style (see p. 32, form β2).

44

(*f*) By additions or insertions—chiefly of interjections:

1. $\frac{4}{4}$ ♩ ♩ | $\frac{2}{4}$ ♫♫ | $\frac{4}{4}$ ♩ ♩ ♩ ♩ | ♪♩. ♩ ‖ (No. 123) (from *a* 2);
   Sej, haj
   ⌣
   Addition

2. $\frac{4}{4}$ ♫♫ ♫♫ | $\frac{2}{4}$ ♩ ♩ | $\frac{4}{4}$ ♪♩. ♩ ‖ (from γ 2).
   Sej, haj
   ⌣
   Insertion

It also occurs that many of these devices are used together. For instance, in lines 1, 2, and 4 of No. 144 we have:

$\frac{4}{4}$ ♩ ♩ ♩ ♩ | ♫♫ ♫ ♩ | $\frac{2}{4}$ ♫♫ | $\frac{4}{4}$ ♪♩. ♩ ‖
⌣
Contraction

which may arise from rhythm (*a*) 1: $\frac{4}{4}$ ♩ ♩ ♩ ♩ | $\frac{2}{4}$ ♫♫ | $\frac{4}{4}$ ♪♩. ♩ ‖ the second and third bars being repeated, but so as to contract into the rhythm ♫♫ ♫ ♩ when rhythm ♫♫ | ♪ ♩. ♩ ‖ first appears—in other words, here we have the three devices *a*, *b*, and *e*.

The evolution of lines 1, 2, and 4 of No. 148 may have been as follows:
A repetition (see above, *e*) changed $\frac{4}{4}$ ♩ ♩ ♩ ♩ | ♩ ♩ ♩ ♩ | ♪♩. ♩ ‖ (that is, δ 2) into $\frac{4}{4}$ ♩ ♩ ♩ ♩ | ♩ ♩ ♩ ♩ | ♩ ♩ ♩ ♩ | ♪♩. ♩ ‖ (*e* 1).

By contraction (see *b*) the tempo of the first bar became quicker; and, quavers replacing the crotchets in bar 3 (see *c*), this bar became ♫♫ ♫♫.

The ending of a tune-line whose syllabic index is even (e.g. ten-syllable) may be strong or weak. Here is one with a weak ending: $\frac{4}{4}$ ♫♫ ♫♫ | ♩ ♩ ‖ (this type is the more frequent; see Nos. 84 and 86); and here is one with a strong ending: $\frac{4}{4}$ ♫♫ ♫♫ ♩ | ♪♩. ♩ | (less frequent; see No. 93). This latter type may be conceived as derived from γ 2 as per (*d*).

The less current rhythm-forms in invariable *tempo giusto* either exist in the old style or might have been derived from forms existing in it by one of the processes described above.

Obviously, tune-lines of twelve syllables or more are not independent formations, but are derived from ten- or eleven-syllable lines. This is shown by the fact that the extra syllables in the corresponding texts consist chiefly of repeated portions of line or of insertions (mostly of adjectives, &c.); by eliminating these repetitions or insertions, lines consisting of twelve, fourteen, sixteen, or eighteen syllables are easily reduced to their

45

original ten-syllable form, and lines consisting of thirteen, fifteen, seventeen, or nineteen syllables to their original eleven-syllable.[1]

The new style is characterized by a remarkable diversity of rhythmic forms. As many as 200 types of lines, all more or less different in rhythm, are available. And the number of strophe-types resulting from combinations of these lines is approximately 380. The tune-strophe types may be classified as follows:

(a) isorhythmic,
(b) heterorhythmic, while still isometric,
(c) heterometric.

The following table gives the comparative frequency of these:

Number of syllables in line (or in outer lines of heterometric types).	Strophes consisting of isometric lines.				(c) Strophes consisting of heterometric lines.	
	(a) Lines isorhythmic.		(b) Lines heterorhythmic.			
	Number of combinations.	Number of tunes.	Number of combinations.	Number of tunes.	Number of combinations.	Number of tunes.
6	3	3	2	4	8	12
7	3	4	3	3	6	8
8	10	18	9	15	7	10
9	7	7	3	3	8	11
10	16	126	7	14	20	22
11	13	108	21	62	44	65
12	7	15	2	4	27	32
13	4	4	1	1	22	26
14	4	21	2	3	27	47
15	5	14	6	8	28	37
16	—	—	—	—	11	13
17	—	—	—	—	10	11
18	—	—	—	—	17	19
19	—	—	—	—	11	11
20	—	—	—	—	1	1
21	—	—	—	—	3	3
22	—	—	—	—	3	3
23	—	—	—	—	1	1
25	—	—	—	—	2	2
In all	72	320	56	117	256	334

Total number of tunes 771

[1] For instance, the original eleven-syllable texts of Nos. 141 and 144 were probably:
(No. 141) Ez a kislány rezet hozott az este,
Rézsarkantyút csináltatott belőle;
Aj de szépen csengett-pengett az este,
Mikor régi babáját beengedte.

46

As shown, most strophes consisting of heterometric lines consist of lines containing eleven syllables or more, but we have no example of an isometric strophe consisting of lines of more than fifteen syllables. This fact shows that the peasant's instinctive sense of proportion was unerringly at work; for strophes consisting of isometric lines of sixteen syllables or more would have proved unendurably clumsy.

We likewise see that the isometric rhythm-forms $(72+56)$ are far more abundantly represented (by $320+117$ tunes) than the heterometric (256 types, but only 334 tunes). The isometric structure first gains ground in association with ten- and eleven-syllable lines. And this fact shows clearly how limited the variety is of tunes constituting the main body of the new-style repertory. About 170 eleven-syllable and 140 ten-syllable tunes—that is, about 40 per cent. of the new-style tunes—are in strophes consisting of isometric lines; and in 30 per cent. the strophe-structure is isorhythmic. In all the first and second lines end with 1 5 except for a very small number of tunes which have 2 or b3. The 56 different rhythmic schemata which we find in them differ only in trifling particulars. And it should be added that in most heterometric structures the inner lines (B-lines) consist of ten or eleven syllables, and the longer outer lines (A-lines) may be considered as derived from ten- or eleven-syllable types. The fact that in over half of these tunes the structure is homogeneous affords the best proof that we are dealing with a style of peasant music that has reached the full strength of its maturity.

In heterometric structures the different lines occur chiefly as follows:

(*a*) Only the third line differs in metre from the others. This occurs in many AA⁵BA forms, some of the AA⁵A⁵A and ABBA forms, and most of the AABA forms (Nos. 110, 111, &c.).

(*b*) The second and third lines are similar in metre and differ from the outer lines. This occurs chiefly in ABBA forms, and—of course—never in AABA forms (Nos. 118, 122).

(*c*) The second and third lines are different from one another and from the outer lines (No. 142).

(*d*) The fourth line is different from (generally longer than) the other three (No. 77).

In heterometric strophes whose outer lines contain from six to eleven syllables, (*a*) is the only possible combination. Then this third line contains a greater number of syllables. In eleven-syllable tunes the conclusion ♪ ♩. ♩

(No. 144) Átulmennék én a Tiszán, nĕm merĕk,
Attul félek, hogy a Tiszábajesĕk;
Lovam hátán férefordul a nyerĕg,
Tisza-Duna habgyai közt elveszĕk.

is often replaced by ♪♪♪♪ ♩ ‖ (e.g. No. 93 *b, c*). Or in six-, seven-, eight- or ten-syllable tunes this line will be a double line (6+6, 7+7, 8+8: No. 76).

In strophes whose outer lines contain twelve syllables or more, combination (*a*) is used chiefly in AABA forms, the B-line becoming a double line. Let it be emphasized that then, if the ending of the outer lines is weak, both halves of this double line have weak endings, and conversely (Nos. 125, 128, 133).[1, 2] A simple third line differing in metre is almost invariably shorter than the other three; the parallelism of the final rhythms of each line is even then noticeable: Nos. 136, 141.

In tunes of twelve syllables or more we encounter combination (*b*). When the final rhythm of the outer lines is weak, the inner lines are ten-syllable; when it is strong, the inner lines are eleven-syllable (No. 117). At times an eleven-syllable inner line with a strong ending may be replaced by a ten-syllable line with a strong ending (No. 122). These formations are really extensions of ten-syllable or eleven-syllable isometric structures, the number of syllables contained in the outer lines having become greater.

Combination (*c*) is a mere offshoot of the above two. The inner lines were originally similar, but the third tune-line was eventually made longer or shorter (No. 142).

There are very few instances of combination (*d*), which occurs only in tunes whose first line contains ten syllables or less. In a few tunes (*d*) is associated with (*a*).

As mentioned before, only the inner lines (and especially the third) can have a feminine final rhythm, which is either ♩ ♩ ♩ ♩ ┊ ♩ ♩ ♩ ♩ ‖, or one of the derived forms ♩ ♩ ♩ ♩ ┊ ♪♪♪♪ ♪♪♪♪ ‖ (No. 110), ♩ ♩ ♩ ♩ ┊ ♩ ♩ ┊ ♩ ♩ ♩ ♩ ‖, &c.

Here are a few more remarks on the patterns of the last bar in lines with a strong masculine ending.

In A-lines this final bar may be:

very frequent   less frequent   scarce

Almost all outer lines containing fifteen syllables or more end with (1) or (2).

The last bar of the second tune-line, when this is an A⁵- or a B-line, may have any one of the above six endings, but higher by a fifth. Exceptionally,

---

[1] ♪♪♪♪ ♩, originating in ♪ ♩· ♩, is a strong ending.

[2] Exceptions occur now and then (Nos. 130, 131). At times the double line has a feminine ending (in the third line of No. 134 we have ♩ ♩ ♩ ♩ ┊ ♩ ♩ ♩ ♩ ‖ twice).

a B-line in that position may end in [musical notation] or [musical notation].

In A-lines with a weak ending the final bar is the stereotyped [musical notation] (in A⁵-lines [musical notation]).

The A-lines of about ten available tunes end with [musical notation] (Nos. 115, 116); more scarce are the endings [musical notation] or [musical notation] These endings are probably the outcome of an external (urban) influence; for in art songs they occur often.

These uniform endings of tune-lines naturally tend to impart a character of uniformity to the tunes; but the variety and often the striking originality of the rhythmic combinations within the lines partly make up for this weakness. In the less numerous tunes in invariable rhythm the endings of the tune-lines are not uniform. Hence these tunes stand out amid the corpus of new-style tunes for the impression of freshness they convey.

Exceptionally, a few new-style tunes are performed *parlando-rubato*: this is probably a survival of old-style tradition, and is the case with one tune whose outer lines are eight-syllable, fourteen tunes whose outer lines are ten-syllable (No. 89), twelve whose outer lines are eleven-syllable (No. 99), and one whose outer lines are nineteen-syllable (No. 146).

In all, the *tempo giusto* $\frac{4}{4}$ [musical notation] is replaced by the *parlando-rubato* rhythm [musical notation] or [musical notation] or [musical notation], &c., the value of [note] being close at times to [note], at times to [note]; the line-ending [musical notation] either remains unaltered or becomes [musical notation].[1]

Ornamentation. In the new-style tunes there are hardly any ornaments; or the ornaments will be melisms consisting of two notes, seldom of three (Nos. 100, 102; eighth bar of No. 122). The *portamento* (or *glissando* towards or from a note) is common.[2]

Relation between tune and text. There can be no definite reply to the

---

[1] The rhythm $\frac{3}{4}$ [musical notation] which occurs now and then in *tempo giusto* tunes (Nos. 97, 115) may have resulted from the hardening of a similar mode of performance *parlando-rubato*.

[2] The *portamento*, an important idiosyncrasy of the peasants' mode of execution, would deserve to be carefully considered. However, it is impossible to go into this question of detail here.

question whether each tune is bound with one text; for there are instances of this and instances to the contrary. Tunes belonging to Class *B* are sung almost exclusively to lyrical texts—texts of love-songs and soldiers' songs, sometimes of match-making songs.

Performance. As the new style is flourishing at the present time, collecting examples of it is far less difficult than collecting examples of old-style tunes. The latter are obtainable from elderly people only, who at times—on account of their age—cannot easily be persuaded to sing, and whose memory is not infallible. It very seldom occurs that we find at the same spot several people who sing old tunes: indeed, we may rejoice if in one village we encounter one person who remembers old tunes. But as regards the new tunes, the position is far different. These are fashionable; every boy and girl knows a good many of them. People sing them in unison while working in the fields or marching, so that indeed in this case we hear 'the spontaneous expression of the peasant's musical instinct', to quote the usual stock-phrase. And we are able accurately to observe the mode of performance. Of course, it is collective singing that provides the most useful opportunity.

The Hungarian peasant uses only chest-notes. Whenever a singer uses head-notes, we may presume that urban influences have been at work. The performance is strongly rhythmed. When marching, singers assign a crotchet to each step: hence ♩ = 100, a pace which we may consider as the normal tempo of new-style tunes.[1] But if only one person is singing, and especially singing to a listener, the pace is often slackened, and sometimes to excess. Hence the normally invariable groups of quavers become adjustable; or—especially when the singer is a young boy—the *tempo giusto* rhythm is altered to a *rubato*.

Another remarkable practice—one might almost say, a malpractice—should be mentioned. It is so common nowadays in the performance of new-style tunes that experienced collectors take hardly any notice of it; but it may perplex tiros so much that they will be unable to recognize the real melodic pattern. It is connected with the steadily growing compass of tunes: in the case of a tune whose compass is 1-♭10 or even 1-12 (so great a compass seldom occurs in the peasant music of any other race) it is not always easy for the singer to select a pitch which will enable him to intone with equal ease all the low and all the high notes. Hungarian peasants do not devote much care to selecting a suitable pitch, but they simplify difficulties in proportion as they occur: whenever a note is too high or too low for them, they transpose it by an octave, regardless of design and rhythmic conditions. This they will do *ad libitum*, perhaps several times in the course

[1] This was probably also the normal pace of old-style tunes in adjustable *tempo giusto*.

50

of one tune. Hence at times the most peculiar leaps of a seventh occur; for instance, instead of the usual ♪♩ we often hear ♩♪ In the course of time this practice has become so usual that many peasants resort to changes of octaves without being driven by need.

Naturally, these accidentally transposed notes should not be noted down as heard, but brought back to the normal. Hence the musical examples in this book contain no illustrations of the practice.

With the diffusion of the new style, the same mannerism has been introduced in the performance of old tunes. But a noteworthy fact is that the Slovaks, who sing many new Hungarian tunes of considerable compass, hardly ever resort to it.

When performing new-style tunes, it is not unusual (especially when the lines comprise more than nine syllables) to repeat the second half of the tune—viz. the third and fourth lines.

The new style is the only one in honour among the younger generation, which tends more and more to ignore the precious legacy of the past. This new current of taste was most plainly observable during the last decades; it mirrors an almost revolutionary change, of which all the relics of our old tunes will gradually be the victims.

This musical revolution has affected not only the Hungarian-speaking zone, but also the Slovak and Ruthenian. Its influence has spread across the country's boundaries over the Moravian and Galician regions, where nowadays young people sing almost exclusively—although, of course, to texts in their own language—either new-style Hungarian tunes or tunes recently born under the influence of that style, and having more or less significant affinities with it. It will not be possible to deal with this interesting fact of evolution except in a projected book on Slovak folk-music.

There are few traces of any influence of the new Hungarian style upon the Rumanians. I shall content myself with giving a few instances which show it at work: two curiously abridged versions of No. 140 appear in the *Chansons populaires roumaines du département Bihar* under Nos. 195 and 196 (see my note on this tune); and a Rumanian variant of No. 143, from the district Maros Torda, is known to us.

Synopsis.

The new style is represented by 770 tunes approximately, not counting variants.[1] There are four architecturally rounded structures that

---

[1] The Színi, Kiss, and Bartalus collections contain in all 48 new-style tunes (apart from a small number of variants); 30 of these are variants of tunes which are also represented in our manuscript collection.

characterize these tunes—and no other tunes—distinctly: AA⁵BA, AA⁵A⁵A (these two are the oldest), ABBA (more recent), and AABA (the newest). Form ABBA is undoubtedly pure Hungarian. The first three have $\boxed{1}\ \boxed{5}\ \boxed{\ }$, the fourth has $\boxed{1}\ \boxed{1}\ \boxed{\ }$. Another characteristic feature is the variable *tempo giusto* rhythm. The rhythmic schemata are either the same as those of the *tempo giusto* schemata of the old-style tunes, or evolved from these.

Lastly, the isometric strophe-structure is characteristic. The apparently heterometric structures that we encounter now and then are reducible to isometric types.

The most common scales are the Dorian, the Aeolian, and the modern major; the Mixolydian is fairly frequent, the Phrygian and the modern minor less frequent.

The number of syllables to a line varies from six to twenty-five; but lines of twelve syllables or more may be considered as extensions of ten- or eleven-syllable lines.

The new style, undoubtedly, is a Hungarian creation. It exercised a considerable influence upon the more recent Slovak and Ruthenian peasant music, but hardly any upon the Rumanian.

The following may be considered as legacies from the old style:

the adjustable *tempo giusto* rhythm;

the isometric strophe-structure;

the many pentatonic turns in tunes in the Dorian or Aeolian scale.

More modern, and probably Western, influences are indicated by:

the rounded architectural structure (especially ABBA);

and the modern major or minor scale.

The tables on pp. 39 and 46 provide statistics. See also p. 51, footnote.

C. OTHER TUNES IN HUNGARIAN PEASANT MUSIC
(Miscellaneous Class)

I HAVE grouped in a special class (which I call the miscellaneous) all tunes lacking one or several of the idiosyncrasies characterizing the two classes hitherto referred to. Hence the class consists of tunes placed together on account of their negative peculiarities, not their positive; in other words, of most heterogeneous elements, no unity of style being discernible.

The more any one of these tunes differs in its characteristics from the tunes belonging to Class *A* or *B*, the more we may suspect that it is of alien origin; if the differences are slight and few, we may believe it to be specifically Hungarian.

For instance, the scale of certain of these tunes is quite obviously pentatonic; the index-figures (of line-endings) and the structural schema are characteristic of the old style, but the strophes are heterometric in structure (Nos. 243, 244, 261). Such tunes stand very close to the old-style tunes of the corresponding sub-class; and it is only on account of their heterometric strophe-structure that they are placed in Class *C*. In others the index-figures, the structural schema (so far as concerns the contents of lines), and the isometric strophe-structure suggest the old style, but the scale cannot be considered as pentatonic in origin.

Again, other tunes are in the variable *tempo giusto* rhythm (in its initial form or further evolved), which is characteristic of the new style; and their index-figures ⌐1⌐ ⌐5⌐ ⌐?⌐ are equally characteristic. But on account of their non-architectural structure (e.g. AABC) they had to go into Class *C*.

The contents of Class *C* is divided into several sub-classes and groups, according as tunes differ more or less from Class *A* or *B*. A few preliminary explanations on general points are needful.

The line-endings vary greatly. We can neither determine a general rule nor even point out a frequent recurrence of any one schema.

The same remark applies to *the scales*. The scales characterizing the other two classes occur: the pentatonic only in a few tunes, heterometric in structure. The modern minor is more frequent than in Class *B*; the Dorian is fairly frequent, the Aeolian and the Mixolydian less frequent, the major most frequent of all. Often the major and the minor scales are represented by 1–5 or 1–6 only. We also encounter the following two scales:

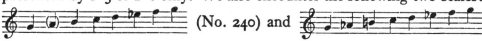

(No. 271); in both, the main melodic notes are ♪. In the

53

second, the notes ab' and b' never follow one another: in other words, the interval of augmented second never occurs. Both are related to the first five degrees of a minor scale starting from c" approximately in the same way as a Mixolydian scale starting from g' is related to the first five degrees of a major scale starting from c". So that one may venture to suppose that these two strange scales originate in the 'plagalizing' of the minor scale (see p. 40, footnote 1). Indeed, we have one example confirming the supposition: No. 218 a in an authentic variant, No. 218 b a plagal. Probably No. 218 a is the original form (anyhow, it is the most widespread) and No. 218 b was derived from it. Likewise, the not very widespread plagal variant, No. 276 b, may originate in the widespread authentic tune in minor, No. 276 a. There is a similar example in Sz.N. 72–75); but there the plagal form, No. 74, is far more widespread than the authentic, No. 72. Nos. 73 and 75 are variants of the former two, differentiated by the use of a major third (73) or sixth (75). In this last group the plagal form should be considered as the original—but the greater or smaller number of available variants is no decisive proof. Often it is impossible to say with certainty which is the primitive form. But as regards the tunes in Class C, which are permeated with obviously alien—West European—elements (and one of these elements is precisely the Western scale, major or minor), we may presume that the authentic forms (major or minor) appeared first, and that the plagal forms are derived forms. 'Plagalizing', by the way, is one of the devices by virtue of which major or minor tunes, whose character is emphatically Western, acquire in Eastern Europe a fresher, almost exotic quality.

We may also presume that certain Dorian, Aeolian, and Mixolydian tunes, especially when their main notes are [music] or [music], are plagal forms of minor or major tunes (Nos. 226, 227; an interesting example appears in Example 299: No. 229 b is a plagal tune in the Dorian or Aeolian scale; No. 229 c, a plagal Mixolydian tune; compare with these the authentic No. 229 a).[1]

It may happen that either of the two scales mentioned above is used *minus* its second or third degree, or the second and third, or the seventh:

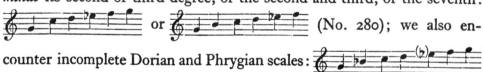

[music] or [music] (No. 280); we also encounter incomplete Dorian and Phrygian scales: [music]

---

[1] The tendency to 'plagalize' is a significant feature in Slovakian tunes, whose function in Slovakian folk-music will be considered in the projected book on Slovakian folk-music.

54

(No. 226) or ♪♪♪♪♪♪ (Nos. 174, 195), &c.

The interval of augmented second appears only in half a dozen tunes or so: its appearance is connected with the raising of the fourth degree in minor (or perhaps Dorian or Aeolian) scales (Nos. 153, 196, 214, 299 a) or of

the seventh degree in the scale: ♪♪♪♪♪♪ (No. 304).

Similar augmented seconds are frequent in the scales used by the Máramaros Rumanians. It is to the influence of these scales that the augmented fourth in No. 196 should be ascribed—possibly the whole tune was taken over from the Rumanian fund of Máramaros.[1] In the other examples doubtless the influence of the augmented seconds which gipsies use to excess in their performances is recognizable. It is perhaps superfluous to point out that these rare appearances afford no sufficient reason for considering the scales with the augmented seconds as specifically Hungarian—quite apart from the fact that the so-called 'Hungarian' scales:

and ♪♪♪♪♪♪ are entirely unknown to Hungarian peasant music: the few examples referred to contain only the augmented second b flat–c sharp or only e flat–f sharp; never do two different augmented seconds appear in one tune.

It is also interesting to note that even then one sometimes finds c used besides c sharp and f besides f sharp, and the intonation of the augmented second is usually rather uncertain—the lower note being a little too high, the upper note a little too low.[2] In No. 153 we find b as well as b flat, c as well as c sharp.

In Class C it often occurs that tunes contain both a natural note and its chromatic alteration (in No. 259 e we have a flat and a, in No. 181 f and f sharp, in No. 241 e flat and e natural, in No. 252 b and b flat, &c.). Chromatic changing-notes are used far more freely than in tunes belonging to Class B (e.g. c sharp in Nos. 176 b and 251, second bar); the changing-note is usually c sharp in major or minor tunes: the interval ♪♪♪ unques

tionably came into being by analogy with ♪♪♪ (as is shown by the second and fifth bars of No. 177).

[1] In the Rumanian musical dialect of the Banat, the augmented second a flat–b occurs very often in the scales of the tunes; but this fact has exercised no influence upon Hungarian peasant music.
[2] The intonation of this interval is equally uncertain among the Rumanians of both the Banat and Máramaros.

A characteristic negative feature is the total absence of the Lydian scale, so widely used in old Slovakian peasant music (No. 274 is not really in the Lydian scale: the characteristic downward movement is lacking—the same occurs in No. 305).

Neither do we encounter here the tunes with latent accompaniment in thirds, which are numerous in the Slovakian fund; these seem to be in the Phrygian scale, and their main notes are . One may adjoin to any of these tunes another tune running parallel to it a third lower, and consisting entirely of notes belonging to the same scale: the tune will then end with the major third .

(These tunes, of Western—probably German—origin, were sung in thirds in the country of their birth and also in the regions through which they first spread. But when they were taken over by races which—as the Slovakian—practise unison-singing only, one of the parts (usually the lower) was left out.)

In Class *C*—or, more accurately speaking, in the sub-classes affected to tunes of alien character—find place most of the so-called 'favourite Hungarian peasant-songs' that are popular among the upper classes in Hungary. These songs, even in Class *C* where evidence of foreign influences is so plentiful and obvious, stand out on account of their alien character; they occur as much in Slovakian peasant music as Hungarian, and again their non-native character is obvious. It is extremely difficult to account for the fact that the upper classes seem deliberately to select, out of all the existing peasant songs, those that are most signally alien in character, and to enjoy none but those.[1]

Class *C* may be divided into seven sub-classes, as follows:
   I. Tune-strophes consisting of four isometric lines, the rhythm being either *parlando-rubato* or an invariable *tempo giusto*.[2]
   II. Tune-strophes of four isometric lines in adjustable *tempo giusto* rhythm.
   III. Tune-strophes of four heterometric lines in invariable *tempo giusto* rhythm.[2]

[1] Indeed, this strange phenomenon occurs in other countries; in Rumania, for instance (see p. 24, footnote 2). It may be supposed, however, that such tunes first acquired popularity among the upper classes and subsequently wormed their way among the peasants. But then it becomes almost impossible to imagine whence and how, in the first instance, they reached the upper classes.

[2] If the tempo be abnormally slow, an adaptation of the rhythm may naturally take place in tunes belonging to this sub-class, as in tunes in invariable rhythm belonging to Class *A* or *B*.

IV. Tune-strophes of four heterometric lines in adjustable *tempo giusto*.
V. Kolomeïka-rhythm (see footnote, p. 73), four-line strophes.
VI. Two-line tune-strophes.
VII. Three-line tune-strophes.

I

The tunes in sub-Class I consist of lines comprising from five to fourteen syllables.

1. Five-syllable lines.

There are only about eight examples of these. In most of them the lines are isorhythmic, the rhythm being either $\frac{3}{4}$ ♩ ♩ ♩ | ♩ ♩ or the variants ♩ ♩ ♩ | ♩ ♩ or ♪♩ ♪♩ | ♩ ♩ (No. 152).

Their structure is ABCD. Two examples are heterorhythmic, the rhythm of one being:

$\frac{3}{8}$ ♪♩ | ♪♩ | ♩. | ♪♩ | ♫♫ | ♪♩ | ♫♫ | ♪♩ | ♪♩ | ♩. ‖

Here we find the so-called Slovakian rhythm-contraction, which will be described hereafter.

2. Six-syllable lines.

(a) *Parlando-rubato* rhythm. We have about 32 examples of such tunes, whose rhythm corresponds exactly to that of the *parlando-rubato* tunes in sub-Class *A* II (Nos. 153–158; Sz.N. 39, 66, 122).

(b) (α) Invariable *tempo giusto* rhythm, lines isorhythmic.
Eleven different rhythmic formulae are known. Of the formulae in Class *A* II (see p. 26) we encounter:

α 1 (Nos. 159–160); α 2 (No. 163); α 3 (No. 161, Sz.N. 43); α 4 (Színi, No. 183); α 5 (No. 162 and the well-known song whose text is 'Szeretnék szántani').

There are also, among others, instances of:

α 8 $\frac{2}{4}$ ♩ ♩ | ♫ ♩ | ♩ ‖ (No. 164);

α 9 $\frac{3}{4}\frac{2}{4}$ ♫ ♩ ♩ | ♩ ♩ ‖;

α 10 $\frac{3}{8}$ ♪♩ | ♪♩ | ♪♩ ‖ (No. 165);

α 11 $\frac{3}{8}\frac{2}{8}$ ♫♫ | ♩ ♪| ♩ ‖ (one tune only; its variants are given in Sz.N. 72–75).[1]

Remark. Most frequent are α 2 (in 16 tunes), α 3 (in 7), and α 1 (in 6); in all likelihood, α 10 is the 'Magyar' adaptation of the German rising rhythm, with up-beat: $\frac{3}{8}$ ♪| ♩ ♪| ♩ ♪| ♩.[2]

---

[1] Three more variants in Bartalus: vol. iii, No. 118, vol. iii, second suppl., No. 1, and vol. iv, No. 90; but all three are set down in entirely incorrect rhythm.

[2] This, in a rhythm similar to the rhythm of the Hungarian examples, is to be encountered also in Slovakian folk-tunes.

57

(b) (β) Invariable *tempo giusto* rhythm, lines heterorhythmic.

About 50 such combinations are known (Nos. 166–178), including the following of the combinations mentioned under *A* II: β 1 (Sz.N. 57); β 2 (Nos. 171–172); and β 4 (the well-known tune whose text is 'Pántlikás kalapom fujdogálja a szél'—Bartalus, vi. 34). It is impossible to describe all these combinations here. The most frequent is β 1, occurring in 5 tunes.

Special attention should be given to the following combination, which we find in 4 tunes (e.g. No. 178):

$$\frac{2}{4}\ \flat\ \flat\ \flat\ |\ \flat\flat\ \flat\ \flat\ |\ \flat\ \|\!:\ \flat\ \flat\ |\ \flat\flat\flat\flat\ :\!\|\ \flat\ \flat\ |\ \flat\flat\ \flat\ |\ \flat\ \|$$

Here ♪♪♩♩ in the second and third lines is in fact the contraction of ♪♪ ♩ ♩ in the first and fourth, ♩ and ♩ having been reduced to two quavers. This rhythm is a characteristic feature of Slovakian peasant music: so that we may definitely assume that any tune of the type under notice in which this 'Slovakian rhythm-contraction' appears is of Slovakian origin (see also Nos. 185 and 205). The arrangement of the text syllables is also peculiar: only two lines are used to a tune, both being repeated. This device is an essential characteristic of this order of tunes.

3. **Seven-syllable** (always in invariable *tempo giusto* rhythm).

(α) Lines isorhythmic.

Of the types mentioned under *A* III, the following occur:
1 (Nos. 179–181), 2, 3 (No. 182), 4 and its variants (No. 183); we also encounter

α 6 $\frac{3}{4}$ ♪♪ ♩ ♩ | ♪♪ ♩ ⌐ ‖ (Színi, No. 78).

α 7 $\frac{6}{8}$ ♩ ♪♩ ♪|♩ ♪♩ ⌐ ‖ (No. 184).[1]

Of these, the most frequent is α 1 (♩♩♩♩ | ♪♪ ♩), of which 27 examples are known. The others occur only in 1 to 4 tunes each.

(β) Lines heterorhythmic.

There are 9 combinations—e.g. the well-known song whose text is 'Falu végén van egy ház', Színi, No. 153.[2]

Undoubtedly No. 185, in the second and third lines of which the Slovakian rhythm-contraction occurs, is of Slovakian origin.

4. **Eight-syllable.**

(a) About 98 tunes are in *parlando-rubato* rhythm, the same rhythm as in the eight-syllable *parlando-rubato* tunes belonging to Class *A* (Nos. 186–193; Sz.N. 31, 32, 70).

[1] Only in one tune, which has Slovakian variants in the same rhythm.

[2] The rhythm of the seventh bar of this song, ♩ ♪♩ ⸳ originates in ♩ ♩ ; so that even the
Hej
third line is to be considered as seven-syllable.

58

(b) (α) Invariable *tempo giusto* rhythm, lines isorhythmic (68 tunes).

The following rhythm-schemata occurring in sub-Class *A* I are represented here:

α 1 (No. 194); α 2 (No. 195); α 4 (No. 197 and the well-known song whose text is 'Debrecenbe kéne menni'); α 5 (No. 196); and α 6 (Sz.N. 25, 89).

We also encounter:

α 8 $\frac{4}{4}$ ♩ ♩ ♩ ♩ | ♩ ♫ ♩ ‖ (the well-known song whose text is 'Kis szekeres, nagy szekeres', Színi, No. 62).

α 9 $\frac{2}{4}$ ♩ ♩ | ♬♬ ♩ | ♩ ♩ ‖ (No. 198).

α 10 $\frac{3}{4}$ ♫ ♩ ♩ | ♫ ♩ ♩ ‖ (No. 199).

α 11 $\frac{2}{4}$ ♩ ♫ | ♩ ♩ | ♩ ♩ | ♩ ‖ (No. 201[1] and the well-known song whose text is 'Gyere be rózsám, gyere be').

α 12 $\frac{4}{4}$ ♫ ♩ ♩ | ♩ ♩ ♩ ♩ ‖·

α 13 $\frac{3}{8}$ ♩ ♪ ♩ | ♪ ♪ ♪ ♪ ♪ ♩· ‖·

Most frequent are α 4 (occurring in 13 tunes) and α 5 (in 9).

(b) (β) Invariable *tempo giusto*, lines heterorhythmic (57 tunes).

Here we find 38 combinations, most of them occurring only in one tune (Nos. 202,[2] 204, 205). Only the following are comparatively frequent:

$\frac{2}{4}$ ♬♬ | ♫ ♩ | ♩ :‖ ♬♬ | ♬♬ | ♬♬ | ♫ ♩ | ♩ ‖

in 7 tunes (e.g. Bartalus, iv, No. 109, and vi, No. 174)

and

$\frac{2}{4}$ ‖: ♩· ♪ ♩ ♩ | ♩· ♪ ♩ ♩ | ♩· ♪ ♩ ♩ | ♫ ♩ | ♩ :‖

in 4 tunes (No. 203 and the well-known tune whose text is 'Ég a kunyhó, ropog a nád').

In this group again we find several instances of Slovakian rhythm-contraction (No. 205).

5. Nine-syllable.

Of these, only 14 examples are known, all in invariable *tempo giusto* rhythm and the lines isorhythmic.

The rhythm-schemata are five:

1. $\frac{2}{4}$ ♬♬ | ♩ ♩ | ♫ ♩ ‖[3] (eight examples; No. 206 and the well-

---

[1] In this ♩ ♫ becomes the triplet ♩ ♩ ♩, and ♩ ♩ becomes ♩ ♩; such transformations of even or angular rhythms into triplets are most characteristic of the Slovakian mode of performance.

[2] This, exceptionally, happens to be a *rubato* performance replacing the more usual *tempo giusto*: ‖: ♬♬ | ♬♬ | ♬♬ | ♩ ♩ | ♩ :‖

[3] A well-known rhythm-formula, frequent in Classes *A* and *B*.

known tune whose text is 'Ezt a kerek erdőt járom én', in Színi, No. 156).

2. $\frac{2}{4}$ ♫♫ | ♫♩ | ♩ ‖ ·

3. $\frac{2}{4}$ ♩ ♩ | ♩· ♪ ♫♫ | ♩ ‖ (Bartalus, i, No. 40).

4. $\frac{2}{4}$ ♫ ♩ | ♫ ♩ | ♩ ♩ | ♩ ‖ (Bartalus, ii, No. 135).

5. $\frac{2}{4}$ ♩· ♪ ♩· ♪ ♩· ♪ ♩ ⌐ ‖ [1] (Bartalus, v, No. 37, in wrongly noted rhythm).

6. Ten-syllable (all in invariable *tempo giusto* rhythm).

(α) Lines isorhythmic (Nos. 207–209; 46 such tunes exist).

Apart from the rhythm-schemata mentioned in sub-Class *A* V and their variants, the following occur:

α 4. $\frac{3}{4}$ ♫ ♩ ♩ ♩ | $\frac{2}{4}$ ♫♫ ♩ | ♩ ♩ ‖ ;

α 5. $\frac{2}{4}$ ♩ ♩ | ♩ ♩ | ♫♫ | ♫ ♩ ‖ ;

α 6. $\frac{2}{4}$ ♩ ♩ | ♩ ♩ | ♫♫ | ♩ ♩ ‖ ;

α 7. $\frac{2}{4}$ ♫♫ | ♩ ♩· | ♫ ♩ | ♩ ‖ ;

α 8. $\frac{3}{8}$ ♫♩ | ♫♩ | ♫♫ | ♩ ⌐ ‖ ;

α 9. $\frac{2}{4}$ ♩ ♫ | ♩ ♩ | ♩ ♫ | ♩ ‖ ·

Remark. α 9 often becomes $\frac{3}{8}$ ♫♩ | ♪ ♩ (No. 208) or ♫♩ | ♩ ♪ (No. 209).

The most frequent are: α 1 (No. 207; 10 tunes); α 3 (7 tunes); α 2 (6 tunes); the remainder are represented by one or two tunes each.

It should be added that some of these tunes are performed *poco parlando*. But this is no essential characteristic: for even then traces of the original *tempo giusto* rhythm remain recognizable.

(β) Lines heterorhythmic.

Here we have six different combinations, each represented by one example only (Nos. 210, 211).

7. Eleven-syllable.

(a) *Parlando-rubato*; about 20 tunes [2] (No. 212).

(b) (α) Invariable *tempo giusto* rhythm, lines isorhythmic. Of this type seven tunes are known. Their rhythm-schemata are:

1. $\frac{2}{4}$ ♫♫ | ♫♫ | ♩ ♩ | ♩ ‖ 5 tunes (Bartalus, vii, No. 179).

---

[1] This particular rhythm-schema, as well as the seven-syllable one given under α 7, is altogether antagonistic to the Hungarian sense of rhythm (see what was said of ♩ ♫ | ♩ ♫ | on p. 27).

[2] Their rhythms correspond exactly to the rhythms of the eleven-syllable tunes in Class *A*.

2. $\frac{2}{4}$ ♩♩♩♩ | ♩♩♩. | ♪♩ ♪‖ [1] = Bartalus, i, No. 67.

3. $\frac{2}{4}$ ♩♩♩♩ | ♩ ♩ | ♩♩♩. | ♩ ‖ = Bartalus, ii, No. 110.

4. $\frac{2}{4}$ ♩ ♩ | ♩♩♩♩ | ♩♩♩. | ♩ ‖ .

(b) (β) Invariable *tempo giusto* rhythm, lines heterorhythmic. Only one example is known.

8. Twelve-syllable.

(a) Rhythm *parlando-rubato*. About 9 tunes [2] (No. 213 and Sz.N. 28; No. 214 and Sz.N. 42, 44; Sz.N. 23, 40).

(b) (α) Invariable *tempo giusto* rhythm, lines isorhythmic. Six tunes, exemplifying five different rhythm-schemata.

(b) (β) Invariable *tempo giusto* rhythm, lines heterorhythmic. Five tunes (among which the well-known song whose text is 'Szücs Marcsa', Színi, No. 53), each in a different rhythm-schema.

9, 10, 11. Thirteen-, fourteen-, and fifteen-syllable.

Represented by 2, 7, and 1 tunes respectively (Nos. 215, 216).

In sub-Class C I the majority of the tunes (about 220) have the structure ABCD; there are 60 instances of AABC, 20 of AABB$_v$, 20 of A⁵B⁵AB, 10 of AABB, 7 of ABBC, 7 of ABB$_v$C, and 6 of AABA. There are about 25 other combinations, each represented by one or two tunes only.

. . . .

Obviously, it is the *parlando-rubato* tunes in sub-Class C I that stand nearest to the old style. We notice differences—probably due to foreign influences—in their scales and in the line-endings; but the *parlando* mode of performance was taken over, practically unchanged, from the old style. No similar *parlando* tunes, no similar *parlando* mode of performance are to be found in the neighbouring countries; so that we may presume that the majority of the above tunes, despite the alien elements that occur in them on a more or less great scale, were evolved on Hungarian soil.

Not so, however, the *tempo giusto* tunes in sub-Class I. Most of these were probably taken over from Slovakia, or cropped up under the influence of tunes taken over; for there is no essential difference between them and the tunes which must have served as models.

This question cannot be considered at greater length here. It would be necessary to go deep into the study of the Slovakian peasant music fund.

---

[1] Corresponds exactly to the *a* 3 rhythm of the ten-syllable examples in Class *A*, except for the extension of one syllable.

[2] Their rhythms correspond exactly to the rhythms of twelve-syllable tunes in Class *A*.

61

Therefore the whole matter will find place in a book on Slovakian folk-music. Let it be pointed out, meanwhile, that most of the invariable *tempo giusto* forms (many represented by the Slovakian variant of the corresponding purely Hungarian tune) are in use in Slovakia.

The so-called Slovakian rhythm-contraction occurs in seven or eight Hungarian tunes only, but in many Slovakian tunes. So that tunes in which it is present may safely be considered as of Slovakian origin.

II

In tunes whose strophes consist of four isometric lines and are in adjustable *tempo giusto* rhythm, the lines may comprise six, seven, eight, ten, eleven, fourteen, or fifteen syllables. Most of their rhythm-schemata were already encountered in tunes in adjustable *tempo giusto* belonging to Class *A* or *B*. Of course, apparently heterometric structures are again to be found (Nos. 220, 222, 223, &c.) in which the longer lines contain additional syllables whose presence does not alter the fundamental character of the rhythm-structure—exactly as is the case with songs in the new style (see pp. 44–46).

1. Six-syllable.

(α) Strophes isorhythmic.

Only one rhythm-schema is known:

$$\frac{4}{4}\ \text{♩ ♩ ♩ ♩ | ♩\ \ ♩ ‖}\quad\text{(2 tunes: No. 217 and Sz.N. 97)}.$$

(β) Strophes heterorhythmic.

Only one tune known.

Remark. The tempo of the above tunes may have been originally quicker, and the rhythm invariable. So that they might be included in sub-Class *C* I, group 2. Later, their tempo and also their rhythm may have changed under the influence of the tunes in adjustable *tempo giusto*, which were becoming more and more popular. We may assume that the same thing happened to the 6, 6, 8, 6 tunes in sub-Class *C* IV, group 6.

2. Seven-syllable.

(α) Lines isorhythmic.

The only rhythm-schema is the well-known $\frac{4}{4}$ ♩ ♩ ♩ ♩ | ♪♩. ♩ ‖. There are 16 such tunes in the minor mode (No. 218), 3 in the Dorian, 4 in the Phrygian, 5 in the Mixolydian (Nos. 219, 220), and 19 in the major (No. 221).

(β) Lines heterorhythmic.

Two rhythm-schemata are known, each occurring in one tune only.

3. **Eight-syllable.**

(α) Strophes isorhythmic.

There is only one rhythm-schema: $\frac{4}{4}$ ♩ ♩ ♩ ♩ | ♩ ♩ ♩ ♩ ‖. Fourteen such tunes are in the minor mode, 4 in the Aeolian (No. 222),[1] 4 in the Dorian, 1 in the Mixolydian, and 19 in the major.

(β) Lines heterorhythmic (9 examples).

Six combinations are known (Nos. 224, 225, Sz.N. 114), each occurring in one or two tunes.

4. **Ten-syllable.**

(α) Lines isorhythmic.

One rhythm-schema: $\frac{4}{4}$ ♩ ♩ ♩ ♩ | ♩ ♩ ♩ ♩ | ♩ ♩ ‖ occurring in 9 examples (Bartalus, iii, No. 157).

(β) Lines heterorhythmic.

Three schemata, each occurring in one or two tunes (Nos. 226, 227).

5. **Eleven-Syllable.**

(α) Lines isorhythmic.

Two schemata, both familiar:

$\frac{4}{4}$ ♫♫ ♫♫ | ♪ ♩. ♩ ‖ and

$\frac{4}{4}$ ♩ ♩ ♩ ♩ | ♩ ♩ ♩ ♩ | ♪ ♩. ♩ ‖.

The first occurs in 5 minor tunes, 1 Dorian, 2 Phrygian, 2 Mixolydian, and 10 major tunes (No. 228); the second in 3 minor, 1 Dorian (No. 229), 1 Aeolian, 1 Phrygian, 1 Mixolydian, 9 major.

(β) Lines heterorhythmic.

Twelve schemata are known. Of these the most frequent (4 examples) is the β 1 type in sub-Class *A* IV (No. 231).[2] We have one example of β 2 (No. 230) and one of β 3 (same sub-class).

We have three instances of:

$\frac{4}{4}$ ‖: ♫♫ ♫♫ | ♪ ♩. ♩ :‖ ♩ ♩ ♩ ♩ | ♩ ♩ ♩ ♩ | ♪ ♩. ♩ |

♫♫ ♫♫ | ♪ ♩. ♩ ‖ (No. 233).

Remark. No. 234 is a very instructive example, in which the metamorphosis process is plainly perceptible. No. 234 *b*, except for a few alterations, is an art-song, which ought to go into group 16 of sub-Class *C* 3. In No. 234 *a* the tune has become isometric, and the rhythm of the third and fourth lines has assumed the primitive schema of the adjustable eleven-syllable rhythm-form.

---

[1] This tune is almost pentatonic, and the question arises whether it does not belong to Class *A*.

[2] In the 2nd and 4th bars the extended form ♫♫ ♩ ⌐ | originates in the primitive ♪ ♩. ♩ ‖.

6. Fourteen- and fifteen-syllable.

We have two examples of the former, three of the latter.

In sub-Class *C* II the most current structure is—as in the foregoing—
ABCD (76 instances); another current one is AABC (40 instances). There are
8 instances of ABCB, and 17 other schemata occur, each in one or two
tunes only.

. . . .

As regards rhythm, the tunes in sub-Class *C* II stand close to the tunes
in adjustable rhythm in Class *A* on the one hand, to those in Class *B* on the
other hand. It is the tunes whose third is minor and whose structure is
ABCD that stand close to those in Class *A* (the line-endings and scales being,
however, more or less different); and the tunes whose structure is AABC (or
some other type not ABCD) or ABCD with major third that stand close to
those in Class *B*—with differences in the structure and in the line-endings.

Their adjustable rhythm—this essentially Hungarian feature—is an
almost absolute proof that they were born on Hungarian soil, although
partly, perhaps, under alien influences. The Slovakian fund comprises
a small number of these tunes: part of them were obviously borrowed from
Hungary, others were born under the influence of the borrowings (more
will be said on this matter in the book on Slovakian folk-music).

III

The sub-class containing tunes whose strophes consist of four heterometric lines, the rhythm being invariable *tempo giusto*, is the richest in
number of tunes and in variety of structural forms.

In order further to classify these tunes into groups, we must observe the
relative differences in the number of syllables to each line.

Each tune usually contains lines of two different lengths. Indicating the
longer line by Z and the shorter by z, we shall use the combination of
letters z, z, Z, z to indicate that in a tune the first, second, and fourth lines
have the same number of syllables, and the third line has a greater number
(e.g. tune No. 246, in which the numbers of syllables are 5, 5, 8, 5). Likewise, Z, Z, z+z, Z will indicate a tune in which the first, second, and fourth
lines are of equal length, but the third is a double line whose two parts are,
singly, shorter than those other lines (e.g. tune No. 237, in which the
numbers of syllables are 11, 11, 5+5, 11). On the basis of the syllabic
proportions, we are able to determine 16 different groups:

1. Z, Z, Z+Z, Z   (e.g. 6, 6, 6+6, 6; Bartalus, iii, No. 135) in 8 cases.
2. z, z, Z+Z, z   („ 6, 6, 8+8, 6;   „   „ 235) „ 5   „
3. Z, Z, z+z, Z   („ 8, 8, 7+7, 8;   „   „ 236) „ 25 „

64

4. Z, Z, z+z, ȥ [1] (e.g. 10, 10, 7+7, 6; Bartalus, iii, No. 240) in 71 cases
5. Z+Z, z, Z+Z, z („   7+7, 5, 7+7, 5;   „   „   244) „ 17   „
6. z, z, Z, z   („   5, 5, 8, 5;   „   „   247) „ 22   „
7. Z, Z, z, Z   („   7, 7, 6, 7;   „   „   249) „ 22   „
8. Z, Z, z, z   („   8, 8, 7, 7;   „   „   250) „ 47   „
9. z, z, Z, Z   („   5, 5, 8, 8;   „   „   253) „ 41   „
10. Z, z, Z, z   („   7, 6, 7, 6;   „   „   256) „ 46   „
11. z, Z, z, Z   („   8, 11, 8, 11;   „   „   261) „ 9   „
12. Z, z, z, z   („   8, 6, 6, 6; Bartalus, iv,   „   61) „ 5   „
13. z, Z, Z, Z   („   6, 9, 9, 9; Bartalus, ii,   „   119) „ 1 case
14. z, z, z, Z   („   8, 8, 8, 12; Bartalus, vii, „   147) „ 12 cases
15. Z, Z, Z, z   („   10, 10, 10, 8; Bartalus, i, „   144) „ 3   „
16. A miscellaneous group; of the tunes it contains, none has
    more than two lines equisyllabic; many have a different
    number of syllables to each line (e.g. 7, 5, 6+6, 5,
    No. 262; 10, 13, 6, 9, No. 266)   „ 85   „

                                                      In all, 419 cases

Remark. For the sake of convenience, all tunes whose structure is Z, Z, Z+Z, z or Z, Z, z+z, z are placed in group 4, all those whose structure is Z+Z, Z, Z+Z, Z or z+z, Z, z+z, Z in group 5.

The specific characters of the tunes in sub-Class *C* III are, on the one hand, quite at variance with what we see in Classes *A* and *B*, which are the most genuinely Hungarian; on the other hand, in the Slovakian, Moravian, and Czech funds, they strike no jarring note (although in all likelihood they are, then, imports from the West, not native growths). Hence we may assume that it is from these three regions that this form of construction came.

Several of these tunes (e.g. Nos. 239,[2] 254, 268) have, in fact, Czech, Moravian, or Slovakian variants. Others (e.g. Nos. 242, 246, 249, 253, &c.) have no known variants of such origin, but the variants may have existed, or still exist. Anyhow, we have many Czech, Moravian, and Slovakian tunes of similar structure. A small number of the tunes in sub-Class *C* III (e.g. Nos. 243, 244, 261) come so close to the tunes of Class *A* through their line-endings, their definitely pentatonic scale, and their characteristic A^5B^5AB structure, that they might be included in the said class. They are, indeed, tunes that appear to originate in the old style, and to have remained untouched in all essentials, although they underwent the influence of certain heterometric strophe-structures (especially of types 5 and 11). Hence, they are to be considered as Hungarian formations, even if they are to be found (as No. 243 is) current in Slovakia.

Even if the heterometric strophe-structures in *C* III correspond exactly,

[1] Here the number of syllables in the fourth line (marked ȥ) is usually shorter than in each part (marked z) of the double line; sometimes it is of the same length (it appeared superfluous to create a separate group to cover this case).
[2] See the remark appended to the text of this song.

in the main, with the similar Czech, Moravian, and Slovakian types of structure, it is interesting to know which structures are most popular among the Hungarians and which among the Czechs, Moravians, and Slovaks.

The scarcity of types 5 and 11 in the Slovakian fund is very striking.

In the Hungarian fund types 4, 9, and 10 occur twice or thrice as frequently as they do in the Slovakian. The reverse obtains as regards types 1, 2, and 3. Type 11 seems to have grown on Hungarian soil. The same cannot be asserted of type 5, which is scarce in the Slovakian fund, but fairly frequent in the Moravian and the Czech.

. . . .

It is not possible to go further into the description of each type of strophe; but a few words should be devoted to the most characteristic, beginning with a few general remarks.

The first type (Z, Z, Z+Z, Z) can be derived from an isometric type, by duplication of the third line of a Z, Z, Z, Z isometric strophe.

The eleventh (z, Z, z, Z) and the fourteenth (z, z, z, Z) are in a way related. In the eleventh the second and fourth lines of the text were extended following upon an extension of the tune-lines; in the fourteenth, the same happened to the fourth only. Both types are scarce in the Slovakian fund.

There also exist relations between type 5 (Z+Z, z, Z+Z, z) and type 10 (Z, z, Z, z), both more scarce in the Slovakian fund than in the Hungarian; and between types 3 (Z, Z, z+z, Z) and 4 (Z, Z, z+z, ʒ) also.

The structure of the fourth type is nearly always AABC (but the second line may be A³, A⁴, or A⁵); the fourth line (marked C or ʒ) generally has the rhythm of the second half or of the end of the A-line (No. 241). So that the whole type seems to have arisen out of Z, Z, z+z, Z by elimination of the first half or of the first three-quarters of the fourth line. Indeed, let us consider in Bartalus the tunes iv. 97, v. 59, and vii. 48: their tune-strophes all belong to the Z, Z, z+z, Z types, and the first half of the fourth line might in all cases be eliminated, so that the strophe-type would become Z, Z, z+z, ʒ without the tune becoming meaningless. There are, moreover, groups of variants consisting of examples belonging partly to type 3, partly to type 4.

A noteworthy fact is that type 3—which is very clumsy—is far more frequent in the Slovakian fund than type 4—whose rhythm is lighter and brisker, and which is the more popular in Hungary. Yet also type 4 is to be considered as a Slovakian product; the demonstration of this point will be given in the book on Slovakian folk-music.[1]

. . . .

[1] The well-known tune 'Azt mondják, nem adnak engem galambomnak' (Színi, No. 92), whose origin is undoubtedly Slovakian, belongs to type 4; so does another tune (Bartalus, iii. 114) closely resembling it.

Type 4 is the most frequent in the Hungarian fund (71 tunes in *C* III; that is, roughly, 17 per cent.); and again most frequent in tunes in which Z is eight-syllable, z six- or seven-syllable, z four- or six-syllable (15 tunes). The eight-syllable Z-line may be:

$$\frac{2}{4} \text{[musical notation]} \quad \text{Ossia} \quad \text{[musical notation]} \quad ;$$

$$\frac{2}{4} \text{[musical notation]} \quad ;$$

$$\frac{2}{4} \text{[musical notation]} \quad , \&c.$$

The rhythm of the z line is usually [musical notation].

The most characteristic arrangement is 8, 8, 6+6, 4:

$$\frac{2}{4} \text{[musical notation]}$$

(Színi, No. 111).

Other tunes belonging to this group are: Sz.N. 27, 64; Bartalus, i. 20; ii. 155, 194; vii. 120, 189, 191, &c.

Type 10 (Z, z, Z, z) is fairly frequent (46 tunes; that is, 11 per cent.), the structure being mostly 7, 6, 7, 6, or 8, 6, 8, 6:

$$\frac{2}{4} \text{[musical notation]} \quad \text{(19 tunes: No. 256, Sz.N. 5, 139); and sometimes 8, 5, 8, 5:}$$

$$\frac{2}{4} \text{[musical notation]} \quad \text{(7 tunes: No. 258).[1]}$$

Both structures show the 'Kolomeïka' rhythm, to which further reference is made under sub-Class *C* V.

Tunes 259 *a*, *b*, *c*, *d*, *e* constitute a most instructive example of tune-transformation (see the remarks appended to this group).

Equally frequent is type 9 (z, z, Z, Z; 47 tunes, or 11 per cent.). It comprises 34 different rhythm-schemes (most of them occurring in one known tune only); and in fourteen tunes the z lines are octosyllabic. To this group belong the well-known tunes 'Két malomra tartok számot' (Bartalus, vi, No. 166), 'Erdő mellett nem jó lakni' (Bartalus, ii, No. 172, rhythm wrongly noted), 'Ezer esztendeje annak' (Bartalus, i, No. 121).

Type 5 (17 tunes) calls for special notice.

The structure of eight tunes is A^5B^5AB, and six of these eight are pentatonic or Dorian (Nos. 243–245; Bartalus, ii, No. 201). Therefore we may consider these tunes as Hungarian products, although all except 244 are fairly current among the Slovaks. The two A^5B^5AB major tunes, No. 242 and Bartalus, i. 95, and generally speaking all the A^5B^5AB major tunes in the other sub-classes of Class *C* may be considered as Slovakian in origin, because

[1] In this particular tune the given number of syllables does not include repetitions.

a great number of such tunes occur in Slovakia. But apart from the examples just mentioned, hardly any Dorian or pentatonic tunes with the structure A⁵B⁵AB are to be found in that country.

The sub-class also comprises six tunes whose structure is ABCD or ABCB (the main caesura being $\boxed{1}$, $\boxed{2}$, or $\boxed{5}$: Színi 57; Kiss, p. 446, No. 1). These we may safely consider as taken over, because many similar forms occur in the Czech, Moravian, and Slovakian funds.

The cross between the Hungarian tune-structure A⁵B⁵AB and the alien strophe-structure Z+Z, z, Z+Z, z may be accounted for as follows:

The tendency to construct isometric tune-strophes of the A⁵B⁵AB type and in the pentatonic scale spread from Hungary westwards. Conversely, the strophe-structure Z+Z, z, Z+Z, z, chiefly in conjunction with the use of the major or minor scale and of main caesura $\boxed{1}$ or $\boxed{2}$, was imported into Czech, Moravian, and Slovakian regions, possibly from Germany; that is, it spread from West to East. Where these two currents bifurcated there arose, on the one hand, the Hungarian A⁵B⁵AB forms whose scale is pentatonic and whose strophe-structure is Z+Z, z, Z+Z, z, and on the other hand the Moravian and Slovakian A⁵B⁵AB forms, whose scale is major and whose strophes are isometric or heterometric.

Type 11 is represented in 9 tunes (the percentage is therefore 2).

Of these nine, the following call for special notice:

$\boxed{1}$ $\boxed{5}$ $\boxed{1}$, 6, 8, 6, 8; structure AB⁵AB (Színi 37; Bartalus, iv, Nos. 96 and 155). This tune occurs in the Slovakian fund also; but it should be considered as a Hungarian formation, because it is comparatively scarce among Slovaks and because its structure is fairly similar to the characteristically Hungarian A⁵B⁵AB.

Two 8, 11, 8, 11 tunes (No. 261 and Bartalus, vi. 111) and one 8, 14, 8, 14 tune. All four lines of their texts are octosyllabic. To the extra notes in lines 2 and 4 are sung refrains such as 'ejeha', 'hajrá haj', 'ricaca', or 'csillagom, galambom'. This shows that the tune-lines were originally isometric —which is further demonstrated by the nature of the melodic additions.[1]

Type 14 is represented by 12 tunes (percentage 3). The same may be said of the extension of the fourth line. Refrains such as 'kis angyalom', 'eszemadta', 'ihajja', 'hej dunárom', 'kedves angyalom' are used under the extra notes; in three instances repeated words occur instead of a refrain. So that again we may assume that this type was derived from an isometric type.[2] Examples: Sz.N. 114; Bartalus, ii. 90; iv. 106; v. 40; vii. 147.

The Miscellaneous (16th) group comprises 85 tunes (percentage 20),

[1] No. 261, with its pentatonic scale and A⁵B⁵AB structure, stands very close to the old style. The other two tunes exemplify the remarkable structure A⁴B⁴AB, which probably originated in a lowering by a degree of the first half of an A⁵B⁵AB form.

[2] The same may be presumed of many heterometric tunes belonging to other types; but it is impossible to consider here each case in detail.

which represent so many types of structure that no classification can be usefully attempted here.

Examples: Nos. 262–268, Sz.N. 3, 12, 20, 35, 38; the tunes whose texts are 'Debrecenben kidobolták, hogy a dongót ne danolják' (Színi, No. 173); 'Ez a kislány megy a kútra' (with the refrain 'Hajnalban, hajnal előtt': Bartalus, v, No. 161), 'Kakas a szemeten annyit nem kapar' (Bartalus, i, No. 129), and 'Én elmentem a vásárra félpénzzel' (Bartalus, i, No. 23).

In sub-Class C III the relatively small proportion of ABCD-structures (about 130) and the relatively great proportion of AABC-structures (about 150; the second line is sometimes A^3, A^4, or A^5) is remarkable. In 14 tunes we encounter A^5B^5AB; eight of these belong to type 5, and four to the sub-class in Kolomeïka-rhythm of type 10 (Sz.N. 139).

In 20 tunes we encounter AABB$_v$ (sometimes the second line is A$_v$; the fourth may be B). Naturally the strophe-type is almost always 8 or 9.

Remarkable, but easily explicable, is the occurrence of schema AABA in three tunes whose strophe-type is 3,[1] and in three tunes whose strophe-types are 1, 4, and 7 respectively. And there are 21 other types, each exemplified by one, two, or three tunes.

IV

The next sub-class is that of tunes whose strophes consist of four heterometric lines, the rhythm being a variable *tempo giusto*. These tunes differ from those in sub-Class III only in the rhythm of the tune-lines. By virtue of their specifically Hungarian rhythm, they are fairly closely related to tunes in similar rhythm belonging to Class B. And most of them—especially those whose variable rhythm is not to be considered as an aftergrowth—may be accepted as Hungarian products. Some of them represent stages of transition between Classes C and B.

Let us, for instance, compare tune No. 273 (Class C) with tune No. 144 (Class B). The structure of the former is the old ABCD, that of the latter is ABB$_v$A. The relationship is obvious, because the third and fourth lines are almost the same in both. It is difficult to determine which of them is older. Both are sung by young folk.

Even more interesting are Nos. 299 *a*, *b*, *c*, which show the beginning, middle, and end of the line leading from Class C to Class B. No. 299 *a*—probably an old art-song—is, syllabically, 10, 10, 8+8, 12; its structure is AABC, its rhythm invariable,[2] and it belongs to sub-Class C III, group 16

[1] It must be noted that many AABA tunes in Class B, in which the third line is a double line, exemplify the very same structure Z, Z, z+z, Z. Their evolution certainly took place under the influence of this type of strophe-structure already tested in the tunes belonging to Class C.

[2] This tune is occasionally performed *parlando*, with a few adjustments of the rhythm.

(miscellaneous). In No. 299 *b* the rhythm has become adjustable, and hence the tune really belongs to *C* IV, group 16; the numbers of syllables remain the same, and the structure is AA⁵BC. In No. 299 *c* we have the last stage of evolution. The line-endings are ⌐1¬ ⌐1¬ ⌐1¬, the syllabic indices are 12, 12, 8+8, 12 (or 14, 14, 10+10, 14), and the structure is AABA. The tune, for these reasons, belongs to Class *B*. It is, in the strict sense of the term, a peasant song, born out of an art song. The assumption that No. 299 *a* is the oldest of the three variants is supported by unquestionable proof: this version was known to old folk only, and the other two only to younger people.[1]

Another remarkable fact is that No. 275 *b* and No. 276 *a* have variants exactly twice as long as the originals, disposed thus: the first line = first and second of the original, the second line is the same as the first, the third = third and fourth lines of the original, and the fourth is the same as the first and second. Hence, out of No. 275 *b* has come a tune which is ⌐1¬ ⌐1¬ ⌐5¬, 19, 19, 12, 19, AABA; and out of 276 *a* one which is ⌐1¬ ⌐1¬ ⌐b3¬, 14, 14, 12, 14, AABA—both belonging to Class *B*.

We also have instances of tunes belonging to sub-Class *C* IV which originate in the abridgement of art songs belonging to Class *B*. Such is No. 151 *b*: ⌐V¬ ⌐5¬ ⌐1¬, 8, 7, 8, 14, ABCD, born out of the second half of No. 151 *a*, an art song, very popular of late among the people. Another interesting example is No. 285, which appears to have originated in the second half of the main subject of the chorus 'Meghalt a cselszövő és elmúlt a viszály' in Franz Erkel's opera 'Hunyadi László' (see remark appended to this tune).

The Slovakian fund also comprises a sub-class corresponding to *C* IV. The relation between this sub-class and the Hungarian *C* IV is not quite clear. Many tunes are common to both (e.g. Nos. 272, 275, 278, 285, 290) and are probably Hungarian in origin.[2] Other tunes show similar strophe-types, the rhythm of the lines and the structure being, however, dissimilar. Of

---

[1] It is only of a very few tunes that we have variants exemplifying all three stages. One can only wonder how many other examples would be available had Hungarian peasant music been collected at an earlier date.

[2] At times this origin is so obvious that no further proof is needed—e.g. when the Slovakian text of a song contains a refrain which is a corrupt form of a Hungarian refrain. Such are:

'Čilagom, rad'agom galambom' (< Ragyogó csillagom, galambom).
'En vad'ok en, zorgo a legeň' (< ?).
'Ej, barna baba' (< Barna babám).
'Látod baba' (< Látod babám).
'And'alom, vilám, dere be,
Fordo čak ed'ser a elembe' (< ?).
'Rin vaj revere
rožám dere be' ⎫
and thence: ⎬ (< Rin vaj revere,
'Leva levele   ⎭   Rózsám gyere be).
ruzan dzerebebe'

these we must surmise that although they were born under Hungarian influences they are native and independent Slovakian formations. More will be said on this matter in the book on Slovakian folk-music.

Special notice should be given to Nos. 269 and 271. Both are to be found in the newer repertory of the Máramaros Rumanian music dialect (see notes to these two songs). They were apparently taken over from Rumania.

No. 270 recalls, in a measure, No. 192 in sub-Class *C* I, and possibly was derived from it.

Of the strophe-types described with regard to sub-Class III, 2, 12, and 15 are not represented here.

Strophe-type 1 is exemplified in Nos. 269,[1] 270, 271.

,,	3	,,	,,	No. 272.
,,	5	,,	,,	,, 274.
,,	6	,,	,,	Nos. 275–279.
,,	7	,,	,,	No. 280.
,,	8	,,	,,	Nos. 281, 282.
,,	9	,,	,,	No. 283.
,,	10	,,	,,	Nos. 284–289, 151 *b*.
,,	11	,,	,,	,, 290–294.
,,	14	,,	,,	the 'Kossuth' song (Szini, No. 186).
,,	16 (miscellaneous) is exemplified in Nos. 295–300.

I shall restrict myself to describing the two main types.

Type 6 (z, z, Z, z).

We know 33 examples of it, 19 of which have the following rhythm:

(Nos. 275–278, Szini 7,[2] 148).

The form marked *ossia* is a remarkable, pseudo-heterometric strophe-structure which may be considered as a transition between the six-syllable isometric type and the heterometric 6, 6, 8, 6. The evolution of the third line probably took place as follows:

Invariable rhythm.   Adjustable rhythm.

1st stage:

2nd ,,

3rd ,,

[1] I have not included in my reckoning the extension of the fourth tune-line over the syllables 'ihaj csuhaj'.   [2] With a few modifications of the rhythm.

The crotchet or minim over 'Hej' in the second stage may in certain cases be considered as an interpolation, and accordingly be omitted from the count[1]; then the strophe may be considered as isometric (as in No. 173). But for the sake of convenience, all tunes that have variants illustrating the third stage of evolution are placed, with their variants, in the group of the heterometric tunes.

In the schema of this third stage the ♩ or ♩ of the second stage become,
hej   hej
respectively, ♫ or ♩ ♩, but the number of syllables in the text-line is increased to eight, so that the interjection 'hej' is suppressed.

Remark. I presume that in the 6, 6, 8, 6 tunes, and the tunes belonging to sub-Class *C* II, group I (see the remark on p. 62), the rhythm, originally, was invariable, and the tempo quicker. Adjustable rhythm and slower tempo probably came later, in all likelihood under the influence of other tunes in adjustable rhythm. The above tunes stand fairly close to the 6, 6, 8, 6 tunes in Class *B*.

Strophe-type 10 (Z, z, Z, z; 15 tunes).

Two rhythm-schemata are known:

1. $\frac{4}{4}$ ‖: ♩ ♩ ♩ ♩ | ♩ ♩ ♩ ♩ | ♩ ♩ ♩ ♩ | ♩   ♩ :‖ , in 8 tunes (Nos. 284, 285).

2. $\frac{4}{4}$ ‖: ♩ ♩ ♩ ♩ | ♩ ♩ ♩ ♩ | ♩ ♩ ♩ ♩ | ♪♩. ♩ :‖ , in 7 tunes (Nos. 286–289 [2]; 151 *b*).

They are fairly frequent in the Slovakian fund. Their origin is difficult to determine.

Structures ABCD and AABC (in the latter the second line may be A³, A⁴, A⁵, or Aᵥ) exist in sub-Class *C* IV in the same proportion as in sub-Class III: of ABCD we have about 70 examples, of AABC about 60. Structure A⁵B⁵AB never occurs. In two tunes the structure is AABBᵥ—a structure which, here as in sub-Class III, is to be found in groups 8 and 9. Six other structures are represented by one tune each.

·   ·   ·   ·   ·   ·   ·   ·   ·   ·

In *C* I–IV we also encounter a remarkable ABCD structure, that of tunes consisting of four statements in a descending sequence, of one pattern (e.g. Nos. 181, 182, 206, 217, 250). Sub-Class I comprises many such tunes in the major mode. Even a greater number are to be found in the Czech, Moravian, and Slovakian funds. So that we suppose this type to have been introduced into Hungary through Slovakian agency. In a very few instances it has found its way into the old style (see p. 35).

[1] In the Slovakian fund we often encounter similar interpolations (e.g. at the beginning of the 2nd and 4th line of a tune). These are never to be counted for the purpose of determining the form: otherwise it would be very difficult to carry out a survey.

[2] The increase in number of syllables noticeable in a few lines of Nos. 288 and 289 was not taken into account.

V. Four-line tunes in Kolomeïka rhythm.

Коломийки [1] is the designation given to certain Ukrainian or Ruthenian dance tunes whose rhythm-schema is as follows:

$\frac{2}{4}$ [musical notation]

First line   Second line

(in the Huzul region the rhythm ♩ ♩ generally becomes ♪ ♩ ♩).

In certain tunes the second line with its text is repeated, the last note alone being different. In the songs of the Ruthenes living on Hungarian soil [2] it is usually the last two bars of the second line that are repeated thus. Or, instead of this repetition, two (or sometimes four) extra bars are filled with a tag sung to some kind of refrain. I shall not say more on the Kolomeïka tunes at present. Their enormous number and their entirely homogeneous structure indicate that they represent an independent, self-contained style.

In the Hungarian fund group 10 of sub-Class III (Z, z, Z, z) contains about 15 tunes whose rhythm is in the main that of the Kolomeïka (No. 256 and the well-known song 'Elvesztettem zsebkendőmet, megver, anyám érte', Színi, p. 174). Probably their origin is not unconnected with the Ukrainian Kolomeïka tunes. They are scarce, their structure lacks unity, and therefore their significance as regards the Hungarian fund is very slight. Their structure may be defined as consisting of four lines, the numbers of syllables being 8, 6, 8, 6 or 7, 6, 7, 6. Hence they take place in sub-Class *C* III.

The Hungarian fund also comprises a greater number of tunes in similar rhythm, but twice as long (29 tunes and many variants).

Here are the four types of tune-line rhythms occurring in the above tunes:

(*a*) 1. [musical notation] (No. 303 *a*).

2. [musical notation] (Nos. 301, 303 *b*).

(*b*) 1. [musical notation] }
2. [musical notation] } (No. 303 *c*).

In the same tune 1 and 2 may alternate, but (*a*) and (*b*) never do.

The chief caesura is: in 1 tune [V],

     „ 14 tunes [1],

     „ 6   „   [5],

     „ 4   „   [♭3],

     „ 2   „   [4],

     „ 2   „   [2].

---

[1] See Lud'keveč, *Halečko-ruški narodni mel'odiji*, Etnografičnej zbirnek, vol. xxi, Lemberg, 1906, published by the Ševčenko Society; 1,525 tunes—pp. 244–283, tunes Nos. 1019–1211.

[2] In my own unpublished collection (81 Ruthenian songs from the districts Máramaros and Ugocsa) are 16 Kolomeïka tunes.

The most frequent structure (16 examples) is AABB (the second and fourth lines occasionally being A,B,). There are 6 examples of AABC. A peculiar structure, A^5A^5AA, standing close to A^5B^5AB, occurs in two instances (the second and fourth lines may also be $A^5{}_vA_v$).

The scale is Dorian or Aeolian, and often may be conceived as almost pentatonic. The scale of No. 302 is quite pentatonic.

This group of tunes, as is seen, stands very close to the old style, and indeed might perhaps be considered as belonging to it. I refrained from following this course for two reasons: firstly, the characteristic structure AABB is very exceptional in the old style; and secondly, the alien origin of the tunes is obvious.

The peculiar extension of the form to twice the length of the Ukrainian Kolomeïka tunes may perhaps be accounted for as follows.

In olden times the isometric four-line strophe was the only one used by the Hungarians. When the two-line Kolomeïka tunes trickled through, they were considered as halves of tunes, and instinctively transformed into the usual type of four-line tune, simply by repetition of each line in turn. Hence the structure AABB instead of the original AB. The repetition may also have occurred with a change of the final note of each line, whence the arrangement into two periods, AA, and BB, (structure AA,BB,). It should be remarked that besides such extended forms a small number of two-line variants are to be encountered; according to the old Hungarian conception, these stand as halves of tunes in comparison with the four-line tunes.

Remark. Possibly the above-mentioned tunes, placed in group 10 of sub-Class *C* III, are likewise halves of tunes. Yet, as their full form is unknown, and they may be considered, by analogy with other tunes, as consisting of four heterometric lines, it appeared preferable to admit them into sub-Class *C* III.

It is possible that these Kolomeïka tunes, after their introduction into Hungary, endured for a time in their original two-line form—or, according to the old Hungarian notion, as halves of tunes—to be extended at a later date. But we may conclude, from the fact that the extended four-line forms stand very close to the old style, that the extension took place far back in the past.

They may have been used as dance tunes, and possibly as tunes of Kanász (swineherd's) dances. At least, that much may be inferred from certain features of their texts (Nos. 302, 303 *b*).

Apart from the aforesaid 29, there are 16 tunes in similar rhythm, but in the modern major. Such are No. 305,[1] Kiss, p. 384; Bartalus, iv. 104, &c. The relation between the two groups is, roughly, the same as between the

[1] Here the rhythm ♩♩♩♩ | ♩♩♩♩ | is changed, at times to ♩♩♩♩ | ♩. ♪ |, at times to ♩♩♫ | ♫ ♩ |. It may be doubted whether this tune actually cropped up under Kolomeïka influences. If so, it should go into sub-Class *C* I on account of its eleven-syllable, isometric lines and of its invariable *tempo giusto*.

isometric *parlando-rubato* major tunes (*C* I) and the corresponding penta-tonic tunes in Class *A*.

The Rumanian dance tunes of the 'Ardeleana' type, without text, prob-ably originate in the Ukrainian Kolomeïka. Hence there exists a certain connexion between them and the Hungarian Kolomeïka form. This con-nexion is perceptible most clearly in No. 303 *c*. The matter can only be dealt with in full in a projected book on Rumanian folk-music.

VI, VII

Comparatively few two-line and three-line tunes are to be found in the Hungarian fund.

Part of the 76 two-line tunes seem to be halves of tunes, some of which belong to the old style and some to the new. Their full, four-line forms are unknown. The origin of the remainder—most of them in invariable *tempo giusto*, as Nos. 306 and 307—is not clear. Whether they are incom-plete tunes, or peculiar independent formations, cannot be ascertained. A few of these occur in the Slovakian fund.

Of the 79 three-line tunes, 51 have their main caesura at the end of the first line, 28 have it at the end of the second.[1]

The three-line asymmetric tune-structure can hardly be considered as a primitive form. It should be either the expansion of a two-line type or the contraction of a four-line type. The very arrangement of the text-lines shows this. A three-line text-strophe in peasant songs is the greatest of rarities, and one never to be encountered in the Hungarian fund; the third line will consist of a repetition of one of the two original lines or of an added refrain.

Whether all three-line tunes actually originate in two-line or four-line tunes cannot be ascertained. Certain Hungarian three-line tunes have four-line variants; e.g. No. 310 (ABC) is to be found in four-line form (AABC) in Vikár's collection. Of Színi, No. 17 (ABC), we have a four-line variant in Bartalus, i, No. 128 (AA⁵BC); and four Slovakian four-line variants of No. 313 (more on this point hereafter). In other words, what occurs in four-line tunes is that the A-line of the three-line ABC structure is repeated in some fashion or other. There is a great likelihood that if a few three-line tunes, curtail-ments of longer tunes, were available, then actual original three-line tunes may have been created in imitation of these.

The structure of three-line tunes whose main caesura is at the end of the first line may usually be compared with the four-syllable type AABC, some-times with the type AABA. For three-line tunes whose main caesura is at the end of the second line, the comparison should be with ABCC.

[1] But in certain cases it is difficult to decide which is the main caesura: so that perhaps it might be better to forgo this mode of classification.

75

Two particular sub-groups arise out of the first-mentioned group:

(1) Major or minor tunes in invariable *tempo giusto*, whose structure is
1̄ |?̄|, ABA, B always being, and A sometimes being, a double line (usually
8+8). Such are: No. 309; the well-known tune whose text is 'Víz, víz, víz,
nincsen olyan víz' (Bartalus gives it, iii, No. 83, to another text); Bartalus,
vi, No. 156, and i, No. 127 (this last, exceptionally, has 2̄ |3̄|).
The texts consist of so-called homologous strophes.[1] The order of the
text-strophes usually is: 1st line, 2nd line, 1st line.

Eight examples in all are known, all of which are obviously of foreign origin.
Indeed this tune-structure often occurs in the Czech songs [2] (probably, it is
of German origin, and reached Hungary through Slovakian channels).

(2) Songs with the refrain 'Libizáré labzom'[3] or some similar refrain
(Nos. 308, 311, 312; Bartalus, i. 114).
The structure of all these is either AA$_v$B or ABC. Their *tempo giusto*
rhythm may originally have been invariable, but the pace of most tunes
became slower—probably not before the modern period—and the rhythm
became variable. A remarkable feature is that the refrain is inserted to
represent the third line. Here is an example which will stand in good
stead of explanations:

Line 1. A mi kutyánk megfázott,
Line 2. Varrtam neki—libizáré labdony
⎵⎵⎵⎵⎵
refrain
Line 3. Labdonyija libidonyi pütyürütyü—nadrágot.
⎵⎵⎵⎵⎵
refrain

Often the second and third lines contain a repetition of the first line
instead of new text, the refrain breaking out in the middle as shown above.
This may have been the original arrangement; for in the very widespread

[1] This word is used, in accordance with Kodály's practice, to designate strophes of poems in
which 'the consecutive strophes contain only one or two dissimilar words, the remainder of the
contents being always the same, but appearing in a new light by virtue of the changed words'.
See Z. Kodály, 'The strophe-structure of the Hungarian folk-tune', Nyelvtudományi Közlemények, vol. 36, Budapest, 1906.
[2] See K. J. Erben, *Nápěvy prostonárodních písní českých*, Prag, 1863, Nos. 26, 213, 318, 384,
485, 499, 744, &c.
[3] The refrain consists of meaningless words (as is often the case with refrains) and perhaps
aims at mimicking some foreign idiom—possibly a gipsy idiom. Apart from this type of refrain,
we have another in two variants: 'sej idrom-fidrom, gálica szikszom' and 'jó igrom-figrom
gránicom szikszom'. Both are to be found in Slovakian tunes of similar structure: 'libezaji
labzom, labzaji bumbum', 'iksom figurom punktom zamurom', and 'iksom fiksom kompaṣarom'.
In the Slovakian examples many other most peculiar refrains occur; e.g. 'Handža mindža
hazatri, za tri metre tri na tri', or 'sumbr jabr maksu sumbr miksu zabr volta gabr', or 'šnip
šnap šnibrdan, šnibiribi zabrdaj'.

Slovakian songs that are related to the examples under notice, this practice is universal to the present day.

When the refrain starts, a break occurs in the melodic line, which resumes its natural course only when the text proper reappears—that is, in the last bar. The portions of the tune affected to the interpolated refrain are themselves interpolations.

At times the two lines of the text are sung in their entirety to the first two tune-lines, and the last two or three syllables of the text are repeated until the end of the tune is reached.

The first tune-line (and, correspondingly, each text-line apart from the refrain) is always heptasyllabic. The texts—in accordance with the nature of the refrain—are always jocular. Eleven examples of such songs are known; they probably are of foreign origin.

A few words must be added as to the origin of No. 313. There exists a Hungarian song—probably an art song in the folk-character—

whose text is 'Kertem alatt faragnak az ácsok' (also in Bartalus, iii. 130, with a few changes and to another text). This song became popular among Hungarian, Slovakian, and Moravian peasants; became, in fact, a peasant song (No. 86 may perhaps be a form of the same tune adapted under rural influences; it stands near the well-known tune sung to the text: 'A Csapuccán véges-véges-végig'). Another probably derived from it is the popular Slovakian one whose text is 'Pri Prešporkom, pri tychom Dunajku', in which the Slovakian rhythm-contraction (see p. 58) is to be seen:

This Hungarian tune, after taking a Slovakian form, passed into Hungary again. Then, by analogy with Hungarian models, the second and third lines were considered as a double line, and the tune accordingly as a three-line tune: so that the first was simply left out so as to obtain a symmetric two-line form instead of a form which Hungarians felt to be asymmetrical. Possibly, the form of the tune given under No. 313 arose in this very way.[1] This is one of the most instructive instances of the changes undergone by a tune during its peregrinations.

[1] It is easy to explain the fact that lines 2 and 3 were conceived jointly, as a double line: not only because the inner lines, with their Slovakian rhythm-contraction, actually behave as one double line, but also because the B-lines in AABA tunes in the new style are generally double lines. It would have been equally logic, when carrying out the alteration, to repeat the first line instead of leaving it out.

In three-line tunes whose main caesura is at the end of the second line (Nos. 315–320), the third line is usually sung either to a refrain or to a repetition (maybe a portion of the foregoing text is repeated several times).

All these songs except one or two are in invariable *tempo giusto* rhythm.

Texts of the songs in Class C. Generally speaking, all that was said of the isometric *parlando-rubato* tunes in Class *A* applies to those in Class *C*; and what was said of the isometric tunes in adjustable *tempo giusto* in Class *B* likewise applies to tunes of a similar kind in Class *C*.

Yet in sub-Classes III and IV tune and text are, organically, more closely connected. Most texts are never sung—or cannot be sung, on account of structural peculiarities—to more than one tune. Most of these texts are jocular (Nos. 238, 260 *a*, 264, 288, 297), some are dance-tune texts (Nos. 246, 250, 281). The texts often consist of homologous strophes (Nos. 252, 257, 305, &c.). Many of them are current among other nations; so that their very character suggests that foreign influences have been at work or at least that they are international in character. These songs, in all likelihood, are derived from alien art-songs, which spread (texts and tunes jointly) among various nations—probably propagated by the upper classes.

Generally speaking, it may be posited that the more truly rural the songs (many tunes of similar structure and texts of similar structure), the less exclusively any one text is associated with any one tune; and the more we are justified in suspecting that urban (but popular) art-tunes have influenced the character of a song, the more close is the organic connexion between tune and text.

Note. Most tunes of the marriage and match-making songs belong to Class *C*.

Synopsis.

The miscellaneous materials in Class *C* contain—as regards structure—very dissimilar tunes. These belong to widely different periods, some being quite ancient in character, whereas others may have cropped up during the last few decades.

Despite more or less obvious traces of foreign influences, many of these tunes are to be considered as properly Hungarian, viz. the greater part of the *parlando-rubato* tunes whose structure is isometric, the greater part of tunes, isometric or not, in variable rhythm—that is, in all, about one-third of the contents of this class. Foreign influences are most clearly asserted in tunes whose strophe-structure is heterometric and whose rhythm is in invariable *tempo giusto*; they are noticeable in the three-line tunes, many of which comprise foreign materials directly taken over.

Evidence of foreign influences is provided mainly by the infiltration of certain musical elements (heterometric strophe-structure, modern major or minor scale, &c.) or even of actual tunes from the Czech, Moravian, or Slovakian regions. The question how far these influences are directly due to the native tradition of these regions, or how far, on the contrary, the said regions simply transmitted to Hungary influences which should primarily be traced back to regions farther afield, will be considered in my book on Slovakian folk-music. Ukrainian influences are noticeable in sub-Class V.

Let us now tabulate the contents of this class divided into sub-classes.

Sub-Class I	(a) *parlando rubato*, six-, eight-, eleven-, and twelve-syllables		.	159
	(b) invariable *tempo giusto*:			
	(α) lines isorhythmic .	. . . . .	.	231
	(β) lines heterorhythmic	. . . . .	.	161
,, II	(α) lines isorhythmic .	. . . . .	.	139
	(β) lines heterorhythmic	. . . . .	.	40
,, III	. . .	. . . . .	.	417
,, IV	. . .	. . . . .	.	180
,, V	scale with minor third	. . . . .	.	29
	major scale .	. . . . .	.	16
,, VI	(two-line tunes)	. . . . .	.	76
,, VII	(three-line tunes) { main caesura at end of first line	. .	.	51
	main caesura at end of second line	.	.	28
	Total	. . . .	.	1,527[1]

One of the most characteristic phenomena as regards peasant music is the number of tunes to be found in each separate region, village, or known to each individual. In this respect, Hungary stands midway between Slovakia and Rumania: on an average a Slovakian village, nowadays, is richer in tunes than a Hungarian village, a Rumanian village poorer. These differences are closely connected on the one hand with the relative age of the tradition of peasant music in these various places, and on the other hand with the more or less conservative disposition of the people.

Nowadays it is only the older people who are acquainted with old-style Hungarian tunes. The tunes in Class *C*, generally speaking, are more widely known, but are being thrown farther and farther into the background owing to the ever-increasing popularity of the new-style tunes. In short, the peasant music which we may hear nowadays consists of a small number of old tunes, a greater number of more recent tunes, and a very great number of new tunes.

As to the quantity of available materials, the following facts may provide an indication: in 1906 and 1907 two careful searches—lasting about a fort-

[1] Here again, as in our synopsis of Classes *A* and *B*, variants are not included. The collections of Színi, Kiss, and Bartalus contain 391 tunes belonging to Class *C*, apart from a small number of variants. Of these 391, 241 are variants of tunes included in the manuscript collections of Hungarian tunes.

night in all—at Felsőireg (District Tolna) yielded 307 tunes; at Nagymegyer (District Komárom) I collected in a week, in 1910, 94 tunes. Let it be emphasized that in this village I did not note down any tune already known. As to the number of tunes known to one singer, I shall say that in 1906 at Békésgyula a girl of eighteen, Panna Illés, provided me with about 80 tunes. This is the greatest number I ever obtained from one singer. But between 1917 and 1920 Mrs. Emma Kodály obtained as many as 130 tunes from Julia Kontz, of Avasujváros (District Szatmár), born in 1894.

Conclusion.

The study of Hungarian peasant music shows that Hungarian peasants have always adhered, and still adhere, to isometric strophe-structure and to certain pentatonic formations. In fairly old tunes as well as in the most recent, a liking for variable *tempo giusto* rhythm is evinced. These three features jointly may be considered as altogether typical: they differentiate Hungarian peasant music from that of any other nation.

The peasantry of Hungary preserved the idiosyncrasies of old native music, but were not hostile to innovation: hence the birth of the new style which is altogether homogeneous, quite different from that of any other peasant music, typical of the race, and closely connected with the no less typical old style. There is, to my knowledge, no other country in which, of late years, a similarly homogeneous new style has cropped up. And the originality—even the very existence—of this new Hungarian style are all the more astonishing when one considers that so many alien elements had penetrated into Hungary before this style began to take shape. That these alien influences did not seriously interfere with the national character of Hungarian peasant music at the new stage in its evolution is the best possible proof of the independence and the creative power of the Hungarian peasantry.

APPENDIX I

Lists of places of origin of the tunes contained in the recent collections (see pp. 5–6)

The first list gives the names in the alphabetical order, and shows how many tunes were found in each, and to which class and sub-class the tunes belong. Column 6 refers to round-dance tunes, to tunes that for some reason or other cannot be included in any class, and to instrumental tunes. Footnotes indicate the instruments upon which the last-named tunes are performed.

The second list gives the names grouped according to districts and to dialect-regions.

The names of the collectors are indicated as follows:

B. = Bartók

G. = Garay

K. = Kodály

K. Z.-né = Mrs. Emma Kodály

L. = Lajtha

M. = Molnár

V. = Vikár

81   G

TABLE I

Locality (District).	Class B.	Class C. Sub-Class.			Class A.	Other tunes.	Total number of tunes per locality.
		II, IV.	I, III.	V–VII.			
Adács (Heves), V.	6	—	1	—	—	—	7
Ajnácskő (Gömör), L. . . .	2	—	—	—	—	—	2
Ákosfalva (Maros-Torda), B. . .	8	3	2	—	1	1	15
Alsóbalog (Gömör), K. . . .	3	3	18	—	2	2	28
Alsófalu (Gömör), K. . . .	1	2	9	1	2	—	15
Alsok (Somogy), V.	2	3	2	—	1	1	9
Alsószecse (Bars), K. . . .	1	1	14	1	1	1	19
Alsóvárad (Bars), K. . . .	3	1	3	—	—	—	7
Andornak (Borsod), V. . . .	4	2	—	—	—	—	6
Andrásfalva (Bukovina), K. . .	6	3	17	—	8	9	43
Apátfalva (Csanád), B. . . .	15	8	1	1	1	—	26
Arad [1] (Arad), B.	5	2	—	—	—	—	7
Árvátfalva (Udvarhely), V. . .	—	1	1	—	—	3[2]	5
Átány (Heves), V.	1	—	—	—.	—	—	1
Avasujváros (Szatmár), K. Z.-né .	77	20	20	—	—	13	130
Babindál (Nyitra), K. . . .	1	1	4	1	—	—	7
Balatonberény (Somogy), B. . .	—	—	2	—	1	—	3
Balogpádár (Gömör), K. . . .	12	9	10	1	2	1	35
Bánffyhunyad (Kolozs), B. . . .	—	5	5	1	2	—	13
Bánffyhunyad (Kolozs), V. . . .	18	4	11	—	—	—	33
Baracs (Fejér), B.	30	6	10	—	6	1	53
Barkaszó (Bereg), B. . . .	—	—	—	—	—	1	1
Bárna (Nógrád), K.	9	—	2	—	—	—	11
Barslédecz (Bars), K. . . .	1	4	29	3	3	6	46
Bátta (Tolna), G.	1	—	—	—	7	1	9
Bazsi (Zala), B.	1	—	—	—	—	—	1
Béd (Nyitra), K.	41	14	28	5	2	5	95
Békésgyula (Békés), B. . . .	65	17	16	5	7	1	111
Békésgyula (Békés), K. . . .	1	1	12	1	2	1	18
Berencs (Nyitra), K.	5	1	7	1	1	—	15
Besenyszög [3] (Szolnok), B. . .	4	—	4	—	—	3	11
Beszterczebánya [4] (Zólyom), B. . .	19	4	—	—	—	1	24
Betfalva (Udvarhely), V. . . .	—	—	—	—	—	13[5]	13
Bodok (Nyitra), K.	3	—	—	—	3	—	6
Bogyoszló (Sopron), B. . . .	1	—	2	—	1	—	4
Boldogfa (Zala), V. . . .	1	1	4	—	—	1	7
Boly (Zemplén), K.	2	1	1	—	—	1	5
Borsodharsány (Borsod), K. . .	1	—	—	—	—	—	1
Bögöz (Udvarhely), V. . . .	—	—	1	—	—	—	1

[1] Sung by soldiers from this region. [2] Whistled. [3] Collected on the Puszta by Felsőszászberek. [4] Sung by soldiers from Region II. [5] Played on the clarinet.

LOCALITY (District).	Class B.	Class C.			Class A.	Other tunes.	Total number of tunes per locality.
		II, IV.	I, III.	V-VII.			
			Sub-Class.				
Bözöd (Udvarhely), V.	5	1	3	—	2	1	12
Bussa (Nógrád), K.	2	—	—	—	—	—	2
Bükszád (Háromszék), V. . . .	—	1	2	1	—	—	4
Czup (Zala), V.	1	1	1	—	—	2	5
Csáb (Hont), K.	11	4	5	—	—	—	20
Csanádapácza (Csanád), B. . . .	2	—	—	—	—	—	2
Csány (Heves), K.	2	—	—	—	—	—	2
Csekefalva (Udvarhely), V. . . .	3	2	11	—	1	4	21
Csíkcsobotfalva (Csík), L. . . .	—	2	—	—	1	—	3
Csíkjenőfalva (Csík), B.	5	6	11	1	7	—	30
Csíkmenaság (Csík), L.	2	1	—	—	4	—	7
Csíkrákos (Csík), B.	9	7	13	4	8	2	43
Csíkszentdomokos (Csík), L. . .	—	—	1	—	3	—	4
Csíkszentmihály (Csík), B. . . .	2	1	2	—	—	—	5
Csíkszentmihály (Csík), L. . . .	2	2	3	2	7	1[1]	17
Csíkszenttamás (Csík), B. . . .	3	4	9	2	9	2	29
Csíkverebes (Csík), L.	1	1	2	—	2	—	6
Csincse (Borsod), V.	14	8	6	—	1	4	33
Csitár (Nyitra), K.	5	1	17	6	2	1	32
Csoknya (Somogy), V.	—	—	1	—	—	—	1
Csomafalva (Csík), B.	1	2	15	3	5	1	27
Csomafalva (Csík), M.	9	7	19	2	11	17[2]	65
Csongrád (Csongrád), B. . . .	—	1	3	—	1	—	5
Csorna (Sopron), K.	1	—	1	—	—	—	2
Csurgó (Somogy), V.	1	—	—	—	—	—	1
Damásd [3] (Hont), K.	4	—	—	—	—	—	4
Dávidháza (Bereg), K.	1	—	—	—	—	—	1
Decs (Tolna), G.	—	1	—	—	3	—	4
Dég (Veszprém), V.	—	1	—	—	—	—	1
Dejtár (Nógrád), K.	1	—	—	—	—	—	1
Dejtár (Nógrád), M.	9	1	—	—	—	1	11
Deménd (Heves), V.	2	1	3	—	—	—	6
Deményháza (Maros-Torda), V. .	1	—	1	1	—	—	3
Derczen (Bereg), B.	4	6	10	1	7	3	31
Derecske (Heves), V.	7	3	4	—	1	2	17
Deresk (Gömör), K.	7	4	13	1	3	—	28
Déva (Hunyad), V.	—	—	—	—	2	—	2
Diósad (Szilágy), L.	10	11	1	—	2	—	24
Doboz (Békés), B.	64	40	37	5	15	3	164
Dombovár (Tolna), K.	—	—	1	—	1	—	2

[1] Played on a shepherd's flute.   [2] 8 tunes played on the violin; 5 on a shepherd's flute; 4 whistled.   [3] Sung by girls whose mother tongue is Slovakian.

83

Locality (District).	Class B.	Class C. II, IV.	Class C. I, III.	Class C. V-VII.	Class A.	Other tunes.	Total number of tunes per locality.
		Sub-Class.					
Dunapentele (Fejér), B.	5	—	3	—	4	1	13
Ecseg (Nógrád), K.	16	9	10	2	—	3	40
Eger (Heves), V.	6	7	6	1	—	1	21
Egervár (Vas), V.	1	—	—	—	—	1	2
Ehed (Maros-Torda), B. . . .	1	3	5	—	4	6[1]	19
Emőd (Borsod), K.	2	—	1	—	—	—	3
Énlaka (Udvarhely), V.	2	—	9	—	1	1	13
Érd (Fejér), K. Z.-né	48	20	42	8	—	21	139
Erdőkövesd (Heves), V.	—	1	4	—	1	—	6
Erdőszentgyörgy (Maros-Torda), V.	—	1	—	—	—	—	1
Értarcsa (Bihar), K. Z.-né . . .	—	—	—	—	1	—	1
Farkasd (Nyitra), K.	5	1	7	1	—	—	14
Farkasfa (Vas), V.	5	2	2	—	—	—	9
Farkaslaka (Udvarhely), V. . . .	—	—	1	—	—	1	2
Felsőboldogfalva (Udvarhely), V. . .	1	3	3	—	3	—	10
Felsőireg (Tolna), B.	123	43	92	4	34	11[2]	307
Felsőnána (Heves), V.	3	—	—	—	2	—	5
Felsőnyék (Tolna), B.	2	—	4	—	—	—	6
Felsőrás (Gömör), K.	5	3	13	1	4	—	26
Felsőszecse (Bars), K.	2	—	5	—	—	3	10
Felsőszeli (Pozsony), K.	8	2	1	—	—	—	11
Felsőtárkány (Borsod), V. . . .	13	1	2	—	2	—	18
Fenyéd (Udvarhely), V.	—	—	2	—	—	—	2
Firtosváralja (Udvarhely), V. . .	—	3	7	2	1	2	15
Fogadjisten (Bukovina), K. . . .	2	1	6	—	2	—	11
Fornos (Bereg), B.	3	5	9	—	4	3	24
Fót (Pest), B.	7	—	3	—	1	—	11
Füzesabony (Heves), V.	13	3	10	—	4	4	34
Füzesgyarmat (Hont), K. . . .	7	4	14	—	3	4	32
Gáborjaháza (Zala), V.	2	1	2	—	—	—	5
Gács (Nógrád), K. Z.-né . . .	8	8	15	1	—	5	37
Garamsalló (Hont), K.	10	4	13	2	3	2	34
Garamszentgyörgy (Bars), K. . .	3	5	18	2	3	—	31
Ghymes (Nyitra), K.	35	14	59	13	13	5	139
Gicze (Gömör), K.	7	5	9	1	2	—	22
Gomba (Pest), K.	—	—	1	—	—	—	1
Gyanta (Bihar), B.	—	2	4	2	4	3	15
Gyergyóalfalu (Csík), K. . . .	3	2	2	—	11	1	19
Gyergyóalfalu (Csík), M. . . .	21	14	20	3	16	38[3]	112
Gyergyóditró (Csík), K.	—	—	6	—	3	—	9
Gyergyóditró (Csík), L.	1	—	2	—	3	—	6

[1] 5 tunes played on a shepherd's flute.   [2] 4 tunes played on a shepherd's flute.
[3] 15 tunes played on a violin; 7 on a shepherd's flute; 5 whistled.

84

Locality (District).	Class B.	Class C. II, IV.	Class C. I, III.	Class C. V-VII.	Class A.	Other tunes.	Total number of tunes per locality.
			Sub-Class.				
Gyergyóremete (Csík), K. . . .	—	—	—	4	7	—	11
Gyergyószentmiklós (Csík), K.. .	10	5	13	2	11	—	41
Gyergyószentmiklós (Csík), M.. .	—	1	—	—	—	—	1
Gyergyóujfalu (Csík), B. . . .	7	6	14	2	16	4¹	49
Gyergyóujfalu (Csík), M. . . .	2	2	3	—	5	5²	17
Gyimes-(bükk ?)³ (Csík), V.. .	—	—	6	1	13	—	20
Gyimes-(bükk ?)³ (Csík), L.. .	—	—	1	1	4	2	8
Gyimesfelsőlok (Csík), L. . .	—	2	—	—	3	6⁴	11
Gyimesközéplok (Csík), L. . .	5	2	2	1	13	—	23
Gyöngyös (Heves), V.	4	1	1	—	—	—	6
Gyulavári (Békés), B. . . .	10	1	5	—	1	1⁵	18
Gyulavári (Békés), K. . . .	2	—	2	—	1	—	5
Gyulavarsánd (Arad), B. . . .	1	—	—	—	—	—	1
Hadikfalva (Bukovina), K.. . .	9	2	11	·—	9	2	33
Haraszti (Verőcze), G.	1	1	3	2	1	—	8
Hasznos (Heves), K..	2	1	—	—	—	—	3
Hatvan (Heves), V.	1	—	—	—	1	—	2
Hegyi (Zemplén), K.	1	—	—	—	—	—	1
Hetes (Somogy), V..	4	1	5	—	5	—	15
Hétfalu⁶ (Brassó), V.	—	1	2	—	—	—	3
Hidalpuszta (Gömör), K. . . .	—	—	—	—	1	—	1
Hollóháza (Abauj), K.	1	—	—	—	—	—	1
Horgos (Csongrád), B. . . .	25	5	4	—	4	2	40
Hottó (Zala), V.	—	3	11	—	4	2	20
Ipolybalog (Hont), K. . . .	4	—	—	—	—	—	4
Ipolybalog (Hont), L.	9	3	2	—	1	1	16
Ipolybalog (Hont), M.	46	16	6	2	—	9	79
Ipolykelenye (Hont), L.. . . .	5	4	2	—	—	—	11
Ipolyság⁷ (Hont), B..	1	—	2	—	4	44⁸	51
Ipolyszécsénke (Hont), L. . .	4	1	4	—	1	1	11
Istenmezeje (Heves), K.. . . .	—	1	1	—	1	—	3
Istensegíts (Bukovina), K. . . .	16	6	42	2	28	6	100
Izsnyéte (Bereg), K..	1	—	—	—	—	—	1
Jakabfa (Zala), V.	6	1	4	—	1	1	13
Jánoshida (Szolnok), B.. . . .	27	8	7	2	1	1	46
Jászberény (Szolnok), B. . . .	19	2	6	1	—	1	29
Jobaháza (Sopron), B.	25	8	2	—	—	2	37

¹ 1 tune played on a shepherd's flute, 1 on a violin.   ² Played on a violin.   ³ Noted down by the collector 'Gyimes'.   ⁴ 5 tunes whistled.   ⁵ Whistled.   ⁶ Common name of the following localities: Bácsfalu, Csernátfalu, Hosszúfalu, Pürkerecz, Tatrang, Türkös, and Zajzon.   ⁷ Sung by cowherds and swineherds from the region.   ⁸ 4 tunes played on a shepherd's flute, 15 on the 'tülök' (swineherd's horn), 25 on the bagpipe.

| | | Class C. | | | | | |
Locality (District).	Class B.	II, IV.	I, III.	V-VII.	Class A.	Other tunes.	Total number of tunes per locality.
			Sub-Class.				
Jobbágytelke (Maros-Torda), B. .	14	10	7	—	6	3[1]	40
Józseffalva (Bukovina), K. . . .	6	4	12	—	7	5[2]	34
Kadicsfalva (Udvarhely), V. . .	—	1	—	1	5	3	10
Kánya (Tolna), B.	6	3	5	—	3	1	18
Kápolnásfalu (Udvarhely), V. . .	3	1	6	3	5	7[3]	25
Kaposfüred (Somogy), V. . . .	4	—	10	1	7	3	25
Kaposujlak (Somogy), V.. . . .	1	—	—	—	3	—	4
Kaposvár (Somogy), V.	3	1	2	1	1	—	8
Karczfalva (Csík), B.	3	4	3	1	10	1	22
Kassa [4] (Abauj-Torna), K. . . .	89	15	6	2	—	4	116
Kászonaltíz (Csík), K.	—	—	1	—	2	—	3
Kászonfeltíz (Csík), K.	—	—	7	1	3	—	11
Kászonimpér (Csík), K.. . . .	—	1	4	—	14	2	21
Kászonjakabfalva (Csík), K. . .	3	2	6	—	3	—	14
Kászonujfalu (Csík), K.. . . .	4	1	22	—	8	7	42
Kecskemét (Pest), V.	3	3	2	—	2	—	10
Kenész (Somogy), G.	—	2	1	—	2	—	5
Kénos (Udvarhely), V.	1	2	6	—	—	6	15
Kerkaszentmihályfa (Zala), V. . .	2	3	2	—	—	—	7
Keszthely (Zala), B.	31	4	1	2	3	—	41
Kibéd (Maros-Torda), B. . . .	12	6	3	3	—	—	24
Kilyénfalva (Csík), B.	3	1	2	1	4	—	11
Kincsestanyahomok (Ung), B. . .	—	1	—	—	—	—	1
Királyrév (Pozsony), K. Z.-né .	4	2	5	5	—	3	19
Kisgörgény (Maros-Torda), B.. .	—	2	4	3	2	1	12
Kisgyarmat (Hont), K.	—	—	11	2	2	—	15
Kisölved (Hont), K..	2	1	9	2	2	—	16
Kisrákos (Vas), V.	4	—	4	—	2	—	10
Kissáró (Bars), K.	—	—	1	—	—	—	1
Kistild (Bars), V.	7	2	2	—	—	—	11
Kisunyom (Vas), K..	3	1	3	—	—	1	8
Kisvisnyó (Gömör), K..	6	5	15	2	2	3	33
Kohány (Somogy), G.	—	—	—	—	2	—	2
Kolon (Nyitra), K.	5	6	15	4	5	2	37
Kolozs (Kolozs), V.	1	1	—	—	—	—	2
Kórógy (Szerém), G.	1	2	3	—	9	1	16
Korond (Udvarhely), V. . . .	1	2	3	—	1	2	9
Körösfő (Kolozs), B.	26	12	10	1	5	6[5]	60
Körösladány (Békés), B. . . .	46	11	5	2	—	3	67
Köröstárkány (Bihar), B. . . .	—	5	15	2	6	4[5]	32

[1] 1 tune played on a swineherd's horn.   [2] 3 tunes played on a shepherd's flute.   [3] Played on the clarinet.   [4] Sung by soldiers from the region.   [5] 4 tunes played on a shepherd's flute.

86

Locality (District).	Class B.	Class C. II, IV.	Class C. I, III.	Class C. V–VII.	Class A.	Other tunes.	Total number of tunes per locality.
		Sub-Class.					
Körtvélyfája (Maros-Torda), L.	—	—	—	—	—	1	1
Köttse (Somogy), V.	1	1	—	—	1	—	3
Kraszna (Szilágy), K.	4	—	—	—	—	—	4
Lelesz (Zemplén), K.	6	—	—	—	—	—	6
Levárt (Gömör), K.	—	—	3	—	1	—	4
Licze (Gömör), K.	1	2	9	—	3	3	18
Lövéte (Udvarhely), V.	1	2	9	—	3	3	18
Lukanénye (Hont), K.	15	1	12	—	5	6	39
Mácsa (Arad), B.	1	—	—	—	—	—	1
Magyaratád (Somogy), V.	3	—	—	—	—	—	3
Magyargyerőmonostor (Kolozs), B.	2	6	11	—	3	—	22
Magyarvalkó (Kolozs), V.	12	2	1	—	—	2[1]	17
Máréfalva (Udvarhely), V.	—	1	—	1	1	—	3
Marosvásárhely[2] (Maros-Torda), B.	41	4	4	3	1	—	53
Martonos (Udvarhely), V.	—	1	4	—	4	1	10
Medesér (Udvarhely), V.	—	1	1	—	—	2[3]	4
Menyhe (Nyitra), K.	40	13	32	9	3	3	100
Mezőkövesd (Borsod), V.	34	15	28	—	12	5	94
Mezőpanit (Maros-Torda), L.	3	—	—	—	—	—	3
Mezőveresegyház (Szolnok-Doboka), K.	1	—	1	—	—	—	2
Mikháza (Maros-Torda), V.	1	—	2	—	—	—	3
Mikosszéplak (Vas), B.	2	1	4	—	—	—	7
Mindszent (Heves), V.	—	—	1	—	1	—	2
Mohi (Bars), K.	16	10	76	4	10	14	130
Nádszeg (Pozsony), K.	1	1	—	—	—	—	2
Nagyborosnyó (Háromszék), L.	1	—	1	1	—	—	3
Nagyfüged (Heves), V.	1	—	—	—	—	—	1
Nagygút (Bereg), B.	—	—	2	1	—	—	3
Nagykáta (Pest), B.	1	—	—	—	—	—	1
Nagykede (Udvarhely), V.	1	1	—	—	—	—	2
Nagykőrös (Pest), V.	—	—	2	—	—	—	2
Nagymegyer (Komárom), B.	2	11	46	12	5	18[4]	94
Nagyod (Bars), K.	1	1	10	—	—	—	12
Nagypáli (Zala), V.	2	1	2	—	1	1	7
Nagypeszek (Hont), K.	11	1	16	—	—	—	28
Nagyrákos (Vas), V.	3	2	11	1	1	—	18
Nagyszalonta (Bihar), K.	104	48	71	4	6	14[5]	247
Nagyszénás (Békés), B.	2	—	2	1	—	—	5
Nagyszentmiklós[6] (Torontál), B.	4	—	2	—	—	—	6
Nemesdéd (Somogy), V.	1	—	—	—	—	—	1

[1] Whistled.   [2] Sung by soldiers from the region.   [3] Played on the violin.   [4] 7 tunes played on the bagpipe.   [5] 6 tunes played on the cither.   [6] Sung by girls from the region.

Locality (District).	Class B.	Class C.			Class A.	Other tunes.	Total number of tunes per locality.
		II, IV.	I, III.	V–VII.			
		Sub-Class.					
Nemesnép (Zala), V.	3	—	4	1	—	1	9
Nemesócsa (Komárom), L.	7	1	19	3	4	8	42
Nógrádverőcze (Nógrád), V.	1	2	2	—	—	—	5
Nyárádköszvényes (Maros-Torda), B.	—	1	7	1	7	12[1]	28
Nyárádremete (Maros-Torda), B.	4	5	11	—	5	12[2]	37
Nyírbéltek (Szabolcs), K.	2	—	—	—	—	—	2
Nyírbogdány (Szabolcs), K.	1	—	—	—	—	—	1
Nyírtass (Szabolcs), K.	1	—	—	—	—	—	1
Nyitracsehi (Nyitra), K.	6	3	16	2	1	4	32
Nyitraegerszeg (Nyitra), K.	8	5	27	5	2	1	48
Nyitragerencsér (Nyitra), K.	20	5	3	2	2	—	32
Olad (Vas), V.	3	1	1	—	—	—	5
Oroszhegy (Udvarhely), V.	—	2	9	—	2	—	13
Őcsény (Tolna), L.	29	9	11	1	5	1	56
Őcsény (Tolna), V.	21	3	5	1	6	3	39
Őriszentpéter (Vas), V.	3	—	5	—	2	—	10
Palást (Hont), V.	10	3	1	—	—	—	14
Pankasz (Vas), V.	1	2	10	—	1	5	19
Pápa (Veszprém), V.	4	7	8	—	1	3	23
Papkeszi (Veszprém), K.	1	—	2	—	—	—	3
Parád (Heves), V.	4	1	2	—	—	—	7
Páskaháza (Gömör), K.	17	9	27	1	—	8	62
Pered (Pozsony), K.	6	1	1	—	—	—	8
Perjése (Gömör), K.	3	5	11	—	3	2	24
Perőcsény (Hont), K.	5	2	8	—	1	1	17
Péterfalva (Ugocsa), B.	—	—	—	—	1	—	1
Petneháza (Szabolcs), V.	—	—	1	—	1	—	2
Pincz (Nógrád), B.	10	2	1	—	—	—	13
Pográny (Nyitra), K.	5	4	12	3	2	—	26
Pográny (Nyitra), V.	4	6	11	2	—	1	24
Pozsony[3] (Pozsony), B.	24	3	1	1	—	—	29
Pürkerecz (Brassó), V.	2	1	4	2	1	—	10
Pusztafalu (Abauj), K.	—	1	—	—	—	—	1
Pusztaföldvár (Békés), V.	—	2	5	—	4	3	14
Pusztakovácsi (Somogy), K.	1	—	—	—	—	—	1
Pusztarádócz (Vas), K.	—	1	—	—	—	—	1
Rafajnaujfalu (Bereg), B.	1	2	15	2	3	2	25
Rákoskeresztúr[4] (Pest), B.	12	6	1	—	1	—	20
Ránkfüred[3] (Abauj-Torna), K.	18	3	3	—	—	2	26
Recsk (Heves), V.	2	1	—	—	—	—	3

[1] 10 tunes played on a shepherd's flute, 1 whistled.   [2] 9 tunes played on a shepherd's flute, 1 on the violin.   [3] Sung by soldiers from the region.   [4] Sung by girls whose mother tongue is Slovakian.

Locality (District).	Class B.	Class C. II, IV.	I, III.	V–VII.	Class A.	Other tunes.	Total number of tunes per locality.
			Sub-Class.				
Resznek (Zala), V.	41	16	26	1	10	5	99
Rudabányácska (Zemplén), K. . .	1	—	—	—	—	1	2
Rugonfalva (Udvarhely), V. . .	3	3	5	1	5	—	17
Sámson (Hajdu), B.	38	13	5	—	2	1	59
Sarud (Borsod), K.	4	—	1	1	—	—	6
Sepsiköröspatak (Háromszék), L. .	—	—	—	—	1	—	1
Siklód (Udvarhely), V.	1	1	14	—	5	4	25
Siménfalva (Udvarhely), V. . . .	1	—	1	—	—	—	2
Sinfalva (Torda-Aranyos), V. . .	2	1	3	—	1	1	8
Somogyszobb (Somogy), V. . .	6	2	8	—	5	—	21
Sümeg (Zala), K. Z.-né . . .	10	3	3	—	—	4	20
Szalakusz (Nyitra), K.	1	—	—	—	—	—	1
Szalócz (Gömör), K.	11	3	7	—	2	1	24
Szárhegy (Csík), K.	—	1	4	1	9	1	16
Szatta (Vas), V.	9	—	5	—	—	1	15
Szécsény (Nógrád), K. Z.-né . .	—	—	1	—	—	—	1
Szeged (Csongrád), B.	30	9	7	—	3	—	49
Szeged (Csongrád), K.	2	—	—	—	—	—	2
Szegvár (Csongrád), V.	11	9	14	—	4	1	39
Székelybetlenfalva (Udvarhely), V.	1	2	2	—	—	1[1]	6
Székelydobó (Udvarhely), K. . .	—	—	4	—	—	—	4
Székelylengyelfalva (Udvarhely), V.	4	3	15	2	4	1	29
Székelyudvarhely (Udvarhely), V. .	8	3	5	1	4	4	25
Székelyvaja (Maros-Torda), B. . .	—	1	9	1	6	3[2]	20
Szentábrahám (Udvarhely), V. . .	2	1	—	—	1	1[3]	5
Szentegyházasfalu (Udvarhely), V. .	2	3	18	1	9	—	33
Szentes (Csongrád), B.	4	3	3	—	4	5[4]	19
Szentgyörgyvölgy (Zala), V. . .	5	3	15	2	2	5	32
Szentlászló (Szerém), G. . . .	1	—	1	—	1	—	3
Szentsimon (Udvarhely), V. . .	—	—	2	—	1	—	3
Szilágyperecsen (Szilágy), K. . .	3	—	—	—	1	—	4
Szilágynagyfalu (Szilágy), K. . .	—	1	1	—	—	—	2
Szilicze (Gömör), K.	18	5	15	—	2	5	45
Szinyérváralja (Szatmár), K. Z.-né .	1	—	—	—	—	—	1
Szólád (Somogy), V.	—	—	—	—	1	—	1
Szombatfa (Zala), V.	6	2	3	—	—	2	13
Szováta (Maros-Torda), V. . . .	—	2	2	—	1	2	7
Szőreg (Torontál), V.	4	1	2	—	—	3	10
Takácsháza (Gömör), K. . . .	—	—	1	—	—	—	1
Taksonyfalva (Pozsony), K. . .	7	—	—	—	—	—	7
Tápiószele (Pest), B.	28	2	2	—	—	—	32

[1] Whistled.   [2] 2 songs performed on a shepherd's flute, 1 whistled.   [3] Played on the violin.   [4] Played on the hurdy-gurdy.

89

Locality (District).	Class B.	Class C.			Class A.	Other tunes.	Total number of tunes per locality.
		II, IV.	I, III.	V-VII.			
		Sub-Class.					
Tekerőpatak (Csík), B.	5	4	9	4	7	5[1]	34
Tekerőpatak (Csík), M.	4	5	5	2	3	1	20
Tergenye (Hont), K.	—	1	3	—	—	—	4
Tiszapély (Heves), V.	16	5	5	—	1	3	30
Tordátfalva (Udvarhely), V.	—	—	4	1	2	1	8
Toroczkó (Torda-Aranyos), B.	2	2	4	—	1	—	9
Tőketerebes (Zemplén), K.	—	—	1	—	—	—	1
Tura (Pest), B.	57	14	47	5	23	5	151
Tusnád (Csík), L.	—	—	—	1	1	—	2
Tyukod (Szatmár), K.	3	1	1	—	—	—	5
Újcsanálos (Zemplén), K.	1	—	—	—	—	—	1
Ujszász (Pest), B.	76	9	42	6	5	17	155
Vacsárcsi (Csík), B.	30	10	14	6	14	1	75
Váczszentlászló (Pest), B.	11	—	1	—	—	—	12
Vágkirályfa (Nyitra), K.	8	3	10	3	—	—	24
Vaja (Szabolcs), K.	3	2	2	—	—	—	7
Vásárosnamény (Bereg), B.	—	—	—	—	—	1	1
Velem (Vas), V.	5	5	10	—	1	5	26
Vésztő (Békés), B.	80	24	19	5	7	3	138
Vicsápapáti (Nyitra), K.	5	4	18	3	5	2	37
Visk (Hont), B.	2	—	—	—	—	—	2
Viszák (Vas), V.	1	4	6	—	3	—	14
Zabar (Gömör), K.	5	2	2	—	4	—	13
Zágon (Háromszék), L.	1	1	—	—	1	—	3
Zajzon (Brassó), V.	—	1	—	1	—	3[2]	5
Zalaba (Hont), K.	6	6	11	2	1	—	26
Zentelke (Kolozs), V.	3	12	11	—	3	1	30
Zetelaka (Udvarhely), V.	3	2	12	—	4	5	26
Zsére (Nyitra), K.	34	15	35	5	5	5[3]	99
Zsida (Vas), V.	1	1	5	1	—	1	9
Zsigárd (Pozsony), K.	10	4	4	—	—	—	18
Fundort unbekannt, B.	10	5	4	2	—	—	21
Fundort unbekannt, K.	10	—	—	1	—	—	11
Fundort unbekannt, M.	1	1	—	—	—	—	2
Fundort unbekannt, V.	6	6	7	1	3	—	23
Total number of tunes	2,675	1,070	2,320	276	836	637	7,814

[1] 4 tunes played on a shepherd's flute. [2] Whistled. [3] 2 tunes played on the bagpipe.

TABLE II

Serial numbers.		Number of tunes.

I

District FEJÉR

1. Baracs B.	. . .	. 53
2. Dunapentele B.	. .	. 13
3. Érd K. Z.-né	. .	. 139

Number of localities: 3   205

District SOMOGY

4. Alsok V.	. . .	. 9
5. Balatonberény B.	. .	3
6. Csoknya V.	. .	1
7. Csurgó V.	. . .	1
8. Hetes V.	. . .	15
9. Kaposfüred V.	. .	25
10. Kaposujlak V.	. .	4
11. Kaposvár V.	. .	8
12. Kenész G.	. .	5
13. Kohány G.	. .	2
14. Köttse V.	. .	3
15. Magyaratád V.	.	3
16. Nemesdéd V.	.	1
17. Pusztakovácsi K.	.	1
18. Somogyszobb V.	.	21
19. Szólád V.	. . .	1

Number of localities: 16   103

District SOPRON

20. Bogyoszló B.	. .	. 4
21. Csorna K.	. .	. 2
22. Jobaháza B.	. .	. 37

Number of localities: 3   43

District SZERÉM

23. Kórógy G.	. .	. 16
24. Szentlászló G.	. .	. 3

Number of localities: 2   19

District TOLNA

25. Bátta G.	. . .	. 9
26. Decs G.	. . .	. 4
27. Dombovár K.	. .	. 2
28. Felsőireg B.	. .	. 307

Serial numbers.		Number of tunes.
29. Felsőnyék B.	. . .	. 6
30. Kánya B.	. . .	. 18
31. Őcsény L., V.	. .	. 95

Number of localities: 7   441

District VAS

32. Egervár V.	. .	. 2
33. Farkasfa V.	. .	. 9
34. Kisrákos V.	. .	. 10
35. Kisunyom K.	. .	. 8
36. Mikosszéplak B.	.	. 7
37. Nagyrákos V.	. .	. 18
38. Olad V.	. .	. 5
39. Őriszentpéter V.	.	. 10
40. Pankasz V.	. .	. 19
41. Pusztarádócz K.	.	. 1
42. Szatta V.	. .	. 15
43. Velem V.	. .	. 26
44. Viszák V.	. .	. 14
45. Zsida V.	. .	. 9

Number of localities: 14   153

District VERŐCZE

46. Haraszti G.	. .	. 8

Number of localities: 1   8

District VESZPRÉM

47. Dég V.	. .	. 1
48. Pápa V.	. .	. 23
49. Papkeszi K.	. .	. 3

Number of localities: 3   27

District ZALA

50. Bazsi B.	. . .	. 1
51. Boldogfa V.	. .	. 7
52. Czup V.	. .	. 5
53. Gáborjaháza V.	.	. 5
54. Hottó V.	. .	. 20
55. Jakabfa V.	. .	. 13
56. Kerkaszentmihályfa V.	.	. 7
57. Keszthely B.	. .	. 41
58. Nagypáli V.	. .	. 7
59. Nemesnép V.	. .	. 9
60. Resznek V.	. .	. 99

Serial numbers.	Number of tunes.
61. Sümeg K. Z.-né . . .	20
62. Szentgyörgyvölgy V. . .	32
63. Szombatfa V. . . .	13
Number of localities: 14	279

District Abauj-Torna

64. Hollóháza K. . . .	1
65. Kassa K.	116
66. Pusztafalu K. . . .	1
67. Ránkfüred K. . . .	26
Number of localities: 4	144

District Bars

68. Alsószecse K. . . .	19
69. Alsóvárad K. . . .	7
70. Barslédecz K. . . .	46
71. Felsőszecse K. . . .	10
72. Garamszentgyörgy K. . .	31
73. Kissáró K. . . .	1
74. Kistild V. . . .	11
75. Mohi K. . . .	130
76. Nagyod K. . . .	12
Number of localities: 9	267

District Bereg

77. Barkaszó B. . . .	1
78. Dávidháza K. . . .	1
79. Derczen B. . . .	31
80. Fornos B. . . .	24
81. Izsnyéte K. . . .	1
82. Nagygút B. . . .	3
83. Rafajnaujfalu B. . .	25
84. Vásárosnamény B. . .	1
Number of localities: 8	87

District Borsod

85. Andornak V. . . .	6
86. Borsodharsány K. . .	1
87. Csincse V. . . .	33
88. Emőd K. . . .	3
89. Felsőtárkány V. . .	18
90. Mezőkövesd V. . .	94
91. Sarud K. . . .	6
Number of localities: 7	161

Serial numbers.	Number of tunes
District Gömör	
92. Ajnácskő L. . . .	2
93. Alsóbalog K. . . .	28
94. Alsófalu K. . . .	15
95. Balogpádár K. . . .	35
96. Deresk K. . . .	28
97. Felsőrás K. . . .	26
98. Gicze K. . . .	22
99. Hidalpuszta K. . . .	1
100. Kisvisnyó K. . . .	33
101. Levárt K. . . .	4
102. Licze K. . . .	18
103. Páskaháza K. . . .	62
104. Perjése K. . . .	24
105. Szalócz K. . . .	24
106. Szilicze K. . . .	45
107. Takácsháza K. . .	1
108. Zabar K. . . .	13
Number of localities: 17	381

District Heves

109. Adács V. . . .	7
110. Átány V. . . .	1
111. Csány K. . . .	2
112. Deménd V. . . .	6
113. Derecske V. . . .	17
114. Eger V. . . .	21
115. Erdőkövesd V. . .	6
116. Felsőnána V. . . .	5
117. Füzesabony V. . .	34
118. Gyöngyös V. . . .	6
119. Hasznos K. . . .	3
120. Hatvan V. . . .	2
121. Istenmezeje K. . .	3
122. Lelesz K. . . .	6
123. Mindszent V. . . .	2
124. Nagyfüged V. . . .	1
125. Parád V. . . .	7
126. Recsk V. . . .	3
127. Tiszapély V. . . .	30
Number of localities: 19	162

District Hont

128. Csáb K. . . .	20
129. Damásd K. . . .	4
130. Füzesgyarmat K. . .	32

Serial numbers.	Number of tunes.
131. Garamsalló K.	34
132. Ipolybalog K., L., M. . .	99
133. Ipolykelenye L. . . .	11
134. Ipolyság B.	51
135. Ipolyszécsénke L. . . .	11
136. Kisgyarmat K.	15
137. Kisölved K.	16
138. Lukanénye K.	39
139. Nagypeszek K.	28
140. Palást V.	14
141. Perőcsény K.	17
142. Tergenye K. . . .	4
143. Visk B.	2
144. Zalaba K. . . .	26
Number of localities: 17	423

District Komárom

145. Nagymegyer B. . . .	94
146. Nemesócsa L. . . .	42
Number of localities: 2	136

District Nógrád

147. Bárna K.	11
148. Bussa K.	2
149. Dejtár K., M. . . .	12
150. Ecseg K.	40
151. Gács K. Z.-né . . .	37
152. Nógrádverőcze V. . .	5
153. Pincz B.	13
154. Szécsény K. Z.-né . .	1
Number of localities: 8	121

District Nyitra

155. Babindál K. . . .	7
156. Béd K.	95
157. Berencs K. . . .	15
158. Bodok K.	6
159. Csitár K.	32
160. Farkasd K. . . .	14
161. Ghymes K. . . .	139
162. Kolon K. . . .	37
163. Menyhe K. . . .	100
164. Nyitracsehi K. . .	32
165. Nyitraegerszeg K. . .	48
166. Nyitragerencsér K. . .	32

Serial numbers.	Number of tunes.
167. Pográny K., V. . . .	50
168. Szalakusz K. . . .	1
169. Vágkirályfa K. . . .	24
170. Vicsápapáti K. . . .	37
171. Zsére K.	99
Number of localities: 17	768

District Pest-Pilis-Solt-Kiskun

172. Tura B.	151
173. Váczszentlászló B. . .	12
Number of localities: 2	163

District Pozsony

174. Felsőszeli K. . . .	11
175. Királyrév K. Z.-né . .	19
176. Nádszeg K. . . .	2
177. Pered K.	8
178. Pozsony B. . . .	29
179. Taksonyfalva K. . .	7
180. Zsigárd K. . . .	18
Number of localities: 7	94

District Ugocsa

181. Péterfalva B. . . .	1
Number of localities: 1	1

District Ung

182. Kincsestanyahomok B. .	1
Number of localities: 1	1

District Zemplén

183. Boly K.	5
184. Hegyi K.	1
185. Rudabányácska K. . .	2
186. Tőketerebes K. . .	1
187. Újcsanálos K. . .	1
Number of localities: 5	10

District Zólyom

188. Beszterczebánya B. . .	24
Number of localities: 1	24

Serial numbers.	Number of tunes.

III
District ARAD

189. Arad B.	7
190. Gyulavarsánd B. . . .	1
191. Mácsa B.	1
Number of localities: 3	9

District BÉKÉS

192. Békésgyula B., K. . . .	129
193. Doboz B.	164
194. Gyulavári B., K. . . .	23
195. Körösladány B. . . .	67
196. Nagyszénás B. . . .	5
197. Pusztaföldvár V. . . .	14
198. Vésztő B.	138
Number of localities: 7	540

District BIHAR

199. Értarcsa K. Z.-né . . .	1
200. Gyanta B.	15
201. Köröstárkány B. . .	32
202. Nagyszalonta K. . .	247
Number of localities: 4	295

District CSANÁD

203. Apátfalva B.	26
204. Csanádapácza	2
Number of localities: 2	28

District CSONGRÁD

205. Csongrád B.	5
206. Horgos B.	40
207. Szeged B., K. . . .	51
208. Szegvár V.	39
209. Szentes B.	19
Number of localities: 5	154

District HAJDU

210. Sámson B.	59
Number of localities: 1	59

Serial numbers.	Number of tunes.

District JÁSZ-NAGYKUN-SZOLNOK

211. Besenyszög B.	11
212. Jánoshida B.	46
213. Jászberény B.	29
Number of localities: 3	86

District PEST-PILIS-SOLT-KISKUN

214. Fót B.	11
215. Gomba K.	1
216. Kecskemét V.	10
217. Nagykáta B.	1
218. Nagykőrös V.	2
219. Rákoskeresztúr B. . .	20
220. Tápiószele B. . . .	32
221. Ujszász B.	155
Number of localities: 8	232

District SZABOLCS

222. Nyírbéltek K.	2
223. Nyírbogdány K. . . .	1
224. Nyírtass K.	1
225. Petneháza V.	2
226. Vaja K.	7
Number of localities: 5	13

District SZATMÁR

227. Avasujváros K. Z.-né . .	130
228. Szinyérváralja K. Z.-né . .	1
229. Tyukod K.	5
Number of localities: 3	136

District TORONTÁL

230. Nagyszentmiklós B. . . .	6
231. Szőreg V.	10
Number of localities: 2	16

IV
District BRASSÓ

232. Hétfalu V.	3
233. Pürkerecz V.	10
234. Zajzon V.	5
Number of localities: 3	18

Serial numbers.	Number of tunes.	Serial numbers.	Number of tunes.
In BUKOVINA		**District HUNYAD**	
235. Andrásfalva K.	43	272. Déva V.	2
236. Fogadjisten K. . . .	11	Number of localities: 1	2
237. Hadikfalva K. . . .	33		
238. Istensegíts K. . . .	100		
239. Józseffalva K. . . .	34	**District KOLOZS**	
Number of localities: 5	221	273. Bánffyhunyad B., V. . .	46
		274. Kolozs V.	2
		275. Körösfő B.	60
District CSÍK		276. Magyargyerőmonostor B. .	22
240. Csíkcsobotfalva L. . .	3	277. Magyarvalkó V. . . .	17
241. Csíkjenőfalva B. . .	30	278. Zentelke V.	30
242. Csíkmenaság L. . .	7	Number of localities: 6	177
243. Csíkrákos B. . . .	43		
244. Csíkszentdomokos L. .	4		
245. Csíkszentmihály B., L. .	22	**District MAROS-TORDA**	
246. Csíkszenttamás B. . .	29	279. Ákosfalva B. . . .	15
247. Csíkverebes L. . . .	6	280. Deményháza V. . .	3
248. Csomafalva B., M. . .	92	281. Ehed B.	19
249. Gyergyóalfalu K., M. .	131	282. Erdőszentgyörgy V. . .	1
250. Gyergyóditró K., L. .	15	283. Jobbágytelke B. . .	40
251. Gyergyóremete K. . .	11	284. Kibéd B. . . .	24
252. Gyergyóújfalu B., M. .	66	285. Kisgörgény B. . .	12
253. Gyergyószentmiklós K., M.	42	286. Körtvélyfája L. . .	1
254. Gyimes(-bükk) L., V. .	28	287. Marosvásárhely B. . .	53
255. Gyimesfelsőlok L. . .	11	288. Mezőpanit L. . .	3
256. Gyimesközéplok L. . .	23	289. Mikháza V. . . .	3
257. Karczfalva B. . .	22	290. Nyárádköszvényes B. .	28
258. Kászonaltíz K. . .	3	291. Nyárádremete B. . .	37
259. Kászonfeltíz K. . .	11	292. Székelyvaja B. . .	20
260. Kászonimpér K. . .	21	293. Szováta V. . . .	7
261. Kászonjakabfalva K. . .	14	Number of localities: 15	266
262. Kászonujfalu K. . .	42		
263. Kilyénfalva B. . . .	11		
264. Szárhegy K. . . .	16	**District SZÍLÁGY**	
265. Tekerőpatak B., M. . .	54	294. Diósad L. . . .	24
266. Tusnád L. . . .	2	295. Kraszna K. . . .	4
267. Vacsárcsi B. . . .	75	296. Szilágyperecsen K. . .	4
Number of localities: 28	834	297. Szilágynagyfalu K. . .	2
		Number of localities: 4	34
District HÁROMSZÉK			
268. Bükszád V. . . .	4		
269. Nagyborosnyó L. . .	3	**District SZOLNOK-DOBOKA**	
270. Sepsiköröspatak L. . .	1	298. Mezőveresegyház K. . .	2
271. Zágon L.	3	Number of localities: 1	2
Number of localities: 4	11		

Serial numbers.	Number of tunes.	Serial numbers.	Number of tunes.
District Torda-Aranyos		315. Lövéte V.	18
299. Sinfalva V.	8	316. Máréfalva V.	3
300. Toroczkó B.	9	317. Martonos V.	10
Number of localities: 2	17	318. Medesér V.	4
		319. Nagykede V.	2
		320. Oroszhegy V.	13
District Udvarhely		321. Rugonfalva V.	17
		322. Siklód V.	25
301. Árvátfalva V.	5	323. Siménfalva V.	2
302. Betfalva V.	13	324. Székelydobó K.	4
303. Bögöz V.	1	325. Székelybetlenfalva V.	6
304. Bözöd V.	12	326. Székelylengyelfalva V.	29
305. Csekefalva V.	21	327. Székelyudvarhely V.	25
306. Énlaka V.	13	328. Szentábrahám V.	5
307. Farkaslaka V.	2	329. Szentegyházasfalu V.	33
308. Felsőboldogfalva V.	10	330. Szentsimon V.	3
309. Fenyéd V.	2	331. Tordátfalva V.	8
310. Firtosváralja V.	15	332. Zetelaka V.	26
311. Kadicsfalva V.	10	Number of localities: 32	386
312. Kápolnásfalu V.	25		
313. Kénos V.	15		
314. Korond V.	9	Origin unknown, B., K., M., V.	57

APPENDIX II

List of Editions and Literature.

Referring to Hungarian folk-music:

Gábor Mátray: *Magyar Népdalok Egyetemes Gyűjteménye.* (General collection of Hungarian Folk-tunes.) Vols. i–iii. Pest, 1852, 1854, 1858. (Songs with piano accompaniments.)

Károly Színi: *A magyar nép dalai és dallamai.* (Songs and tunes of the Hungarian Folk.) Pest, 1st edition 1865, 2nd edition 1872; Gustav Heckenast. (200 tunes.)

István Bartalus: *Magyar Népdalok, egyetemes gyűjtemény.* (Hungarian Folk-tunes, a general collection.) Vols. i–vii. Budapest, 1873–96. (About 800 songs with piano accompaniments.)

Áron Kiss: *Magyar Gyermekjáték-gyűjtemény.* (Collection of Hungarian children's songs.) Budapest, 1891; Viktor Hornyánszky.

Gyula Káldy: *Kurucz dalok XVII. és XVIII. század.* (Kurucz songs of the 17th and 18th centuries.) n. l. n. d. (Songs with piano accompaniments.)

Gyula Sebestyén: *Regös-énekek.* (Regös songs.) *Magyar Népköltési Gyűjtemény.* (Collection of Hungarian Folk-poems.) Vol. iv. Budapest, 1902. (28 tunes.)

Zoltán Kodály: *A magyar népdal strófa-szerkezete.* (The strophe-structure of Hungarian Folk-song.) Nyelvtudományi Közlemények. (*Journal of Philology*.) Vol. xxxvi. Budapest, 1906. (4 tunes.)

Béla Bartók and Zoltán Kodály: *Magyar Népdalok.* (Hungarian Folk-tunes.) Budapest, 1906; Karl Rozsnyai. (20 tunes with piano accompaniments.)

Zoltán Kodály: *Ötfokú hangsor a magyar népzenében.* (The pentatonic scale in Hungarian Folk-music.) Zenei Szemle (*Musical Review*). Vol. i. Temesvár, 1917. (19 tunes.)

Béla Bartók and Zoltán Kodály: *Népdalok* (Erdélyi Magyarság). (Folk-tunes, Erdély Hungaria.) Budapest, 1923; Népies Irodalmi Társaság. (150 tunes.)

Referring to Czech folk-music:

K. J. Erben: *Nápěvy prostonárodních písní českých.* (Tunes of Czech Folk-songs.) Prague, 1st edition 1863, 2nd edition 1886; Alois Hynek. (About 800 tunes.)

Referring to Moravian folk-music:

František Sušil: *Moravské Národní Písně.* (Moravian Folk-songs.) Brno, 1859; Karol Winiker. (1,890 songs.)

E. Peck: *Valašské národní písně.* (Walachian Folk-tunes.) Brno, 1860. (About 300 songs.)

František Bartoš: *Nové Národní Písně Moravské.* (New Moravian Folk-songs.) Brno, 1882; Karol Winiker. (400 tunes.)

František Bartoš: *Národní Písně Moravské.* (Moravian Folk-songs.) Brno, 1889; 'Matica moravská'. (About 1,050 songs.)

František Bartoš: *Národné Písně Moravské.* (Moravian Folk-songs.) Prague. In two parts:

1899 and 1901. Published by the Czech Franz-Josephs Academy of Sciences. (About 2,100 songs.)

N.B. With an introductory essay by Leoš Janáček, containing 58 tunes. Bartoš's three collections are quoted thus: Bartoš I, Bartoš II, Bartoš III.

Joža Černík: *Zpěvy Moravských Kopaničárů.* (Songs of the Moravians.) Prag, 1908; J. Otto. (313 tunes.)

Referring to Slovakian folk-music:

Jan Kollár: *Národnié Zpiewanky čili Pjsně Swětské Slowákůw W Uhrách.* (Folk-songs or secular songs of the Slovakians in Hungary.) I–II. Bd. Buda, 1834, 1835. (Words only, no tunes.)

Sborník Slovenských národních piesni. (A collection of Slovakian Folk-songs.) Vienna, 1870; 'Matica Slovenská'. (66 tunes.)

Slovenské Spevy. I–III. Bd., Túróczszentmárton, 1880, 1890, 1899; 'Priatelia Slovenských Spevov'. (About 1,800 tunes.)

Karol A. Medvecky: *Detva (monografia).* Rózsahegy, 1905. (50 tunes.)

Referring to Ukrainian folk-music:

St. Lud'keveč: *Halećko ruśki narodni meľodiji.* (Folk-songs of the Galicia Ruthenians.) Etnografičnej Zbirnek, vol. xxi. Lemberg, 1906. Published by the Ševčenko Society.

F. Kolessa: *Melodien der ukraïnischen rezitierenden Gesänge (Dumy).* Beiträge zur ukraïnischen Ethnologie, vols. xiii, xiv. Lemberg, 1910, 1913. Published by the Ševčenko Society.

Referring to Rumanian folk-music:

Béla Bartók: *Chansons populaires roumaines du département Bihar (Hongrie).* Bukarest, 1913. Published by the 'Academia Română'. (371 songs.)

Béla Bartók: *Volksmusik der Rumänen von Maramureş.* Sammelbände für vergleichende Musikwissenschaft, vol. iv. Munich, 1923; Drei-Masken-Verlag. (365 tunes.)

Referring to Arabian folk-music:

Béla Bartók: *Die Volksmusik der Araber von Biskra und Umgebung.* Zeitschrift für Musikwissenschaft, vol. ii. Leipzig, 1920.

APPENDIX III

This book deals with the music of the Hungarian peasant class only. There is a cogent scientific reason for dealing with this peasant music quite apart from any other kind of folk-music (including the repertory of popular art songs).

We have seen that, from the scientific point of view, the most important folk-songs are those that belong to one or several definite classes, characterized by the fact that they exhibit common features. For obvious reasons, such songs arose only among the peasant class. In constitution, aspect, form, and character, these peasant songs are different from any other type of folk-music. And unless one studies them separately, the result will be obscurity and confusion—the very thing that science must strive to avoid.

Hence the necessity to devote this book—which is not, and does not pretend to be, anything but a study on Hungarian Peasant Music—to Hungarian peasant music only. Investigation of the music of other classes I leave to those who are interested in that music.

I have but little to say here on the functions of Gipsy musicians.

What do Gipsy musicians play in Hungary?

Mostly Hungarian popular art tunes (Hungarian because they were written by Hungarian composers), seldom Hungarian peasant songs, often (by request) light art music from Western Europe, such as waltzes, &c. Their programmes, generally speaking, are adjusted to the preferences of the classes for whom they happen to be catering: to the middle and upper classes they play popular art tunes or light music from Western Europe, to peasants they may also play, now and then, peasant tunes.

They perform all music with an excess of *rubato* and ornaments. Their repertory is not particularly extensive; it is, indeed, mostly restricted to the tunes in fashion at the moment.

There have even been a few Gipsy musicians (such as Bihari and Dankó) who enriched Hungarian popular art music with tunes of their own invention. These tunes are similar in character to all the tunes of the same category written by Hungarian composers. Accordingly the so-called 'Gipsy music' is not Gipsy music at all, but Hungarian music, from miscellaneous sources, performed by Gipsies. One would be justified, at most, in speaking of Gipsy methods of performance—a subject, I repeat it, which I leave to those whom it may attract.

How did the Gipsies become the principal performers of music in Hungary?

It is very difficult to reply to this question. One may be almost certain that originally—perhaps a few centuries ago—our peasant class had only its own native peasant musicians, who were hired on festive occasions (dances, weddings, &c.) to play dance music. They used, according to regions, the native bagpipes, flutes, hurdy-gurdies, &c. I found sporadic traces of the survival of this state of things along the northern border of the Hungarian-speaking zone, at the beginning of the present century. It is far more current, even nowadays, in certain Rumanian regions (e.g. in the districts of Bihar and Hunyad) in which no single Gipsy musician could be found. In Bihar peasant musicians use violins, in Hunyad bagpipes or peasant flutes.

How, when, and why Gipsy musicians gradually supplanted these peasant musicians is a question that cannot be solved without protracted historical investigations. The reply—if there can be one—will have to show whether the Gipsies were accepted at first by the ruling classes and thence penetrated among the peasant class, or whether the contrary occurred.

SONG TEXTS

FULL TEXTS OF THE SONGS

1

Sír a kis galambom, sírok én magam is,
Sírunk mind a ketten igën keservesën.
Anyám, édës anyám, mért üldözesz engëm,
Mért nem hagytad ezt a kis lëányt elvennëm?

When my little dove weeps, I also weep,
We both shed bitter tears.
Mother, dear mother, why torment me,
Why not let me marry this little maiden?

2

Kemény kősziklának könnyebb meghasadni,
Mint két édes szűvnek egymástól megválni.
Mikor két édes szűv egymástól megválik,
Még az édes méz es keserűvé válik.

It is easier to split a hard stone cliff
Than to part two loving hearts.
When two loving hearts are parted,
Even the sweetest honey tastes bitter.

3

Sirass éldes anyám, mig előtted járok,
Mer aztán sirathatsz, ha tőled elválok.
A jó isten tudja, hol történ halálom,
A jó isten tudja, hol történ halálom.

Weep, mother, so long as I am with thee:
You will weep more bitterly when I am far
away.
|: God All-merciful knows where death awaits
me. :|

4

1. Nem arról hajnallik, amerről hajnallott,
   Magam sorsa felől szomorú hirt hallok.
2. Árad napról-napra bánatja szivemnek,
   Már végire jártam szabad életemnek.

1. Day does not dawn where I awaitest dawn,
   But a direful message comes to me.
2. Alas, ever my heart is full of woe,
   Ended is my life of freedom.

5

Istenöm, istenöm, szerelmes istenöm,
Mi ennek az oka, mi ennek az oka:
Szép sejöm karincám végig elhasada,
Szép sejöm karincám végig elhasada.

My God, my God, O God whom I love,
What has happened, what has happened?
|: My beautiful silk apron is all torn!: |

6

Verje meg az isten a mészárosokat,
Mér vagdalták el a kis borjulábakat!
A szegény kis borju nem tud lábra állni,
Nyom orult bakának a hátán kell vinni.

May the Lord smite the butchers
Who cut off the little calf's feet:
The little calf no longer can stand on his legs,
So the soldier must carry the poor thing on
his back.[1]

7 a and b

Mikor guláslegény voltam,
Gula mellett elaludtam.
Fölébredtem éjféltájba:
Ëgy barmom sincs az állásba.

I was a cowherd,
I slept by my cows,
I awoke in the night,
Not one beast was in its stall.

7 c

1. Megállj pajtás, hogy panaszolom el sorsom,
   Miként áll az állapotom:
   Inyësfinyës a putlikom,
   Harmadnapba sincs prófontom.

1. Stop, comrade, and hear my tale of woe,
   Hear how Fate has treated me.
   Empty is my ration-tin,
   And for three days not a single loaf.

[1] i.e. a knapsack made of the calf's hide.

2. Panaszolom a tisztemnek: [1]
   Nincs ereje a testemnek.
   Mérges száját rám forditja,
   Jézus-Krisztusomat szidja.

2. I complained to my officer:
   No strength remains in my body.
   Angrily he stands abusing me,
   Inveighing against the name of the Lord.

8

1. Elment Simon disznót lopnyi,
   Nem jó helyre talált mennyi.
   Ottan várja egy pár fegyver:
   Ugy jár, kit az isten megver.

2. Nincs Simonnak siratója,

   Nincs is annak pártfogója;

   Cifra szűre koporsója,

   Bikkfalevél takarója.

1. Simon went to steal a pig,
   But came not to the right spot.
   For there two guns were ready for him,
   God's punishment was in store for him.

2. None will weep for Simon,
   None take his part:
   His embroidered cloak is his coffin,
   Beech-leaves are his pall.

9

1. Hallottátok-e már hírül
   Kaszai Sanyi legénységül?
   Bicskával vágja ja nyárfát,
   Hogy ne hallják dobogását.

2. Fel-felveszi a vállára,
   Viszi Róza ablakára:
   — Kelj fel Róza, itt a májfa,
   Egész éjjel vigyázz rája!

3. Az anyja jaz ajtót nyitja,
   Az apja ja gyertyát gyujtja,
   Róza a kendőt keresi,
   Sanyi a májfára köti.

1. Have you already heard the story
   Of that fellow Kaszai Sanyi?
   He felled a poplar with his knife,
   So that no noise should betray him.

2. He carried it away on his shoulder,
   Beneath the window of Rosie's room:
   'Hullo, Rosie, here's the May-tree,
   Watch well upon it throughout the night.'

3. Mother opens wide the door,
   Father lights the candles,
   Rosie fetches a kerchief,
   Sanyi ties it to the May-tree.

10

1. Minden ember szerencsésen,
   Csak én élek keservesen;
   Fejem lehajtom csendesen,
   Csak ugy sirok keservesen.

2. Ne sirj, kedves feleségem,

   Ne zokogj, édes gyermekem!
   Gondodat viseli-az [2] isten,
   Kiszabadulok még egyszer.

1. All men appear happy,
   Yet I am full of woe.
   Silently I bow my head,
   Bitterly I weep.

2. Do not weep, my darling wife,
   Do not sob, child of my heart!
   God will have good care of thee,
   And bring freedom to me.

[1] The portion of the tune marked [1] is left out at this place.
[2] 'li-az' pronounced as one syllable.

Arra gyere, a mőre én;
Maj mëgtudod, hol lakok én:
Csipkebokorrózsa mellett, —
Gyere babám, megölellek.

A cseroldalt összejártam,
Sehol párom nem találtam.
Ez a hat forintos nóta,
Kinek tetszik, járja rea.

Napom, napom, fényës napom,
Homályban borult csillagom.
Süss még ëgyszër világosan,
Ne süss mindíg homályosan.

Eddig vendég jól mulattál;
Ha tetszenék, elindulnál!
Szaladj gazda, kapjál botra,
A vendéget indítsd útra.

1. Harangoznak vecsërnyére,
   Gyere pajtás az erdőre,
   Az új útnak tetejére,
   Az új útnak tetejére.

2. Mindën embërnek mëghagyom,
   Sötét rëggel fát ne vágjon;
   Mert én sötét rëggel vágtam,
   Szerëncsétlen órán jártam.

3. Testem törött a bokorba,
   Vérem kihullott a porba;
   A madarak pásztorolták,
   Énekszóval virrasztották.

4. Azt a gazdája megtudta,
   Mindgyár utána indula.
   Meg van a koporsó festve,
   Uti Miska fekszik benne.

5. Nyisd ki apám a kapudat,
   Halva hozzák szép fiadat;
   Sirass anyám, ne bízd másra,
   Most siratsz meg utoljára.

Erdők, völgyek, szűk ligetek,
Sokat bujdostam bennetek.
Bujdostam én az vadakkal,
Sirtam a kis madarakkal.

11 a

Come, follow where I go.
You will soon know where I live:
By the hedge of hawthorn,
Come, my love, unto my arms.

11 b

I walked along the bush,
I could not find my love:
This is the song of six florins,
Let who likes it dance to it.

12

Sun, O Sun, my splendent Sun,
My bedimmed star:
Shine in all thy brightness,
Not in mist enshrouded.

13

Up till now the guest was well entertained.
May he please to go his way.
Rise, host, and grasp your staff;
Show the guest his way.

14 (var. 21)

1. The vesper bells are tolling;
   Come, friend, to the forest,
   Along the new road to the crest,
   Along the new road to the crest.

2. All men I instruct:
   On a dim morning, fell no tree.
   But I on a dim morning felled one,
   Ill fated was the hour.

3. The branches tore my body;
   The dust was caked with my blood,
   Over which the birds kept watch,
   Gaily singing as they watched.

4. 'His master heard of it
   And followed him swiftly.
   The coffin is there, all painted,
   For Uti Miska to lie in.'

5. Father, open your door,
   Behold your bonny son is dead.
   Weep, mother, leave it not to others:
   Now you mourn me for the last time.

15

Forests, valleys, groves,
Long through you I fled,
Fled with the wild beasts,
Wept with the little birds.

Ha kiindulsz Erdély felől,
Ne nézz rózsám visszafelé:
Szivednek ne lëgyën nehéz,
Hogy az idegën földre mész.

Crossing the borders of Transylvania,
Do not look backwards, my sweetheart:
For your heart will grieve
At your being in a foreign land.

Megmondtam én bus gerlice:
Ne rak' fészket az útszélre,
Mert az uton sokan járnak,
A fészkedből elvadásznak.

Let me warn you, turtle dove:
Build not your nest by the roadside,
For many people passing by
Will scare you off your nest.

Fölmëntem a szilvafára,
Elrededt a gatyám szára.
Huszul b . . . . . . az irgalmát,
Maj mëgvarrja az én babám.

Climbing the plum-tree,
I tore my breeches,
D . . . it all, b . . . it all,
My little girl will mend them.

Gyulainé édës anyám!
Engedje mëg azt az ëgyet:
Hogy kérjem mëg Kádár Katát,
Jobbágyunknak szép lëányát.

Hearken, Dame Gyulaı, mother mine,
But one boon I crave of thee:
Permission to woo Katie Kadar,
Our farmer's beautiful daughter.

1. Szántani kék, tavasz vagyon,
   A szerszámom széjjel vagyon.
   A szerszámom széjjel vagyon,
   Ekém szarva Szarvason van.

2. A tengelye Tengelyesen,
   A kereke Kerepesen,
   Az patingom fa tövibe,
   Ostornyelem a hegyibe.

3. Szegje, járma Gyarmaton van,
   Az al-fája Alfáron van,
   A béldeszkám Békésen van,
   Járomszögem Szögeden van.

4. A béresem az Bácskában,
   A baltája az Bánátban,
   Szép hat ökröm az vásárba,
   De nem tudom, hol az ára.

1. It's time to plough, it's springtime,
   But my implements are scattered,
   Aye, my implements are scattered:
   In Szarvas is the ploughtail.

2. In Tengelyes the shaft;
   In Kerepes the wheels,
   Under a tree the axle,
   On the tree-top the whip-handle.

3. Bolts and harness are in Gyarmat,
   The body is at Alfár,
   The flanges at Békés,
   The yoke at Szöged.

4. My boy is at Bácska,
   My hatchet in the Bánát.
   My six fine oxen are in the market,
   And I don't know where the purchase-
   money is.

Romlott testëm a bokorba,
Piros vérem hull a hóba;
Hull a vérem, hull a hóba,
Piros vérem hull a hóba.

I lie wounded in the thicket,
My red blood trickles on the snow,
My blood trickles, trickles on the snow,
My red blood trickles on the snow.

1. Mikor a nagy erdőn kimész,
Arra kérlek, vissza ne nézz,
Ne legyen szűvednek nehéz,
Hogy az idegën földre mész.

2. |: Idegën föld az én hazám,
Ferenc Jóska éldes apám, : |

3. |: Fehér sziju az mejemen, : |
|: Rezes csákó a fejemen. : |

4. Jaj istenem, én istenem!
Jaj, hát Csíkból ki kell mennem,
|: A babámat itt kell hagynom. : |

5. |: Katonának vagyok írva,
Meghal éldes anyám sírva; : |

6. |: Katonaságom sem bánom,
Csak éldes anyám sajnálom. : |

1. Would you get out of the big forest,
Look not behind you,
Lest your heart be heavy
When you set foot in a foreign land.

2. |: This foreign land is my own home
And Ferenc Jóska[1] is my father. : |

3. |: A white strap across my shoulders, : |
|: A burnished shako on my head. : |

4. O my Lord, O God my Lord,
Now I must away from Csik,
|: And leave behind my darling child. : |

5. |: If I must a soldier be,
My mother will die of grief. : |

6. |: I can't stand being in the army,
I bewail my poor mother's fate. : |

23 (var. 24, 29, 32)

A fekete halom alatt
Fehér László lovat lopott,
Lovat lopott szerszámostul,
Cifra nyeregkantárostul.

Under yonder murky hills,
Fehér László stole a white horse,
Stole a horse with all its harness,
With its saddle and its bridle.

24 (var. 23, 29, 32)

Fehér László lovat lopott
A fekete halom alatt;
Fehér Lászlót ott megfogták,
Tömlöc fenekére zárták.

Fehér László stole a horse
Under yonder murky hills.
As soon as Fehér László 's caught
He is cast into the deepest dungeon!

25

Túl a vizön, a töngörön,
Rózsa teröm a kendörön;
Mindön szálon kettő-három, —
Van szeretőm tizenhárom.

O'er the water, o'er the sea
Roses grow upon the hemp,
Two and three upon one stem,
I have thirteen sweethearts.

26

1. Tova mënyën három árva,
Tőlük kérdi a Szűz Márja:
— |: Hova mëntëk három árva? : |

2. — Álljatok mëg, három árva,
Adok néktek arany vesszőt,
|: Csapjátok meg a temetőt. : |

3. — Kelj föl, kelj föl, édes anyánk,
Mer elszakadt a gyászgunyánk!
— Nem kelhetek, édes fiam,
Elrothadtak az inaim.

4. Elrothadtak az inaim,
Két karjaim s két lábaim;
A vérem is elároklott
S a lelkem is elbucsuzott.

1. Three orphans were going along,
The Virgin Mary asked them:
|: 'Where go you, orphans three? : |

2. Wait, you orphans three,
I'll give you a golden rod,
|: Strike with it the burial-ground.' : |

3. 'Arise, arise, beloved mother:
Our mourning clothes are torn.'
'I shall not rise, dear children,
My sinews have turned to dust.

4. My sinews have turned to dust,
And both my arms and legs;
My blood is clotted,
My soul has left me.'

[1] The emperor Franz Joseph.

5. — Adja ide, édes anyáın,
A koporsójának kócsát,
Had' zárjam ki koporsóját,
Csókoljam meg kezét, lábat.

6. — Tova mënyën egy menyecske,
Két orcája ki van festve;
A'llesz néktek mostohátok.
Aki fejért ad rëátok.

7. Mikor fejért ad rëátok,
Vérrel virágzik hátatok;
Mikor kenyert ad kezedbe,
Hull a könyved kebeledbe.

5. 'Give me, dear mother,
The key of your coffin,
I'll open the coffin,
Kiss your hands and feet.

6. 'There goes a young woman.
Her cheeks are painted.
She'll be your step-mother,
Give you clean clothing.

7. 'And when she gives you clean clothing,
Blood will ooze from your backs,
When she gives bread into your hands,
Tears fall upon your breast.'

27 (var. 193)

1. Egy hete-e, vagy már három,
Mióta a gazdám várom?
Amott jön már, amint látom,
Egy deresszőrű szamáron.

2.[1] Jónapot, jó bojtárom!
Van-e hibád, van-e károd?

— Se nem is vót, se nem is lesz,
Míg a nyáj a kezemen lesz.

3. — Dehogy is nincs, de bizony van!
Hát a vezérürüd hol van?
Vezérürüd harangostul,
Rózsás szamár kantárostul?

4. — |: Zsidó elvitte a bőrit,
Magam megettem a testit. :|

1. Have I not for a week, aye, for three,
Been awaiting my master?
And here he comes, I see,
Riding a grey donkey.

2. 'Good day, my good shepherd.[1]
Any mistakes? Any losses?'
'None there have been, none there shall be
So long as I'm in charge of the flock.'

3. 'There are none? Indeed there have been:
For where is the leader of the flock,
The wether with his bell,
And the rose-pink donkey with its bridle?'

4. |: 'The Jew took their skins,
I ate their flesh.' :

28

1. Cigány vagyok, rest a nevem,
Ha dolgozom, fáj a fejem,
— Cigány, cigány, mért vagy cigány,
Mért jársz a magyar lány után?

2. — |: Azért járok én az után:
Szebb a magyar, mint a cigány. :|

1. 'I'm a gipsy, lazy is my name.
If I do work, it gives me a headache.'
'Gipsy, gipsy, why, O gipsy,
Do you run after Hungarian girls?'

2. |: 'I run after them
Because Hungarian girls are prettier than
gipsies.' :|

29 (var. 23, 24, 32)

1. Fehér László lovat lopott
A fekete halom alatt,
Hatot fogott suhogóra,
Görc városa csodájára.

2. Rajta, rajta Görc városa,
Fehér László meg van fogva.
Verjünk vasat a kutyára,
Jobb kezére, bal lábára.

1. Fehér László stole a horse
Under yonder murky hills.
Six he caught
And the city of Görc wondered at the
deed.

2. Arise, arise, city of Görc,
Fehér László is caught.
The cur will be put in irons,
His right hand chained to his left foot.

[1] Sung to variant 1.

3. — |: Kutya betyár, add meg magad,
Vagy azt mondd meg, kinek hínak. : |

4. — Az én lovam keselylábú,
Az én húgom Fehér Anna.
— Nem kérdjük mink a lovadat,
Sem azt a büszke húgodat.

5 = 3.

6. — Az én lovam keselylábú,
Az én nevem Fehér László.
— Verjünk vasat a kutyára,
Jobb kezére, bal lábára.

7. |: El is vitték jó messzire,
Sötét börtön fenekére. : |

8. Fehér Anna meghallotta,
Hogy a bátyja be van fogva.
Parancsolja kocsisának:
— Kocsisom, fogj be hat lovat,

9. Kocsisom, fogj be hat lovat,
|: Tégy fel egy véka aranyat, : |
Kiszabadítom bátyámat.

10. Fehér Anna nem nyúgodott,
Felszaladt a vasajtóra:
— Bátyám, bátyám, Fehér László,
Aluszol-e vagy nyúgodol?

11. — |: Se nem alszok, se nem nyugszok,
Húgom, rólad gondolkozok. : |

12. Fehér Anna nem nyúgodott,
Felszaladt a vasajtóra:
— Bátyám, bátyám, Fehér László,
Hogy hívják itten a bírót?

13. — |: Ez a bíró Horvát bíró,
Az akasztófára való. : |

14. Ekkor megyen Fehér Anna
Horvát bíró ablakára:
— Bíró, bíró, Horvát bíró,
Szabadítsd ki a bátyámat,

15. Szabadítsd kí a bátyámat,
Adok egy véka aranyat.
— Nem kell nékem az aranyad,
Csak hálj vélem egy éjcaka.

16. Fehér Anna nem nyúgodott,
Felszaladt a vasajtóra:
— Bátyám, bátyám, Fehér László,
Azt mondta nekem a bíró:

17. |: 'Kiszabadul bátyád még ma,'
Háljak véle egy éjcaka. : |

3. |: 'Dog of an outlaw, give yourself up,
Or tell me what is your name.' : |

4. 'My horse has piebald legs,
My young sister is Fehér Anna.'
'I do not inquire about your horse,
Nor about your proud sister.'

5 = 3.

6. 'My horse has piebald legs,
And my name is László Fehér.'
'Let 's put the fetters on the cur:
Tie his right hand to his left foot.'

7. |: And they led him far away,
And they thrust him in a dark prison.: |

8. Fehér Anna heard the news
That her brother was caught.
So she told her coachman:
'Coachman, bring forth six horses,

9. Coachman, bring forth six horses,
|: And a bushel of gold pieces, : |
For me to buy my brother's freedom.'

10. Fehér Anna did not tarry,
She went to the iron door.
'Brother, brother, Fehér László,
Are you asleep, or are you resting?'

11. |: 'I am neither asleep nor resting,
Little sister, I think of you!' : |

12. Fehér Anna did not tarry,
She went to the iron door:
'Brother, brother, Fehér László,
Tell me who is judge here.'

13. |: 'The judge here is Judge Horvát,
A gallows-bird indeed!' : |

14. Thereupon went Fehér Anna
Under Judge Horvát's window.
'Hearken, Judge, Judge Horvát!
Set my brother free,

15. Set my brother free,
I shall give you a bushel of gold pieces.'
'I do not want a bushel of gold pieces,
I only want a night with you!'

16. Fehér Anna did not tarry,
She went to the iron door.
'Brother, brother, Fehér László,
This the judge said to me:

17. |: "Your brother will be set free at once.'
But I must spend the night with him.': |

18. — Húgom, húgom, Fehér Anna,
    Ne hálj véle egy éjcaka;
    Szüzességedet elveszi,
    A bátyádnak fejét veszi.

19. Fehér Anna nem nyúgodott,
    Elment a bíró házához,
    Véle is hált egy éjcaka
    Az aranyos nyoszolyába.

20. Éjféltájban egy órakor
    Csörgés esett az udvaron.
    — Bíró, bíró, Horvát bíró,
    Mi csörömpöl az udvaron?

21. — |: Kocsisom lovat itatja,
    Annak csörög zabolája. :|

22. Fehér Anna nem nyúgodott,
    Felszaladt a vasajtóra:
    — Bátyám, bátyám, Fehér László,
    Aluszol-e vagy nyúgodol?

23. — Húgom, húgom, Fehér Anna,
    Ne keresd itt a bátyádat:
    Zöld erdőbe, zöld mezőbe,
    Akasztófa tetejébe!

24. Akkor megyen Fehér Anna
    Horvát bíró ablakára:
    — Bíró, bíró, Horvát bíró,
    Lovad lába megbotoljon,

25. |: Lovad lába megbotoljon,
    Tégedet a földhöz vágjon. :|

26. Tizenhárom szekér szalma
    Rothadjon el az ágyadban,
    Tizenhárom esztendeig
    Nyomjad az ágyad fenekit.

27. Tizenhárom doktor keze
    Fáradjon ki sebeidbe.
    Tizenhárom sor patika
    Ürüljön ki a számodra.

28. Ugy-e bíró, jót kivánok:
    Mosdóvized vérré váljon,
    Törülköződ lángot hányjon,
    Isten téged meg ne áldjon!

18. 'Sister, sister, Fehér Anna,
    Do not spend the night with him.
    He will rob you of your maidenhood,
    And cut off your brother's head.'

19. Fehér Anna did not tarry,
    Went to the judge's house,
    And she spent the night with him
    In his golden bed.

20. And at the hour of midnight
    A clatter arose from the courtyard.
    'Hearken, Judge, Judge Horvát,
    What is this clatter arising from the
    courtyard?'

21. |: 'My coachman is watering my horse,
    And so the bit is rattling.' :|

22. Fehér Anna did not tarry,
    She went to the iron door.
    'Brother, brother, Fehér László,
    Are you asleep or are you resting?'

23. 'Sister, sister, Fehér Anna,
    Do not seek your brother here,
    But in the green woods, in the green
    fields,
    Hanging from the gallows.'

24. Thereupon went Fehér Anna
    Under Judge Horvát's window.
    'Hearken, Judge, Judge Horvát,
    May your horse stumble on his feet,

25. |: May your horse stumble on his feet,
    And you be thrown to the ground! :|

26. May thirteen cartloads of straw
    Rot away in your bed!
    May you for thirteen years
    Lie upon it in cruel illness!

27. May thirteen doctors work
    At dressing your wounds,
    Thirteen shelves of drugs
    Be emptied on your account!

28. Indeed, Judge, I wish you well:
    May your washing-water turn to blood,
    Your towel spit flames,
    And God never bless you!'

30

Elment a pap almát lopni,
Elfelejtett zsákot vinni;
Levetette a gatyáját,
Teletömte a két szárát.

The priest went to steal apples,
But he forgot to bring a bag:
So he took off his drawers
And stuffed both legs full.

1. Nem loptam én életembe,
   Csak hat tinót Debrecenbe.
   Hazahajtottam a tinót,
   Mind a hat daruszőrű volt.

2. Elhajtottam a vásárra,
   Elhajtottam szerencsésen.
   Jászberényi Becsalinál
   Elejbem áll kilenc zsandár.

3. Asz kérdezi, mi a nevem,
   Hol az útazólevelem?
   — Várjál zsandár, megmutatom,
   Ha a lájbim kigombolom.

4. Kigomboltam a lájbimat,
   Kirántom a pisztolyomat,
   Kettőt mingyán fejbelőttem:
   — Itt az útazólevelem!

Fehír László lovat lopott
A feKéte halom alatt,
Mindën nyerëgszerszámostul,
Csikófékes kantárostul.

1. Elhervadt cidrusfa
   A magas hegytetőn, —
   Én is elhervadtam
   A börtön fenekén.

2. Kilencfontos vasat
   Nyolcat elszaggattam,
   Kilencediket is
   Jól elvásítottam.

3. — Anyám, kedves anyám,
   Kérjed levelemet,
   Kérjed levelemet,
   Szabad életemet.

4. — Anyám, kedves anyám,
   Mit mondtak az urak?
   — Azt mondták az urak,
   Hogy felakasztanak.

5. — Ó te drága anyám,
   Kár vóna azt tenni,
   Szép göndör hajamat
   Szélnek ereszteni

6. Sem egyért, sem másért:
   Két szürke pejkóért,
   Hozzátartozandó
   Sallangos szerszámért.

1. Never in my life did I steal anything,
   Except for six calves in Debrecen.
   I drove the calves to my own home,
   All six of them were grey.

2. I drove them to market,
   I drove them successfully,
   But at the Becsal inn at Jasberenyi
   Nine policemen stood before me.

3. They asked who I was,
   And where was my passport.
   'Wait, policeman, I will show it:
   But I must unbutton my vest.'

4. And I unbuttoned my vest,
   And I pulled out a pistol,
   Shot two forthwith through the head.
   'Here is my passport!'

32 (var. 23, 24, 29)
Fehír László stole a horse
Under yonder murky hills,
With its saddle and its bridle,
And with trappings all complete.

33 a

1. A cedar tree is withering
   On the high mountain.
   I too am withering
   In a grim prison-cell.

2. Nine-pound fetters
   I broke eight times,
   And a ninth time
   I have worn them thin.

3. Mother, beloved mother,
   Ask for my discharge,
   Ask for my discharge,
   Ask for my freedom.

4. Mother, beloved mother,
   What did the gentlemen reply?
   'The gentlemen replied
   That you will be hanged.'

5. O my dear, dear mother,
   'Twould be a pity indeed
   If my beautiful curly hair
   Were scattered to the winds.

6. Not for this, not for that,
   But for six grey horses,
   And the beautiful saddles
   That go with them.

1. Kérették nénémet
   Szép királyfiának,
   Engem is kérettek
   Egy kódus fiának.
2. Elvitték nénémet
   Szép aranyhintóba,
   Engem is elvittek
   Egy kóduskordélyba.
3. Ётették nénémet
   Szép arany csészéből,
   Engem is ётettek
   Moslékos sajtárból.
4. Fektették nénémet
   Szép királyfi mellé,
   Engem is fektettek
   Egy kandisznó mellé.

1. My sister is woo'd
   By a beauteous prince,
   But I am woo'd
   By a beggar's son.
2. My sister is taken away
   In a golden carriage,
   I am taken away
   In a beggar's barrow.
3. My sister eats
   Off a plate of gold,
   While I must eat
   Off a slop-basin.
4. My sister lies
   By the beauteous prince,
   And I must lie
   By an ugly boar.

Lёszállott a páva
Vármegyeházára,
Szájjába visz vizet
A rabok számára.

Down came a peacock
By the town-hall,
In his beak he carries water
To each of the prisoners.

1. Angoli Borbála
   Kis szoknyát varatott,
   Elül kurtábbodott,
   Hátul hosszabbodott.
2. Elül kurtábbodott,
   Hátul hosszabbodott,
   Szép karcsú dereka
   Egyre vastagodott.
3. — Lányom, lányom, lányom,
   Angoli Borbála,
   Mi dolog lehet a':
   Kerek aljú szoknya
4. Elül kurtábbodik,
   Hátul hosszabbodik,
   Szép karcsú derekad
   Egyre vastagodik?
5. — Szabó nem jó szabta,
   Varó nem jó varta.
   Ez a szobaleány
   Reám nem jól adta.
6 = 3; 7 = 4.
8. — Anyám, anyám, anyám,
   Vándorvári Kati,
   Fojóvizet ittam,
   Attól vastagodom.

1. Angoli Borbála
   Bought a little frock,
   The front became rather short,
   The back became rather long.
2. The front became rather short,
   The back became rather long.
   Her beautiful slim hips
   Grew gradually broader.
3. 'My daughter, my daughter,
   Angoli Borbála,
   What has happened?
   The circular hem of your frock
4. Has become rather short in front,
   And at the back rather long,
   And your beautiful slim waist
   Has grown gradually broader?'
5. 'The tailor has cut it badly,
   The seamstress sown it badly,
   And the chambermaid
   Has adjusted it badly.'
6 = 3; 7 = 4.
8. 'Mother, mother, mother,
   Vándorvári Kati,
   I drank water from the river
   And therefore I am swollen.

9 = 3; 10 = 4.

11. — Mit tűröm-tagadom,
Csak ki kell vallanom:
Gyöngyvári úrfitól,
Attól vastagodom.

12. — Pandúrok jőjjetek,
|: Fogjátok, vigyétek, :|
Börtönbe tegyétek:

13. Tizenhárom napig
|: Sem enni, sem inni, :|
Sem pedig aludni!

14. Tizenharmadnapra
Előjön az anya:
— Eszel-e vagy iszol,
Vagy pedig aluszol?

15. — Nem eszem, nem iszom,
Sem pedig nem alszom;
Csak egy órát engedj,
Levelem had' írom,

16. Levelem had' írom
Gyöngyvári úrfinak,
Gyöngyvári úrfinak,
Kedves galambomnak.

17. — Jó estét, jó estét
Ösmeretlen anyám!
Hol vagyon, hol vagyon
Az én kedves babám?

18. — Kinn van a kis kerben
Gyöngyvirágot szedni,
Bús koszorút kötni,
A fejére tenni.

19. — Nincsen ott, nincsen ott.
Ösmeretlen anyám.
Mondja meg, hol vagyon
Az én kedves babám?

20. — Mit tűröm-tagadom,
Csak ki kell vallanom:
Benn van a szobában
Fekete-szín padon.

21. Bemegy a vőlegény,
Bemegyen sietve,
Veszi a nagy kését,
Szegezi szivének:

22. — Vérem a véreddel
Egy patakot mosson,
Szívem a sziveddel
Egy sírba nyugodjon.

9 = 3; 10 = 4.

11. 'I can't go on lying,
And I must confess:
It is Squire Gyöngyvári
Who is the cause of my swelling.'

12. 'Come here, you Pandurs,
|: Take her, drag her away, :|
Throw her into prison.

13. For thirteen days
|: No food, no drink, :|
And even no sleep.'

14. Thirteen days elapse
And the mother comes.
'Do you eat, do you drink,
Or at least do you sleep?'

15. 'I eat not, I drink not,
And even I sleep not,
But grant me one hour
For to write a letter,

16. For to write a letter
To Squire Gyöngyvári,
To Squire Gyöngyvári,
To my well-beloved.'

17. 'Good evening, good evening,
My newly-met mother!
Where is she, where is she,
My dearly beloved?'

18. 'She went into the garden
To pluck lilies of the valley,
To weave a dismal wreath,
And wear it round her head.'

19. 'She is not there, not there,
My newly-met mother.
Do tell me, where is she,
My dearly beloved?'

20. 'I can't go on lying,
And I must confess:
She is up there in the room,
In her black coffin.'

21. In went the bridegroom,
In went he quickly,
And drove his big knife
Straight into his heart.

22. 'My blood with thy blood
Runs in one stream,
My heart and thy heart
Will rest in one tomb.

I

23. Szívem a sziveddel
    Egy sírba nyugodjon,
    Lelkem a lelkeddel
    Egy istent imádjon!

23. My heart and thy heart
    Will rest in one tomb,
    My soul and thy soul
    Will pray to one God.'

34 b (var. 176 a)

1. Kérettelek téged
    Szalai Rózsika,
    Sëm ëgyszer, sëm kétszer,
    Hanëm tizënkétszer.

1. I have wooed you,
    Szalai Rózsika,
    Not once, not twice,
    But twelve times.

— — — — — —

2. — Húzd rá cigány, húzd rá
    A te muzsikádat,
    Arannyal, ezüsttel,
    Mindennel szolgálok.

2. 'Play away, you Gipsy,
    Give us your tunes,
    Gold and silver
    Will be your payment.

3. — Hadd el cigány, hadd el
    A te muzsikádat,
    Arannyal, gyémánttal,
    Mindennel szolgálok.

3. 'Stop, you Gipsy, stop
    Playing your tunes:
    Gold and diamonds
    Will be your payment.

4. — Fogd be apám, fogd be
    A te lovaidat,
    Kien [1] had' vigyék be
    A te szép lányodat.

4. 'Harness, father, harness
    Your horses,
    For to bring home
    Your beautiful daughter.

5. — Bontsd le anyám, bontsd le
    Halottas ágyodat,
    Kire had' tegyék fel
    A te szép lányodat.

5. 'Prepare, mother, prepare
    The death-bed
    Upon which to lay out
    Your beautiful daughter.

6. Húzd le anyám, húzd le
    Kopogós cipőmet,
    Mer bizony teli van
    Piros aludt vérrel.

6. 'Pull off, mother, pull off
    My boots that go tapping.
    See, indeed they are covered
    With red, trickling blood.

7. Vedd le anyám, vedd le
    Halottas tükrödet,
    Kibe had' nézzem meg
    Elfásult szememet.

7. 'Take down, mother, take down
    The mirror of death
    For me therein to see
    My palsied eyes.

8. — Csináltatsz-e anyám
    Diófakörösztöt?
    — Bizony csináltatok
    Márványkűkörösztöt.

8. 'Will you order, mother,
    A cross of walnut wood?'
    'Indeed I will order
    A cross of marble.'

9. — Csináltatsz-e anyám
    Diófakoporsót?
    — Bizony csináltatok
    Márványkűkoporsót.

9. 'Will you order, mother,
    A coffin of walnut-wood?'
    'Indeed I will order
    A coffin of marble.'

10. — Behuzatod-e anyám [2]
    Fekete fátyollal?
    — Behuzatom bizony
    Fekete bársonnyal.

10. 'Will you deck it, mother,
    In black crape?'
    'Indeed I shall deck it
    In black velvet.'

[1] = Akin.

[2] Line sung to variant 1.

11. — Megsiratsz-e anyám
Ahol senki se lát?
— Bizony megsiratlak
Ahol mindenki lát.

12. — Kikisérsz-e anyám
Sírom fenekére?
— Bizony kikisérlek
A Jézus nevébe.

11. 'Do you mourn for me, mother,
Where none may see you?'
'Indeed I mourn for thee
Where all may see me.'

12. 'Will you follow me, mother,
To my darksome tomb?'
'Indeed I shall follow you
In the name of Jesus.'

35

1. Virágos kendërëm
Kiázott a tóba, —
Ha haragszol, babám,
Ne jőjj a fonóba.

2. Elejtem az orsóm,
Nem lesz, ki fëladja,
Bánatos szívemet
Ki megvígasztalja.

1. My hemp in bloom
Is steeping in the pool.
If you are angry, my love,
Go not to the spinning-room.

2. If I drop my spindle,
None will pick it up,
None my aching heart
Will comfort.

36 (var. 278)

1. Az én lovam Szajkó,
Magam pedig Jankó;
Mind a négy lábáról
Leesett a patkó.

2. Csak egy maradt rajta,
S az es kotyog rajta;
Kovács jó barátom,
Igazítson rajta.

1. My horse is Szajkó,
And I am Jankó.
From all his four hoofs
The horse-shoes have fallen.

2. One still hangs on
But it's very loose;
The smith, my good friend,
Will adjust it all.

37

1. Sütött ángyom rétest,
Nem ettem belűle,
Levitte ja kerbe
Rózsás keszkenőbe.

2. Utánna ja bácsi
Uj galléros szűrbe,
Megcsolkolta gyángyit
A ker' közepébe.

1. My cousin has made cakes,
But I ate them not:
She took them into the garden
In a rose-coloured cloth.

2. Uncle followed her.
He was wearing a new cape,
And he kissed her
Right in the middle of the garden.

38

Add oda angyalom
A . . . . . . szomszédját,
Majd én is od' adom
A . . . . . bimbóját.

Give me, my angel,
The neighbour of your b . . . ,
And I shall then give you
The rosebud of my t . . . .

39

Szeretnék szántani,
Hat ökröt hajtani,
Ha a rózsám jönne
Az ekét tartani.

I should love to plough,
To drive six oxen,
If my love would come
And hold the plough.

40

1. Imhol kerekedik
   Egy fekete fölhő,
   Abban tollászkodik
   Sárgalábú holló.

2. Állj meg holló, állj meg.

   Had' üzenek tőled

   Apámnak, anyámnak,
   Jegybéli mátkámnak.

3. Ha kérdik, hogy vagyok,
   Mondd, hogy beteg vagyok.
   Győri temetőbe
   Nyugodni akarok.

1. See there looming
   A black cloud,
   In which is preening his plumage
   A yellow-legged raven.

2. Stay, you raven, stay:
   Take a message with you
   To my father and mother,
   To my betrothed.

3. If they ask how I am,
   Say I am ill,
   And that in the churchyard
   I long to find rest.

41

1. Megkötöm lovamot
   Szomorú fűzfához,
   Lehajtom fejemet
   Két első lábához.

2. Lehajtom fejemet
   A babám ölébe,
   Hullajtom könnyeim
   Rózsás kötényébe.

1. I tie my horse
   To the weeping willow.
   I bow my head
   Towards his forelegs.

2. I bow my head
   Towards the lap of my love,
   And I shed tears
   Upon her flowery apron.

Elmëgyëk, elmëgyëk,
Vissza sëm tekintëk,
Ennek a falunak
— — — —

I'm off, I'm off,
Never look back
Towards the village
— — — —

1. Egy kicsi madarka
   Hozzám kezde járni,
   Virágos kertemben
   Fészket kezde rakni.

2. De azt az irigyek
   Eszre kezték venni,
   Kicsi madár fészkét
   Széjjel kezték hánni.

3. Elment a madarka,
   Üres a galicka, —
   Azt izente vissza,
   Visszajő tavaszra.

4. De nem jöve vissza
   A kicsi madarka,
   S talán az ő szíve
   Más párra talála.

1. A little bird
   Often came to see me,
   In my flower garden
   Started building his nest.

2. But the envious
   Became aware of it,
   The little bird's nest
   They tore away.

3. The bird flew away,
   Empty are the branches,—
   It sent a message,
   That it will return in spring.

4. But it came not back,
   The little bird:
   Perhaps its heart
   Has found elsewhere a mate.

5. Hogyha vissza nem jő,
   Tudom, mást keresett,
   Az ő fájó szíve
   Tudom, mást szeretett.

6. Hogyha vissza nem jő
   Buzapiroslásra,
   Akkor, tudom, nem jő
   Többet soha vissza.

5. If it does not return,
   I know, it sought another.
   Its aching heart,
   I know, loved another.

6. If it does not return,
   Until ripe is the grain,
   I know, that never then
   Will it come back here.

44

Lefeküdtem csak alig,
Nem egészen a falig;
Jól megölelj engemet,
Le ne essem mellőled!

I lie barely poised on the bed,
Not quite against the wall;
Throw your arm well around me,
Lest I fall down.

45

Sarjut eszik az ökröm,
Ha jóllakik, békötöm;
Úgy menyek a babámhoz,
Tudom, elvár magához.

My ox is eating the after-grass,
When he has done I'll tie him up;
Then I'll go to my sweetheart,
I know that she awaits me.

46

Télen nem jó szántani,
Nehéz ekét tartani,
Jobb az ágyban maradni,
Menyecskével jáccani.

To plough in winter is hard work:
One can hardly hold the plough.
'Tis better to remain abed,
Disporting with a young woman.

47

Szép a leány ideig,
Tizennyolc esztendeig;
De a legény mindaddig,
Míg mëg nëm házasodik.

A girl is handsome awhile,
Until she is eighteen:
But a boy is handsome so long
As he does not get married.

48

A bú sírjon a fagyon,
Bánat üttessék agyon,
Ma örömnapja vagyon,
Mi es örvendjünk azon.

Sorrow may weep on the frozen ground,
Distress should be killed.
To-day is a day of joy,
Let us go rejoicing.

49

— Elmész ruzsám? — El biz én!
— Itt hagysz engem? — Itt biz én!
— Ha te elmész, én is el,
Mind a ketten menjünk el.

Going, my love?—Yes indeed!
You forsake me?—Indeed I do!
If you go, I go,
Let 's together go.

50

1. Vékony cérna, kemény mag, —
   — Jaj, de kevé' legény vagy!
   Fűnek-fának adós vagy,
   Egy pénznek ura nem vagy.

1. Thin yarn, hard grain,—
   —What a proud fellow you are!
   To all you owe
   Own not one penny.

2. — Ne bánd, édes virágom,
   Hogy igy élem világom!
   Éljed téses,¹ nem bánom,
   Szívemből azt kévánom.

3. Félre tőlem, búbánot,
   Nem élek én több nyárot;
   Ha érek es, csak hármot,
   Nem rakok én kővárot.

2. Don't worry, sweetheart,
   That thus I live:
   My wish to you is
   That you too should live thus.

3. Away with sorrow,
   I shan't live another summer,
   Or if I do, not more than three:
   I shan't build a stone castle.

51

Kertem alatt selyemrét,
Beleszokott két ökrész.
Hajtsd be biró az ökrét,
Vasald meg az ökrészét.

In my garden grows silky grass,
Two cowherds make free with it.
Judge, drive in their cattle
And put them both in chains.

52

Ugy ég a tűz, ha lobog, —
Ugy élek én, ha lopok.
Loptam csikót, lopok is,
Ha felakasztanak is.

While a fire burns, flame must rise,
While I live, I must steal.
I stole and shall steal foals,
If I must swing for it.

53

Még az este jó voltál,
Lefeküdtél, aludtál;
Haza jöttél vizessen,
Csókot adtál szivessen.

You were good and sweet at night,
You lay down and slept,
Having come home drenched
And kissing me warmly.

54 ᵃ

Dunyhám, párnám de hajlik,
Bejjebb babám a falig;
Öleljük egymást hajnalig,
Mig édes anyánk aluszik.

My coverlet and pillow are sagging,
Move back, my love, towards the wall.
Let us remain fondly clasped until dawn,
So long as my mother is asleep.

54 ᵇ

Tulsó soron, innend is
Áldjon meg az isten is,
Téged rózsám, engëm is,
Még aki fölnevelt is.

Far and near and night and day
May the Lord bless you,
You, my love, and me,
And them who brought you up.

55

Ha tudtad të, kis angyalom, nëm szeretsz,
S mér nëm kűdtél ëgy szomorú levelét?
S tetted volna a leggyorsabb postára,
S hogy jött volna Kalotaszenkirájra.

If you did know, my angel, you loved me not,
Why not write me a farewell letter?
You could have sent it by the quickest post
For me to get it in Kalotaszenkiráj.

56

Édös anyám, temetőben eredj ki,
A legárvább sirhalmot ott keresd ki,
Ára burujj, azon sirasd fiadat,
Ára ültesd tavaszkor virágodat.

Dearest mother, go to the churchyard,
Seek the most forlorn grave in it:
There bend down and mourn for your son,
There plant flowers in the spring.

¹ = te is.

57

Elmentem a kútra vizet merítni,
Odajött a kis gerlice csacsogni;
Körme között hozott egy kis ujságot,
Hogy mind elfogták az éfiúságot.

I went to the spring to fetch water,
There came a little turtle-dove to chat with
me.
She carried in her claws the news
That all youths would be taken (to serve in
the army).

58

Asz hittem, hogy nem kellek katonának,
Gondját viselem az édes anyámnak.
De mán látom, katonának kell lenni,
Ferenc Jóska csákóját kell viselni.

I was sure I should not have to be a soldier,
But might take care of my mother;
And now I see I have to be a soldier,
I have to carry the badge of Ferenc Jóska.[1]

59

Száraz fábul könnyű hidat csinálni,
Jaj de bajos szép szeretőt találni!
Találtam én szeretőre, de jóra,
Ki elviszen a bánatos hajóra.

It 's easy to build a bridge of dry wood,
But difficult to find a beautiful sweetheart.
I found a sweetheart loving,
Who will sail with me on the ship of sadness.

60

Októbërnak, októbërnak elsején
Nem süt a nap Csíkkarczfalva mezején,
Elbúcsúzom a madártól s az ágtól,
Azután a csíkkarczfalvi lányoktól.

In October, on the first of October,[2]
There 's no sunshine of the meadows of Csík-
karczfalva.
I part from the birds and the trees,
And also from the maidens of Csíkkarczfalva.

61

1. A Tiszából a Dunába foj a víz, —
— Mi dolog az, kis angyalom, hogy te
    sírsz?
— Hogy ne sírnék, hogy ne rínék, drága
    kincs:
Most akartalak szeretni, már elmész.

2. Ha te elmész, kis angyalom, kívánom,

Hogy az út előtted rózsának váljon;
Még a fű is piros almát teremjen,

A te szíved soha el ne felejtsen.

1. From the Tisza to the Danube waters flow,
I would know, my darling, why you weep.
'How can I not weep, and sob, my be-
    loved?
Just when I long to love you, you go
    away!'

2. If you must go, beloved, my wish is
That your path should be strewn with
    roses,
And that red apples should grow where
    you tread,
And that your heart should never forget.

62

Édes anyám, be szépen felneveltél,
Mikor engem karjaiddal rengettél.
Akkô mondtad, bévesznek katonának,
Felesketnek egy szép magyar huszárnak.

Kind mother, you brought me up beautifully,
And you rocked me in your arms,
And you said I'd become a soldier,
Now I'm sworn in as a fine Hungarian hussar.

[1] See p. 107, footnote.   [2] The day on which the recruits join their regiments.

63

Ujkorába megrepedjen a csizsmám,
Ha én járok többet a babám után!
Eddig is csak azért jártam én oda,
Hogy a babám kökényszeme csalt oda.

May my new boots burst
If I go again to see my little girl!
Up to now that which drew me towards her
Was the sheen of her sloe-like eyes.

64

Mikor éngem férhez adtak,
Tizënhárom pendelyt adtak,
Tra la la la la la la la la la la!
Tizënhárom pendelyt adtak, tralala.

When I was married
I was given thirteen smocks,
Tra la la la la la la la la la!
I was given thirteen smocks, tralala.

65

Édes anyám, mi vagyon a zsebébe?
— Három alma. — Adjon egyet belőle.
Ugy sem eszem sokáig az almáját,
Viselem a Ferenc Jóska csákóját.

My mother, what is in your pocket?
'Three apples!' Give me one of them.
For a long while I shall eat no more apples:
I must wear the shako of Ferenc Jóska.

66

1. Amott látszik egy piros tűz magába,
   Ott tüzelget szógalegény űnálla.
   Gyerünk pajtás! tán nem járunk hiába:
   Ott legelész szép hat csikó magába.

1. See over there the lonely red fire,
   There a farm-boy warms himself.
   Let's go, friend! Perhaps we shan't go
      in vain:
   Over there pasture six fine colts, alone.

2. Kúcsot tegyél vágott szűröd ujjába,
   Gyerünk pajtás! tán nem járunk hiába.
   Eriggy pajtás, fogd fel azt a hat csikót,
   Hagy veszem le a lábárul a békót.

2. Stick a wrench under your cloak-sleeve,
   Let's be off, friend: we shan't go in vain.
   Come, friend! you will hold the six,
   And I shall take the hobbles off their feet.

3. Ha levágtam a lábárul a békót,
   Majd elvégzem én a többi bajárul;
   Majd elvisszük, amerre a nap szölke,
   Ott aggyák a sok szép uj bángót érte.

3. When the hobbles are off their feet
   We shall play a good trick with them.
   We shall take them where the sun is
      brighter,
   For them we'll receive many fine gold pieces.

67

Béreslegény, jól mëgrakd a szekeret,
Sarjutüske böködi a tenyered!
Mennél jobban böködi a tenyered,
Annál jobban rakd mëg a szekeredet.

Farm-boy, load your cart well full,
Though the prickly aftermath sting your
   hands,
Ever more fully if it sting your hands,
Ever more fully load your cart.

68

1. Kondorosi szép csárdásné háza előtt
      van egy szomorufűzfa,
   Arra kötöm a lovamat
      jövő szombat hajnalba.
   Üjj föl hát most kondorosi szép csárdásné
      egyetlenegy édes kedves Marcsa
      nevű leánya a lovamra.
   Elviszlek az eszterházi számadónak
      legelső tanyájára.

1. By the house of the beautiful hostess at
      Kondoros
   Stands a weeping willow,
   There I'll tie my horse
   Next Saturday at dawn.
   Hey, you peerless beloved Marcsa,
   You daughter of beautiful hostess of
      Kondoros,
   My sweet maid, ride my horse,
   I'll take you to the farm
   Of the Esterhazy's bailiff.

2. Kondorosi szép csárdásné
   adjon isten jó estét![1]
Elnyertem az Uristentől
   a legnagyobb szerencsét,
Mert elvettem kondorosi szép csárdásné
   egyetlenegy édes kedves
   Marcsa nevű leányát,
Ez szerette három évig
   eszterházi [2] számadónak
   a legszebbik bujtárját.

2. Beautiful hostess of Kondoros,
   God give you joy this evening.[1]
May the Lord grant me
   The supreme joy
   That I should take you to wife,
You of the beautiful hostess of Kondoros,
   The peerless daughter Marcsa
Who for three years has loved
   The handsome shepherd [2]
   Of the Esterhazy bailiff.

69

Bereg Náni veres pántikája
Nem illik a szép sárig hajába.
— Tedd el, Náni, a ládád fiába,
Majd jó lësz a leányod hajába.

Nani, this red ribbon
Does not suit your golden hair.
Put it away in your chest,
It may suit a daughter of yours.

70

Azér, hogy a szeretőm elhagyott,
Én azér egy csöppet sem búsulok.
A rózsa se nyilik ki ëccere,
Lesz szeretőm vasárnap estére.

Because my love has forsaken me
I shall not worry in the least.
Roses may not bloom always,
Yet I'll have found love by Sunday night.

71 a

Fekete föld termi a jó buzát,
Sűrű erdő neveli a bëtyárt,
Sűrű erdő a bëtyár lakása,
Szép csárdásné gondot visel rája.

The black earth carries a good crop of corn,
The deep forest fosters the outlaw,
The deep forest is the outlaw's home,
And on his behalf the beautiful hostess is
   concerned.

71 b

Félre tőlem bubánat, bubánat,
Kancsót vágok utánad, utánad,
Szélës világ csufjára, csufjára,
Mëgfujtlak ëgy pohárba, pohárba.

Away with worry, with worry,
I'll throw a jar at you, at you,
The whole world will deride you, deride you,
You'll drown in a drinking glass, drinking
   glass.

72

Ketten mentünk, hárman jöttünk, tedd rá,
Jaj de hamar sokan lettünk, nyomd rá.
Lehuzták a jegykötőt előle,
Ugy takarták a gyermeket bele.

Two of us went, three came back, so there!
Quickly indeed do we add to our numbers.
The bridal pinafore was quickly taken,
To serve to swaddle the baby.

73

Akkor szép az erdő, mikor zöld,
Mikor a vadgalamb benne költ.
A vadgalamb olyan, mint a lány,
Maga jár a szép legény után.

Lovely is the forest when it is green,
When turtle-doves people it.
The turtle-dove is like a maid,
Who goes after a bonny boy.

[1] Here the part of the tune marked [1] is omitted.
[2] Here the part of the tune marked [2] is repeated.

74 a

Az ürögi ucca sikeres,
Benne pajtás szép lányt ne keress,
Mer aki van benne, mind görbe,
Kinek a szája széle csempe.

The street of Ürögi is straight:
Friend, you'll find no pretty maid there,
All who live there are hunchbacked,
The corners of their mouths are jagged.

74 b

Oh én édös pintös üvegöm,
Süvegöm előtted lëvöszöm.
Ahol szép lánt látok, köszöntök,
Ojjat iszom, csak úgy nyöszörgök.

Oh my dear pintful,
I doff my hat to thee,
And I make my bow to the pretty maids,
And will drink until I groan.

74 c

Nem messzi van innen Uzora,
Csak egy órajárás az útja,
Vasas kocsim, réz a szegjei,
Kis angyalom csalfa szemei.

Not far from here is Uzora,
One hour's walk from here;
My cart is iron bound, with copper nails,
My beloved has wily eyes.

75

1. Jaj de beteg vagyok,
   Talán meg is halok,
   Talán bizony a szeretőm édes anyja
   Engem megátkozott.

1. Alas I am ill,
   Perhaps near death,
   Perhaps indeed my sweetheart's mother
   Has cast a curse upon me.

2. Ne átkozzon engem
   A szeretőm anyja,
   Azér, hogy a kökényszemű barna fiát
   Nem szerettem soha.

2. Let her not curse me,
   My sweetheart's mother,
   Because her sunburnt, blue-eyed son
   Was never loved by me.

3. Ha szerettem vóna,
   Hozzá mentem vóna,
   Az őcsényi magos templom tornya alatt
   Mögesküdtünk vóna.

3. Had I loved him,
   I'd have married him,
   Under the high steeple of Őcsény
   We should have been united.

76

1. Csütörtökön este
   Nálad voltam lesbe;
   Láttam, hogy pánkót sütöttél,
       engem bé nem eresztettél,
   Pedig éhes voltam.

1. On Thursday evening
   I saw you, unobserved.
   You were cooking pancakes,
   You did not allow me in
   Although I was hungry.

2. Még szombaton este
   Nálad voltam lesbe,
   Láttam, hogy ágyat vetettél,
       engem bé nem eresztettél,
   Pedig álmos voltam.

2. On Saturday evening
   I saw you, unobserved.
   You were making your bed,
   You did not allow me in
   Although I was sleepy.

3. Még vasárnap este,
   Nálad voltam lesbe,
   Láttam, hogy jegyet váltottál,
       engem a szívedből kitagadtál:
   Verjen meg az isten!

3. On Sunday evening
   I saw you, unobserved.
   You were plighting your troth
   And you drove me out of your heart . . .
   May the Lord strike you!

77

Biró Marcsa libája
Belement a Tiszába;
Kettőt lépett utána:
Kilátszott a Biró Marcsa
    piros alsó szoknyája.

Biró Marcsa's geese
Walked into the Tisza.
Two steps she took after them.
See Biró Marcsa's
    Red petticoat flap.

78

A rátóti legények
Libát fogtak szegények.
Nem jól fogták a nyakát, a nyakát, sej, a nya-
    kát:
Elgágintotta magát.

Boys from Rátót
Stole a goose,
Gripped it clumsily by the neck, the neck,
And the goose gave out a squeak.

79

1. Nincsen szebb a magyar lyánynál,
  Vékony karcsú dërëkánál;
  Olyan vékony, mint a nádszál,
  Maga jár a legény után.

2. Maga mondja a legénynek,
  Válassza szeretőjének.
  — Jó van, kis lyány, én nem bánom,
  Csak az anyád ne sajnáljon.

3. Még az anyja nem is tudja,
  Hogy a lyánya milyen csalfa.
  Maj megtudja nemsokára,
  Legény jár az udvarába.

1. Nothing is lovelier than a Magyar girl,
  Slim and strong ánd slender,
  As slender as a bulrush,
  See her following the boys.

2. And to a boy she says:
  'Take me for your sweetheart.'
  —Indeed, girlie, I have no qualms,
  Provided your mother does not object.

3. The mother may not know
  What a rogue the girlie is.
  Soon after she will hear
  That a boy visits her courtyard.

80

1. Tollfosztóban voltam az este,
  Az én rózsám azt is kileste;
  Mindig csak azt hányja-veti szememre,
  Kivel beszélgettem az este.

2. Nem beszélgettem én senkivel,
  Feleségem testvéröccsivel;
  Avval sem beszélgettem én sokáig:
  Éjfél után három óráig.

1. I went to the feather-trimming last night,
  And my love found it out;
  She is always upbraiding, asking
  With whom I was talking there.

2. I talked with nobody
  But with my wife's younger brother,
  Nor did I find the talk too long
  At three o'clock in the morning.

81

Érik a ropogós cseresznye,
Viszek a babámnak belőle,
Viszek a babámnak, tyuhaj, belőle,
Ha beteg, gyógyuljon meg tőle.

They have come, the crisp cherries,
I'll carry some to my love,
I'll carry some to my love, huzzah!
If she is ill, she will be made better.

82

Jaj de szépen esik az eső,
Jaj de szépen zöldül a mező,
Közepibe legel a juhom, —
Katona jaz édes galambom.

Alas, how beautifully falls the rain!
Alas, how beautifully green is the field!
Around me my flock is grazing,—
My beloved, alas, is soldiering.

1. Váradiné lánya Mariska
   Kiállott az úcasarokra.
   — Eredj be te, sej, haj, göndörhajú zsi-
   dólány,
   Mer megfog a rendőrkapitány.

   ♩. ♪ (sic!)

2. Asz kérdi a rendőrkapitány
   ♩. ♪
   — Mi a neved göndörhajú lány?
   — Az én nevem, sej, haj, Sári, Mári,
   Kalári, ♩ ♩
   Tudom szeretnél hozzám járni.

   ♩ ♩ (sic!)

3. Asz kérdi a rendőrkapitány:
   ♩ ♩
   — Hol lakol te göndörhajú lány?
   — Ott lakok a lent a, lent a, lent a
   ♩ ♩
   legsarkon,
   ♩. ♪ ♪ ♩.
   Zöld sarugátéros a gangom.

4. Zöld sarugátéros a gangom
   Alatta sétál a galambom:
   — Jobb volna, ha sírnál, sírnál-rínál,
   ♩ ♩
   édesem,
   ♩. ♪ ♪ ♩.
   Nem leszek a tiéd sohasem.

A gőzösnek pattog a kereke,
Barna kis lány hajlik ki belőle;
A fátyolát fujja a szél, —
Látod babám, hogy menyasszony lettél.

1. Este van már, csillag van az égen,
   Varga Julcsa mezitláb a jégen,
   Sajnálja a cipőjit felhúzni,
   Garzó Péter nem vesz többet néki.

2. Garzó Péter elment katonának,
   Acélfegyvert csináltat magának;
   Acélfegyver, rózsafa a nyele,
   Rá van írva Varga Julcsa neve.

Idelátszik a temető széle,
Abba nyugszik az én szëmem fénye;
A koporsó öleli helёttem,
Mos tudtam mёg, milen árva lёttem.

---

1. Dame Váradi's daughter Mariska
   Stands at the corner of the street.
   —Hey, in with you, curly-haired Jewess,
   Or the police-captain will take you.

2. And the police-captain will ask:
   'What is your name, curly-haired maiden?'
   'My name is, hey, Sári, Mári, Kalári,
   I know you wish to come with me.'

3. And the police-captain will ask:
   'Where do you live, curly-haired maiden?'
   'I live down there, down there,
   Green blinds has the house.

4. Green blinds has the house,
   And there my beloved roves about.'
   'Better were it for you to sob and weep,
   my dear,
   For I shall never be yours.'

The car rolls, the wheels clatter,
At the window a dark-haired maid appears;
The wind blows her veil about,
You are going to be a bride, my dear.

1. Night falls, the sky is starry,
   Varga Julcsa goes barefoot on the ice,
   To spare her footwear,
   For Garzó Péter will not provide a new pair.

2. Garzó Péter is in the army,
   A steel rifle was made for him,
   A steel rifle with a rosewood butt
   On which is written Varga Julcsa's name.

From here is seen the graveyard's border
Where rests she who was the light of my eyes.
The grave holds her, whom I would hold.
Now only I know how thoroughly I am
orphaned.

Az ürögi sűrü erdő alatt
Barna legény rozmaringot arat,
Én vagyok a rozmaring szedője,
Barna legény igaz szeretője.

Down in the deep forest of Ürög
A brown youth is cutting rosemary,
And I collect the rosemary,
For I love the brown youth dearly.

Reggel korán kimegyek a kútra,
Leteszem a zsajtárom az útra.
Arra ment a vármegye hajduja,
Belelépett, eltörött alatta.

In the early morning I went to the spring,
I put down my pitcher on the path.
The district Hajduk passed by,
He trod on it and broke it.

1. Lemberg alatt van egy magas erdő,
   Közepibe van egy gyásztemető,
   Abban fekszik százhúszezer baka:
   Eltemette gyászos Galicija.

2. Édes anyám kapott egy levelet,
   Abban írják az én holt híremet;
   Sírhat-ríhat szegény bánatába,
   Nem borul a fia sírhalmára.

3. Nincsen kereszt a sírom elején,
   Mint a vadak elásva fekszem én;
   Ott fekszem egy nagy nyárfa tövébe,
   Mint a vadak erdő sűrűjébe.

4. Köppenyem a gyászos szemfedelem,
   Nem szép hazám földje takar engem,
   Oroszország földje borul reám,
   Sírhat-ríhat szegény édes anyám.

1. Under Lemberg is a tall forest,
   In the midst of it is a dismal cemetery,
   There lie a hundred thousand warriors
   Given by hapless Galicia.

2. My mother received a letter
   Bringing the news of my death,
   And she will weep and sob in misery,
   For she cannot weep over her son's grave.

3. No cross stands upon my tomb,
   I lie buried like the beasts of the fields,
   Here, under a high poplar tree,
   Like the beasts in the midst of the forests.

4. My greatcoat is my shroud,
   Not my country's earth holds me,
   But in Russian soil I lie,
   My poor mother weeps and sobs.

Nem messze van ide Kismargita,
Hortobágynak vize körülfolyta;
Közepibe koponyai csárda,
Ott iszik egy nagy betyár bujába.

It is not far to Kismargita,
Around it flows the Hortobágy;
In the middle is the inn,
There a great highwayman drinks sadly.

Kiöntött a Tisza a partjára,
Kis pej lovam térdig jár a sárba,
Sáros kantárszára a kezembe, —
Gyere kis angyalom az ölembe.

The Tisza is in spate,
My little brown horse treads knee-deep in
     mud,
I am holding his dirty reins.
Come, sweetheart, sit on my knees.

Érik a, érik a búzakalász, —
Nálamnál szebb szeretőre nem találsz.
Szállj ide, szállj oda fecskemadár,
Kérd meg a rózsámtól, mért csapodár.

Ripe, ripe is the wheat . . .
You'll find no prettier one to love than me
Fly here, fly there, you swallow,
Find out why my beloved is faithless.

93 a

Kedves lánya voltam az anyámnak,
Mégis odaadott egy oláhnak;
Annak adott, akit nem szerettem,
Gyász lesz véle az egész életem.

I was my mother's dear daughter,
Yet I was given away to a Wallachian;
She gave me to him whom I loved not,
To be with him saddens my whole life.

93 b

Jaj de sokat arattam a nyáron,
De keveset aludtam az ágyon!
Vesd meg rózsám, vesd meg a slingölt ágyadat,
Had pihenjem ki magam az alatt.

Alas, long have I reaped in summer,
Little have I slept in my bed,
Prepare, my love, prepare your bed,
So that I may rest therein.

93 c

A vacsárcsi halastó, halastó,
Belejestëm lovastó, kocsistó.
Jaj istenëm! ki vësz ki, hej de ki vësz ki?
Sajnál-e még éngëmët valaki?

In the stewpond, stewpond at Vacsárcsi
I lay with horse and cart.
O Lord, who will pull me out, pull me out?
Will any one have pity on me?

94

1. A kertmegi laposon, laposon
   Horvát István ül vason, ül vason;
   Este-reggel zörgeti a vasat,
   Hej, Gál Róza szíve majd meghasad.

2. Hej, te Róza, ne hidd el magadat,
   Ne rázd olyan keményen a farodat;
   Alsó ruhád kilátszik tenyérnyire,
   Ülhetsz még a Horvát István ölibe.

1. On the flat ground at Kertmeg
   István Horvát lies in fetters, lies in fetters;
   Night and day he rustles his fetters
   So that Gál Róza's heart is breaking.

2. Hey, Róza, don't fancy yourself so much,
   Don't wriggle your hips:
   Under your skirt your underwear shows,
   You will again sit on Horvát István's knees.

95

Sej, felszállott a kakas a meggyfára,
Kukorékol hajnalhasadtára.
Hajnal hasad, fényes csillag ragyog,
Sej, én még most is a babámnál vagyok.

Hey, the cock crows in the cherry tree,
Crows at the break of day.
Daylight spreads, yet a bright star shines,
Hey! I am still with my sweetheart.

96

Károly király bánatába, de igazán,
Kisétál a Dunapartra, de igazán.
Ráborúl a koronára:
Sej, hova lett a katonája, de igazán.

King Charles was in distress, aye indeed,
Tramped the banks of the Danube, aye indeed,
And he said, bending over his own crown:
'Hey, where are my soldiers, aye indeed?'

97 (var. 288)

1. Jánoshidi vásártéren
   Legényvásár lesz a héten. .
   Ezresekér adnak egyet,
   Jaj de drága, mégis vesznek.

2. Jánoshidi vásártéren
   Kislányvásár lesz a héten.
   Két krajcárér adnak egyet,
   Jaj de olcsó, mégsem vesznek.

1. On the market-place at Jánoshida
   Young men are on sale this week,
   A couple of thousand is the price for one,
   Lord, how dear! Yet you buy.

2. On the market-place at Jánoshida
   Young girls are on sale this week.
   Two groats is the price for one,
   Lord, how cheap! Yet none buys.

Öreg baka afférol a szobába,
A babája siratja a konyhába.
— Ne sirj babám, kérjed a jó teremtőt,
Adjon néked egy remunda szeretőt.

In the room the old soldier is taking leave,
In the kitchen his sweetheart is weeping.
'Weep not, my love, but pray to the Maker
That I give you a good remount.'

Szép csárdásné kisétál az uccára,
Rajta van a nyári piros szoknyája,
Rajta van a nyári piros szoknyája,
Kutya szolgabiró sétál utána.

The beautiful hostess takes a walk in the
    street,
She wears a red summer-frock,
She wears a red summer-frock.
That dog of a judge is following her.

Megyen már a hajnalcsillag lëfelé.
Az én babám mos megyen hazafelé.
Lábán van a lagosszárú kis csizsma;
Rásütött a hajnalcsillag sugara.

The morning star already is setting,
My love is going back home.
And his top-boots are so finely polished
That they reflect the light of the star.

Az őcsényi templom piros bádogos, —
Az én kedves kis angyalom de magos.
Ha magos is, nem kell arra gondulni,
Maj lehajul, ha meg akar csókulni.

The Öcsényi church has a red tin roof.[1]
My well-beloved is very tall.
However tall he is, no need to worry:
He'll stoop if he wishes to kiss me.

Kását ettem, megégettem a számat; —
Ki viseli gondját az én anyámnak?
Én már látom, nëm viselem szegénynek,
Oltalmára bizom a jó istennek.

I ate porridge, burnt my mouth;
Who is going to take care of my mother?
I see indeed that I cannot look after the un-
    fortunate one:
May the Lord take her in His care.

1. Darumadár utnak indul hajnalba,
Levelet hoz ide Jánoshidára;
Az van írva a levél belsejébe:
El kell menni huszonkettedikére.

1. A crane takes its flight at dawn,
Brings a letter from Jánoshida;
Inside the letter is the news
That we must leave on the twenty-second.

2. Jánoshidi köves uton zörögnek,
Kohner Adolf nagy kocsijai jönnek.
A sok kufer már össze van pakolva,
Tót Pál József házához van az hordva.

2. There's a loud clatter in the streets of
    Jánoshida.
Adolf Kohner's big carts come,
Many trunks are packed together in them,
They are being taken to Tót Pál József's
    house.

3. Isten, áldjon, Jánoshida, elmegyünk,
Négy hónapig Felsőszászberken leszünk.
Majer Sándor, az uradalmi kasznár
Tót Pál Etelnek csak ezeket mondja:

3. God bless Jánoshida! We are going,
We shall be four months in Felsőszász-
    berek.
Majer Sándor, the steward,
Spoke thus to Tót Pál Etel:

4. — De szép summás, jaj, de erős leányok
Ezek a jánoshidai summások!
Ugy örülök, úgy szeretlek titeket,
Isten áldjon, segítsen benneteket!

4. 'Handsome and strong are the maids,
The maids of Jánoshida!
I rejoice, and I like you all,
May the Lord protect you.'

[1] Often the first line of a poem refers to a setting or an object, not necessarily connected with the subject of the song (see, e.g., nos. 111, 116, 123, etc.).

5. — Kasznár uram, szépen kérjük mi magát,
Áldja meg az isten minden birtokát,
Szeresse ja jánoshidai summást,
Mi meg jó szívvel folytatjuk a munkát.

6. Tót Pál Etel, ha kimegy a pusztába,
Rátekint a jánoshidi summásra.
Ha rátekint, azt gondolja magába:
De szép summásaim vannak sorjába.

7. Gazsi Károly nagyvendéglő termébe
De szépen szól Horvát Kálmán zenéje!
Ugyan kinek szól így ez a muzsika:
Tót Pál Etel summásai mulatnak.

5. 'Sir Steward, we humbly pray
That God grant you all blessings,
As you are well disposed towards us,
We shall carry on the work with zest.'

6. When Tót Pál Etel goes along the fields
She keeps watch on the Jánoshida maids,
She watches, and thinks:
Fine indeed are my girls in their ranks.

7. In the hall of Gazsi Károly's big inn
Gaily resounds Horvát Kálmán's music:
To whom does this music play?
Tót Pál Etel's maids have a good time.

104

Jaj de széles, jaj de hosszi az az út,
Akin az a kilenc betyár elindult,
Akin az a kilenc betyár elindult,
Pápainé udvarára befordult.

Open and long indeed is the road
Along which the nine robbers are going,
Along which the nine robbers are going
Towards dame Pápai's farm.

105

1. Már mikor én tizennyolc éves voltam,
Már én akkor házasodni indultam.
Tizenkét szép lánya volt egy anyának,
Mind a tizenkettőt kértem magamnak.

2. Az elsőnek kicsi voltam, az vót baj,
A másiknál csalfa voltam, az vót baj.
A harmadik, hogy a szemem kéket nyit,
Negyediknek kacsintásom nem tetszik.

3. Ötödiknél: miért nincs édesanyám,
Hatodiknál: mért nem jöttem paripán,
Hetedik a pipafüstöt nem állja,
Nyolcadikat lebeszéli mamája.

4. Kilencedik: miért nincs édesapám,
Tizediknél: mért nem jöttem hamarább,
Tizenegyediket atyja nem adja,
Tizenkettedik nem mén férjhez soha.

5. Igy már nékem házasodnom nem lehet,
Szomorúan kell élni életemet.
Beizentem a budai bírónak:
Irasson be engemet katonának.

1. When I was eighteen years old,
I took steps to get married:
Twelve fine daughters a mother had,
All twelve of them I wooed.

2. For the first I was small, that was the
trouble;
For the second I was sly, that was the
trouble.
The third couldn't stand my blue eyes,
And my winks displeased the fourth.

3. The fifth said I was motherless,
The sixth that I did not come on horse-
back;
The seventh objected to my pipe,
The eighth was dissuaded by the mother.

4. The ninth said I was fatherless,
The tenth that I showed no haste in
coming;
The eleventh the father would not give
away,
The twelfth would never marry.

5. And so it is I cannot marry,
So I must live alone and sad.
I shall send word to the Buda magistrate
That he should write me down for the
army.

106

Békót veretëk a lovam lábára,
Mert nem ügyel a gazdája szavára.
Békóba ver engem is a szerelëm,
Amióta ezt a kis lányt szeretëm.

I fetter my horse's feet,
Because he does not obey his master:
And I myself am in love's fetters
Ever since I fell in love with this little girl.

107

Elmennék én tehozzátok egy este,
Ha az anyád az ablakon nem lesne.
De az anyád, ez a csalfa menyecske
Kihallgatta, mit beszéltünk az este.

I should come to your house of an evening
If your mother were not at her window:
Your mother is a wily woman,
She has heard we talk together in the evening.

108

Egyet-kettőt füttyentett a masina,
Gyere velem, babám, ki a vasútra!
— Nem mehetek, rózsám, szivem meghasad:
Egyedül kell visszajönnöm magamnak.

Once and twice the engine whistles,
Come with me, my love, to the station.
'I cannot go, my love, my heart will break . . .
I should have to return alone!'

109

Zsindelyezik a kaszárnya tetejit,
Mind elviszik a legénynek elejit.
Marad itten kettő-három nyomorult:
Rátok lányok még az ég is beborult.

Shingles are laid on the barrack's roof,
All the young men are taken away.
Only two or three cripples are left ;
Over the girls' heads the very sky is clouded.

110

Kimegyek a doberdói harctérre,
Föltekintek a csillagos nagy égre.
Csillagos ég, merre van a magyar hazám,
Merre sirat engem az édes anyám ?

I go towards the battle-field of Doberdo,
I look up to the starry sky.
Starry sky, where is my home, Hungary ?
Where does my dear mother weep ?

111

Apró szëme van a kukoricának,
Szép termete van a kedves babámnak.
Szép termetét el sem tudom felejteni:
Igy jár az, aki igazán tud szeretni.

The maize is bearing little grains,
Fine and tall is my beloved.
So fine and tall, I cannot forget her ;
Thus it is, when one loves truly.

112

1. Stolac alatt van egy magos sirhalom,
   Abban nyugszik az én kedves pajtásom.
   Levágta a török szegénynek a jobb karját,
   Kivel mindig ölelte a babáját.

1. Under Stolac there is a big graveyard,
   There rests my beloved friend !
   Poor fellow, the Turks hacked his right
   arm off,
   The arm with which he used to clasp his
   love.

2. — Irjál pajtás az én kedves babámnak,
   Választhat már más szeretőt magának.
   Levágta a török ártatlan jobb kezemet,
   Kivel mindíg írtam a levelemet.

2. Write, friend, to my love
   That she may now elect to love another.
   I had my innocent right hand hacked off
   by the Turks,
   With which I wrote letters to her.

113

Túl a Tiszán juhászlegény vagyok én,
Harminchárom birkára vigyázok én.
Gyere babám, téritsd meg a birka elejét,
Ne jegye le a bodorka levelét.

O'er the Tisza I'm a shepherd,
Three and thirty flocks I tend.
Come, love, drive the forward flocks on,
Lest they eat all the clover.

114

Végigmentem az ürögi nagy uccán,
Betekintek kis angyalom ablakán.
Épen akkor sejehaj,
    vetëtte föl az ágyát,
Rozmaringgal söpörte *ja* szobáját.

I went along the great street in Ürög,
And I peeped into the window of my beloved,
And saw her tidying her bed,
And sweeping her room with rosemary
    boughs.

115

Kisdobozi kerek erdő de magos,
Közepibe barna kis lány aranyos.
Hogyha én az erdőnek a
    szélső fája lehetnék,
A babámnak vállaira borulnék.

Around Kisdoboz is a high forest,
In it is a gold-brown maiden.
Could I be the farthest tree in this forest,
I should rest upon my love's shoulder!

116

Belényesi állomáson keresztül
Tizenhárom fehér galamb átrepül.
Tizenhárom fehér galamb, fehér galamb,
    csuhaj páratlan, —
Én utánam bitang legény ne járjon.

Over the Belényes station
Thirteen white doves are flying.
Thirteen white doves, aye, an uneven num-
    ber!
I'll have nothing to do with a ne'er-do-well.

117

Sej, haj, édes anyám, huszár a szeretőm,
Elvitte *ja* zsebjébe *ja* kendőm.
Csak a nevëm rá ne volna írva,
Sej, haj, hogy a szivem ne sajogna érte.

Hey, mother dear, a hussar I love,
He's got my kerchief in his pocket.
If only my name was not written on it,
Hey! Then in my heart I should not fret.

118

Sej, jaj de széles, jaj de hosszú az az út,
Amelyiken barna legény elindult.
Barna legény, térj vissza az utadra,
Sej, emlékezz a szombat esti szavadra.

Hey, broad and long is the road
Along which the swarthy youths started:
Swarthy youths, wend back your steps,
Hey, think of the words you spoke on Satur-
    day night!

119

Hej, édes anyám, kedves édes anyám,
Szedje össze nékem a gyászgunyám,
Szedje össze, akassza a szegre, ej, huj,
Három kerek évig nem veszem testemre.

Hey, mother, dearest mother mine,
Get me all my robes of mourning,
Get them, hang them on the nail.
Alas, for three years I shall not wear them.

120

Csillagok, csillagok, szépen ragyogjatok,
A szegény legénynek utat mutassatok;
Mutassatok utat a szegény legénynek,
Nem találja házát a szeretejének.

Stars, stars, brightly shine,
Show the way to the poor fellows;
To the poor fellows show the way,
Or they'll not reach the house of their love.

121

Ennek a kislánynak rövid a szoknyája,
Mondtam az anyjának, varrjon fodrot rája.
Asz mondta az anyja, nem varr fodrot rája,
Akinek nem tetszik, ne járjon utána.

This little girl's frock is too short;
I said to her mother, 'Sew flounces round it.'
She said to me, 'I'll sew no flounces round it;
Who disapproves need not walk after her!'

122

Fekete cserepes a mi házunk teteje,
Vadgalamb szállott a tetejébe,
Vadgalamb, turbékold el a nótám:
Hogy a csárdás tubicám szeret-e még igazán?

Of black tiles is the roof of our house made,
A wood-pigeon settles on the top.
Wood-pigeon, coo me a song:
Whether my handsome lover loves me truly.

123

Sej, huj, vikcos csizma a lábomat szorítja,
Barna kis lány a szivem szomorítja.
Ne szomorídd az én árva szivemet,
Sej, huj, szenvedhetek három évig eleget.

Hey, hey, my polished boots hurt my feet,
A dark-haired maiden saddens my heart:
Do not sadden my lonesome heart,
Aye, aye, I shall suffer enough for three years.

124

Végigmentëm a tárkányi, sej, haj, főuccán,
Betekintettem a babám ablakán.
Épen akkor vetëtte meg paplanos ágyát,
Rozmaringgal sëprëtte ki pingált szobáját.

I went all along the main street, heigh, ho, of
      Tárkány,
I peeped through my love's window:
Just as she had placed the counterpane on
      her bed
And swept her room with rosemary.

125

Az ürögi faluvégen szól a muzsika,
Gyere kedves kis angyalom, menjünk el, oda.
Ott mulatok kedvemre,
      babám sír keservesen,
Ropogós csolkja rajtam szárod, nem felejtëm
      el.

At the far end of the Ürög village, music
      sounds.
Come, my beloved, let us go there.
There I shall rejoice heartily,
My love shall weep bitterly,
Her kisses will dry on my lips, but I shall
      never forget her!

126

Ha felülök, Bözsikém, a fekete gőzösre,
Isten tudja, hol szállok ki belőle.
Majd kiszállok a svaromlénia jelőtt,
Ott vár engem, Bözsikém, a szép gyászos
      temető.

If I get into the black train, my Bözsi,
God knows when I'll get out of it.
Soon I'll get out, in front of the vanguard:
There awaits me, my Bözsi, the beautiful sad
      graveyard.

127

Kiesett a, kiesett a szivar a zsebemből, —
Kitagadott, kitagadott babám a szivéből,
Kitagadott, azért vagyok árva; —
Jaj de szépen szól a zene Gyula városában.

Fallen, fallen is the cigar from my pocket,
Driven, driven am I from my love's heart.
Driven, and therefore solitary,—
Alas, lovely sounds the music over there in
      Gyula town.

128

Nagyváradi kikötőben megállt a gőzhajó,
Tetejibe ki van tűzve a nemzeti zászló;
Fujja a szél, fujja,
      hazafelé fujja,
Az egybeli öreg bakák jönnek szabadságra.

At the landing at Nagyvárad stops the steam-
      ship,
Over her floats the country's flag.
Blowing wind, unfurl it towards our country,
For we old soldiers all together are going on
      furlough.

Csuhaha, lehajlott a diófának az ága,
Csuhaha, ráhajlott a vizitáló szobára.
De sok, édes anya sírva jár el alatta:
Ihajla, hogy a fia három évig katona.

Huhaha! The branches of the nut-tree droop
low.
Huhaha! They hang over the inspection-
room.
How many mothers are weeping down there
Because their sons three years a soldier will be.

Esik eső szép csendesen, tavasz akar lenni,
De szeretnék a babám kertjébe rózsabimbó
lenni.
Nem lehetek én rózsa,
    elhervaszt Ferenc Jóska
Budapesti háromemeletes magas kaszárnyába.

Gentle rain is falling, spring is ready to burst
forth.
Would I were a rosebud, in my sweetheart's
garden.
I can never become a rose,
    Ferenc Jóska keeps me withering
In the three-story-high barracks of Budapest.

A gyulai nagy pavillon fel van pántlikázva,
Az ablaka, az ajtaja sarkig ki van nyitva.
Abba ülnek azok az urak,
    akik engem be is soroztak;
Besoroztak három évre, harminchat hónapra.

In Gyula the big pavilion is beflagged,
All the windows and the doors stand open.
Inside are seated those gentlemen
    who have recruited me,
Recruited me for three years, six and thirty
months.

Barna kis lány levelet ír,
    ráborul az asztalra,
Oda megy az édes anyja,
    kérdi tőle: mi baja?
— Ne kérdezze édes anyám, nincs semmi
bajom,
Jól tudja, hogy árva vagyok,
    galambomat siratom.

A little brunette writes a letter,
She throws herself athwart the table,
To her comes her mother,
Asks her: what is the matter?
'Ask not, mother: nothing is the matter;
But well you know I am forsaken,
I weep for my sweetheart.'

Már Kistilden, már Kistilden
    régën lëjesëtt a hó, —
Azt gondoltam, kis angyalom,
    véled lëjesëtt a ló,
Kitörött a jobb kezed,
    mivel ölelsz engemet? —
Édes kedves kis angyalom,
    nëm lëhetëk a tied.

In Kistild, in Kistild
Long ago snow started falling,
And I think, my sweetheart,
That from your horse you've fallen.
If you've broken your right arm,
Will you still be able to clasp me?
O darling, sweetheart mine,
I cannot become yours!

Ha bemegyek, ha bemegyek
    a baracsi csárdába,
Cifranyelű kis bicskámat
    vágom a gerendába.
Aki legény, az vegye ki,
    aki bátor, az teheti:
Még az éjjel zsandárvérrel
    irom ki a nevemet.

When I go, when I go,
To the wine-house at Baracs,
My ornamented knife
I'll drive into the rafters.
Who is the brave boy who'll do it,
The fine fellow who'll pull it out?
To-night in the blood of the gendarmes
Will I write out my name.

Ferenc József, az apostoli király
  szereti a regutát,
Két sorjába maga mellé
  állítja a századát.
Két sorjába ég a gyertya,
  közepibe a szép feszület,
Ferenc József, az apostoli király
  jaj be szépen esküdtet.

Francis Joseph, apostolic king,
  Likes his new soldiers,
He marshals his regiments,
  Two by two beside him.
And two by two the candles burn,
  In the midst a great crucifix.
Francis Joseph, apostolic king,
  How beautifully he makes us swear in!

136

Mikor szürkébe öltöztem,
  azon kezdtem gondolkozni:
Ki lesz az én utitársam,
  ha *ja* harctérre kell menni?
Majd lesz utitársam az én jó pajtásom,
Ki megássa a síromat
  doberdói hegyaljában.

When I donned the grey
This is what I started thinking:
Who will march by my side,
When shall I reach the battle-field?
My good comrade will march by my side,
He will lay me in my grave
At the foot of the Doberdo mountains.

137

Erdő, erdő, kerek erdő,
  jaj de messzire ellátszik,
Közepibe, közepibe,
  két szál rozmaring virágzik,
Egyik hajlik a vállamra,
  másik a babáméra,
Ráhajtom a bús fejemet
  babám ölelő karjára.

Forest, forest, circular forest,
From afar one can see thee.
In thy midst, in thy midst,
Two sprigs of rosemary blooming.
One droops upon my shoulder,
The other over my sweetheart.
I lay my weary head
On the clasping arms of my sweetheart.

138 (var. 191)

1. Mikor megyek Románia felé,
  még a fák is sírnak,
Rezgő nyárfa hullatja levelét,
  az is engem sirat,
Sirass, sirass, rezgő nyárfa,
  boruljál a babám vállára,
Súgjad néki bele a fülébe:
  fáj, fáj, fáj a szívem érte, babám,
  fáj, fáj, fáj a szívem érte.

1. When I go to Rumania
  The very trees will weep,
The quivering poplars will let fall their
    leaves
And weep for my sake.
Weep, weep, quivering poplar,
Drooping over my sweetheart's shoulders,
Whisper into her ear:
Woe, woe is my heart, my love,
Woe, woe is my heart.

2. Édes anyám rózsafája,
  én vagyok egy ága,
Én vagyok a Károly király
  vitéz katonája.
Százhúsz éles nyomja a vállam,
  szívemet a búbánat:
El kell menni messze a csatába,

2. Of my mother's rose-tree
I am a sprig,
And of King Charles
I'm a soldier brave.
A hundred and twenty cartridges weigh
  on my shoulders,
Grief is in my heart:
Now I must go to the war.

szívemet megöli a bánat, babám,
szívemet megöli a bánat.

3. Édes anyám levelet írt

katona fiának:

— Gyere haza kedves fiam,

nem jó katonának.

Károly király azt felelte,

hogy nem mehetek haza:
Elveszett a nagy iroda kulcsa,
                          (sic!)
nem szabadulok meg soha, babám,
nem szabadulok meg soha.

My heart will be killed by grief, my love,
My heart will be killed by grief.

3. My mother writes a letter
    To her soldier son:
    'Come home, beloved son,
    It is not good to be a soldier.'
    King Charles he replies
    That I may not return home:
    Lost is the key of the war office,
    Never shall I be free again, my love,
    Never shall I be free.

Kis kertemben, seje huja haj,
    egy rózsafát ültettem,
Este, reggel, ihaj csuhajja,
    könnyeimmel öntöztem.
Megártott a tövének,
    seje huja, gyenge levelejének; —
Már én többet, ica hejre haj,
    nem hiszek a legénynek.

139

In my little garden—Hey, huya, hey!
    I plant a rose-tree,
And morning and evening—hey, huya hey!
    I water it with my tears.
He has injured its roots,
    hey, huya, hey—and its tender leaves.
Never again, lackaday,
    shall I trust a boy.

Gáborgyházi Telëk alatt
De sok gyalog utak vannak.
Minden kislány eggyet csinál,
Sej, kja szeretűjéhez jár.

140

Across the fields of Gáborgyháza
Lie many tracks.
Each young maiden makes her own
As she goes towards her sweetheart.

Ez a kis lány, ez a barna kis lány
    rezet hozott az este,
Rézsarkantyút, hej de rézsarkantyút
    csináltatott belőle.
Aj de szépen csengett-pengett csütörtök este,
Mikor azt a régi jó babáját
    ajtaján beengedte.

141

This young maiden, this young brunette,
Brought copper last evening.
Copper jugs, aye, copper jugs
She had made out of it.
How they'll cling and clang on Thursday
    nights,
When her good lover of long standing
    she lets in through her door.

Ha csakugyan, csakugyan,
    ha csakugyan nem találok szeretőt,
Felszántatom a csorvási temetőt.
Vetek belé rozmaringot,
Az én babám, a babám,
    az én babám mással éli világát.

142

If indeed, if indeed,
If indeed I can find no sweetheart,
I shall plough the churchyard at Csorvás,
And therein sow rosemary.
For my beloved, for my beloved,
For my beloved is happy with another.

143

Már minálunk babám, már minálunk babám,
   az jött be szokásba,
Nem szedik a lányok, nem szedik a lányok
   meggyet a kosárba.
Felmegy a legény meggyfa tetejébe,
Lerázza ja meggyet, te pejg babám szedjed
   rózsás kötényedbe.

Here with us the custom is:
The girls pluck not, the girls pluck not
   Basketfuls of cherries:
But the boys go up the cherry-trees,
And shake down the cherries; you, my love,
Shall collect them in your pink apron.

144

Átulmennék én a Tiszán, nëm merëk,
   nëm merëk, de nëm merëk,
Attul félek, hogy a Tiszábà jesëk,
   hogy a Tiszábà jesëk.
Lovam hátán, sejehaj,
   férefordul a nyerëg,
Tisza, Duna habgyai közt elveszëk,
   a babámé nëm lëszëk.

I'd like to swim across the Tisza, but dare not,
   But dare not, but dare not.
I fear that I may sink in the Tisza,
   That I may sink in the Tisza.
On my horse's back, alas,
   The saddle wobbles:
In the waters between Tisza and Danube I'll
   vanish,
   And never belong to my sweetheart.

145

Debrecenyi nagy kaszárnya,
   csuhaja, sárgára van meszelve,
Három évet, nyolc hónapot,
   csuhaja, én is eltöltök benne.
Rá van írva csákómra,
   csákóm mind a két oldalára:
Három hónap van még hátra,
   csuhaja, ebb' a komisz ruhába.

In Debrecen the big barracks,
Heya, hoo, all painted yellow,
Three years and eight months,
Heya, hoo, must I spend there.
It is written on my shako,
On both sides of my shako:
Another three months to spend,
Heya, hoo, in the regulation garb.

146

A tamási, a tamási,
   a tamási nagyvendéglő de magos,
Abba sétál, abba sétál,
   abba sétál a regemenc főorvos.
Tárd ki babám két karodat, ölelj meg,
Hogy a felcser, kutya felcser,
   kutya felcser ne vizitálhasson meg!

At Tamási, at Tamási,
At Tamási, how big the inn is!
There walking, there walking,
Walking goes the military doctor-in-chief.
Throw both thine arms around me, love,
So that the doctor, the hound of a doctor,
The hound may not examine me.

147

Kedves édes anyám, kedves édes anyám,
   mért szültél a világra?
Mért nem vetettél a, mért nem vetettél a
   Tisza vize alája?
Tisza vize vitt vóna ja Dunába,
Mostan nem is vónék, mostan nem is vónék
   senki megunt babája.

Well-beloved mother, well-beloved mother,
Why hast thou brought me into the world?
Why hast thou not thrown me into the
   Tisza's waters?
The Tisza's waters would have carried me to
   the Danube,
And now I should not be, now I should not be
Derided as nobody's sweetheart.

148

Ha bemegyek, ha bemegyek,
  ha bemegyek a dobozi csárdába,
Leülök a, leülök a,
  leülök a cseresznyefalócára.
Kocsmárosné, arra kérem rögtön jőjjön ki,
Ezt a csekély adósságom,
  borom árát ki akarom fizetni.

When I go, when I go,
When I go into the inn at Doboz,
I shall sit on the, sit on the,
Sit on the bench of cherry-wood.
Hostess, I ask you, come out at once,
This trifling debt of mine,
On account of my wine, I wish to settle.

149 (the text is lacking)

150

A kányai biró háza de magos,
  köröskörül kilenc zsalugátëros,
Tizediken maga néz ki a biró:
  — No legények, megjött már a behivó!
Engëm babám ne sirass,
  értem könnyet ne hullass,
Beírták a nevemet a nagy könyvbe
  a tamási 'Korona' vendéglőbe.

Lofty is the house of the mayor at Kánya,
Around it are nine windows with blinds.
Out of the tenth the mayor himself is looking:
'Well, boys, now you are called up!'
Weep not, my beloved,
Let not thy tears fall:
My name is written down in the big book,
At the Crown inn at Tamási.

151 a

Szegény asszony fia vagyok,
Minden kocsmába tartozok.
Jaj istenem, hogy adjam meg,
Hogy a babám ne tudja meg.

A poor woman's son am I,
In debt with every innkeeper.
O good Lord, how can I pay,
So that my sweetheart know nothing of my
  plight!

151 b

1. János bácsi hegedűje
   Maradt vóna az erdőbe,

2. Hogy ne szólna olyan búsan,
   Nem lönnék szerelmes soha.

1. If only Uncle János's fiddle
   Had been left in the forest,

2. It would not be singing so sadly,
   Nor would I ever be falling in love.

152 (var. 316)

1. Szántottam gyöpöt,
   Vetëttem gyöngyöt,
   Hajtottam ágát,
   Szëdtem virágát.

2. Az erdün járó
   A Márton Szidi,
   Utána járó
   A Vörös Dezső.

3. Mit nézëk rajta,
   Nem fekszëk rajta;
   Bús az ő szíve,
   Gyönggyel van kirakva.

1. I was ploughing the sward,
   I was sowing pearls,
   I was bending boughs,
   I was plucking flowers.

2. Through the forest roving
   Went Márton Szidi,
   Behind her roving
   Came Vörös Dezső.

3. Why do I look?
   It's none of my business:
   Sad is her heart,
   Inlaid with pearls.

Elment az én rózsám
Idegen országba,
Azt izente vissza,
Menjek el utána.

Gone is my beloved
Into foreign countries,
He sent a message
That I should follow him.

Sohasë láttalak,
Nëm is ösmertelek,
Csak hired hallottam,
Má mëgszerettelek.

I never saw thee,
Did not know thee,
But when I heard of thee
I fell in love at once.

1. Hirës bëtyár vagyok,
   Patkó az én nevëm,
   Tizënhárom mëgye
   Rég kerestet engëm.

2. Pedig ott is járok,
   Ahol nem gondolják,
   Hirës paripámat
   Mindenütt csodálják.

3. Ha megsarkantyúzom,
   Sok határt átugrok,
   Pandurok kezébe
   De sohase jutok.

1. A famous highwayman am I,
   Patkó is my name.
   Thirteen districts
   Have long been seeking me.

2. And often I go
   Where none expect me,
   My beautiful charger
   Is everywhere admired.

3. By spurring him on
   I could jump over many borders,
   Into the hands of the Pandurs
   I should never fall.

1. Hérvadni kezdettem,
   Mint ősszel a rózsa,
   Mert bokros búbánat
   A szívemet járja.

2. Csak azt szánom-bánom,
   Tőled mëg këll válnom,
   Sok utánad való
   Járásim sajnálom.

3. Vagy mëghalok érted,
   Vagy magamnak tëszlek,
   Vagy piros vérëmmel
   Födet festëk érted.

4. Nem azért kívánom
   Rózsám, elvesztedet,
   Hogy meguntam volna
   Világon éltedet:

5. Velem nem tölthetted
   Gyönyörűségedet,
   Mással se tölthesd el
   Világon kedvedet.

1. I am beginning to wither
   Like the rose in autumn,
   For deep sadness
   Is in my heart.

2. If I fret and grieve
   It is because I must leave thee:
   That many times after thee
   I walked I regret.

3. I must either die for thy sake,
   Or get thee for my own.
   Or with my red blood
   Dye the earth for thy sake.

4. I have wished thy death,
   Beloved, but not because
   I might grow tired
   Of you if you lived.

5. If you cannot share
   With me your joy,
   You shall not share it
   With any one else

1. Mënyecske, mënyecske,
   Te barna mënyecske,
   Rég mëgmondtam nékëd,
   Ne mënj a cserésbe.[1]

2. Bémënt a cserésbe,
   Lefeküdt a fűbe,
   Sárig [2] hasú kigyó
   Bébútt kebelébe.

3. — Anyám, édes anyám,
   Kedves és jó dajkám,
   Sárig hasú kigyó
   Bébútt kebelëmbe.

4. Arra kérem magát,
   Vegye ki belőle,
   Szerelmes szivemët
   Mëgemészti benne.

5. — Nem veszem leányom,
   Kezemet mëgmarja,
   Az én kicsi gyënge
   Ujjam leszakajsza.

6. Inkább elleszek én
   Jó leányom nélkül,
   Hogysem én ellegyek
   Gyënge karom nélkül.

7. — Bátyám, édes bátyám,
   Kedves és jó bátyám,
   Sárig hasú kigyó
   Bébútt kebelëmbe.

8 = 4.

9. — Nem veszem testvérem,
   Kezemet megmarja,
   Kezemet megmarja,
   Ujjam leszakajsza.

10. Inkább elleszek én
    Jó testvérem nélkül,
    Hogysem én ellegyek
    Gyënge karom nélkül.

11. — Kedvesem, kedvesem,
    Hűséges kedvesem,
    Sárig hasú kigyó
    Bébútt kebelëmbe.

12. Arra kérem magát,
    Vegye ki belőle,
    Tüdőmet, májamat
    Mëgemészti benne.

[1] cserjésbe.

1. Young woman, young woman,
   You dusky young woman,
   Indeed I tell you
   Go not into the coppice.

2. She went into the coppice,
   Lay down on the grass,
   And a yellow snake
   Crept up to her bosom.

3. 'Mother, dearest mother,
   Thou who lovest me so,
   A yellow snake
   Is lurking on my bosom!

4. I ask you, indeed,
   Take it away,
   Or it will devour
   The poor heart in my breast.'

5. 'I shall not pull it away, daughter,
   For it might bite my hand,
   And my slender, tender
   Fingers wrench away.

6. Rather will I live
   Indeed without a daughter,
   Than with one arm
   Without a hand.'

7. 'Brother, dearest brother,
   Thou who lovest me so,
   A yellow snake
   Is lurking on my bosom!'

8 = 4.

9. 'I shall not pull it away, sister,
   For it might bite my hand,
   It might bite my hand,
   Wrench my fingers away.

10. Rather will I live
    Indeed without a sister
    Than with one arm
    Without a hand.'

11. 'Sweetheart, beloved sweetheart,
    Thou my faithful sweetheart,
    A yellow snake
    Is lurking on my bosom!

12. I ask you, indeed,
    Take it away,
    Or my liver and my lungs
    By it will be devoured.'

[2] = sárga.

13. Erre az éldese
Mëg is keseredett,
Gyënge karjaira
Ruhát tekergetett.

14. Bényult kebelibe,
Kivette belőle:
Sárig hasú kigyó
Aranyalma leve.

15. S így hát az éldese
Jobb, mint hív szülöttje,
Tizenkét éve, hogy
Mind őtet kereste.

158

1. Dombon van a házam,
Szélnek van fordítva,
Kerëk az ablakja,
Ingem lesnek rajta.

2. Ne búsulj, ne bánkódj,
Ne is síránkozzál,
Mëgsegít a jó isten,
Csak jól imádkozzál.

159

Hërvadj, rózsám, hërvadj,
Mer az enyim nem vagy.
Ha az enyim volnál,
Különbet nyilonnál.

160

Haza, gazda, haza,
Bé van a ló fogva,
Vármegyeházánál
Szól a csengő rajta.

161 (var. 34 a, 165)

1. Egy özvegy asszonynak
Volt tizenkét lánya,
A tizenkettedik
Londonvár Ilonka.

2. — Londonvár Ilonka
Mi annak az oka,
Zöld selemszoknyádnak
Hosszabb a hátulja?

3. — Szabó nem jól szabta
Varó nem jól varta:
Verje meg az isten,
Jaj de elrontotta!

— — — —

13. Thereupon her sweetheart,
Full of bitterness,
Around his tender hand
Wound pieces of cloth,

14. Clutched at her breast
In order to pull the snake away,
But the yellow snake
Turned into an apple of gold.

15. And thus her sweetheart
Was better than her faithful parents,
He who for twelve years
Wooed her, and her only.

1. On the hill is my house,
Turned to the wind;
Round are its windows,
From which I am watched.

2. Be not sad, do not fret,
And do not shed tears:
God in His mercy will help,
If only we pray well.

Fade away, rose, fade away,
That art not mine.
If thou wert mine,
Thou wouldst blossom far better.

Homewards, master, homewards!
Here is the horse ready,
By the Komitat-hall
His bells are tinkling.

1. A widowed woman
Had twelve daughters,
The twelfth was named
Londonvár Ilonka.

2. 'Londonvár Ilonka,
What is the reason that
Your green frock of silk
Is longer at the back?'

3. 'The cutter cut it badly,
The seamster sewed it badly:
May the Lord strike him
Who, alas, has spoilt it.'

— — — —

139

4. — Hóhérok, hóhérok,
   Vigyétek lányomat,
   Vigyétek lányomat
   Az akasztófára!

5. — Jó anyám, jó anyám,
   Várjál egy félórát,
   Várjál egy félórát
   Vagy pedig egy némutát.[1]

6. — Fecskékém, fecskékém,
   Vidd el a levelem,
   Vidd el a levelem
   Kis Király Miklóshoz.

7. Ha ebéden éred,
   Asztalára teszed,
   Ha vacsorán éred,
   Tányérjára teszed.

8. — Kocsisom, kocsisom,
   Fogd be a hat lovat,
   Fogd be a hat lovat
   A szebbet és jobbikat!

9. Úgy menjünk, mint a szél,
   Vagy mint a gondolat,
   Ha élve találjuk
   Londonvár Ilonkát.

10. — Jó anyám, jó anyám,
    Ismeretlen anyám,
    Hol van az én babám,
    Londonvár Ilonka?

11. — Lement a patakba
    Lábát mosogatni,
    Lábát mosogatni,
    Magát vigasztalni.

12. — Nincsen ott, nincsen ott,
    Ismeretlen anyám,
    Hol van az én babám,
    Londonvár Ilonka?

13. — Lement a kis kerbe
    Virágokat szedni,
    Virágokat szedni,
    Koszorúba kötni.

14 = 12.

15. — Átment a szomszédba
    Szomszédasszonyához,
    Szomszédasszonyához
    A leánypajtáshoz.

16 = 12.

---

4. 'Hangmen, hangmen,
   Take my daughter away,
   Take my daughter away,
   Away to the gallows!'

5. 'Kind mother, kind mother,
   Wait one half-hour,
   Wait one half-hour,
   Or one more minute!'

6. 'O swallows, you swallows,
   Carry this my letter,
   Carry this my letter,
   To Kis Király Miklós.

7. 'If you find him at dinner,
   Put it on the table;
   If you find him at supper,
   Put it on his plate.'

8. 'My coachman, my coachman,
   Harness my six horses,
   Harness my six horses,
   The finest and best!

9. 'Let them go like the wind,
   As swift as the very mind,
   May I find alive
   Londonvár Ilonka!'

10. 'Good mother, good mother,
    Mother whom I knew not,
    Where is my well-beloved,
    Londonvár Ilonka?'

11. 'She went down to the brook
    To bathe her feet,
    To bathe her feet
    And to find solace.'

12. 'She's not there, she's not there,
    Mother whom I knew not,
    Where is my well-beloved,
    Londonvár Ilonka?'

13. 'She went down to the garden
    To pluck flowers,
    To pluck flowers,
    To make them into a wreath.'

14 = 12.

15. 'She went down to the neighbour's,
    To see the lady-neighbour,
    To see the lady-neighbour,
    To see the girl, her friend.'

16 = 12.

[1] = minutát (= percet).

17. — Nincs tűrés-tagadás:
Benn van a szobába,
Ki is van terítve
Zöld selem párnára.

18. Bemén a vőlegény,
Bánat-örömébe,
Bánat-örömébe
Kést nyomott a szivébe.

1. Elejbe, elejbe,
Sárga ló elejbe,
Hogy bé në ugorjon
Virágos kis kerbe!

2. Bé talál ugornyi,
Le találná szönnyi,[1]
Rózsafa bimbaját
Le találná törnyi.

1. Itt van az ideje,
Házasodni kéne,
Nem tudom, kit vegyek
Fiatalt vagy vénet.

2. Ha jöreget veszek,
A'mmindíg szomorú,
Annak minden szava
Egy égi háború.

3. Ha kisasszonyt veszek,
Szeret cifrán járni,
Én fogom ruházni,
Más fog véle hálni.

4. Ha gazdagot veszek,
Asz fogja mondani:
Az övébe vagyok,
El talál hajtani.

5. De ha szegényt veszek,
Magam is az vagyok,
Egy koldusból kettőt
Csak úgy csinálhatok.

6. Jobb inkább így vesznem,
Kraslomba [2] kell mennem,
Az apácák között
Páterrá kell lennem.

[1] = szedni.

17. 'Lies are of no avail:
She 's in there, in her room,
She lies on bed
On a pillow of green silk.'

18. In went the betrothed,
Distressed and rejoicing,
Distressed and rejoicing,
And drove his knife into his heart.

1. Forwards, forwards,
At the yellow horse forwards,
Lest he jump
Into my flower-beds.

2. He may go jumping,
He may go pulling off
The buds on my rose-trees,
He may go wrecking them.

1. Is it time
For me to get married?
I do not know whom to take,
A young one or an old one?

2. If I take an old one,
She'll be always sullen,
And whenever she holds forth
It will be a thunderstorm.

3. If I take a young maiden,
She'll like to go about in fine clothes,
I shall find the clothes for her,
Another will spend the nights with her.

4. If I take a rich one,
She may start saying:
I live on her money,
And drive me away.

5. But if I take a poor one,
I myself shall be poor.
Of one beggar to make two
Is the one result I shall achieve.

6. Far better than to take one,
Let me go into a cloister,
And amid the nuns
Be a reverend father.

[2] = klastromba.

1. Két út van előttem,
   Melyikre induljak?
   Három szeretőm van,
   Melyiktől búcsuzzak?

2. Ha jegytől búcsuztam,
   Kettő megharagszik;
   Igy hát az én szivem
   Soha meg nem nyugszik.

1. — Jónapot, jónapot
   Homródi nagyasszony!
   Hol vagyon, hol vagyon
   Homródi Zsuzsanna?

2. — Elküldtem, elküldtem
   Az virágmezőben,
   A rózsamezőbe,
   A virágos kerbe,

3. |: Virág vizsgálgatni,
   Magát múlatozni. :|

4. — Jónapot, jónapot
   Te kis kertészlegény!
   Hol vagyon, hol vagyon
   Az én hív kedvesem?

5. — |: Nem tudom, nem tudom,
   Tennap mind itt jára. :|

6 = 1.

7. — Elküldtem, elküldtem
   Az Duna martjára,
   Aranyhalat fogni,
   Magát múlatozni.

8. — Jónapot, jónapot
   Te kis hajószlegény!
   Hol vagyon, hol vagyon
   Az én hív kedvesem?

9. — |: Nem tudom, nem láttam,
   Tennap idejára. :|

10 = 1.

11. — Mi tűrés-tagadás,
    Látom, ki kell valljam,
    Elvitték, elvitték
    Az virágmezőbe,

12. Az virágmezőbe,
    A hóhér kezébe,
    Hogyha tegye belé
    A fekete fődbe.

1. Two roads are in front of me,
   Which shall I follow?
   Three sweethearts I have,
   Which shall I part from?

2. If I part from one,
   Two will be angry,
   So that my heart
   Will never be at rest.

165 (var. 34a, 161)

1. 'Good day, good day,
   Lady Homródi,
   Where is, where is
   Homródi Zsuzsanna?'

2. 'I sent her, I sent her
   Into the flower-meadow,
   Into the rose-meadow,
   Into the flower-garden,

3. |: To look upon the flowers,
   And enjoy herself.': |

4. 'Good day, good day,
   You young gardener!
   Where is, where is
   My faithful well-beloved?'

5. |: 'I know not, I know not,
   Yesterday she was there all day.' :|

6 = 1.

7. 'I sent her, I sent her
   To the banks of the Danube,
   To catch golden fishes
   And enjoy herself.'

8. 'Good day, good day,
   You young fisherman!
   Where is, where is
   My faithful well-beloved?'

9. |: 'I know not, I saw her not.
   Yesterday she was here.' :|

10 = 1.

11. 'What do lies avail?
    I see I must confess it:
    She was carried, she was carried
    Into the flower-meadow.

12. 'Into the flower-meadow,
    Into the hangman's hands,
    So that he should lay her
    Into the black earth.'

13. — Jónapot, jónapot
Te kis hóhérlegény,
Hol vagyon, hol vagyon
Az én hív kedvesem?

14. — |: Itt vagyon, itt vagyon
Az fekete fődben. :|

15. — Akajsz fel éngem is,
Tégy egy sírba véle,
Hogy a patak mossa
Mü piros vérünket.

1. Vetettem vijolát,
Várom kikeletjét,
Várom a babámnak
Hazajövetelét.

2. Kikőtt a vijola,
De nem igen teljes;
Hazajött a babám,
De nem igen szeret.

3. Hervad az a fűszál,
Kit a kasza levág,
Hervad az a kis lány,
Kit babája elhágy.

Igyunk itt, mert van mit,
Jó gazda lakik itt;
Nem csurog, nem csëpeg,
Elmulathatunk itt.

1. Áldja meg az isten
Azt az édes anyát,
Aki katonának
Neveli a fiát!

2. Húsz évig neveli
Világ pompájára,
Húsz éves korába
Öltözteti gyászba.

— — — — —

3. Szólnak ott az ágyúk,
Csattognak a kardok,
Lelkem éldes anyám,
Most mingyárt meghalok.

4. Hogyha a nagy isten
Rajtunk nem könyörül,
A vitézek közül
Még egy sem menekül.

13. 'Good day, good day,
You hangman's boy:
Where is, where is
My faithful beloved?'

14. |: 'She's here, she's here,
In the black earth!' :|

15. 'Then hang me too,
Put me in the same grave,
So that the river may run
Red with our blood!'

1. I have sowed violets,
I await their growing,
I await my beloved,
I await his home-coming.

2. The violets have closed,
They are not luxuriant;
My beloved is home,
But he is not very loving.

3. Faded is the grass
Which the scythe mows down,
Faded is the maid
Whom her lover forsakes.

Drink away, here is drink:
A good host lives here.
Rainproof is the roof,
Let us linger here.

1. May the Lord God bless
The good mother,
Who to be a good soldier
Will bring up her son.

2. For twenty years she'll bring him up,
For the world's pride,
When he's twenty years old,
Dresses him in mourning.

— — — — —

3. Now the cannon roars,
Now the swords clink,
O my beloved mother,
I shall forthwith die.

4. If God the Lord
Have no pity on us,
Of our heroes
Not one shall escape.

5. — Nohát pajtás, áşsál
   Sírt én kardhegyemmel,
   Takard bé szememet
   Az én zsebkendőmmel.

6. — Ások pajtás, ások
   Sírt én kardhegyemmel,
   Bétakarom szemed
   Az én zsebkendőmmel.

7. — Nohát pajtás, írd meg
   Szomorú halálom,
   Hol történt halálom
   Idegen országon.

8. Ki levelem kapja,
   Jajszóval olvassa,
   Én éldes anyámnak
   Bánatját újítja.

9. Kedves éldes apám,
   Tehozzád fordulok,
   Katona létemre
   Utoljára szólok:

10. Éltemet áldozom
    Az magyar hazámért,
    Véremet kiontom
    Az magyar nemzetért.

11. Ne félj, Magyarország,
    Isten vigyáz rëád
    Ellenség kezibe
    Nem adja határát.

169

Jelmetsztem az ujjam,
Folyik piros vérëm;
Messze van galambom,
Ki kötyi mëg nékem?

170

(a) Ultettem ibolyát,
    Rozmaring mi vyšou;
    Özvegy embert vártam,
    Mládenec mi prišou.

(b) 1. Hol voltál, kde si bou
      Tento malý juhás?
      Mér nem jöttél te
      Včera večer u nás?

   2. Ha eljöttél volna
      Včera do kostola,
      Megláttad volna,
      Aká son ti bola.

5. 'Well then, friend, dig
   A tomb with the point of your sword,
   And cover my eyes
   With your handkerchief.'

6. 'I'll dig, friend, I'll dig
   The grave with the point of my sword,
   And I'll cover your eyes
   With my handkerchief.'

7. 'And then, friend, write
   Of my sad death,
   Of my death that took place
   In a foreign country.

8. 'And they who receive the letter
   Will lament as they read it,
   Of my dear mother
   The grief will be revived.

9. 'And to thee, dear father,
   To thee I turn,
   I who became a soldier
   Address thee for the last time.

10. 'My life I sacrificed
    For Hungary, my country,
    My blood I shed
    For the Hungarian people.

11. 'Fear not, Hungary,
    God will protect thee,
    Into the hands of thy foes
    Not give away thy frontiers.'

I have cut my finger,
My red blood is flowing.
Far away is my beloved,
Who will bind my wound?

(a) I have planted a violet,
    Rosemary came up;
    A widower I expected,
    A young man came to me.

(b) 1. Where were you, where indeed,
      Tell me, young shepherd?
      Why did you not come
      Yesterday evening to our house?

   2. Had you but come
      Yesterday to church,
      You would have seen
      How (pretty) I was there.

144

1. — Járjad pap a táncot,
   Adok száz forintot.
   — Nem járom, nem tudom,
      nem illik, nem szabad
   Papnak táncot járni.

2. — Járjad pap a táncot,
   Szép hat ökröt adok.
   — Nem járom, nem tudom,
      nem illik, nem szabad
   Papnak táncot járni.

3. — Járjad pap a táncot,
   Szép menyecskét adok.
   — Járom is, tudom is,
      illik is, szabad is
   Papnak táncot járni.

1. 'Go, priest, go and dance:
   I'll give you a hundred florins.'
   'I shan't go, I can't dance,
      It 's not meet, not allowed
   That a priest should go and dance.'

2. 'Go, priest, go and dance:
   I'll give you six fine oxen.'
   'I shan't go, I can't dance,
      It 's not meet, not allowed
   That a priest should go and dance.'

3. 'Go, priest, go and dance:
   I'll give you a pretty maiden.'
   'I shall go, I can dance,
      It is meet, it 's allowed
   That a priest should go and dance.'

1. Egyszer egy királyfi
   Mit gondolt magába:

2. Föl kéne öltözni
   Kocsisom ruhába,

3. El kéne most menni
   Szoda városába,

4. Meg kéne kéretni a
   Szolgabíró lányát.

5. — Jóestét, jóestét
   Szolgabíró lánya!

6. — Jóestét, jóestét
   Szegény kocsislegény!

7. Újjön le minálunk
   Festett kanapéra.

8. — De nem azért jöttem,
   Hogy én itt leüljek,

9. Hanem azért jöttem:
   Jössz-e hozzám, vagy nem?

10. — Nem menek, nem menek
    Szegény kocsislegény:

11. Van a szomszédunkban egy
    Kosárkötő lánya.

12. — Jóestét, jóestét
    Kosárkötő lánya!

13. — Jóestét, jóestét
    Szegény kocsislegény!

14. Újjön le minálunk
    Hófehér padkára.

1. Once there was a prince
   Who thought within himself:

2. Now I must dress up
   In my coachman's clothes,

3. And I must go forthwith
   To the town of Szoda.

4. There I must woo
   The Judge's daughter.

5. 'Good evening, good evening,
   Daughter of the Judge!'

6. 'Good evening, good evening,
   Poor young coachman!

7. 'Sit down in our home,
   On this painted seat.'

8. 'I came not in order
   To sit on this bench,

9. 'But I came in order to ask:
   Will you come with me or not?'

10. 'I shan't go, I shan't go,
    Poor young coachman:

11. 'But in the next house there is
    A basket-maker's daughter.'

12. 'Good evening, good evening,
    Basket-maker's daughter!'

13. 'Good evening, good evening,
    Poor young coachman!

14. 'Sit down in our home
    On this snow-white little bench.'

15, 16 = 8, 9.

17. — Elmenek, elmenek
Szegény kocsislegény.

18 = 1.

19. Föl kéne öltözni
Királyi ruhába.

20–22 = 3, 4, 5.

23. — Jóestét, jóestét
Király őfelsége!

24. Üjjön le minálunk
Zöld selem dívánra.

25, 26 = 8, 9.

27. — Elmenek, elmenek
Király őfölsége.

28. — Kellesz a fenének,
Annak is a vénnek:

29. Van már nékem egy más,
Kosárkötő lánya.

30–34 = 12, 23, 7, 8, 9.

35. — Nem menek, nem menek
Király őfölsége,

36. Van már nékem egy más,
Szegény kocsislegény.

37. — Én vagyok az a más,
Csókoljuk meg egymást.

15, 16 = 8, 9.

17. 'Yes, I'll go, yes, I'll go,
Poor young coachman.'

18 = 1.

19. Now I must don
My princely robe.

20–22 = 3, 4, 5.

23. 'Good evening, good evening,
Your Royal Highness!

24. 'Sit down in our home
On this green silk divan.'

25, 26 = 8, 9.

27. 'Yes, I'll go, yes, I'll go,
Your Royal Highness!'

28. ''Tis a Devil that wants you,
And an old one at that:

29. 'I have already another one,
The basket-maker's daughter.'

30–34 = 12, 23, 7, 8, 9.

35. 'I shan't come, I shan't come,
Your Royal Highness,

36. 'I have another one already,
A poor young coachman.'

37. 'I am that other one,
Let us kiss one another.'

173

1. Béres vagyok, béres,
Béresnek szegődtem;
Sej, itt az újesztendő,
Jön a szekér értem.

2. Sajnálom ökrömet,
A járomszögemet,
Sej, cifra ösztökémet,
Barna szeretőmet.

---

1. I'm a hired farm-boy,
I've pledged myself as such.
Hey, when comes the New Year,
Comes the cart to fetch me.

2. I grieve for my oxen,
For my nail-studded yoke,
Alas, my polished goad,
And my dark-haired sweetheart.

174

1. Volt-e olyan juhász,
Héj huj tirajlárom,

2. Ki meg tunná őrözni
Farkastul a bárányt?

3. — Voltak-e farkasok?
— Hej, bizony nem angyalok.

4. — Gyöttek-e az erdő felül?
— Hej, nem a templom felül.

---

1. Was there ever such a shepherd,
Hey, huy, tirylarom,

2. Who knew so well to keep away
From the wolf his lambs.

3. 'Have wolves been here?'
'Oh! surely not angels!'

4. 'Came they from out the forest?'
'Oh! surely not from out the temple.'

5. — Vittek-e el bárányt?
— Hej, bizony nem is hoztak.

6. — Fojt-e el a vére?
— Hej, bizony nem a teje.

Két szál pünkösdrózsa
Kihajlott az útra,
El akar hervadni,
Nincs ki leszakítsa.

1. — Jónapot, jónapot
Sári bírónénak,
Sári bírónénak,
A Kati lányának!

2. — Jőjj be, Kati lányom,
Legények hivatnak,
Sári városában
Lakodalmat laknak.

3. — Nem mék anyám, nem mék,
Mer tudom, nem jó lesz,
Árvadi Jánosnak
Lakodalma most lesz.

4. — Vedd föl, Kati lányom
Finom selyem szoknyád,
Húzd a lábaidra,
Húzd karmazsin csizmád.

5. Tíz pár aranygyűrűd
Rakd az ujjaidra,
Had' szakadja szívit
Kedves galambodnak.

6. — Jóestét, jóestét
Árvadi Jánosnak!
Én is megérkeztem
A lakodalomba.

7. — Gyere velem táncra,
Egy kis mulatságra.
— Nem megyek én kenddel,
Mer zsíros az ingujj.

8. — Gyere velem táncra,
Egy kis mulatságra.
— Elmegyek én kenddel,
Nem zsíros ingujja.

9. — Huzd rá cigány délig,
Déltül fogva estig,
Estétül hajnalig,
Világos viradtig.

5. 'Took they lambs away?'
'Oh! they surely did not bring them here.'

6. 'Was it their blood that flowed?'
'Oh! surely it was not their milk.'

175

Two roses of June
Are blooming in the lane,
They are ready to fade,
No one will pluck them.

176 a (var. 34 b)

1. 'Good day, good day,
Wife of the mayor of Sári,
Wife of the mayor of Sári,
Kati, her young daughter.'

2. 'Come in, Kati my daughter,
Young men are calling you,
In the town of Sári
A marriage feast takes place.'

3. 'I shan't go, mother, I shan't go;
I know it is no good:
Of Árvadi János
It is the marriage feast.'

4. 'Put on, Kati my daughter,
Your fine silk frock,
And thrust your feet
Into your red top-boots.

5. 'Ten pairs of gold rings
Put on your fingers.
This will rend the heart
Of him you love.'

6. 'Good evening, good evening,
Árvadi János!
Here I have come
To attend your wedding.'

7. 'Come and dance with me
And a while rejoice.'
'No, I shan't go with you,
Your sleeve is greasy.'

8. 'Come and dance with me
And a while rejoice.'
'Yes, indeed I'll come,
Your sleeve is not greasy.'

9. 'Play away, gipsy, till noon,
And from noon till night,
And from night till morning,
When will rise the sun.'

10. — Eresszen kend mán el,
　　Mer mingyán meghalok,
　　Finom selyemszoknyám
　　Testemhöz ragadott.

11. — Nem bánom, meghalsz is,
　　Világból kimégysz is,
　　Ha enyém nem lettél,
　　Másé se lehessél.

12 = 9.

13. — Eresszen kend mán el,
　　Mer mingyán meghalok,
　　Tíz pár aranygyűrű
　　Ujjamra dagadott.

14 = 11.

15. — Eresszen kend mán el,
　　Mer mingyán meghalok,
　　A csizmám szárában
　　A vér megaludott.

16. — Nem bánom, meghalsz is,
　　Világból kimégysz is,
　　Ha enyém nem lettél,
　　Másé se lehessél.

17. — Húzd rá cigány délig,
　　Déltül fogva estig,
　　Estétül hajnalig,
　　Míg ki nem terítik.

18. — Fogjál kocsis, fogjál,
　　Gyerünk hamar haza.
　　— Nyisd ki anyám, nyisd ki
　　Leveles kapudat.

19. Bontsd el anyám, bontsd el
　　Paplanos ágyadat,
　　Hadd pihentessem el
　　Fáradt tagjaimat.

20. — Jónapot, jónapot
　　Sári bírónénak,
　　Sári bírónénak,
　　A Kati lányának!

21. |: Ugyan kedves anyám,
　　Hogy van már a Kati? :|

22. — Jól van már a Kati,
　　Nincs is semmi baja,
　　Ki is van terítve
　　A ház közepibe.

10. 'Let me go, let me go,
　　Or I shall die.
　　My fine silk frock
　　Is sticking to my body.'

11. 'I don't care if you die,
　　And vanish from the world:
　　If you be not mine,
　　You'll not be another's.'

12 = 9.

13. 'Let me go, let me go,
　　Or I shall die.
　　My ten pairs of gold rings
　　Bite into my swollen fingers.'

14 = 11.

15. 'Let me go, let me go,
　　Or I shall die.
　　In the legs of my boots
　　My blood is flowing.'

16. 'I don't care if you die,
　　And vanish from the world:
　　If you be not mine,
　　You'll not be another's.

17. 'Play away, gipsy, till noon,
　　And from noon till night,
　　And from night till morning,
　　Until we lay her out.'

18. 'Harness, coachman, harness,
　　Let us quickly go home.
　　Open, mother, open
　　Your creeper-covered door.

19. 'Open, dear mother, open
　　The blankets on the bed,
　　So that I may rest
　　My weary limbs.'

20. 'Good day, good day,
　　Wife of the mayor of Sári,
　　Wife of the mayor of Sári,
　　And Kati, your daughter.

21. |: 'And pray, good mother,
　　How is Kati now?' :|

22. 'Quite well is Kati now,
　　She is not in any pain,
　　Now that she lies
　　In the middle of the room.

23. — Csináltatsz-e neki
Diófa-koporsót?
— Csináltatok, anyám,
Márványkő-koporsót.

24. Meghúzatod-e már
A hármas harangot?
— Meghúzatom, anyám,
Mind a tizenhatot.

25. — Kiviteted-e hát
Valamily gödörbe?
— Kivitetem, anyám,
Gyászos temetőbe.

26. — Kiviteted-e hát
Valamily koldussal?
— Kivitetem, anyám,
Tizenhat zsandárral.

27. Átkozott az apa,
Hétszerte az anya,
Ki egyetlen lányát
A bálba bocsátja.

28. Este ereszti,
Reggel sem keresi,
Harmadnapra pedig
Halva viszik neki.

Jóestét, jóestét
Tollasiné asszonyság!
Hol van az az ügyes lány,
Ki az este hozzám járt?

Látod ruzsám, látod
Ezt a száraz ágat,
Ha ez kivirágzik,
Akkor leszek párod.

1. |: Csinálosi erdőn :|
|: Van ëgy fiatal fa, :|

2. |: Az alatt fojik egy :|
|: Csendes patakocska, :|

3. |: Oda jár fürödni :|
|: Egy pár galambocska. :|

4. |: Az egyike, mintha :|
|: Majoránna volna, :|

5. |: A másika, mintha :|
|: Teljes szegfű volna. :|

6. |: Az ágya dëszkája :|
|: Majoránna fája. :|

23. 'Will you have made for her
A shell of walnut wood?'
'I'll have made for her, mother,
A shell of marble.'

24. 'Will you have rung for her
Three bells?'
'I shall have rung for her
All sixteen bells.'

25. 'Will you have her carried
To some pit?'
'I shall have her carried, mother,
To the dismal churchyard.'

26. 'Will you have her carried
By some beggar?'
'I shall have her carried
By sixteen gendarmes.'

27. Accursed be the father
And seven times accursed the mother,
Who their only daughter
Let go to the ball.

28. At night they let her go,
In the morning fetch her not,
And on the third day
They bring her back dead.

176 b

Good evening, good evening,
Lady Tollasi!
How is your dear daughter
Who came to me at eventide?

177

See, my sweet rose, see
This withered bough:
When it bears blossoms,
Then shall I be thine!

178

1. |: In the forest of Csinálos :|
|: There is a young tree; :|

2. |: At its foot there runs :|
|: A peaceful little brook. :|

3. |: There come to bathe :|
|: A pair of little doves. :|

4. |: One of them is like :|
|: To marjoram sweet, :|

5. |: The other one is like :|
|: A garden carnation in full bloom. :|

6. |: Their bedstead is made :|
|: Of marjoram stems. :|

149

1. Guta maga egy város,
   Van abba egy mészáros;
   Van két lova, jó hámos,
   Bagaria szerszámos.

2. Alsó Gellér — bóhasár,
   Főső Gellér — mind takács.
   Bogya mellett megállhatsz,
   Tetűt, bóhát találhatsz.

3. Alista és Felista,
   Tőnye jó kis falucska,
   Sok pogácsát, rétesként
   Sütnek ott a menyecskék.

4. Ekel és Nemesócsa,
   Híres vót ez valaha,
   Sok krumpli termett benne,
   Csallóközbe tőtötte.

5. Aranyos és Nagy-Kisbér,
   Van ottan egy himpellér,
   Van ott sok fehér kenyér,
   Nagybélünkbe belefér.

1. Guta is this very town,
   There there is a butcher;
   There are two horses, well harnessed
   With Russian leather ornaments.

2. Alsó Gellér—it is mere dirt,
   Főső Gellér—there all are weavers.
   Hang around Bogya town,
   You'll encounter lice and fleas.

3. Alista, Felista,
   Tőnye are pretty little villages:
   Many cakes and crumpets
   Do the young women bake there.

4. Ekel and Nemesócsa
   Famous were in olden times;
   Many potatoes grow there,
   That go to provision Csallóköz.

5. Aranyos and Nagy-Kisbér,
   There there is a bungler;
   There there is plenty of white bread
   That will fill our insides.

1. Öreganyád igen jó,
   Télen csikó, nyáron ló;
   Ha felül a tűzhelyre,
   Onnan mondják: ne ló, ne!

2. Kivezetëm a gyöpre,
   Szántok rajta egyesbe;
   Adok neki pozdorját,
   Had múlassa ki magát.

1. Your grandmother is very kind,
   In winter a foal, in summer a horse,
   And when she sits by the hearth
   They all call:
   'Woah! my horse, woah!'

2. Let's go on to the sward,
   There I'll plough away,
   And I'll give her chaff
   So that she may rejoice.

Kivirágzott már a nád, —
S nekem ígért vót anyád.
Fődbe veszett a retek, —
Más az, akit szeretek.

The rushes are in bloom,—
Your mother promised you to me.
In the soil the radish rots,—
Another I shall love.

|: Hej, sár elő, sár elő,
Sánta Beke állj elő! :|

|: Hey, out with you, out with you!
Limping Beke, out with you! :|

Ëgy kis kertet kerítëk,
Abba rózsát ültetëk;
Szomszéd asszon kis lánya
Rákapott a rózsára.

A little garden I fenced,
Therein I planted roses;
And my neighbour's young daughter
Helps herself to the roses.

1. Borbély Bábi nagy beteg,
   Nem eheti a levest;
   Vizet inna, vize sincs,
   Kútra kűdjön senki sincs.

2. Van neki egy vak ipa,
   Asz kűdte el a kútra.
   Még az ipa kútra járt,
   A vasárus véle hált.

3. Kérdi tűlle az ipa:
   — Ki hevert az ágyomba?
   — Cica fogott egeret,
   Avval jádzott öleget.

4. Borbély Bábi udvara
   Kövéccsel van kirakva;
   Ne menj arra íccaka
   Ibrent fekszik az ipa.

|: Bakonyerdő gyászba van, :|
|: Rózsa Sándor ágyba van. :|

Elindula három árva,
A három kis csiporkával
Az erdőbe epröt szedni,
Az erdőbe epröt szedni.

1. Békés város de szép helyt van,
   Mert a templom közepén van;
   Ajtajába rózsacsipke,
   Rászállott egy bús gerlice.

2. — Ne búsulj te bús gerlice,
   Jön még neked párod ide.
   — Mit ér nekem a más párja,
   Ha az enyém el van zárva!

1. Ideje bujdosásimnak,
   Eljött már utazásimnak,
   Sok okai vadnak annak
   Az én elbujdosásimnak.

2. Ződ az útnak a két szélje,
   De bánatos a közepe,
   Masérodzom búval benne,
   Masérodzom búval benne.

1. Borbély Bábi is very ill,
   She will not eat anything,
   Craves for water, has no water,
   And has no one to send to the well.

2. She has a blind father-in-law,
   Him she sends to the spring,
   And while he goes to the spring
   The ironmonger sleeps with her.

3. The father-in-law asks her:
   'Who has lain upon my bed?'
   'The cat caught a mouse,
   And with it played a long time.'

4. Borbély Bábi's courtyard
   Is all strewn with flints:
   Do not go there at night,
   The father-in-law is lying in wait.

|: The Bakony forest is in mourning, :|
|: Rózsa Sándor is on his (death) bed. :|

Three little orphans were going along,
All three were carrying little pots,
For to pluck strawberries in the wood,
For to pluck strawberries in the wood.

1. Békés town is a beautiful place,
   For the temple stands in its middle;
   Around its gate are rose-bushes,
   Upon which came to settle a mournful
   turtle-dove.

2. 'Mourn not, mournful turtle-dove,
   Soon will come to thee a mate.'
   'I have no use for another's sweetheart,
   When my own is captive.'

1. The time has come to rove,
   To start journeying,
   And many reasons there are
   For me to go roving.

2. Green are both sides of the road,
   Sad in colour the middle,
   And I march along it with sadness,
   And I march along it with sadness.

3. A két lábam masérodzik,
   A két szemem búsalkodik;
   A két lábam masérodzik,
   A két szemem búsalkodik.

4. Fejem fëlett az nagy fëlhő,
   De nem abból hull az esső,
   A két szemem sűrű fëlhő,
   Mind onnét csurog az esső.

5. Idehaza a legénynek
   Nincsen becsüje szegénynek,
   Mert itthon inkább kedveznek
   Az idegën jövevénynek.

6. Ha a tengeren túll menyek,
   Ott ës jó hírt-nevet szerzek;
   Ha a tengeren túll menyek,
   Ott ës jó hírt-nevet szerzek.

7. De itthon nem fogják tudni,
   Szegény fejem él-e, hal-e,
   Szegény fejem él-e, hal-e,
   S az életbe módja van-e?

8. Isten veled, jó pajtásim,
   Barátim s feletkezetim!
   Akik velem jót tettetek,
   Isten fizesse meg nektek!

9. Akik velem jót tettetek,
   Isten fizesse meg nektek,
   Hosszabbítsa meg éltetek,
   Hogy őtet dicsérhessétek!

10. Angyalidat, én istenem,
    Küldjed, vezerijjen éngem,
    Hogy őrijzen, s óltalmajzon,
    Ahol nem ismérnek éngem.

11. Áldás a szentháromságnak,
    Isten fia szent anyjának,
    Ki angyalt küld kalauznak,
    Az igaz úton járóknak.

3. With my two feet I march,
   With my two eyes I weep;
   With my two feet I march,
   With my two eyes I weep.

4. Above my head a great cloud,
   But not from it falls the rain:
   Both my eyes are heavy clouds,
   It is from them that rain falls.

5. In this country young men
   Are not valued if they're hapless;
   For here are far preferred
   Strangers who come from afar.

6. If I go beyond the sea,
   There I'll be held in honour.
   If I go beyond the sea,
   There I'll be held in honour.

7. But here no one will ever know
   If I, the poor one, am alive or dead,
   If I, the poor one, am alive or dead,
   If I have means of livelihood.

8. God be with thee, good comrades,
   My friends, my companions,
   Who so well have stood by me,
   May God reward you greatly!

9. You who well have stood by me,
   May God reward you greatly,
   Lengthen your life
   So that you sing His praise.

10. Thine angels, O Lord my God,
    Send to me, and guide me,
    May they watch on me and protect me,
    Where nobody knows me.

11. Blessed be the Holy Trinity
    And the Holy Mother of God the Son,
    Who send angels to guide
    Us in the right path.

189

1. Mikor megyek Debrecenbe,
   Debreceni törvényszékbe,
   Látom a sok urat írni,
   Rámtekintett valamennyi.

2. Le is írták a tíz évet,
   Szabadulnék, de nem lehet,
   Irok haza jó anyámnak,
   Hozzon ruhát a fiának.

3. Elhozta ja tiszta ruhám,
   Jaj, de zokogva borult rám,
   — Sírhatsz anyám jajszóval is,
   Egy fiad volt, rab lett az is.

1. When I came to Debrecen,
   To the law-court at Debrecen,
   I saw many gentlemen writing
   And all of them stared at me.

2. They put me down for ten years,
   I'd fain go free, but it can't be done:
   I wrote home to my good mother
   To bring clothes for her son.

3. She brought me clean clothes,
   And bitterly she wept for me.
   'Weep, dear mother, bewail my fate:
   You have one son, and he is a captive.

4. — Ne sírjon kend, édes anyám,
   Gyűjjön, nézze meg a szobám:
   Két szál deszka a nyoszolyám,
   Itt halok meg, éldes anyám.

5. Vasrostélyos az ablakom,
   Nyújtsd be karod, kis angyalom,
   Had' fogjam meg utoljára,
   Búcsút veszek nemsokára.

1. Szógalegény a pusztába
   Gondolkozik ő magába,
   Gondolkozik ő magába,
   Hova szálljon éccakára?

2. Hova szálljon éccakára?
   Özvegyasszony lakásába.
   Bekopogtat patrólmódra:
   — Idehaza-e a gazda?

3. — Nincs idehaza a gazda,
   Kerülj rózsám az ajtóra;
   Készen az ágy, meg van vetve,
   Gyere rózsám, feküdj bele!

4. — Nem megyek be a házadba,
   Nem fekszek le az ágyadba,
   Kimegyek az istállóba,
   Ott fekszek le a jászolba.

1. Keseredett az az anya,
   Kinek két fia katona.
   Egyik káplár s a más húszár,
   Pesti kaszárnyába sétál.

2. Pesti kaszárnya repedj meg,
   Kedves babám szabadulj meg!
   — Szabadulnék, de nem lehet,
   Szabadságom el van zárva.

3. Szabadságom el van zárva
   Ferenc Jóska ládájába;
   Elveszett a láda kócsa,
   Ki se szabadulok soha.

1. Mihelyt, mihelyt férhez mentem,
   Mingyár búsulni kezdёttem;
   Én uramat nem szerettem,
   Egy komámmal megöltem.

2. Erdőszádba kivitettem,
   Nyírfák alá eltemettem.
   Azt egy ember meglátta vót,
   A tiszteknek hirré adta.

4. 'Do not weep, dear mother,
   Come in, behold my room:
   Two boards make my bed,
   And here I shall die, dear mother.

5. 'There are iron bars to my window.
   Put your hand through them, my beloved,
   That I may grasp it for the last time
   And soon thereafter bid you farewell.'

190

1. A servant boy on the Puszta
   Is thinking within himself,
   Is thinking within himself,
   Where will he go to-night?

2. Where will he go to-night?
   To the widow's house.
   He knocks after the fashion of a patrol:
   'Is the master at home?'

3. 'No, the master is not at home.
   Come round, my love, to the door.
   Ready is the bed, it is made:
   Come, well-beloved, lie down on it.'

4. 'I shall not come into the house,
   I shall not lie on the bed,
   I'll go to the stable
   And there I'll lie in the manger.'

191 (var. 138)

1. The mother is grieving
   Whose two sons are soldiers:
   One a corporal, the other a hussar,
   In the Pest barracks walk about.

2. Pest barracks, collapse,
   Let my dear one be free.
   'I'd fain be free, but it cannot be,
   My freedom is in iron bars.

3. 'My freedom is in iron bars,
   In Francis Joseph's coffer.
   Lost is the coffer's key
   And never shall I be free.'

192

1. As soon, as soon as I got married
   I began forthwith to grieve.
   My husband I loved not,
   I had him killed by a crony of mine.

2. To a clearing in the forest I dragged him,
   Under birch-trees I buried him.
   One man saw me do it,
   To the officers he gave warning.

153

3. Rákosfalvi ucca végén
Két ágú fa föl van ásva,
Két ágú fa föl van ásva.
Nincsen semmi írás rajta.

4. Azér nincsen írás rajta:
Benkő Julis függ le róla,
Azér nincsen írás rajta:
Benkő Julis függ le róla.

3. Where the Rákosfalva road ends
There 's a two-limbed tree,
There 's a two-limbed tree.
There is no writing on it.

4. And for this reason there 's no writing
on it:
Benkő Julis is hanging from it.
And for this reason there 's no writing
on it:
Benkő Julis is hanging from it.

193 (var. 27)

1. Már két hete vagy már három,
Hogy a számadómat várom.
Amoda gyün, amint látom,
Fecskehasú szamárháton.

2. — Jónapot, édes bojtárom!
Van-e hibám, vagy sok károm?
— Nincsen hibád, de nem is lesz,
Még a nyáj az karomon lesz.

3. — Még azt mondod, nincsen hiba!
Hát a vezérürü hunn van?
— Maj megkerül kikeletkor,
Mikor a juh legel, akkor.

1. For two weeks, aye, for three,
I've been awaiting the owner of my flock.
There he comes, I see,
Riding a white-bellied donkey.

2. 'Good day, my dear shepherd boy.
Any mistakes? Any losses?'
'No mistakes, nor will there be any
So long as I'm in charge of the flock.'

3. 'You say, there are no mistakes:
But where is the wether, the leader?'
'He'll come back in the spring,
When the sheep graze, that 's the time!'

194

— Kelj fel kandász! elaludtál,
Elment a nyáj s itt maradtál.
— Adsza szűröm meg a baltám,
Had menjek a nyájam után.

'Up with you, swineherd! you sleep,
Your herds run away, and you tarry.'
'Give me my cloak and my hatchet,
And I'll go after them.'

195

Kukorica, kukorica,
Pattogatott kukorica;
Ë 'sszép asszon pattogtatta,
Hej, szeretője ropogtatta.

Oh, the maize, the maize,
The roasted maize!
A pretty woman roasted it,
Hey! her lover cracked it.

196

Arra vigyázz öreg asszony,
Hogy az ördög el ne kapjon,
Bihalbőrbe őtöztessen,
Pokolba bedöcögtessen.

Have a care, old woman,
Lest the devil take you.
In a bullock-skin he'll roll you,
And to hell he'll drag you.

197

Nem láttam én télbe fecskét,
Most öltem meg egy pár csürkét;
Ettem annak szűvit, máját, —
Csókolom galambom száját.

I'll see no swallows in winter.
Now I'll kill a brace of cockerels,
Eat their hearts and livers,
And kiss the lips of my beloved.

Hajtják a fekete kecskét,
Verik a barna menyecskét.
Ha verik is, megérdemli,
Ki az urát nem szereti.

The black goats are driven,
The dark-haired young wife is beaten.
If she's beaten, she deserves it,
For she loves not her husband.

1. Hej, Vargáné káposztát főz,
   Kontya alá ütött a gőz;
   Hányja-veti fakanalát:
   Kinek adja Zsuzsa lányát?

2. Nem adja az más egyébnek:
   Kara István őkelmének.
   Még akkor neki igérte,
   Mikor bölcsőbe rengette.

1. Hey, Mother Varga cooks cabbage,
   The steam goes under her topknot.
   She swings about her ladle.
   To whom will she give Zsuzsa, her
   daughter?

2. She'll give her to no one
   But to Kara István,
   For to him she promised her
   When she was still being rocked in her
   cradle.

Fehér Laci lovat lopott
A fekete hegyek alatt;
Utána ment Gönc városa
Falujustul, hadnagyostul.

Fehér Laci stole a horse,
On the slopes of the black hills;
After him went the whole town of Gönc,
All the people and the lieutenants.

Csicseriborsó, vadlencse, —
Feketeszemű menyecske;
Most adta isten kezemre,
Mos járom vele kedvemre.

Chick-peas, wild lentils,—
Black-eyed young woman:
God has given her into my hands,
Now I'll dance with her joyfully.

— Hogyha elmész katonának,
Moñ mëg fiam, hol kaplak mëg?
— Jeresz ki Galiciába
S ott mëgkapsz ëgy korcsomába.

'When you go to be a soldier,
Tell me, son, where to find you?'
'You will go to Galicia,
There you'll find me in a wine-shop.'

1. Elbúsultam én magamat,
   Itt kell hagynom galambomat;
   Már én akármerre járok,
   Szép rózsára nem találok.

2. Szeress éngöm édös kincsöm,
   Tudod: azt fogadtad néköm,
   Hogy enyém lész mindhalálig,
   Szíved tőlem meg nem válik.

3. Ha megnyeröm szabadságom,
   Szívem gyöngyöm, szép virágom,
   Elvëszlek én esztendőre,
   Esztendőre vagy kettőre.

1. I am full of grief,
   For I must leave my beloved;
   And wherever I wander
   I shall meet no lovely rose.

2. Love me, my beloved, my precious one,
   Know it: I have your oath,
   That you'll be mine until death,
   That you'll never cease to love me.

3. When I am free again,
   My heart, my pearl, my beautiful flower,
   I shall take you away within a year,
   Within a year, or two at most.

204

1. Híres város Kolozsváros,
   Van kapuja kilenc záros,
   Abban lakik egy mészáros,
   Kinek neve Hires János.

2. Kordován csizma lábába,
   Sárig sarkantyú van rajta.
   Kapum előtt összeveri,
   Víg szívemet keseríti.

3. Kapum előtt összeveri,
   Víg szívemet keseríti.
   — Kapum előtt ne veregesd,
   Víg szívemet ne keserítsd.

1. Famous is Kolozsváros town,
   It has a gate with nine locks,
   There lives a butcher
   Whose name is Hires János.

2. He wears boots of Cordova leather,
   Upon which are yellow spurs.
   Those in front of my door he clinks,
   Thereby saddening my cheery heart.

3. Those in front of my door he clinks,
   Thereby saddening my cheery heart.
   'Clink them not in front of my door,
   Sadden not my cheery heart.'

205

1. |: A Mátrában a hegyek közt : |
   |: Egy leányzó pávát őrzött. : |

2. |: Jöttek hozzá jövevények, : |
   |: Három ifijú legények. : |

3. |: Hítták őtet sétálásra, : |
   |: Tisztességes barátságra. : |

4. |: — Ha véletek utam veszem, : |
   |: A pááváim hova teszem ? : |

5. |: Ha a pávám eltévedne, : |
   |: Érte szívem megrepedne. : |

6. |: — Páváid hajtod forrásra, : |
   |: Mert azt nem bízhatod másra. : |

1. |: In Mátra, amid the mountains : |
   |: A maiden is watching over peacocks.: |

2. |: There to her came foreigners, : |
   |: Three young fellows. : |

3. |: They asked her to come for a walk, : |
   |: Suggested meet and seemly friend-
   ship. : |

4. |: 'If with you I go walking, : |
   |: Where shall I leave my peacocks ? : |

5. |: 'If my peacocks went astray : |
   |: Then indeed my heart would burst.' : |

6. |: 'Drive your peacocks to the spring, : |
   |: For you can trust them to no other.' : |

206

Elvitte jaz árviz az pallout,
Kirül gyënge rózsám beléhout.
Në fél rózsám, në fél, nëm hadlak,
Nyujtsad a kezedët, kihúzlak.

The flood has carried away the bridge
From which my love has fallen.
Fear not, my love, I shan't forsake you,
Hold out your hand, I'll pull you out.

207

Párta, párta, feneette párta,
Hogy a menkű régen meg nem vágta.
Elszaggattam tizënhárom pártát,
Fene látta a gatyának szárát.

Wreath, wreath, accursed wreath,
May a thunderbolt strike you!
I've worn out thirteen wreaths
And the devil of a pair of breeches did I see!

208 (var. 237)

Hopp ide tisztán szép palútt dëszkán,
Nem lëszek többé nyoszolólëány;
Ha lëszek, lëszek, menyasszony lëszek,
Annak is pedig legszebbje lëszek.

Jump here on the beautiful polished board,
I shan't be a bridesmaid any more.
But I'll be, I'll be, a bride I'll be,
And the loveliest of all I'll be!

1. Elmënt a két jány virágot szënnyi,
   Elindulának, kezdének mënnyi,
   Egyik másiknak kezdi mondanyi:
   — Vót-ë valaki tígëd kíretnyi?

2. — Már engëm mátkám tízen kírettek,
   Már az tíz közül melyikhëz mënjek?
   Adjá' tanácsot árva fejemnek,
   Hogy virág helyëtt kórót ne szëdjek.

3. Szántottam fődjit, vetettem gyöngyit,
   Hajtottam ágát, szedtem virágját.
   Az igazmondás nem emberszólás,
   Hogy a rossz férfi holtig való gyász.

4. Első a János annak a neve,
   Annak szívembe megvan szerelme;
   Inkább szeretném őtet kedvembe,
   Ha lépett volna Lénus [1] kertjibe.

5. Másik Sámuel, avval én szívem
   Meg nem nyughatik vele én lelkem;
   Lám azelőtt is legküsebb vétkem
   El nem szenvedte ok nélkül nékem.

6. A harmadiknak a neve Zsigmond,
   Ha megharagszik, ő k . . . . nak mond,
   Leszen kezibe korbács és dorong,
   Száll a fejemre keserves nagy gond.

7. A negyediknek a neve Istvány,
   Abban az a kár, hogy igen hitvány,
   Ha lefekszik is a jobboldalán,
   Ő nyugodalmat sohase talál.

8. Ötögyik Pétër, az igën fösvíny,
   Annak a háza tudom, hogy sövíny,
   Ha ahhoz mégyëk, perpatvar lészën,
   Jaj lészën nékëm egísz életëm.

9. Hatogyik Ferenc, bátyja Jánosnak,
   Az nem szereti nyelit ásónak,
   Nem is rossz fia a sernek, bornak,
   Felit sem alussza ki éjszakának.

---

1. Went two maidens to pluck flowers,
   Started off, started on their way.
   The one said to the other:
   'Has any one wooèd you?'

2. 'Indeed, there have been ten to woo me:
   But out of the ten, to whom was I to go?
   Give advice to my poor head,
   So that instead of flowers I pluck not dry
   stalks.

3. 'I dug the ground, I sowed pearls,
   I pulled branches down and plucked
   flowers.
   And this true saying is no slander,
   That a bad man means grief to the end
   of life.

4. 'The name of the first is János.
   In my heart I love him still:
   I should have favoured him
   Had he but stepped into the garden of
   Venus.

5. 'The second is Sámuel, with him nor my
   heart
   Nor my soul were satisfied.
   For, behold, even my slightest trespasses
   He could not tolerate, and without any
   reason.

6. 'The name of the third is Zsigmond,
   When he grows angry he calls me a
   w . . . . .
   He holds in his hand a whip and a
   scourge,
   On my head would fall deep sorrow and
   worry.

7. 'The name of the fourth is Istvány,
   It's a pity he's such a weakling.
   When he lies on his right side
   He can never find peace.

8. 'The fifth, Péter, is very miserly:
   His house, I know, is made of laths.
   If I go there, there will be quarrels,
   And woe to me my whole life long.

9. 'The sixth, Ferenc, the brother of János,
   He likes not the handle of the spade.
   He's not a bad one at beer and wine,
   He never spends half a night sleeping.

[1] = Vénus.

157

10 Gábort szeretem, mert nem utolsó,
Látom kezibe van boros korsó,
Szíp leányokkal igen játszodózó,
És azok után igen haldosó.

11. Györgyöt szeretném, az jó játékos,
Annak ruhája tudom aranyos,
Paripája is hatvan talléros,
A konyhája is mindenkor zsíros.

12. Kilencedik András, ki hűségesen,
Ki hűségesen szedte hálóját,
Hogy megfoghassa kedves galambját,
Régenn ohajtja kedves galambját.

13. Tizegyik Mihál, most is ohajtom,
Velem tett jókér meg is síratom,
Mert ő volt nékem igaz gyámolom,
Ő szíp személit magamnak tartom.

10. 'Gábor I like, for he 's not the last,
I see in his hand a wine-pitcher;
He plays about with the pretty girls,
And is for ever dying for them.

11. 'György I love, he is very playful.
His clothes, I know, are of gold,
His horse is worth sixty crowns,
His kitchen is well stocked with fats.

12. 'The ninth is András, who faithfully,
Who faithfully sets his net
In order to catch his well-beloved,
Who long has desired his well-beloved.

13. 'The tenth is Mihál, him I desire,
I weep, because he was so kind to me.
He was my real protector:
His beautiful self I keep for myself.'

210

1. Letörött a pécsi torony gombja; —
Megszomjult a Rákop Jóska lova.
Eredj, rózsám, hozzál néki vizet,
Rákop Jóska az Alföldre siet.

2. Rákop Jóska a lovát nyergeli,
Szeretője az ablakon lesi.
— Ne lesd, rózsám, gyászos iletemet,
Mind teérted szenvedem ezeket!

3. Rákop Jóska mindig csak azt mondja,
Senki őtet soha meg nem fogja.
— Kilenc zsandár fogott meg engemet,
Megkötöztek s Fehérvárra vittek.

4. — Szépen kérem fehérvári bírót,
Nem raboltam egyebet, csak zsidót;
Engedje meg szabad életemet,
Utonállást nem cselekszem többet!

1. Collapsed has the point of the steeple at Pécs,
Thirsty is Rákop Jóska's horse.
Up, my love, give him water,
Rákop Jóska must to Alföld hasten.

2. Rákop Jóska saddles his horse,
His love from the window looks at him.
'Look not, my love, at my sad life,
I suffered everything for your sake!'

3. Rákop Jóska always says
That never will he be caught.
'Nine gendarmes caught me,
In fetters they took me to Fehérvár.

4. 'I shall plead to the judge at Fehérvár,
I've never robbed any one but Jews:
Allow me to go free in life,
I shall never again commit highway robbery.'

211

1. Fehér habgya vagyon a Dunának,
Kedves fija voltam az anyámnak,
Kedves fija voltam az anyámnak,
Mégis besoroztak katonának.

2. Ha tunnának, el akarnak vinni,
Bodor hajam le akarják vágni.
Bodor hajam nem hagyom levágni,
Evvel fogom a császárt szógálni.

1. White waves are on the Danube;
I always have been my mother's beloved,
I always have been my mother's beloved,
Yet they call me up to be a soldier.

2. They want to send me away,
Cut the hair of my head off.
I shan't let them cut my hair short,
With long hair I can serve the Emperor.

158

3. Bodor hajam mikoron levágták,
Kedves rózsám kötényébe hányták;
Nem volt annyi a hajamnak szála,
Mint a mennyi könnyem hullott rája.

A szëgszárdi szőllők alja homokos,
Arra járnak arany-, ezüstgombosok.
Azok hajtják el a sárga csikókat,
Azon vesznek arany, ezüst gombokat.

Szërnyű nagy romlásra készül Pannonia,
Kinek mint tëngërnek megáradó hobja.
Sok búnak, bánatnak környülvëtte árja,
Mert a vitézëknek esëtt ma ëgy héjja.

1. |: Ha folyóvíz vónék, bánatot nem tud-
nék : |
|: Hëgyek, völgyek között szép csëndesën
folynék, : |

2. |: Martot mosogatnék, füvet újítanék, : |
|: Szomjú madaraknak innyok adogat-
nék. : |

1. Ó én szegény kis madár, mire vetemëdtem,
Mikor a szalmában én szëmet szëdeget-
tem!
Tőrben estek lábaim, oda szabadságim,
Kötve vadnak szárnyaim, oda vigasságim.

2. Én, ki eddig szabadon éltem az világon,
Mindennapi dalomat fúttam a zöld ágon,
Számomra is egy szoba el vagyon készítve,
Eledelem cukorral fël van elegyítve.

3. Mégsem tetszik az nékem, jut eszembe
fészkem,
Hogy százszor jobb volt nékem zöld erdő-
ben élnem.
Patakoknak vizei jobbízűek voltak,
A lucsfának gyöngyei édesebbek voltak.

4. Megraktam a fészkemet, más éli munká-
mat,
Megvettem az ágyamat s más fekszi pár-
námat;
Tarka nyakú páromat más öleli társam,
Szerelmébe nem veszi, csak úgy moso-
logja.

---

3. When they cut my hair,
They fell into my sweetheart's apron,
And my hair were not so many
To the tears that fell from my eyes.

212

Of the Szegszárd vineyards the soil is sand,
Where people come and go with gold and
silver buttons.
Those who steal our yellow foals,
Buy from them gold and silver buttons.

213

Towards a great disaster Pannonia is heading,
It comes like the rush of a stormy sea.
Much sorrow and distress is in store for her,
For one of her heroes is missing to-day.

214

1. |: Were I a brook, I'd know no sorrow,: |
|: Through hill and dale I'd gently flow,: |

2. |: Playfully hug the banks, bring forth new
plants, : |
|: Quench the thirst of the little birds.: |

215

1. O poor little bird I, what was with me,
That I sought grains of corn amid the
straw?
My leg encountered a trap, gone is my
freedom.
Pinioned are my wings, gone is my cheer-
fulness.

2. I, who until now lived free in the world,
Who daily sang my songs on the green
branches,
For me one room is made ready,
And my food is mixed with sugar.

3. All this pleases me not, I think of my nest.
It were better for me to live in the green
woods,
The water of the brooks tasted sweeter,
The seeds of the spruce were better food.

4. I built my nest, another enjoys it.
I made my bed, another rests on my
pillow,
Another hugs the motley neck of my mate,
Not loving her, but only making merry.

159

5. Édes madártársaim, ma veletek voltam,
   Még ma utoljára is én köztetek jártam;
   Nem leszek már veletek a tiszta időbe,
   Nem csicsergek én többé a koránkelésbe.

216

Nám megmondtam kis lëány, ne menj el az
   erdőbe,
Ott a jáger maj megfog, beletësz a zsebjébe.
|: Belele, belele, beletësz a zsebjébe. :|

217

1. Látom a szép eget
   Fölöttünk fémleni,
   Békesség csillagát
   Rajtunk lengedezni.

2. Talán vérmezőbe
   Háromszínű zászló,
   A seregek ura
   Legyen oltalmazóm!

3. Nem szánom véremet
   Ontani hazámér.
   Méges fáj a lelkem,
   Az én otthonomér.

4. A bús harangok es
   Néma hangon szólnak,
   Mikor indúlni kell
   Szegény katonának.

5. Sír az egyik szemem,
   Sírjon a másik es,
   Sírjon mind a kettő,
   Mint a záporesső:

6. Mer még a fecske es
   Ahol nevelkedik,
   Búsan énekel, ha
   Indulni këlletik.

7. Fëlkötöm a kardot
   Apámért s anyámért,
   Megforgatom én a
   Szép magyar hazámért.

218 a

1. — Hej, halászok, halászok,
   Mit fogott a hálótok?
   — Nem fogott az egyebet:
   Vörösszárnyú keszeget.

5. Sweet birds, my companions, I was with
   you to-day,
   Even to the last I was among you.
   Now I shan't be with you in the lovely
   weather,
   Nor ever sing with you in the early dawn.

Indeed I tell you, little maid, go not into the
   wood:
There the huntsman will come, stick you into
   his pouch.
|: Right into, right into his pouch. :|

1. I see the beautiful sky,
   Everywhere shining,
   The star of peace
   Appears in the sky.

2. Perhaps on the battle-field
   The tricolour flag,
   Master of armies,
   Shall protect me.

3. I grudge not my blood
   To shed for my country,
   Yet my heart grieves
   On account of my home.

4. And sadly the bells
   In muffled tones chime,
   When they must call to war
   The unfortunate soldiers.

5. One of my eyes weeps,
   Let the other weep too.
   Let both of them weep
   As a cloud-burst:

6. For even the swallow
   Where she was brought up,
   Stands singing sadly
   When she has to fly away.

7. I shall gird my sword
   For my father and mother's sake,
   And I shall draw it
   For the sake of Hungary, my beautiful
   fatherland.

1. 'Hey, fisherman, fisherman,
   What did you catch in your nets?'
   'We caught nothing but
   White fish with red fins.'

2. — Hát a keszeg mit eszik,
Ha ja bárkába teszik?
— Nem eszik az egyebet,
Csak szerelemgyökeret.

3. — Hát az öreg íl-e még?
Hát a foga jó-e még?
Rád-e, rád-e, rád-e még,
Rád vicsorítja-e még?

2. 'And what does the fish eat
When it 's in the well of your boat?'
'Nothing does the fish eat
But love-roots.'

3. 'And is the old one still alive?
Do his teeth still work well?
And at you, at you, at you,
At you does he still grin?'

218 b

1. — Héj, halászok, halászok,
Mére mén az hajótok?
— Törökkanizsa felé,
Viszi a víz lëfelé.

2. — Hát a halak mit ësznek,
Ha ja bárkába tësznek (sic!)?
— Nem ëszik az ëgyëbet:
Vërësszárnyú keszegët.

1. 'Hey, fisherman, fisherman,
Whereto goes your boat?'
'Towards Törökkanizsa
The water carries it down.'

2. 'And what do the fish eat
That go into your boat?'
'They eat nothing but
White fish with red fins.'

219

1. Most jövök én Gyulárul,
A gyulai vásárrul;
Ott hallottam ezt a szót:
— Nyisd ki babám az ajtót.

2. — Nyitom biz én, nyitom is,
Melléd fekszëk magam is,
Melléd fekszëk magam is.
Hogyha talán këllëk is.

3. — Bontsd fël, babám, az ágyat,
Vánkost is tégy vagy hármat.
— Tëszëk biz én hatot is,
Melléd fekszëk magam is.

1. Now I come from Gyula,
From the market at Gyula,
There I hear the words:
'Open, my love, the door.'

2. 'Indeed I 'll open, indeed I shall!
And indeed I 'll lie by you,
And indeed I 'll lie by you,
Even as mayhap you wish it.'

3. 'Prepare the bed, my love,
Put thereon a pillow, even three.'
'I shall put six of them thereon,
And I 'll come and lie by thee!'

Ez a kis lány gyöngyöt fűz,
Ég a szëme, mint a tűz.
Ha jaz enyim úgy égne,
Csuhaha, barna legény szeretne.

220

This young maid is stringing pearls,
And her eyes shine like a flame.
If mine shone as brightly,
Hahaha, the dark young man would love me.

— Te kis lëány, te, te, te,
Hány esztendős lëhetsz te?
— Tizënhárom meg egy fél,
Talán tizënnegyedfél.

221

'O you little maid, O you, you,
How many years old are you?'
'Thirteen and a half,
Maybe fourteen minus a half.'

Elment az én babám Pestre,
Póstáslegény lett belőle,
Csej, haj, mindenkinek kűd ujságot,
Nekem csak szomorúságot, igaz a.

222

My beloved has gone to Pest,
He has become a postboy.
Hey, hie, to all sends news,
To me nothing but sad news, aye indeed!

Végigmentem a rózsám udvarán,
Bétekintëk a rózsám ablakán.
Rózsa nyilik a cserépbe,
Láttalak, rózsám, a más ölébe.

223

I paced the whole courtyard of my love's
    house,
I peeped into my love's window.
A rose in a bowl was opening its petals,
And I saw you, love, in another's arms.

Édes volt az anyám teje,
Keserű a más kenyere;
Úgy elmaradtam szegénytől,
Mint a nyárfa levelétől.

224

Sweet was my mother's milk,
Bitter is the strangers' bread.
Thus was I torn away from her, the poor one,
As from the aspen a leaf.

Fel van a lovam nyergelve,
Magam ülök a tetejébe.
Enyím vagy tehát drága gyöngyvirág,
Elmegyek én tehozzád.

225 a

Here stands my horse saddled,
And I shall ride it myself.
And mine art thou at last, beloved lily of the
    valley,
I'm coming to thee.

Le van a szivem láncolva,
Nincsen aki feloldozza.
Oldozz fel hát gyönyörű virágszál,
Akkor leszek szabad madár.

225 b

My heart is in chains,
None shall break them.
O break them, my beautiful blossom,
Then shall I be as free as a bird.

Megkötték már nékem a koszorút,
Ága-buga rozmaringból való.
Ága-buga a vállamra burolt,
Sok vig napom szomorúra fordolt.

226

The wreath is wound around me,
Of wisps of rosemary 'tis made.
The wisps weigh heavy on my shoulders,
My day of joy has turned into pain.

Szegény vagyok, szegénynek születtem,
A rózsámat igazán szerettem;
Az írigyek elrabolták tűlem,
Igy lett igazi árva belülem.

Széna teŗëm, széna terëm a réten, —
Nem beszéltem a babámmal a héten.
Nála van a zsebkendőm a zsebjében,
Előlveszi: arrul jutok eszébe.

Kis pej lovam nëm szereti a zabot,
Kocsmárosné árpájára rákapott.
Mer az árpa nëm is olyan, mint a zab, —
Igaz kis lány nëm is kell a magyarnak.

A Vargáék kapujukon nincsen zár,
Ez a híres Garzó Pista oda jár.
Kapufához kötözi meg a lovát,
Míg Julcsával kibeszélgeti magát.

Zöld az árpa, zöld a buza, kukoricaszár, —
Jaj de kevély, jaj de büszke a dejtári lány;
Környöskörül kivarrott a köténye,
Rá sem nézhet a vidéki legényre.

Életemben eccer voltam nálatok,
Akkor is szemetes volt a házatok.
Rézsarkantyúm felszedte a szemetet, —
Kis angyalom, mér csaltál meg engemet?

Sárgabélű görögdinnye hasadj mëg; —
Ha nem szeretsz, kis angyalom, üzend mëg;
Üzenetëd oly szivesen fogadom,
Árva szivem, babám, másnak ajánlom.

Dombon van a házam, dombon lakom én,
Piciny a galambom, piciny vagyok én.
Ha piciny is, lehajlok én utána,
Megcsókolom menyasszonyi ruhába.

227
Poor am I, poor was I born,
And my sweetheart I loved truly.
But envious ones stole her from me,
And I remain lonely at heart.

228
The hay is ready, ready on the meadow,
I spoke not with my sweetheart for a week.
He has a kerchief of mine in his pocket:
When he pulls it out, I shall be in his mind.

229
Little brown horse, you don't enjoy your oats,
You fancy the hostess's barley:
For oats are not the same thing as barley,
And the Hungarians want not a faithful maid.

230
The Varga gate has no bolts.
The famous Garzó Pista often comes to it,
To the post he ties his horse,
While he chats with Julcsa.

231
Green is the barley, green the wheat, green
    the maize stems,
Alas, how proud, how haughty are the maids
    of Dejtar.
Their pinafores are embroidered all round,
But not once do they look at the boys of the
    next village.

232
Once in my life I was at your house,
And then your house was all in mist.
My brass spurs stirred up the mist.
My darling, why did you deceive me?

233
Yellow water melons, ready to burst.—
If you don't love me, darling, say so now.
And this your news I'll store within my heart,
My lonely heart, my darling, I'll offer to
    another.

234 a
My house is on a hill, on a hill I live.
Tiny is my sweetheart, tiny am I too.
I don't mind her smallness: I stoop down to
    her,
And I kiss her as she stands in her bridal
    robes.

Gyócsból van az ingöm, gyócsból a gagyám,
Tizenhárom este varrta a babám.
Egyik szára rövid vót,
    a másik meg hosszú vót.
Ejnye te babám! Nem jól szabtad a gagyám.

Of linen is my shirt, of linen my drawers;
Thirteen evenings my love spent sewing
    them.
One leg is a bit long,
    And the other is a bit short:
Now then, my love, you have not cut my
    drawers well.

235

Ez a bor nëm drága:
Hat krajcár az ára.
Ergye rózsám, hozz ëgy messzőt,
    had danoljak még ëgy versöt,
Azután elmegyünk.

The wine is not dear:
Seven kreutzers is its price.
Go, my love, bring a pint,
    Then I'll sing a little song,
And after that we'll go.

236

Dömötör felé jár az idő,
A gulásnak számolni kő:
Van néki két üszője,
    azon két csöngetője,
Aztat hajtja aláfelé.

Saint Dimitri's day is nearing,
When the cowherd's accounts are settled.
He has two young heifers,
    They wear two bells,
He drives them down the valley.

237 (var. 208)

Lassan, lassan kis lány a pallásszobán,
Nem leszek én többet nyoszolóleány.
Ha leszek, leszek,
    menyasszony leszek,
Vőlegényem mellett szemérmes leszek.

Slowly, slowly, little maid in the garret,
Never again shall I be a bridesmaid,
    But I'll be, I'll be,
    I'll be a bride,
And by the bridegroom's side be coy!

238

1. Feleségem olyan tiszta,
    Egyszer mosdik egy hónapba.
Refr. { Sej, dinom-dánom,
           míg élek is bánom,
        Hogy megházasodtam.

2. A fejibe olyan tetyű,
    Mint egy közönséges kesztyű.

3. Kenyeret is jól tud sütni:
    Ötször-hatszor befűt neki.

1. My wife is so clean
    That only once a month she washes,
Burden { Hey, let's be merry,
          All my life I'll worry
        because I got married!

2. On her head are lice as big
    As a glove which any one could wear.

3. Well indeed she knows how to bake bread:
    Five times, six times lights the fire.

239

1. — Hol jártál Ruzsicskám ilyen korán,
Hogy ilyen harmatos a rokolyád?
    — Zöld erdőben jártam,
        zöld füvet arattam,
    Édes rózsám.

'Where did you go, my Rosy, so early,
That your frock is so wet with dew?'
    'In the green forest I went,
        The green grass I gathered in,
    O my well-beloved.'

2.[1] Jászburi ruzsicska ü szi bujár
O szi szi szicsmiska zaresztellá
Zare sztem dávicsko
    mula szto mámicsko
Dusa mojá.

240

Ne hagyj el angyalom, megöregszem,
Lábaim nem birnak, megbetegszem.
Támadékom te legyél,
    nálam nélkül ne legyél,
Panaszimnak higyjél.

Forsake me not, my angel: I am growing old,
My legs no longer carry me, I am ailing.
Be my support,
Go not away from me,
Do not mistrust my complaints.

241

— Hová mégy te szőke kis lány?—Az erdőbe
Száraz ágér, sütni, főzni menyegzőbe.
— Száraz ág ellobban,
    a szerelem jobban,
Eszemadta.

'Where go you, fair-haired maiden?' 'To the
    forest,
For firewood, to boil and bake for the wed-
    ding.'
'Firewood burns quick,
    But love even quicker,
    O my beloved.'

242

1. Ma van husvét napja,
    másodéccakája,
  Jól tudjátok,
  Kinek első napján,
    Jézus feltámadván
  Dicsőségbe.

2. Márija, Zsuzsánna,
    Rebeka, Borbála,
  Kegyes szűzek,
  Keljetek fel ágyból,
    cifra nyoszolyából,
  Mit alusztok?

3. Hímes tojás lészen
    tizenkét pár készen
  Mi számunkra,
  Ha az úgy nem lészen,
    vizi puskám készen,
  Rátok lövök.

1. To-day is Easter Day,
  The second night of Easter,
  Know it well!
  And on the first day of Easter
  Jesus arose from the dead,
  In His glory.

2. Maria, Susanna,
  Rebecca, Barbara,
  Pious maidens,
  Arise from your beds,
  Your ornamented beds.
  Why are you asleep?

3. Of painted eggs there are
  Two dozen all ready
  For us.
  If it be not the case,
  My water-squirt is ready,
  I'll besprinkle you.

---

[1] This verse is an almost unrecognizable perversion of the following well-known Slovakian text:

— Anička, dušička, kde si bola?
Kde si si čižmičky zarosila?
— Bola som v hájičku,
    žala som trávičku,
Duša moja!

And the first verse of No 239 is an almost verbatim translation of the Slovakian lines.

4. Ha reátok lövök,
       ha reátok lövök,
   Mind össz' áztok,
   Híres Látrijába (?)
       volt régen szokásba
   Ifijak közt.

5. Ződ plánták ujulnak,
       termőfák virulnak,
   Virágoznak,
   Még a madarak is
       hangicsálnak ők is,
   Vigadoznak.

6. Adjon isten jókat,
       koronázzon sokat
   Az egekbe,
   Végre az egekbe
       vigye fel menyekbe
   Dicsőségbe.

Zörög a kocsi,
    pattogtat Jancsi,
Talán értem jönnek.
Jaj, édes anyám,
    szerelmes dajkám,
De hamar elvisznek.

Szőlőhegyën körösztül
    megy a kis lány öccsöstül,
Dunárul fuj a szél;
Ha Dunárul fuj a szél,
    szegény embërt mindig ér,
Dunárul fuj a szél.

Héj, héj, mit tegyek,
    Pozsony alá hogy menjek,
Ott egyedül éjjek?
A szeretőm elhagyott,
    a szivibül kizárott
Egy kis bolondságért.

1. — Keresd meg a tűt,
   Én meg a gyűszűt,
   Had' vargyam meg a babámnak
   A pergál üngit.

2. — Meg is varrtam már,
   Rá is adtam már,
   Barna piros két orcáját
   Megcsolkultam már.

4. And if I besprinkle you,
   If I besprinkle you,
   You'll all be drenched,
   As in Latrija (?) the famous
   The custom was in olden times,
   Among young people.

5. The green plants bring forth new leaves,
   The fruit-trees are in bloom,
   Covered with blossoms,
   And the little birds
   Twitter and sing
   In glee.

6. God grant His blessings,
   And crown many
   In heaven.
   Finally, in heaven,
   Raise them
   To glory.

243

The cart rattles,
Jancsi cracks his whip,
Perhaps they come for me!
Alas, dear mother,
Beloved one who nursed me,
Soon they'll carry me away.

244

Along the sloping vineyards
Goes a little maid with her brother,
From the Danube the wind blows.
And when from the Danube the wind blows
It always catches the poor folk.
From the Danube the wind blows.

245

Hey, hey, what shall I do,
So that I go down to Pozsony,
There to be lonesome?
My beloved has left me,
Driven me out of her heart
On account of a single mad prank.

246

1. You'll seek the needle
   And I the thimble,
   Let me sew for my beloved
   A cotton shirt.

2. Now I've sewn it,
   And given it him,
   And both his brown cheeks
   I've kissed.

166

Én víg nëm vagyok,
Szomorú vagyok,
Apri kácse måle dutye,
Ó jaj ne bugyre.

I am not cheerful,
I am distressed.

1. Az én ludaimak
   Tizënketten voltak,
2. Mind a tizënketten
   Szép fehérek voltak.
3. Elhajtotta a sas
   Nádnak sürejébe.
   — — — — — — — —

1. My geese
   Were twelve,
2. All twelve
   Were beautifully white.
3. The eagle drove them
   Into a thicket of rushes.
   — — — — — — — —

1. Este van már, nyóc óra,
   Ég a világ a bótba,
2. Ott mérik a pántlikát,
   Tüdőszínű pántlikát.
3. Jakuts Pista méreti,
   Az asztalra leteszi.
4. Biró Róza felveszi,
   A hajába biggyeszti.
5. Biggyeszd Róza, nem bánom,
   Ugyis te vagy a párom.

1. It is evening, eight o'clock,
   Light burns in the shop.
2. There they measure ribbons,
   Liver-coloured ribbons.
3. Jakuts Pista measures them,
   On the table puts them down.
4. Biró Róza takes them up,
   In her hair puts them, carelessly.
5. Do it, Róza, I don't worry,
   For indeed we are betrothed.

1. Kalamajkó annak neve,
   Ugrándozik, mint a fene,
   Hányja-veti lábait,
   Nem sajnálja inait.
2. Csörög ott a rézsarkantyú,
   Járja, járja barna fattyú,
   Járja, járja még az is,
   Még a terhes asszony is.

1. Kalamajkó is its name,
   Jumps about like the devil,
   Up, and swings its feet,
   Spares not its sinews.
2. There the brass spurs clink,
   Stamping go the dark-haired bastards,
   Stamping, stamping go,
   Even the pregnant women.

1. Hármat tojott a fekete kánya; —
   Engëm szeret a kend barna lánya.
Refr. { Kikityenbe, Kukutyonba,
       { Gyere rózsám a kocsimba.
2. Nem ülök én a kend kocsijába,
   Nem köll nékem a kend barna lánya.

1. The black kite has laid three eggs,
   Your dark-haired daughter loves me.
Burden { To Kikityen, to Kukutyon,
        { Come, my love, into my cart.
2. I shan't sit in your cart,
   And I don't want your dark-haired
        daughter.

¹ The last two lines are meaningless.

1. — Adj el anyám, adj el, mer itt hallak!
— Në hagyj itten lányom, férhöz adlak!
— Tyuh, |: had' halljam, hogy kinek ád
   kend. : |

2. |: — Odajadlak, lányom, egy bérësnek.: |
— Tyuh, nem köll nékëm az a tahó,[1]
Az a sok csizma-szaggató!

3. |: — Odajadlak, lányom, egy kanásznak. :|
— Tyuh, nem köll nékëm az a kanász,
Az a fényes, tükrös baltás!

4. |: — Odajadlak, lányom, egy gulyásnak. : |
— Tyuh, nem köll nékëm az a gulyás,
Az a szennyes ingös-gatyás!

5. |: — Odajadlak, lányom, egy kis csősz-
   nek. : |
— Tyuh, nem köll nékëm dülőmászó,
Az a sok ember-gyalázó!

6. |: — Odajadlak, lányom, egy drótosnak. : |
— Tyuh, nem köll nékëm az a drótos,
Mer a haja igen kócos!

7. |: — Odajadlak, lányom, egy zsidónak. : |
— Tyuh, nem köll nékëm az a zsidó,
Mer az uccán végig sipô!

8. |: — Odajadlak, lányom, egy juhásznak. : |
— Tyuh! az köll nékëm, baromőrző,
Az a szép asszonynevellő!

1. 'Give me away, mother, give me away.'
'Don't go away, daughter, I'll find you a
   husband!'
'Well, |: let 's hear to whom you'll give
   me.' : |

2. |: 'I'll give you, daughter, to a farm-
   hand.' : |
'Oh, I've no use for a lout,
A wearer and tearer of top-boots.'

3. |: 'I'll give you, daughter, to a swine-
   herd.' : |
'Oh, I've no use for a swineherd,
With his sharp, shining knife.'

4. |: 'I'll give you, daughter, to a cowherd.': |
'Oh, I've no use for a cowherd,
With his dirty shirt and breeches.'

5. |: 'I'll give you, daughter, to a field-
   guard.' : |
'Oh, I've no use for a clodhopper,
He'll always make a nuisance of himself.'

6. |: 'I'll give you, daughter, to a wire-
   binder.' : | (tier)
'Oh, I've no use for the wire-binder,
With his hair all bristly.'

7. |: 'I'll give you, daughter, to a Jew.' : |
'Oh, I've no use for a Jew,
Who'll always be whistling along the road.'

8. |: 'I'll give you, daughter, to a shepherd.':|
'Ah, he'll suit me, he who watches his flock
Will be a good educator for his wife.'

— Hogy a csibe, hogy?
Hát az ára hogy?
— Mit kérdezi, mi az ára,
Belévágom a markába!

' How much the chicken, how much?
Now then, what is their price?'
'Why do you ask what the price is?
I'll throw it into your hand.'

1. Csëpëreg az esső,
Nem akar megállni —
Ez a barna kislány, ihaja,
Hozzám akar jönni, valaha.

2. Téged, barna kis lány,
Addig el nem veszlek,
Míg az oltár előtt, ihaja,
Essze nem esküdnek, valaha.

1. Rain is falling,
It will not stop.
This dark-haired maiden, hahaha,
Wishes to marry me, some time or other.

2. You, dark-haired maiden,
I shall not take, so long
As in front of the altar, hahaha,
We are not betrothed, some time or other.

[1] = buta, bárgyú.

168

255

Haj, haj, haj, letörött a galy,
Haj, haj, haj, letörött az ág;
Fölmentem a fára az almáért,
Nem adnám az anyját a lányáért.

Hie, hie, hie, broken is the branch,
Hie, hie, hie, broken is the limb.
I'll climb the tree for apples,
I wouldn't give the mother for the daughter.

256 (var. 259 e)

(a) 1. Virág Erzsi az ágyát
Magosra vetette,
Váczi Gábor kalapját,
Rajta felejtette.

2. — Hozd ki Erzsi kalapom,
Had' tegyem fejembe,
Hogy ne nézzen minden lány
Ragyogó szemembe.

3. Ki is hozta kalapját,
Fejébe is tette,
Nem is nézett minden lány
Ragyogó szemébe.

(b) 1. Láttál-e mán valaha
Csipkebokor-rózsát?
Csipkebokor-rózsa közt
Két szál majorannát?

2. Egyik szál majoránna
Varga Julcsa lenne,
Másik szál majoránna
Kara István lenne.

(a) 1. Virág Erzsi her bed
Has made very high,
Váczi Gábor his hat
Has forgotten on it.

2. 'Bring, Erzsi, my hat,
So that I put it on my head,
Lest every maiden look
Into my shining eyes.'

3. And she brings the hat,
He puts it on his head,
So that no maiden can look
Into his shining eyes.

(b) 1. Have you ever seen
Wild roses,
And among wild roses
Two stalks of marjoram?

2. One stalk of marjoram
Would be Varga Julcsa,
The other stalk of marjoram
Would be Kara István.

257

1. Hogy veti el a paraszt
Lassankint a zabot?
Igy veti el a paraszt[1]
Lassankint a zabot.

2. Hogy vágja le a paraszt
Lassankint a zabot?
Igy vágja le a paraszt
Lassankint a zabot.

3. Hogy nyomtatja el a paraszt
Lassankint a zabot?
Igy nyomtatja el a paraszt
Lassankint a zabot.

4. Hogy issza meg a paraszt
Lassankint az árát?
Igy issza meg a paraszt
Lassankint az árát.

1. How does the peasant sow
Gently the oats?
Thus does the peasant sow[1]
Gently the oats.

2. How does the peasant mow
Gently the oats?
Thus does the peasant mow
Gently the oats.

3. How does the peasant thresh
Gently the oats?
Thus does the peasant thresh
Gently the oats.

4. How does the peasant drink
Gently the price of them?
Thus does the peasant drink
Gently the price of them.

[1] At each verse suitable gestures illustrate the action.

1. Beteg az én rózsám szegény,
   Talán meg is hal,
   Ha meg nem hal, kínokat lát,
   Az is nékem baj.

2. A te súlyos nyavalyádból
   Adjál nékem is,
   Hadd érezzük mind a ketten,
   Érezzem én is.

1. Ill is my poor sweetheart,
   Near her death perhaps;
   And if not, to see her suffer
   Distresses me so.

2. Of your crushing illness
   Give a share to me,
   So that we feel it together,
   And I feel it too.

259 a

Ëgy icce bor, két icce bor,
Mëginnám kedvemre,
Hogy ha látnám, hogy a babám
Leülne melléje.

One half-bottle of wine, two half-bottles,
I'd drink with joy,
If I could see that my sweetheart
Was sitting by my side.

259 b

1. Szépen szól a kis pacsirta
   Fönn a magasba,
   El köll mennem katonának,
   Lányok siratnak.

2. Nyiregyházán nyirik le a
   Göndör hajamat,
   Csernovicban nyergelik a
   Kis pej lovamat.

3. Nem jól nyergelte fel az a
   Huncut cseh gyerek:
   Lovam hátán fére-fére-
   Fordul a nyereg.

1. Beautifully sings the little lark
   High up above,
   And I must become a soldier,
   The girls weep for me!

2. In Nyiregyháza they'll cut
   My curly hair,
   In Csernovic they'll saddle
   My little brown horse.

3. Badly he's saddled
   By the rascally young Czech,
   On my horse's back right and left
   The saddle wobbles.

259 c

1. Varga Zsuzsa bű szoknyája
   Mëgakadt a kapufába.

2. Nëm a kapufa fogta meg,
   Kara István markolta meg.

3. — Ereszd István a ruhámat,
   Ne szomorítsd az anyámat.

1. Varga Zsuzsa's wide frock
   Remained hanging on the door-post.

2. But the door-post held it not,
   Kara István got hold of it.

3. 'Let go my dress, István,
   Do not distress my mother.'

259 d

1. A csikósok, a gulyások
   Kis lajbliban járnak; —
   Azok iélik világukat,
   Kik párostul járnak.

2. Hát én szegény szógalegény
   Csak magam egyedül
   Hogy iélek meg, ha nem lopok,
   Fehér huszas nélkül!

1. Horse-drivers and cowherds
   Go about in short jackets;—
   Only those live happy
   Who have found their mate.

2. And I, poor hireling,
   I am all alone,
   Could I live if I didn't steal,
   Be without beautiful silver coins!

1. Zúg az erdő, zúg a mező,
   Nem tom, mi zúgása?
   Talán bizony Fábján Pista
   Az lovát ugratja?

2. Víg az lova, víg ő maga,
   Víg a paripája,
   Vígan várja az babája
   Megvetett ágyára.

3. Selem Kati hat párnáját
   Magasra vetette,
   Fábján Pista kis kalapját
   Rajta felejtette.

4. — Hozd ki Kati, kis kalapom,
   Tegyed a fejemre,
   Hogy ne nézzen kutya pandúr
   Kacsingós szemembe.

1. — Édes kedves feleségem!
   — Mi baj, angyalom?
   — Mit keres itt a nyerges ló
   Az udvaromon?

2. Néz az asszony jobbra-balra:
   — Hol van itt a nyerges ló?
   A tehenet kötötte meg
   Borcsa szolgálló.

3. — Tehén hátán sárga nyerget
   Aj, ki látott már,
   Mióta a nagy magas ég
   És a nagy világ.

4. — Édes kedves feleségem!
   — Mi baj, angyalom?
   — Mit keres itt a kék dolmány
   Az én ágyamon?

5. Néz az asszony jobbra-balra:
   — Hol van itt a kék dolmány?
   Ágyteritőm penészedett,
   Aztat tettem rá.

6. — Ágyteritőn sárga gombot
   Aj, ki látott már,
   Mióta a nagy magas ég
   És a nagy világ.

7. — Édes kedves feleségem!
   — Mi baj, angyalom?
   — Mit keres itt a pár csizma
   A fogasomon?

1. The forest rustles, the fields rustle,
   I know not why they rustle.
   It is perhaps Fábján Pista
   Training his horse to jump.

2. Joyous is the horse, joyous is he himself,
   Aye, joyous is his steed.
   Joyfully his love awaits him,
   On her prepared bed.

3. Selem Kati's six cushions
   Piled up high,
   Fábján Pista's little hat
   Is resting forgotten thereon.

4. 'Bring, Kati, my little hat:
   I'll put it on my head
   So that the dog of a Pandur may not see
   My winking eyes.'

1. 'Dear beloved wife mine!'
   'What's the trouble, my love?'
   'Why this horse all saddled
   In my courtyard?'

2. The wife stares right and left:
   'Where is there a saddled horse?
   The cow was tied there
   By Borcsa, our maid.'

3. 'A cow bearing a yellow saddle?
   Woe, who ever saw one,
   So long as the heaven above
   And the wide world have existed?'

4. 'Dear beloved wife mine!'
   'What's the trouble, my love?'
   'Why this blue dolman
   Upon my bed?'

5. The wife stares right and left:
   'Where is there a blue dolman?
   My bedspread had become mildewed,
   So I spread it out.'

6. 'A bedspread with yellow buttons:
   Woe, who ever saw one,
   So long as the heaven above
   And the wide world have existed?'

7. 'Dear beloved wife mine!'
   'What's the trouble, my love?'
   'Why this pair of top-boots
   On my clothes-rack?'

8. Néz az asszony jobbra-balra:
   — Hol van itt a pár csizma?
   A szolgáló köcsögök hejt
   Azt rakott oda.

9. — Köcsögökön rézsarkantyút
   Aj, ki látott már,
   Mióta a csillagos ég
   És a nagy világ.

10. — Édes kedves feleségem!
    — Mi baj angyalom?
    — Mit keres itt a katona
    Az én ágyamon?

11. Néz az asszony jobbra-balra:
    — Hol van itt a katona?
    A szolgálóm hideg lelte,
    Az feküdt oda.

12. — Szolgálónak pörge bajszát
    Aj, ki látott már,
    Mióta a csillagos ég
    És a nagy világ.

13. — Édes kedves feleségem!
    — Mi baj, angyalom?
    — Még az éjjel bált csinálok,
    Hogyha akarom.

14. Néz az asszony jobbra-balra:
    — Milyen lesz itt az a bál?
    — Ajtó megett ázott kötél
    És egy nagy bot áll.

8. The wife stares right and left:
   'Where is there a pair of top-boots?
   The maid has put a couple of milk-jugs
   Right over there.'

9. 'Milk-jugs with brass spurs?
   Woe, who ever saw one,
   So long as the starry sky
   And the wide world have existed?'

10. 'Dear beloved wife mine!'
    'What's the trouble, my love?'
    'Why is there a soldier
    In my bed?'

11. The wife stares right and left:
    'Where is there a soldier?
    The maid has caught a chill
    And there she lies.'

12. 'A maid with a waxed moustache?
    Woe, who ever saw one,
    So long as the starry sky
    And the wide world have existed?'

13. 'Dear beloved wife mine!'
    'What's the trouble, my love?'
    'I'll give a ball here to-night,
    I will indeed.'

14. The wife stares right and left:
    'What kind of a ball will it be?'
    'Behind the door there are a wet rope
    And a big stout cudgel.'

260 b

1. A tamási faluvégen,
   Zsíros bunda lóg a szegen.

2. Zsíros bunda lobba esett,
   Springer Kati terbe [1] esett.

3. Springer Kati mén a kútra,
   Mentiben bement a bótba.

4. Jónapot mond a zsidónak:
   Van-e nála babadunna?

5. — Minek magának a dunna?
   Nincsen még magának ura.

6. — Ha nincs uram, van már kontyom,
   Van is a dunnára gondom.

1. At the end of the village of Tamási
   A greasy fur hangs on a peg.

2. The greasy fur caught fire,
   Springer Kati was with child.

3. Springer Kati went to the well,
   On her way entered the shop.

4. Bade good-day to the Jew,
   Asked whether he had swaddling-clothes.

5. 'What need have you of swaddling-
   clothes?
   You have no husband.'

6. 'I have no husband, but I've put my hair
   up:
   It's time for me to think of swaddling-
   clothes.'

[1] = teherbe.

172

Dunaparton van egy malom,
Bubánatot őlnek azon, ejeha!
Nékem is van bubánatom,
Odaviszem, lejáratom, ejeha.

Nem láttam én molnárcsókot,
De maj látok most!
Héj, huj, Pindes Lenor,
 héj, huj, Fodor József,
Majd kitetszik most.

1. Elmënt uram a Putnára,
 Hazajő hónaputánra.

2. Ha hazajő, hazavárom,
 Az ágy alá jól bévágom.

3. Főzök neki jó vacsorát,
 Köménymagos istennyilát.

1. Elveszett a tarka tyúkom,
 Agyoncsapta a szomszédom.
 Refr. { Tojj, tojj, tojj tojjál már,
    { Tojjál idehaza már.

2. Gyere haza, tarka pizse,
 Íg a számodra a zsizse.

3. Én kazalom alját vásod,
 Másnak adod a tojásod.

(a) 1. Virágéknál ég a világ,
  Sütik már a rántott békát.

2. Váczi Gábor odakapott,
 Békacombot ropogtatott.

3. Puskás Gábor későn jutott,
 Neki csak a fara jutott.

(b) 1. Varga Borcsa kapujába
  Fölforrott a tej magába.

2. Azér forrott föl magába,
 Bátor Mihályt odavárja.

3. Bátor Mihály arany gólya,
 Rászállott az aranytóra.

4. Összeszedte a békákot,
 Ropogtatta, mint a mákot.

261

By the Danube there 's a mill
That grinds worries to shreds, hey ha!
I have many worries,
I'll take them there and have them ground,
 hey ha!

262

I never saw a miller engaged in kissing,
But I'm going to see one now!
Hullo, Pindes Lenor,
 Hullo, Fodor József,
Soon it'll all come to light.

263

1. My husband has gone up Putná,
 He'll be back the day after to-morrow.

2. When he comes back I'll be waiting,
 And under the bed I'll drive him.

3. And I'll cook him a good supper
 —Well flavoured with caraway seed, I
  swear it.

264

1. Lost is my speckled hen,
 My neighbour has done him to death.
 Burden { Lay, lay, lay an egg,
    { Lay an egg right here.

2. Come home, speckled, blunt-beaked one,
 Kindling-wood is burning for you.

3. You go scratching round my rick,
 But give your eggs to others.

265

(a) 1. At the Virág's burns a light,
  They are preparing to bake frogs.

2. Váczi Gábor gets them,
 Cracks the frogs' legs.

3. Puskás Gábor comes too late,
 And only the back parts remain for him.

(b) 1. At Varga Borcsa's door
  The milk is on the boil.

2. And for this reason it is on the boil:
 It awaits Bátor Mihály.

3. Bátor Mihály is a golden stork,
 Flies away to a golden pool,

4. Gets hold of all the frogs,
 Cracks them as if they were poppy-
  seeds.

5. Hazavitte, kiokádta
   Varga Borcsa tányérjára.
6. Varga Borcsa mosogatott,
   Békacombot szopogatott.

5. Brings them home, disgorges them
   In Varga Borcsa's plate.
6. Varga Borcsa does the washing-up,
   Sucking the frogs' legs the while.

266

Erre, arra, a boronya iélén
Kinyíllott a tulipán a kalapom sziélén.
Egy-két szál, három szál,
Álnok voltál babám, mëgcsaltál.

Right along the harrow's ridge,
A tulip on my hat opened its petals.
One and two stalks, three stalks,
Love, you were untrue, you deceived me.

267

Ettem szőllőt, most érik, most érik, most
   érik, —
Virág Erzsit most kérik, most kérik, most
   kérik.
Kihö' ment a levele?
   Garzó Pista kezébe,
Hej, rica, rica, rica, hej Pista te!

I was eating grapes, just ripe, ripe, ripe,
Virág Erzsi has just been wooed, wooed,
   wooed.
To whom then goes her letter?
   Into Garzó Pista's hands.
Hey! Rica, rica, rica, hey you Pista!

268

A zsidónak nincs Krisztusa,
   nincs is annak mennyben jussa,
Van néki egy rossz papucsa,
   avval csoszog a pokolba.
Icca igyunk rája, ugy is eljön a sír szája,
Ott lesz fáradt testünk csendes hazája, ha, ha.

The Jew has no Christ,
   No right to Heaven,
He has shabby slippers,
   With which he slouches down to Hell.
So let's drink on it, until we reach the gaping
   grave,
There our weary body will find a quiet home,
   ha, ha!

269

Ugy ég a tűz, ha lobog, —
Ugy élek én, ha lopok.
Se nem lopok, cserélek,
   mégis igazán élek,
Ihaj, csuhaj, mégis igazán élek.

So long as the fire is alight, it blazes.
So long as I am alive, I steal.
I don't steal, I barter,
   And indeed, indeed I live,
Heyaho, and indeed I live.

270

1. Jönnek, jönnek, majd elvisznek,
   Hol a pártám, hogy készüljek?
   Ökörszekér a kapuba,
      a vőlegény az ajtóba,
   A menyasszony az ablakba.

2. Nyisd ki ajtód, kit bézártál,
   Most jön, akit régen vártál,
   Régen vártál, óhajtottál,
      régen vártál, óhajtottál,
   Szívedbe is béfogadtál.

1. They come, they come, soon they'll lead
      me away.
   Where 's my wreath, that I make ready?
   The cart with the oxen is at the gate,
      The bridegroom is at the door,
   The bride stands at the window.

2. Open the door, which you closed.
   Now he comes, whom you awaited long,
   Awaited long, and longed for,
      Awaited long, and longed for,
   Enclosing him within your heart.

174

3. — Édes anyám, gyújcs gyertyára,
Hozzád jövök vacsorára.
Forralj nekem édes tejet,
    forralj nekem édes tejet,
Morzsálj belé lágy kenyeret.

4. Forralj nekem édes tejet,
Morzsálj belé lágy kenyeret,
Had egyem egy víg vacsorát,
    had egyem egy víg vacsorát,
Amit édes anyám csinált.

Ugy elmegyek, meglássátok,
Soha hírem sem halljátok ;
Se híremet, se nevemet,
    felejtsetek el engemet,
Felejtsetek el engemet.

Esik eső karikára,
Barna legény kalapjára.
Tilos a szerelem,
    a babám ölelem,
Mer én igazán szeretem.

Harmatos a kukorica levele; —
Utóljára, jártam hozzád az este.
Utóljára, ej huj haj,
    fogtam ajtód húzóját,
Kis angyalom, kivánok jó éjcakát.

De sok eső, de sok sár,
    de sok legény mëgcsalt már,
Tra da da da da da da :
Ha még egyszer ugy mëgcsal,
    s mëgátkozom, hogy mëghal,
Tra da da da da da da da tra da da.

1. Elszaladt a lovam
Cidrusfaerdőbe,
Jelszakadt a nyalka csizsmám
A lókeresésbe.

2. Në keresd a lovad,

Mer be vagyon fogva:

Félegyházi szőlők alatt
Szól a harang rajta.

3. 'Mother dear, light the candles,
Now I come to supper:
Heat sweet milk for me,
    Heat sweet milk for me,
And crumble in it soft bread.

4. 'Heat sweet milk for me,
Crumble in it soft bread,
That I may eat joyously one supper,
    That I may eat joyously one supper
Which my dear mother has prepared.'

271
Wherever I go, you'll see,
Never shall you hear tidings of me,
Neither tidings nor my name,
    So forget me,
Forget me.

272
Rain is falling all around,
On the dusky fellow's hat.
Forbidden is love,
    I embrace my sweetheart,
Because I love her truly.

273
Dewy are the maize leaves; —
A last time I went to thee at eventide,
A last time, ah, lackaday!
    I grasped the door-handle:
My darling, I wish thee good night.

274
How much rain, how much mud,
    How many boys deceived me,
Tra da da da da da da,
If another one deceives me,
    I'll curse him so that he dies,
Tra da da da da da da.

275 a (var. 276 a)
1. My horse has run away
To the cedar wood,
I've torn my beautiful top-boots
In my quest for my horse.

2. Seek not your horse,
He 's already caught:
By the vineyards at Félegyháza
Tinkle the bells he wears.

175

1. A temetőkapu
   Mind a kettő nyitva,
   Bárcsak engem oda temetnének,
   Sej, abba a fekete földbe!

2. A sírom tetején
   Piros rózsa nyílik,
   A baracsi piros barna lányok
   Sej, rulam szedik a virágot.

3. Szedjétek, szedjétek,
   Rulam a virágot,
   Csak azt az egy fehér liliomot,
   Sej, rulam le ne szakítsátok.

1. The churchyard doors
   Both stand open,
   If only they had buried me there,
   Hey! deep in the black earth!

2. At the head of my grave
   A red rose is blooming,
   And the peach-coloured, dark-haired
       maidens of Baracs,
   Hey, are plucking its blossoms.

3. Pluck them, pluck them,
   The blossoms on the tomb,
   But only the one white lily,
   Hey, you must not take away.

276 a (var. 275 a)

1. Elvesztettem lovam
   Cidrusfaerdőben,
   Elnyűttem már hat pár csizmát
   A nagy keresésben.

2. Megvan már a lovam,
   Be is van már fogva,
   A kertmegi istállóba
   Szól a csengő rajta.

3. Megismerem lovam
   Csengő szólásárul,
   Megismerem a babámat
   Pörge bajuszárul.

1. I have lost my horse
   In the cedar wood,
   I've worn out six pairs of top-boots
   In my long quest.

2. Here is my horse,
   He has been caught.
   In the stable at Kertmeg
   Tinkle the bells he wears.

3. I know my horse
   By the sound of the bells,
   And I know my love
   By his pointed moustache.

276 b

Körözsfői ucca
Végig tiszta buza,
Arra jár el a galambom,
Majd learatgatja.

By Körözsfő, all along
Nothing but corn, pure corn,
There went my beloved
For to harvest it.

277

1. Mikor Rózsa Sándor
   Felül a lovára,
   Lobog rajta gyócsgatyája,
   Ej, haj, uszik a Dunába.

2. Fujd el szellő, fujd el
   A Dunának habját,
   Hogy ne találja föl senki,
   Ej, haj, Rózsa Sándor nyomát.

1. When Rózsa Sándor
   Is on his horse,
   His linen breeches go flapping,
   Hey, hie, he swims the Danube.

2. Blow, you breeze, blow away
   The foam on the Danube,
   So that nobody may find,
   Hey, hie, Rózsa Sándor's track.

1. Hosszúfarkú fecske, —
   Szép barna menyecske,
   Hogy tudtál eljutni erre,
   Ez idegen földre?

2. — Nem jöttem én gyalog,
   Kis pej lovam hozott;

   Kis pej lovam négy lábárul

   A patkó lehullott.

3. Csak egy maradt rajta;

   Az is ugy lóg rajta;

   Kovács, gyere, jó pajtásom,

   Igazítsd meg rajta.

4. — Meg is igazítom,
   Meg is kopogtatom,
   Még az éjjel a babámat

   Körülcsókolgatom.

278 (var. 36)

1. Long-tailed swallow,—
   Beautiful dark young woman,
   How did you manage to reach this spot,
   This foreign region?

2. 'I came not on foot,
   I used my little brown horse,
   And from my little brown horse's four feet
   The horseshoes fell off.

3. 'Yet one is still on,
   But it is very loose:
   Blacksmith, come, my good friend,
   Fix it up well.'

4. 'I'll fix it up well,
   I'll hammer it well,
   And at night my well-beloved
   I'll cover with countless kisses.'

279

Jól van dolga a mostani huszárnak,
Nëm këll szénát kaszájjon a lovának,
Mer a széna porcióba van kötve, van
   kötve, de van kötve,
Gyere rózsám, tëdd a lovam elébe.

All is well with the hussar to-day,
He need not cut the hay for his horse,
For the hay in rations is tied, is tied, is
   tied.
Come, love, put it in front of my horse.

280

1. Pej paripám rézpatkója de fényës,
   Madarasi csárdás lánya de kényës!
   Kényës cipője, kapcája,
   De sok pénzömet kóstálja, hiába.

2. Pej paripám hányja fejét kényëssen, —
   Vártalak, rózsám, az este szivëssen.
   Ugyan rózsám hová lettél?
   Már két estve el nem jöttél én hozzám.

1. My brown horse's copper shoes are
      shining,
   The wench at the Madaras inn is dainty,
   Dainty her footwear, her stockings,
   How much of my money it has cost, all in
      vain!

2. My brown horse tosses his head daintily,—
   I awaited you, my love, at night so eagerly.
   And where, my love, were you?
   For two evenings you came not to me.

281

1. |: Kihajtottam én ludamat :|
   |: A zöld pázsitdombra. :|

1. |: I drove out my goose :|
   |: On to the grassy green hill. :|

177   N

2. |: Arra jött a biró fia :|
|: Arany bozogánnyal, :|

3. |: Agyonsujtá én ludamat, :|
Gondos gunaramat,
Legszebbik ludamat.

4. |: Elmegyek én a biróhoz, :|
|: Panaszt teszek néki. :|

5. — Isten jónap, biró gazda!
— Fogadj isten, Gyöngy Ilona!
|: Üljön le minálunk. :|

6. |: — Sem ülhetek, sem állhatok, :|
|: Mert nagy panaszom van. :|

7. |: — Mondja meg hát, Gyöngy Ilona, :|
|: Mi légyen a panasz? :|

8 = 1, 9 = 2, 10 = 3.

11. |: — Mondja meg hát, Gyöngy Ilona, :|
|: Mi legyen az ára? :|

12. |: — Minden tolla, szőre szála, :|
|: Egy arany az ára. :|

2. |: There came the mayor's son :|
|: With the golden mace. :|

3. |: He struck dead my goose, :|
My good gander,
My most beautiful goose.

4. |: I'll go to the mayor, :|
|: Complain to him. :|

5. 'God's blessing, Mayor, good host.'
'God bless you, Gyöngy Ilona!
|: Sit down with us.' :|

6. |: 'I shall not sit, I shall not stand, :|
|: I have a big grievance.' :|

7. |: 'Speak, then, Gyöngy Ilona, :|
|: What is the grievance?' :|

8 = 1, 9 = 2, 10 = 3.

11. |: 'And tell me, Gyöngy Ilona, :|
|: What shall the price be?' :|

12. |: 'For every feather, every bit, :|
|: One gold piece is the price.' :|

282

1. Lement a vacsoracsillag,
Babám a Főszërre ballag;
Az hitetlen de régen, de régen
Nem járt el az Alszëren.

2. Hamis a zuzája, mája,
Nem is köll a pántlikája:
Kiülök én a hóra, — ra, hóra,

♩ ♩

Péntekre vërradóra.

3. Pörög az orsóm kereke,
Vékony szálat nyujtok vélle,
Jó lesz lobogós üngnek, — nek, üngnek,
Aki elvësz engemet.

1. The evening star has set,
My love at the upper end of the village
lingers.
Unfaithful one, how long, how long,
He came not to lower end of the village!

2. False are his stomach and liver,
I've no use for his ribbons.
I shall sit in the snow, in the snow,
Of a Friday at dawn.

3. My spinning-wheel turns,
I draw a slender thread.
'Twill be good for to make a flapping shirt
For him who marries me.

283

Piros kukorica szára, —
Házasodom nemsokára.
Igazán, csakugyan, nem tagadom,
A babámat soha el sem hagyom.

Red are the maize stems—
I shall soon be married.
Yes, indeed, it is so, I'm not lying:
My beloved I'll never forsake.

284

1. Sugármagas, sugármagas
A nyárfa teteje,
Halványsárga, de halványsárga
Annak a levele.

1. Tall and slender, tall and slender
The poplar tree stands,
Pale yellow, yes, pale yellow
Are its leaves.

2. Én is olyan, én is olyan
   Halványsárga vagyok,
   Volt szeretőm egy piros-barna kis lány,
   De már rég elhagyott.

3. Ha majd egykor, hűtlen babám,
   Ujra találkozunk,
   Ugy elmegyünk mi egymás melett,   (sic!)
   Még csak nem is szólunk.

4. Te mész jobbra, hűtlen babám,
   Én meg megyek balra;
   Sárba taposom a fényképedet,
   Nem veszlek el soha.

285

1. Szépen szól a kis pacsirta
   Fent a levegőbe, —
   El köll menni katonának
   Három esztendőre.

2. El köll menni katonának
   Három esztendőre,
   Itt kell hagyni a rózsámat
   A legszebb időben.

3. Terád hagyom jó pajtásom,
   Éld vele világod,
   Míg én oda három évig,
   A császárt szógálom.

286

1. Jászkunsági gyerek vagyok,
   Jászkunságon születtem,
   Kiskoromtól nagykoromig
   Benne fëlneveledtem.

2. Kilenc zsandár kísér engem,
   A prágai főuccán,
   Véletlenül betekintek
   Kis angyalom ablakán.

2. And I likewise, likewise
   Am pale and yellow.
   I had a sweetheart, a red and brown young
     maiden,
   But long ago she left me.

3. And if at any time, faithless maiden,
   Once again we meet,
   Then we'll pass by one another
   Without exchanging one word.

4. You'll go to the right, faithless maiden,
   And I shall go to the left,
   And in the dirt I'll trample your photo-
     graph,
   Never shall I take you.

285

1. Beautifully sings the little lark
   High up in the air,
   And I must become a soldier
   For three years.

2. I must become a soldier
   For three years,
   I must forsake my sweetheart
   At the loveliest time.

3. To you I leave her, good friend,
   You may rejoice with her
   While over there for three years
   I serve the emperor.

286

1. I'm a child of Jászkunság,
   I was born in Jászkunság,
   From early childhood to manhood
   There I was brought up.

2. Nine gendarmes escort me
   Through the main street of Prag,
   And by chance I catch a glimpse
   Of my sweetheart at her window.

3. Még onnan is azt kiáltja:
— Hatvannyolcas, gyere be!
Adj egy csókot, egy utolsót,
Kacsintsál a szemembe!

4. — Nem mehetek kedves babám,
Mer be vagyok sorozva,
A prágai nagy kaszárnya
Nyitva van a számomra.

1. Most jöttem én a harctérről,
El van lőve a jobb karom.

2. Nincsen orvos, sem szanitéc,
Ki bekösse a vérző sebeimet.

3. Gyere babám, te kötözd be,
Ha meggyógyul, megszolgálom.

4. Ha meggyógyul, megszolgálom,
Jövő ősszel te leszel a párom.

1. — Jánoshidi vásártéren
Legényvásár lesz a héten.

2. Én is oda fogok menni,
Szőkét, barnát választani.

3. — Szőkét ne végy, mer beteges,
Pirosat se, mer részeges.

4. Barnát vegyél, az lesz a jó,
Az lesz a csókra hajlandó.

Recsegős a csizmám, a melet te vettél,
Ezüst patkó a sarkán,
Valahányszor lépek, annyiszor recsegi:
Kedvesem, sohase szerettél.

3. And therefrom she calls:
'Recruit of the sixty-eighth, don't go:
Give one kiss, one last one,
One fond glance into my eyes.'

4. I can't do it, well-beloved,
For now I am enrolled,
The big barracks at Prag
Are open to receive me.

287

1. Now I came from the battle-field,
My left arm was shot off.

2. No doctor, no nurse
To bind up my bleeding wounds.

3. Come, my love, bind them up.
If I am cured, I shall repay you.

4. If I am cured, I shall repay you:
Next autumn I shall wed you.

288 (var. 97)

1. At the market at Jánoshid
The boy-market takes place this week.

2. And thither I shall go,
A fair one, a dark one select.

3. Don't buy a fair one, he'll be too weak;
Nor a red one, he'll be too fond of drink;

4. 'Buy a dark one, he'll be all right,
He'll be to kissing inclined.'

289

Creaky are my top-boots, which you bought
for me.
Of silver are the heel-pieces.
At every step I take, they creak:
My beloved, you never have loved me.

290

Sárga kukoricaszál
Kapálatlan, kapálatlan maradtál.
Szőke legény, barna lány,
Öleletlen, csókolatlan maradtál.

Yellow maize-stem
Uncut, uncut you remained.
Fair boy, dark girl,
Unhugged, unkissed you remained.

291

Menyek az uton lefelé,
Senki sem mondja; gyere bé! angyalom.
Mikor jöttem vissza felé,
Babám azt mondja: gyere bé! angyalom.

I go down the road,
None says: come in, my love.
When I went back,
My sweetheart said: Come in, my love.

292

Ha tudtad, hogy nem szerettél,
Az öledbe mér ültettél, tyuhajja?
Mér csókoltad meg az én szám,
Mér nem hagytál békét, rózsám, tyuhajja?

If you knew that you loved me not,
Why did you remain in my arms, heigh-ho?
Why did you kiss my lips,
Why didn't you leave me in peace, my sweet,
  heigh-ho?

293

1. Megájj, megájj, te küs madár,
   Beteg szüvem mer riég hogy vár.
   Beteg vagyok szerelmembe,
   Enyhítsd lelkem keservembe.

2. Ládd a kerek erdőt amott,
   Alatta a küs fojlomot,
   Fojlomon túl van egy falu
   Azzal, kiér emészt a bú.

3. Abban lakik a nagy uccán,
   Gólyafiészek van a házán,
   Léces küs kert ablakj' alatt
   Mos meszelték bé a falat.

4. Vidd oda a küs cédulát,
   Repdesd körül az ablakját.
   De ha kérdi, hogy hogy vagyok,
   Érte is hogy mennyit sírok:

5. Visszasiess egyszeribe,
   Ölömbe szájj le egyenest,
   Megölellek, megcsókollak,
   Hűségedért jól is tartlak.

1. Stay, stay, you little bird,
   My ailing heart has long awaited you.
   Sick I am with love,
   Comfort the sadness of my soul.

2. See over there the surrounding forest,
   And down there the little river:
   Beyond the river is a village,
   There lives she on whose account I grieve.

3. There she lives, in the main street,
   There 's a stork's nest on the roof,
   And a little garden under the windows,
   And the walls are newly painted.

4. Carry thither this little note,
   Flutter by the window,
   And if she asks how I am,
   And how much I weep on her account,

5. Hurry back at once,
   Come straight to my arms,
   I shall hug you, I shall kiss you,
   For your faithfulness well entertain you.

294

Azt akartam én megtudni,
Szabad-e másét szeretni?
Tudakoztam, de nem szabad,
Így a szivem gyászban marad.

I wished to learn whether
It was permissible to love another's sweet-
  heart.
I asked: and it is not permissible;
And so my heart remains sad.

1. Tiszáninnen, Dunántúl,
   Túl a Tiszán van egy csikós nyájastul.
   Kis pejlova ki van kötvel
   Szűrkötéllel pakróc nélkül gazdástul.

2. Tiszáninnen, Dunántúl,
   Túl a Tiszán van egy gulás nyájastúl.
   Legelteti a guláját,
   Odavárja a babáját gyepágyra.

3. Tiszáninnen, Dunántúl,
   Túl a Tiszán van egy juhász nyájastul.
   Ott főzik a jó paprikást,
   Meg is eszik kis vellável,
     fakalánnyal bográcsbul.[1]

4. Tiszáninnen, Dunántúl,
   Túl a Tiszán van egy kanász nyájastul.
   Ott sütik a jó malacot
   Cserfahéjjon, bükkfanyárson, ihajja.

Tiszáninnen, Dunántúl,
Ott sütik a kis malacot
   cserfatűzön, bikkfanyárson,
Tiszáninnen, Dunántúl, —
Gyere kedves kis angyalom az ágyhoz.

Dëszkakapu, kerítés,
Az alatt esik jó ölelés.
Ölelj babám, ölelj kedvedre,
Sohasëm vetëm a szemedre.

Megdöglött a biró lova,
Megnyúzta ja biró maga.
Jó lesz a bőre dudának,
A négy lába pikulának,
   a feje meg kocsonyának, csihajla.

1. Kónyár Verka házeleje
   Márványkővel van kirakva.

   ♪ ♩·♪♩· ♩· ♪♩ ♩

2. Az is azér van kirakva,
   Szabó Jóska jár majd oda.

1. This side of the Tisza, beyond the Danube,
   Beyond the Tisza is a young herdsman.
   His grey horse is fettered,
   Tied with a rope, without a rug, by his
     master.

2. This side of the Tisza, beyond the Danube,
   Beyond the Tisza there is a cowherd.
   He pastures his cattle,
   He awaits his sweetheart on the grass bed.

3. This side of the Tisza, beyond the Danube,
   Beyond the Tisza there is a shepherd.
   There they cook good paprika-stew,
   They eat it with little forks
   And wooden ladles out of the stew-pot.

4. This side of the Tisza, beyond the Danube,
   Beyond the Tisza there is a swineherd.
   There they bake good pork
   Over strips of oak-bark, on a spit of beech-
     wood, heigh ho!

This side of the Tiszá, beyond the Danube,
There is cooking a little sucking-pig,
On a fire of oak-wood, on a spit of beech-
   wood.
This side of the Tiszá, beyond the Danube,
Come, my beloved sweetheart, to bed.

Gate made of planks, fence,
Behind them one cuddles comfortably.
Cuddle me, love, cuddle me tenderly,
Never shall I hold it up against you.

The mayor's horse dropped down dead.
The mayor himself skinned it.
The skin will make a good bag for the bag-
   pipes,
The four leg-bones will make fifes,
And of the head will be made brawn, heigh-ho!

1. The front of Kónyár Verka's house
   Is all covered with marble;

2. And it is covered thus,
   Because Szabó Jóska is soon coming there.

[1] Repeat here the tenth bar of the tune.

Búza, búza, kerëk dülő búza,
Fölnyőtt benne két szál levendula.
Levendula közepibe; —
    gyere babám az ölembe,
Ugyis tudom, babám, nem szeretsz igazán.

Corn, corn, corn all around,
Standing in the corn, two stems of lavender.
Lavender right in the middle;
    Come, my love, to my arms,
Indeed I know, my sweet, you do not love
    me truly.

1. Onnand alul jön egy vándorföcske,
Körme között van egy levelecske.
Nincsen, aki elolvassa,
    nem is magyarul van irva; —
Csárdás kis angyalom, el köll masíroznom.

2. Onnand alul jön egy üveghintó,
Abba ül a kutya szolgabíró.
Nem vétettem a kutyának,
    mégis beírt katonának! —
Csárdás kis angyalom, el köll masíroznom.

1. Down comes a wandering swallow,
Between its claws is a little letter.
There's no one who can read it through:
Not a word of Hungarian is written in it [1] —
My beloved, my pretty, I must march away.

2. Down comes a carriage with glass panes,
Therein sits the judge, the hound.
We've done nothing to the hound,
And yet he writes us down as soldiers.
My beloved, my pretty, I must march away.

(a) Erdő, erdő, erdő, marosszéki kerek erdő,
Madár lakja asztat, madár lakja tizenkettő.
Cukrot adnék annak a madárnak,
    dalolja ki nevét a babámnak,
Csárdás kis angyalom, érted fáj a szivem
    nagyon.

(a) Forest, forest, forest, round forest of
    Marosszék,
There live birds, live twelve birds.
I'll bring sugar to those birds,
For them to sing my sweetheart's name.
My beloved, for thy sake my heart grieves
    deeply.

(b) (From Ipolybalog [Hont], 1912, M.; — sung to Variant 1.)

♩ ♩ ♩ ♩
Búza, búza, búza, be nagy tábla búza!
♩ ♩ ♩ ♩
Az én kis angyalom az arató gazda.
Ki fogja azt learatni,
    ha már nekem el kell menni
Sopron városába, huszárkaszárnyába.

Corn, corn, corn, great field of corn;
My beloved owns the harvest,
But who shall reap it,
When now I am compelled to go
To Sopron town, to the Hussar's barracks?

Amoda megy, amoda megy három legény,
Turi Sándor, Turi Sándor a közepén.
Sárga bársony nadrágja,
    lagosszárú csizmája,
Molnár Julcsa a babája.

Over there go, over there go three youths,
Turi Sándor, Turi Sándor in the middle.
Of yellow velvet are his breeches,
Of patent leather the tops of his top-boots,
Molnár Julcsa is his sweetheart.

Megfogtam egy szúnyogot, nagyobb volt a
    lónál,
Kisütöttem a zsírját, több volt egy akónál.
|: Aki aztat elhiszi, szamarabb a lónál. :|

I caught a gnat, it was bigger than a horse.
I melted its fat, there was over a hogshead of it.
|: Who believes this, is a donkey—worse than
    a horse. :|

[1] Summons to recruits were issued in German.

Juki disznu a berektül csak a fülö látszik,
Kanászlegény a bokorba menyecskékkel ját-
    szik.
Elveszëtt a siskája kilenc malacával,
Utána ment a kanász üres tarisznyával.

In the woods, only the ears of the swine show,
While in the thicket the young swineherd
    plays with young women.
A sow with nine piglets got lost,
He goes after her with an empty knapsack.

303 a

Sosem láttál az oláhnak nagyobb virtusságát:
Incse máre la pandure,[1] felakasztja magát.
Az oláhok, az oláhok facipőbe járnak,
Azok élik világukat, akik ketten hálnak.

No one ever saw Wallachs do noble deeds:
They go into the wood,[1] hang themselves.
The Wallachs, the Wallachs wear wooden
    clogs,
Only those rejoice, who sleep two in a bed.

303 b

— Csóri kanász mit főztél? — Tüdőt ká-
    posztával.
— Mivel rántottál belé? — Hasaszalonával.
— Hát az öreg eszik-e? Tőtsd neki tálba.
Ha nem eszik belőle, vágd a pofájáho!

'Swineherd of Csór, what are you cooking?'
    'Lights with cabbage.'
'And how are you cooking them?' 'With fat.'
'Then the old one will eat it? Fill the dish
    for him.
If he does not eat out of the dish, hit him on
    the cheek.'

303 c

Tiéd voltam, tiéd leszek, de már nem vagyok,
Azt is tudod, sokszor mondtam, érted meg-
    halok.
De mivelhogy nem szeretsz, soha fel nem
    lelsz,
Még Rózsafát völgyében velem egybekelsz.

I was yours, shall be yours, but am not yours
    just now.
Well you know, often I told you, for your
    sake I die.
But because you love me not, you shall not
    meet me
Until in the valley of Rosafat you marry me.

304

1. Kecskemét is kiállítja nyalka verbunkját,
   Csárda előtt ki is tűzi veres zászlóját.
   Gyertek ide fiatalok, tessik beállnyi,
   Nyolc esztendő nem a világ, lehet pró-
       bálnyi.

2. Amott sétál egy kis leány nagy vidámsággal,
   Utánna megy a rózsája nagy bátorsággal.
   — Lassan siess, lassan sétálj, kedves an-
       gyalom,
   Fényes kard az oldalomon ne csillámoljon.

3. Kardomnak a markolatja nem csupa réz-
       bül,
   Ki van öntve csillagosra sárga jezüstbül.
   A finyes nap, hogyha rásüt, szépen tün-
       döklik.
   Kis angyalom, ha rátekint, elszomorodik.

1. Kecskemét calls up a splendid set of
       guards:
   In front of the inn is the bright red flag.
   Come along, young people, enter,
   Eight years are not a lifetime, you may
       ascertain it.

2. Over there walks a young girl in high glee,
   After her goes her suitor, full of boldness.
   Go slowly, walk slowly, my beloved,
   Lest the bright sword at my side should
       shine no more.

3. My sword's handle is not of mere brass,
   In it are cast stars of yellow silver.
   And when the sun shines bright, it shim-
       mers beautifully.
   My sweetheart, seeing it, is sad.

[1] Here the text is a corrupt form of a Rumanian sentence, probably running thus: Încă (?)
mere (= merge) la pădure = He goes into the wood.

1. — Hol háltál az éjjel, cinëgemadár?
   — A kapudban háltam, szivem asszony-
   kám.
   — Mér bejjebb nem jöttél, cinëgemadár?
   — Uradtól nem mertem, szivem asszony-
   kám.

2. — Nincs itthon az uram, cinëgemadár,
   Folyópatakra jár, uj hidat csinál.
   |: — Jó lova van annak, gyakran hazajár.:|

3. — Hol háltál az éjjel, cinëgemadár?
   — Ablakodban háltam, szivem asszony-
   kám.
   — Mér bejjebb nem jöttél, cinëgemadár?
   — Uradtól nem mertem, szivem asszony-
   kám.

4 = 2.

5. — Hol háltál az éjjel, cinëgemadár?
   — Az ágyadon háltam, szivem asszony-
   kám.
   — Mér bejjebb nem jöttél, cinëgemadár?
   — Uradtól nem mertem, szivem asszony-
   kám.

6 = 2.

1. 'Where did you spend the night, little tit-
   mouse?'
   'On your door-sill, beloved little house-
   wife.'
   'Why didn't you come in, little titmouse?'
   'I dared not face your husband, little lady.'

2. 'My husband is not at home, little titmouse.
   He's gone to the river, he builds a new
   bridge.'
   |: 'He's got a good horse, comes home
   often.' :|

3. 'Where did you spend the night, little tit-
   mouse?'
   'On your window, beloved little lady.'
   'Why didn't you come in, little titmouse?'
   'I dared not face your husband, beloved
   little lady.'

4 = 2.

5. 'Where did you spend the night, little titmouse?'
   'On your bed, beloved little lady.'
   'Why didn't you come in the bed, little
   titmouse?'
   'I dared not face your husband, beloved
   little lady.'

6 = 2.

1. Teríti egy lány a vásznat
   Így meg így, ippen így.[1]

2. Sulykolja a lány a vásznat
   Így meg így, ippen így.

3. Jön egy öreg a kunyhóból
   Így meg így, ippen így.

4. Kezd a lánynak integetni
   Így meg így, ippen így.[2]

5. De a lány is visszaintett
   Így meg így, ippen így.[3]

6. Jön egy fiatal lóhátas
   Így meg így, ippen így.

7. Kezd a lánynak integetni
   Így meg így, ippen így.[2]

1. A maiden is spreading the linen,
   Thus, thus, thus she does it.[1]

2. A maiden is beetling the linen,
   Thus, thus, thus she does it.

3. Comes an old man out of the hut,
   Thus, thus, thus he comes.

4. He starts signalling to the maiden,
   Thus, thus, thus he does it.[2]

5. And the maiden signals back,
   Thus, thus, thus she does it.[3]

6. Comes a young horseman,
   Thus, thus, thus he comes.

7. He starts signalling to the maiden,
   Thus, thus, thus he does it.[2]

[1] Suitable gestures accompany the singing of the burden.
[2] Beckoning.   [3] Gestures expressing refusal.

8. De a lány is visszaintett
Így meg így, ippen így.[1]

307 (var. 315)

1. — Anna, Anna, Molnár Anna,
Jere vélem hosszú útra!

2. — Nem mëhetëk Sajgó Márton,
Vagyon nékem tüzem, házam,

3. Tüzem, házam, jámbor uram,
Karonülő kicsi fiam.

4. |: Éjjel-nappal csak a sírás. :|

5. Elindula Molnár Anna,
Elindula hosszú útra.

6. Amint mentek, addig mentek,
Egy fa alá le is ültek.

7. — Anna, Anna, Molnár Anna,
Nézz egy kicsit a fejembe!

8. Nézni kezdett Molnár Anna,
Sajgó Mártonnak fejibe.

9. Sírni kezdett Molnár Anna,
A könny lehull a fejére.

10. — Mért sírsz, mért sírsz, Molnár Anna?
— Nem sírok én, Sajgó Márton:

11. Faharmatja, faharmatja
Hullott-e a te fejedre?

308

1. Falu végin van egy ház,

2. Abba lakik egy asszony,

3. Van annak egy szép lánya,

4. Julcsa annak a neve.

5. Sütött Julcsa pogácsát,

6. A Pistának od'atta,

7. A Pista azt megette,

8. A hideg is kilelte.

309

1. — Mestereknek mestere, mestere,
mondd meg, mi az az egy?
— Egy az Isten, a jó Isten,
Aki minket alkotott, alkotott,
mindörökké ámen!

8. And the maiden signals back,
Thus, thus, thus she does it.[1]

1. 'Anna, Anna, Molnár Anna,
Come with me along the road.'

2. 'I can't go, Sajgó Márton,
I have a hearth and home,

3. 'My hearth, my home, my faithful husband,
In my arms my little son.

4. |:'Day and night nothing but weeping.':|

5. Away went Molnár Anna,
Went along the road.

6. And as they went, so far they went,
They sat down under a tree.

7. 'Anna, Anna, Molnár Anna,
Look to my hair a bit for lice.'

8. And she looks, does Molnár Anna,
To Sajgó Márton's hair.

9. Molnár Anna starts weeping,
Her tears fall upon his head.

10. 'Why weep you, why weep you, Molnár Anna?'
'I am not weeping, Sajgó Márton:

11. 'Dew from the tree, dew from the tree
Is falling upon your head.'

1. At the end of the village there is a house,

2. Therein lives a woman,

3. She has a pretty daughter,

4. Whose name is Julcsa.

5. Julcsa is baking cakes,

6. She gives some to Pista,

7. Pista eats them up,

8. And develops a fever.

1. 'Our master, master, master,
Tell me, what is one?'
'One is God, All-merciful God,
Who has created, created us,
World without end, Amen!'

[1] Gestures expressing assent.

186

2. — Mestereknek mestere, mestere
mondd meg, mi az a kettő?
— Kettő Mózes táblája,[1]
egy az Isten, a jó Isten,
Aki minket alkotott, alkotott,
mindörökké ámen!

3. — Mestereknek mestere, mestere,
mondd meg, mi az a három?
— Három a pátriárka,[1]
kettő Mózes táblája,[1]
egy az Isten, a jó Isten,
Aki minket alkotott, alkotott,
mindörökké ámen!

2. 'Our master, master, master,
Tell me, what is two?'
'Two are the tables of Moses,[1]
One is God, All-merciful God,
Who has created, created us,
World without end, Amen!'

3. 'Our master, master, master,
Tell me, what is three?'
'Three are the Patriarchs,[1]
Two are the tables of Moses,[1]
One is God, All-merciful God,
Who has created, created us,
World without end, Amen!'

310

(*a*) 1. A kertmegi káposzta
Kiborult az asztalra;

2. Mán az öreg nem eszi,
Csak a husát keresi.

(*b*) A kertmegi gölödin [2]
Görög a dülő végin.

(*c*) A kertmegi kocsonya,
Beledöglött a béka.

(*a*) 1. The cabbage of Kertmeg
Are poured out upon the table;

2. But the old man eats them not,
Fishes out the meat only.

(*b*) The dumpling of Kertmeg
Rolls to the end of the field.

(*c*) The brawn of Kertmeg
Has choked a frog.

311

1. A Vargáék ablakja
Rózsábul van kirakva, kirakva.

2. Azér van az kirakva,
Garzó Péter jár ide, jár oda.

3. — Hej te Julcsa, gyere ki,
Vár mán Péter ide ki, ide ki!

4. — Tudnám én azt, ha várna,
Mert a szívem dibegne-dobogna.

1. The window at Varga's
With roses is covered, covered.

2. For this reason it is covered,
That Garzó Péter is passing by.

3. 'Hey you Julcsa, come along,
For Péter is here, is here.'

4. 'Well I'd know it, if he were,
For my heart would be going pit-a-pat.

312

1. Két krajcárom volt nékem,
Nékem, nékem, volt nékem.

2. Elvittem a malomba,
-Lomba, -lomba, malomba.

3. Megőröltem a búzát,
(sempre simile)

4. Hazavittem a lisztet,

5. Süttem vele perecet,

6. Megették a gyerekek.

1. Three pennies I had,
I had, had, had.

2. I took them to the mill,
To the mill, mill, mill.

3. Had the corn ground,
(sempre simile)

4. Brought the flour home,

5. Baked it into bretzels,

6. The children ate them up.

---

[1] These half-lines are sung to the bars given at 1. [2] = gombóc.

187

Piros alma leesett a sárba,
Ki felveszi, nem veszi hiába.

The red apple fell into the dirt,
Who picks it up will not be unrewarded

1. Megérett a meggy a fán, —
Férhe ment a Varga lány.

2. Megérett a cseresznye, —
Kara István elvette.

3. — Montam István, ne vedd el,
Nem győzöd azt méderrel.[1]

4. — Ha nem győzöm méderrel,
Majd meggyőzöm kötéllel:

5. Kötelet a lábára,
Zsineget a nyakára.

1. The cherries are ripe on the tree,
Married is the Varga girl.

2. The cherries are ripe,
Kara István has married her.

3. 'I told you, István, don't take her,
You can't afford her many bodices (?).'

4. 'If I can't afford her many bodices,
I shall buy a ribbon,

5. 'A ribbon for her feet,
And a rope for her neck.'

1. A katona a menyecskét
Erdőszélbe csalogatta.

2. Addig-addig csalogatta,
Erdőszélbe csalogatta.

3. Leültette a menyecskét,
Ölébe hajtotta fejét.

4. Gondolkozik a menyecske,
Hogyan váljon meg most tőle.

5. Kihuzta jaz egyik kardját,
Avval vágta le a nyakát.

6. Fölöltözött ruhájába,
Ugy vágtatott hazájába,

7. Ugy vágtatott hazájába,
Bíró uram udvarára.

8. — Bíró uram, adjál szállást,
Lovamnak éjjeli állást.

9. — Nem adhatok én most szállást,
Lovadnak éjjeli állást.

10. Mert nincs nékem feleségem,
Ki jó vacsorát készítsen.

11. — Nem kell nékem jó vacsora,
Csak kell nékem meleg szoba.

12. — Húzd le, fiam, a csizmámat,
Szárogasd meg a kapcámat.

13. — Apám, apám, édesapám,
Ez ám az én édesanyám!

1. The soldier the young woman
To the edge of the wood entices.

2. Far, far away entices,
To the edge of the wood entices her.

3. And he asks the young woman to sit down,
And lays his head on her lap.

4. She sits thinking, the young woman,
Could I but get away from him.

5. She draws out one of his swords,
With it cuts his throat.

6. She puts on his clothes,
And so runs home,

7. And so runs home
Into the mayor's courtyard.

8. 'Mayor, give me hospitality,
And to my horse for the night shelter.'

9. 'I can't give you hospitality,
Nor to your horse for the night shelter.

10. 'For I have not my wife here
For to prepare a good supper.'

11. 'I have no need of a good supper,
I only need a warm room.'

12. 'Draw off, my son, my boots,
And dry my foot-rags.'

13. 'Father, father, dear father,
It is indeed my dear mother!

[1] = mider? (fűző?).

188

14. Megismerem a lábárul,
    Bogárfekete hajárul.
15. — Nincs teneked édesanyád,
    Mer elcsalták a katonák.
16. Kigombolja a dolmányát,
    Ugy szoptatja kis árváját.

14. 'I know her by her feet,
    By her raven-black hair!'
15. 'No, you have no dear mother:
    She 's been enticed away by a soldier.'
16. She unbuttons her dolman
    And gives the breast to the little child.

316 (var. 152)

Szántottam gyöpöt, vetëttem gyöngyöt,
Hajtottam ágát, szëdtem virágát,
Ej, huj, rózsám, gyere velem.

I ploughed the turf, I sowed pearls,
I bent branches, I plucked flowers:
Heigh ho, my love, come to me!

317

1. Eger felé megyen egy út,
   Kin Klimkó Erzsi jelindult,
   |: Klimkó Erzsi :| jel-elindult.
2. Beért Eger városába,
   Citromszínű rokolyába,
   |: Citromszínű :| rokolyába.
3. Benéz a legelső boltba,
   Válogat a viganóba,
   |: Válogat a :| viganóba.
4. — Válogasson a kisasszony,
   Ne siessen olyan nagyon,
   |: Ne siessen :| olyan nagyon!
5. — Sietek én, görög uram,
   Még sokfelé van az utam,
   |: Még sokfelé :| van az utam.

1. Towards Eger leads a road,
   Along it goes Klimkó Erzsi.
   |: Klimkó Erzsi :| goes along.
2. She walks through Eger town
   In a lemon-yellow frock,
   |: A lemon-yellow :| frock.
3. She enters the very first shop
   To select petticoats,
   |: To select :| petticoats.
4. 'Make your choice, young lady,
   Do not hurry so much,
   |: Do not hurry :| so much.'
5. 'I must hurry, Sir Greek,
   In many directions lies my way,
   |: In many directions :| lies my way.'

318

(a) Mënyasszony, vőlegény, de szép mind
    a kettő,
    Olyan mind a kettő, mint az arany-
    vessző.

(b) A mënyasszony sánta, a vőlegény görbe,
    Násznagy uram hátát köszvény kive-
    tëtte.

(c) 1. Az gondullod ruzsám, hogy igen sze-
      retlek,
      Pedig édes ruzsám, könnyen elfelejtlek:

2. Në bizd el magadat, hogy utánnad
   estem,
   Barna szëmiledet szeretgetni kezdtem.

3. Már biz, édes ruzsám, elmëhetsz mel-
   lettem.
   Kezedet sëm fogom, hogy üjj le mel-
   lettem.

(a) You bride, you bridegroom, you are
    both beautiful,
    Both as beautiful as the golden rod.

(b) The bride limps, the bridegroom is
    hunchbacked,
    The best man's back is twisted by gout.

(c) 1. You think, my dear, I love you well.
      But, my dear, I can easily forget you:

2. Do not persuade yourself I fell in love
   with you,
   And started loving your brown face.

3. But believe, my dear, you may pass by
   me,
   I shan't grasp your hand, ask you to sit
   by me.

4. Te tettél fogadást én előttem, nem más,
   Hogy énrajtam kívül sohasëm szeretsz
   mást.

5. Csipkefa, rózsafa, nem árt neked a'ttél—
   Köszönöm édesem, hogy eddig szerettél.

4. It was you, and no other, who swore
   That none but me you would ever love.

5. Hawthorn, rose-bush, suffer not from
   winter-frost—
   I am thankful, my dear, that up to now
   you loved me.

319

1. Sárga csikó, csengő rajta,
   Vajon hova megyünk rajta?

2. Majd elmegyünk valahova,
   Kocsis Róza udvarukra.

3. Betekintünk az ablakon,
   Ki kártyázik az asztalon?

4. Kovács Jani karosszékben,
   Cigánykártya a kezében.

5. Kocsis Róza fésülködik,
   A tükörbe biggyeszkedik.

6. — Ugye Jani, szép is vagyok?
   Épen neked való vagyok.

7. — Szép is vagy te, jó is vagy te,
   Csak egy kicsit csalfa vagy te.

8. Kocsis Róza vetett ágya
   Pallást éri a párnája.

9. Kovács Jani görbe lába
   Nem tud felmászni az ágyra.

10. Majd felmászik a kis székről,
    A meszes dézsa füléről.

1. Yellow foal, decked with bells,
   I wonder where we shall go with it.

2. Soon we'll arrive somewhere:
   At Kocsis Róza's courtyard.

3. And we'll see through the window,
   Who plays cards on the table.

4. Kovács Jani sits in the arm-chair,
   Holding gipsy's cards in his hand.

5. Kocsis Róza is combing her hair,
   She looks at herself in the glass.

6. 'Well, Jani, am I beautiful?
   Am I suitable for you?'

7. 'Beautiful are you, good are you,
   But a wee bit treacherous are you.'

8. Kocsis Róza makes the bed,
   The pillows reach up to the attic.

9. Kovács Jani with the bandy legs
   Cannot climb up the bed.

10. First he climbs upon a stool,
    On to the handles of the whitewash tub.

320

1. Nézd a bakát, mikor az masírozik,
   Négyesivel sorába,
       büszke káplár utána,
   Iceg-biceg a baka a nagy sárba.

2. Én meg csak úgy huszárosan, csinosan,
   Csizmám szára lagosan,

       sarkantyum tallérosan,
   Ölelem a babámat huszárosan.

1. See the infantry on the march,
   Four by four in files,
       a proud corporal in the rear,
   The infantry floundering through deep
   mud.

2. But I'm as smart as a hussar should be,
   My top-boots are well polished,
       my spurs as large as crown pieces.
   I'll cuddle my love as a hussar should.

ERRATA IN MUSICAL EXAMPLES

No. 10 : *Add key-signature*

„ 22 : *For* Csíkvacsárcsi *read* Vacsárcsi

„ 93c : *Add* IV (to indicate dialect-region)

„ 97 : *For* II *read* III

„ 106 : *Add* IV (to indicate dialect-region)

„ 130 : *Add time-signature* $\frac{4}{4}$

„ 130 : *The second bar should read*

„ 195 : *For* III *read* I

„ 209 : *Add* II (to indicate dialect-region)

„ 218b : *Add* III (to indicate dialect-region)

„ 272 : *For* IV *read* III

„ 294, last line of Hungarian text : *For* Íg *and* íg *read* Így *and* így

MUSICAL EXAMPLES

MUSICAL EXAMPLES

Explanation of signs used

(1) The small notes (except for short grace-notes) must be given their full value, which accordingly has to be subtracted from the value of the main note with which they are connected by a slur; e.g. 𝄞 is to

be read 𝄞 . The use of small notes merely indicates that these notes are to be sung with less insistence, a lesser accentuation—passed over lightly, so to speak. But if they are connected by ⌢ with the main

note, each of them must be given its actual value; e.g. in 𝄞 .

Melisms, i.e. groups of notes to be sung to one syllable, are indicated by slurs; where there is no slur, one note is affected to each syllable.

(2) The sign ⌒ (e.g. ♪, ♭) indicates a slight extension of value, and the sign ⌣ (e.g. ♪, ♭) a slight curtailment. The pause (⌒) gives a note at least twice its original value.

(3) The signs ⬂ and ⬀ indicate a *glissando* or *portamento*; ⌐⬂ indicates a *glissando* beginning at the pitch of the note, and immediately after the note is given out, extending approximately to the note belonging to the point of the stave at which the *glissando* sign ends (in other words, the *glissando* covers the whole value of the note); ⬂ indicates a similar *glissando* beginning later (approximately with the second half of the value of the note); ⬀ means a *glissando* from the point of the stave from which the sign starts to the note which the sign reaches (the duration of the *glissando* corresponds approximately to half the value of the note). The

sign ~~~ over two or more notes (⬂) indicates a *glissando* beginning slightly before the first note and ending slightly beyond the last, the two written notes standing out to a certain extent. ⌐ indicates a faint *tremolando*.

(4) The key-signatures include only such signs as obtain throughout a song. Generally, no time-signature is given for *parlando-rubato* tunes.

(5) The sign ↑ over a note indicates a slight rise in pitch, and the sign ↓ a slight lowering, both smaller than a quarter-tone: $^b/_2$ indicates a lowering by a quarter-tone.

(6) Notes considered as ending the first, second, and third tune-lines are marked accordingly (e.g. ⌐1⌐ ⌐5⌐ ⌐1⌐, &c.).

(7) The syllables in italics are non-integrant parts of the text, not included in the count of syllables. The sound indicated by ə corresponds, roughly, to the English ŭ, or Rumanian ă. The italic *j* indicates a sound introduced to avoid a hiatus, *ñ* a nasal *n*.

(8) The heading of each tune gives (from left to right): firstly, the index-number of the phonographic record (if any), followed either by Mus. F. (to indicate that the record belongs to the Ethnographical section of the Budapest National Museum) or by F. (to indicate that it is the collector's private property). Then come: the roman figure indicating the dialect-region; the name of the village; that of the district (in brackets); the name of the performer or performers, with their age so far as known; the year of collection; and an initial indicating the collector (B.=Bartók; G.=Garay; K.=Kodály; L.=Lajtha; M.=Molnár; V.=Vikár).

N.B. The tunes collected by Vikár and Garay were written down by Bartók.

The order of the tunes is not the lexical order described in the Introduction; they are arranged in the order of the main types mentioned in the Essay.

The texts marked, at the beginning, 1, 2, or *a* or *a* 1 are but the first of several strophes which will be found under the corresponding numbers in the text section. The texts in that section contain neither the burdens nor such repetitions of lines as occur uniformly in each strophe.

In the course of these strophes a number of indications of rhythm occur, to show deflexions from the rhythm used in the first strophe as written down.

Remarks on the examples

A I

1. Sung by a man of about 50. The same example in Sz.N. 63. Has no variant. On account of its AABB$_v$ structure, it differs to a certain extent from the songs characteristic of the old style. It is almost to be doubted whether it belongs to Class *A*.

2. Sung by an old woman. Var.: Sz.N. 83; for one half: Sz.N. 56; see also Bartalus, iii. 8, 9, 19, vi. 4 (this last in altogether inaccurately noted rhythm). There are about another 44 known variants (of which 16 are half-tunes), all from the four Székely districts.[1] The melodic pattern recalls, to a degree, those of Examples 16 and 59.

---

[1] viz. Csík, Háromszék, Maros-Torda, and Udvarhely. There has been hardly any collecting in Háromszék; but we may assume that this tune (and likewise a few of those to which the same remark is appended) might have been in use there.

3. Sung by an old man. Var.: Sz.N. 90. Also one variant from district Maros-Torda.

4. Var.: Sz.N. 125. 18 variants from regions I–IV. The structure is ABCD, and in sequences. Cf. Nos. 5, 23, 62.

5. Two variants from district Maros-Torda. Cf. p. 20, note 1. Same structure as the foregoing. Cf. Nos. 23 and 62.

6. One variant from district Hont.

7. *a* sung by a young boy. 9 variants from region I.

8. Sung by an old man. One variant from district Tolna.

9. Match-making song. No variant. On account of its Mixolydian scale, may perhaps not belong to Class *A*.

10. 25 variants from regions I–III. Pattern recalls No. 70.

11. *a* sung by a man. Var.: Sz.N. 22. A dance tune.—*a* is included in Class *A*, exceptionally, despite its end-note ⌊2⌋. This form occurs only in region II (3 other variants), and thence passed into the Slovakian and Moravian repertory. Three manuscript Slovakian variants; likewise *Slovenské Spevy*, i. 281, 478; Bartoš,[1] ii. 334, iii. 1281 (this last a half-tune). The form with ⌊5⌋: *b* was found only in the four Székely districts. Var. of this last: Sz.N. 22 (7 more variants).

12. Var.: Sz.N. 52. 10 more variants from the four Székely districts only. One Rumanian variant from Maros-Torda (borrowed from the Hungarian).

13. Dance tune. No variant.

14. Sung by an old woman. Var.: Sz.N. 61. 6 more variants from the four Székely districts only. A few of these are turned into three-line tunes by the omission of the third line.

15. Sung by an old woman. 11 variants from region I (one of these has the main caesura ⟦4⟧); 2 from region IV, and 1 from region III. Most of those from region I have an unsteady third.

16. Sung by an old woman. The same tune: Sz.N. 91. Var.: Sz.N. 88. 9 more variants from the four Székely districts only. Passed into the Rumanian repertory, which includes many variants (e.g. Bartók, *Chansons populaires roumaines du département Bihar*, Nos. 231, 233, 234, 236, 237). The pattern recalls Examples 1 and 59.

17. The same tune: Sz.N. 89. 7 variants from region IV.

18. Sung by an old man. Probably a dance tune. No variant.

19. Sung by an old woman. Var.: Sz.N. 105. 11 more variants from the four Székely districts and Bukovina only. In the Rumanian region adjoining that of the Székely, a few Rumanian variants (borrowed from the Hungarian).

20. Sung by an old man.

[1] See Bibliography, p. 97.

21. Sung by a man of about 50. Variants: Sz.N. 113; Bartalus, vi. 145, vii. 88. 24 more variants from region IV, and 2 from region III (one of these is to be found in Bartók and Kodály, *Magyar Népdalok*, 1906, No. 1). One Rumanian variant from the Mezőség is known (borrowed from the Hungarian). Its structure is A⁵B⁵AB; but in all variants the end note of the third line dropped from the original *d* to *b* flat.
22. Sung by an old woman. Var.: Sz.N. 119. Another variant from district Kolozs.
23. Var.: Bartalus, iii. 7, iv. 49, vi. 1, vii. 2. Possibly Sz.N. 127 is also related to this. About 25 variants from regions I–III; a few variants, more similar to Sz.N. 127, from region IV. Structure: ABCD, in sequences; cf. examples 4, 5, 62.
24. One variant from district Tolna.
25. Var.: Sz.N. 146; another from Bukovina.
26. Sung by an old woman. Var.: Bartalus, vi. 20. 21 more variants from regions I–IV. Often, the main caesura of the variants from regions I–III is ⓑ₃ . Four Rumanian variants from districts Hunyad and Torda-Aranyos. These are obviously borrowed from the Hungarian, for the main caesura ⑤ is very exceptional in Rumanian tunes.
27. Var.: Bartalus, v. 180. 9 more variants from regions I–III, one from region IV. Passed on to the Slovakians and thence into Moravia. Three manuscript Slovakian variants, likewise *Slovenské Spevy*, ii. 200; Susil, 799 m (the third on p. 667); Bartoš, iii. 2056.
28. One variant from district Szerém; one Rumanian variant from Máramaros (Bartók, *Volksmusik du Rumänen von Maramureș*, No. 128).
29. 11 variants from regions II–IV.
30. 4 variants from regions II–III (mostly in *parlando-rubato* rhythm).
31. One variant from district Borsod.
32. Sung by a man of about 75. No variant.

A II

33. *a* sung by a man of about 35; *b* by a woman of about 70. Var.: Sz.N. 67. 7 more variants from regions I–III.
34. 19 variants from regions I–IV. Three manuscript Slovakian variants (from districts Hont and Zólyom) which doubtless were borrowed from the Hungarian.
35. Sung by an old woman. Var.: Sz.N. 9 (main caesura Ⅶ); 3 more variants from districts Csík and Kolozs.
36. Var.: Sz.N. 77 (*poco rubato*), 102; 6 more from district Csík.
37. Sung by an old woman. Var.: Kiss, p. 364, No. 34 (the last note wrongly written down one degree too low).

38. A dance tune (?). No variant.
39. No variant.
40. Var.: Sz.N. 111 (in this, which comes from region IV, the main caesura $\boxed{\flat 3}$ and not $\boxed{5}$, despite the A⁵B⁵AB structure. Cf. remark to example 21).
41. Var.: Sz.N. 145; another from region IV, and 2 from region II.
42. No variant. Last line of text missing.
43. Var.: Sz.N. 150. Another from district Csík, another from Bars.

A III

44. A dance tune (?). No variant.
45. Sung by a woman. Var.: Bartalus, v. 143. 11 more variants from regions I and IV. Similar Rumanian tunes: Bartók, *Volksmusik der Rumänen von Maramureș*, No. 45 *a* and *b*. One manuscript Slovakian variant.
46, 47, 48, 49. (The last sung by an old man.) No variants.
50. No Hungarian variant. Rumanian variant: *Volksmusik der Rum. von Mar.*, No. 104 ($\boxed{5}$, $\boxed{\flat 3}$, $\boxed{1}$).
51. Sung by an old man. Var.: Bartalus, iii. 88 (with the rhythm incorrectly given); iv. 120. 11 more variants from regions I–IV, most of them in variable *tempo giusto* (i.e. slower) rhythm. A few even show an extension of the rhythm of the last three lines: ♩♩♩♩ ♩ ♩ | ♪ ♩. ♩ | instead of the original ♩ ♩ ♩ ♩ | ♪ ♩. ♩ ‖. Notice the repetition of the fourth line with a different cadence.
52. Sung by an old man. One variant from district Szerém. One Rumanian variant (*Volksmusik der Rum. von Mar.*, No. 107, $\boxed{7}$ $\boxed{\flat 3}$ $\boxed{1}$) (borrowed from the Hungarian).
53. Var.: Bartalus, ii. 91. 5 more variants from regions I, II, and IV. It is doubtful whether this example belongs to the old style or to Class *C*. In Brahms's 10th *Hungarian Dance* the tune is used as second theme, with the ending disfigured thus:

54. Sung: *a*, by an old woman; *b*, by a man of 70. No variant. In the third and fourth lines of *a* an unusual increase in the number of syllables, with a corresponding alteration of the rhythm.

A IV

55. Var.: Sz.N. 6, 17, 18; the main caesura of No. 6 being $\boxed{VII}$, and the scale of No. 18 having strangely become Mixolydian. 8 more variants

from region IV, most of them in *tempo giusto*: the *parlando-rubato* of one example is exceptional.

56. Var.: Bartalus, v. 157. 16 more variants from regions I–IV (only one from region IV). A few of these are ten-syllable; most of them have the major third, one has the major seventh. A peculiar structure of the $A^5A^5{}_vAA_v$ type, in which the final note of $A^5{}_v$ is $\boxed{1}$ instead of $\boxed{5}$. (In the statistical allocation it is treated as ABCD, which is the structure of most of its variants.)

57. Var.: Sz.N. 82, 99. 28 more variants from region IV.

58. Sung by a young boy. 9 variants from regions I, II, III, and 1 from region IV. Part of the former show the influence of the modern minor scale.

59. Var.: Sz.N. 100. 7 more variants from region IV. The melodic line is similar to that of examples 2 and 16.

60. Sung by an old woman. 7 variants, from districts Csík and Udvarhely only: one of these with $\boxed{4}$, five with $\boxed{5}$.

61. Var.: Sz.N. 120. Two more from districts Kolozs and Torda-Aranyos.

62. Sung by an old woman. Var.: Bartalus, vi. 10, 79, i. 136; this last, on account of a peculiar lengthening of the lines, contains lines of 14 syllables. 8 more variants from region IV, one from region I. The melodic line (structure: ABCD, with sequences) resembles that of Examples 4, 5, and 23.

63. Var.: Sz.N. 106. 4 more from region IV. The main caesura is $\boxed{\flat 3}$ in all variants, which are in *tempo giusto*: so that the divergences in this example ($\boxed{4}$ instead of $\boxed{\flat 3}$, and *parlando*) are exceptional.

64. Sung by an old woman. Same tune: Sz.N. 129. Two variants from the four Székely districts.

65. Var.: Sz.N. 134. Five more from regions I–IV.

66. One variant from district Csongrád (in *tempo giusto*).

67. Sung by a man. One variant from district Tolna (with the main caesura $\boxed{\flat 3}$). The structure is really $A^5A^5{}_vAA_v$, as in examples 71 *a* and 74 *a*.

68. No variant. There are a few further examples of similar jocular lengthenings of lines, but with only the first and fourth lines, or only the first, lengthened (e.g. Bartalus, vii. 198, $\boxed{8}$ $\boxed{\flat 3}$ $\boxed{5}$).

A V

69. Var.: Sz.N. 115; Bartalus, ii. 88, iii. 157. It is to be noticed that the song was found among Bukovinian Csángós, who had settled in Déva. 15 more variants from regions II–IV; the main caesura of most of these is $\boxed{\flat 3}$.

70. Sung by a man of about 55. Var.: Bartalus, i. 60, v. 150, vi. 159, vii. 44. 13 more variants from regions I–III. The slow tempo of all variants, and the ensuing variability of rhythm, are uncommon. On account of these features, it would have been necessary (but for the fact that it is reasonable to consider the slowness of the tempo as a mannerism introduced at a later date) to write down the tune in values twice as long. Compare Example 72, in similar rhythm, but in twice as quick a tempo. The melodic line resembles that of Example 10.

71. *a* sung by a man. No variant. The structure of *a* is really A⁵A⁵ᵥAAᵥ (the final note of A⁵ᵥ is ⒤ instead of ⒌). The structure of *b* is ABBC. Similar structural deviations are noticeable in Examples 74 *a, b,* and *c.* Compare 71 *a* and 74 *a,* 71 *b* and 74 *c*; and also 71 *a* with 67.

72. Var.: Bartalus, iv. 132, vii. 169. Two more variants from regions I and II. This tune appears in the Allegro of Liszt's 13th Hungarian Rhapsody, of which it is the first theme, but in the following altered form (transposed here for purposes of comparison):

The flourishes in semiquavers, which remind one of the ornamental runs in eighteenth-century West European music, are entirely foreign to Hungarian peasant music: they are to be ascribed to the methods of gipsy players.

A VII

73. Var.: Színi, 158. In the above-mentioned Rhapsody by Liszt this tune, in the following altered form:

becomes the second theme of the Allegro section. The last bar introduces, very illogically, an ending on E flat. This distortion—also imputable, without doubt, to gipsy practice—arises from an incapacity to understand or to feel the structure of the tune, and utterly spoils the satisfactory effect produced by the real ending on G, the structure being A^5B^5AB. It also tends arbitrarily to imitate, in the 4th (B) line, the not unusual alteration of the main caesura (2nd line) from $\boxed{5}$ into $\boxed{\flat 3}$; and in consequence, one of the main pillars of the structure—the final note of the 4th line—is knocked down.

N.B. The 7th, 8th, 10th, and 11th bars in our example seem imperfect; Színi gives:

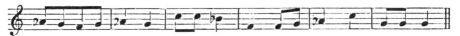

which is certainly better.

74. *c* sung by an old man. One variant, similar to *c* (with the main caesura $\boxed{5}$), from district Szerém. In the third variant in this example a curious transformation in the structure is noticeable: $a = A^5A^5{}_vAA_v$ (as in Example 71 *a*); $b = ABCC_v$; $c = ABBC$ (as in Example 71 *b*). Considering the variant from Szerém (3rd bar: [music] , 5th and 6th

bars: [music] , bars 10–12: [music]),

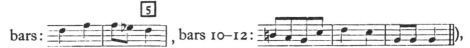

we notice that its structure $\boxed{1}$ $\boxed{5}$ $\boxed{\flat 3}$, 9, ABB_vA_v stands very close to the ABBA structure of Class II. Compare also with No. 67.

B [1]

75. Slovakian variant: *Slovenské Spevy*, ii. 129; another manuscript.
77. Var.: Bartalus, iv. 140, vii. 121.
78. Slovakian variant: *Slovenské Spevy*, iii. 457; another manuscript.
79. Three manuscript Slovakian variants.
80. Peasant variant of the well-known song 'Csak egy kislány van a világon' composed by Elemér Szentirmay, which is used by way of second theme in Sarasate's 'Hungarian Gipsy-Tunes'. Here we have a characteristic instance of the process by which a tune belonging to 'popular' art music becomes a peasant song. The minor scale becomes an Aeolian one with pentatonic turns, the ending of the first line changes from $\boxed{2}$ to $\boxed{1}$, and the fourth line becomes similar to the first. The

[1] As regards Classes *B* and *C*, I have not generally given the numbers of manuscript Hungarian variants, nor particulars as to singers.

gipsy *rubato* of the tempo becomes *tempo giusto*, the third line has eleven syllables (the original ♪♪♪ becoming ♪♪♪): in other words, the form becomes ⑴ ⑸ ⑺, 9, 9, 11, 9, ABBA. The unpleasant flavour of sentimentality that characterized the original is dispelled by the freshness of the country-side style: the result is a genuine, powerful peasant song.

    N.B. The peculiar changes in rhythm by which the fourth line differs from the first are an exceptional feature.

81. Var.: Bartalus, iii. 140. Another manuscript Slovakian variant.
82. Well known in district Békés. No variant from other regions.
84. Two manuscript Slovakian variants.
85. Match-making text.
86. Possibly a variant of the widely known song whose text is 'A Csap uccán véges-, véges-végig' (see p. 77, paragraphs 4–5). Compare with Example 313. Three manuscript Slovakian variants; another, *Slovenské Spevy*, i. 24. Moravian var.: Bartoš, iii. 592 *b*; Černík, 142.[1]
88. Has also variants in the major mode, e.g. Bartalus, i. 134 (second half of the tune only). Slovakian var.: *Slovenské Spevy*, ii. 603 (in the major mode), and three in manuscript.
90. Appears to be one of the oldest of the ABBA songs. Never sung to other words. See p. 43, paragraph 1.
91. Two manuscript Slovakian variants.
92. Originates in the well-known 'art song', 'Érik a, érik a buzakalász', whose composer is unknown:

The structure only is altered, ⑵ having become ⑴, and ABCD having become the usual ABBA. Although invariably ♩ ♪♪│♩ ♪♪ from end to end, the rhythm has remained unchanged, and is of a type that entirely disagrees with the Hungarian peasants' sense of rhythm. Accordingly, the transformation was less thorough than in the case of Example 80. There are five manuscript Slovakian variants whose structure is the same.

93. See p. 40, footnote 1. *a* has 3 manuscript Slovakian variants; another is printed in *Detva*,[2] p. 281.

[1] Joža Černík, *Zpěvy Moravských Kopaničárů*, Praha, 1908.
[2] Karol A. Medvecky, *Detva* (a monograph). Detva, 1905.

94. Match-making text.—There exist manuscript tunes of similar structure, with $\boxed{1}$ $\boxed{2}$ $\boxed{3}$; another, manuscript, is to be found in the Slovakian repertory, and two are in the Moravian: Bartoš, ii. 136 c, iii. 271 d.

96. 7 manuscript Slovakian variants; one Moravian: Černík, 126.

101. 1 manuscript Slovakian variant.

103. The words are quite recent, as shown by the reference they contain to peasants who have contracted to work for landowners for the summer (these labourers are called in Hungarian 'summások') going to work, working, &c. There are several such texts.

104. There is a variant from district Vas in which the ♩ in the second beat is replaced by ♩. (probably a more primitive reading), making the time $^3/_4$ instead of $^5/_8$.

105. One variant with the main caesura $\boxed{b3}$ (see p. 41, par. 1).

107. One manuscript Slovakian variant.

108. Sung by soldiers in Beszterczebánya.

109. Three manuscript Slovakian variants; two Moravian: Bartoš, ii. 265 b, iii. 592 a. More will be said of the curious Slovakian variants, with their admixture of fragments of Czech tunes, in the forthcoming book on Slovakian peasant music.

110. See p. 42, last par.

112. One manuscript Slovakian variant.

114. The third line is appreciably different from the second. Yet we stick to the designation BB for these, because the analogy of the first bar in both points clearly to the connexion of their content and to their common origin. Compare with Example 273, and see p. 69, under IV.

115. One variant with main caesura $\boxed{b3}$.

116. Two manuscript Slovakian variants.

119. In determining the form, the first line was considered as twelve-syllable, by analogy with the fourth. There is a manuscript Slovakian variant.

120. One manuscript Slovakian variant.

121. One manuscript Slovakian variant.

124. One manuscript Slovakian variant (a half-tune).

125. One manuscript Slovakian variant.

128. A very widespread song. Two manuscript Slovakian variants, another in *Detva*, p. 296 (second tune); Moravian variant: Černík, 278.

131. Compare with Example 149.

132. See p. 42, par. 2.

134. Two manuscript Slovakian variants. One Moravian: Černík, 276.

135. One peculiar three-line Slovakian variant (manuscript). In determining the form, the first line was considered as fifteen-syllable by analogy with the second.

136. Sung by soldiers in Kassa.

139. In recent times the A and A⁵ lines in this tune were extended thus:

140. Very popular since 1914, but was known far and wide before that: in fact two curiously abridged Rumanian variants were collected in 1909. See *Chansons populaires roumaines du département Bihar* (Hongrie), Nos. 195, 196. No. 195 is:

which corresponds to the second half of the Hungarian original. The part of the song that has the burden is practically unaltered (moreover, the Rumanian burden is an almost verbatim translation of the Hungarian). This tune was probably derived from the song 'Piros bort ittam az este', composed by Elemér Szentirmay. There is one manuscript Slovakian variant.

143. One manuscript Rumanian variant from district Maros-Torda. Probably derived from an art song.

144. There exists a variant in which the A-lines have an authentic cadence.

147. One manuscript Slovakian variant (a half-tune).

149. The second part of this tune, sung to the words 'Megállj, megállj, kutya Szerbia' (Stop, stop, hound Serbia), was very popular in the autumn of 1914. The example, giving the tune in full, is from the beginning of 1914. It was not possible to write down the words. Of the second part of the tune there is one manuscript Slovakian variant. Cf. Example 131.

150. Lines 1, 2, and 4 were also sung with authentic cadences.

151. See p. 70, last par. Of 151 *b* there are 2 manuscript Slovakian variants.

1

152. Match-making text.

2

153. Var.: Sz.N. 47.
154. Wedding text.—Slovakian variants: 11 manuscript; further: *Slovenské
Spevy*, i. 21, 69, 561; ii. 213, 299, 364, 372; iii. 252. Borrowed from
the Slovakian.
157. Var.: Sz.N. 41; Bartalus, vi. 11.
159. Dance tune; a so-called 'bagpipe tune'.
160. Probably a 'bagpipe tune'. 8 manuscript Slovakian variants. Moravian variants: Bartoš, i. 99, ii. 20, 50 *c*, 161, 830, iii. 627, 821, 1260,
1551; further p. lxxxvii, No. 26. Borrowed from the Slovakian.
165. Has two kinds of authentic variants: either the last bar becomes

, or the tune remains quite unaltered, but is given the addi-

tional following tune-line: . In the latter

case, the third and fourth lines of the original may be considered as
forming one double line (6+6); and the tune, accordingly, will go into
C III, sub-Class 1. A very well-known song.
166. The second half is in a variable rhythm; so that the tune might as
well go into sub-Class *C* II.
167. Var.: Színi, No. 184; Bartalus, iii. 61. Structure A⁵B⁵AB. Might go
into Class *A*. Very widespread in region II, and has many Slovakian
and Moravian variants (probably borrowed from the Hungarian):
Slovenské Spevy, i. 87, 224, 524, iii. 296, 423; Bartoš, i. 57, 148, ii. 642,
iii. 22.
168. Var.: Bartalus, ii. 122. One of the most widespread songs (about 20
manuscript variants are available). Might be admitted into Class *A*.
In the example the *rubato* is exceptional: usually the song is sung in
tempo giusto, as indicated below the staves. Slovakian variants: 2
manuscript; *Slovenské Spevy*, i. 272, ii. 197, iii. 50; *Detva*, p. 291;
Moravian var.: Sušil, 646; Bartoš, 140.
169. Known only in region II, and in 2 variants. Slovakian var.: 2 manuscript; *Slovenské Spevy*, i. 138, 291, ii. 538, 560, iii. 68; Moravian
var.: Sušil, 593, 680 *d*; Bartoš, ii. 41, 53 *a*, iii. 110 *a*; Peck,[1] 182.
170. Var.: Bartalus, vii. 76 (to different words). In this example the

[1] E. Peck, *Valašské Národní písně*, Brno, 1860.

mixture of languages (a so-called 'macaronic' mixture) is remarkable: one line of Hungarian alternates with one of Slovakian throughout. It is most interesting to note that a macaronic variant of the first strophe of *b* is to be found in Kollár's collection of Slovakian folk-poems,[1] vol. ii, No. 178. (There is also another Slovakian-Hungarian text.) Such mixtures in texts are comparatively uncommon. A very well-known one is the Hungarian-Slovakian variant of the text: 'Sárga uborkának zöld a levele'. Only two other examples are known: a Slovakian-Hungarian text from Zólyom and one from Nyitra. Cf. the words of Example 239, and remark to Example 303 *c*.

172. Var.: Bartalus, i. 17 ([V] [3] [4]). A very well-known tune, always sung to the same text or to variants of it. The variants show the greatest variety of line-endings, e.g. [3] [III] [2], [8] [V] [3], [V] [3] [V], [V] [5] [2], and [1] [8] [5]: practically as many different main caesuras as there are variants of the tune.

173. Var.: Színi, 132; Bartalus, iii. 162 (in the latter the rhythm of bars 6 and 7 is incorrectly given. By comparing the records of Színi and Bartalus, one sees clearly how very much better Színi understood Hungarian folk-tunes). In this example the variable rhythm and the slow tempo is undoubtedly ascribable to incorrect singing. Cf. p. 150, par. 3.

175. Match-making text.

176. One of the most widespread tunes, always sung to the ballad text 'Sári (or Sági) biróné'. In all likelihood the form *b* (in the major scale) is the oldest, out of which may have been derived, by substitution of the plagal, the Mixolydian variants with the ending

 . Variant *a*, with its pentatonic turns,

comes close to the old style.

177. Slovakian var.: *Slovenské Spevy*, ii. 157.

178. Slovakian var.: *Slovenské Spevy*, i. 33.—Borrowed from the Slovakian (see p. 58, pars. 1–2).

3

179. Var.: Bartalus, iv. 144. Moravian var.: Bartoš, ii. 987, iii. 82; Černík, 12.

180. Has been given the name 'Bagpipes Polka'.

181. Dance tune. The singer called it 'sima sebes forgató'. The structure is ABCD.

182. A jocular game-song. Sung at parties, the singer limping the while. A similar one in Bartalus, i. 26.

[1] Jan Kollár, *Národnié Zpiewanky*, Ofen, 1834–5,

183. Structure ABCD and in sequences. Cf. Examples 206 and 250. There are one Slovakian variant and one Rumanian, both manuscript; Moravian var.: Bartoš, iii. 1224; Peck, 142.

184. Var.: Színi, No. 86; Bartalus, iv. 60. The other variants have the main caesura $\boxed{1}$ or $\boxed{V}$. Mostly sung to the words of the example. One manuscript Slovakian var., one Ukraïnian. Probably of German origin. The text has Slovakian variants, sung to similar or other tunes.

185. Variants with a few differences ($\boxed{5}$ $\boxed{8}$ $\boxed{4}$): Bartalus, iii. 13, vi. 8. Never sung to other words. Very widespread. Slovakian variants: 8 manuscript; *Slovenské Spevy*, i. 62, 246, 394, ii. 169, 475, iii. 163, 220, 380; Moravian variants: Sušil, 821 *b*; Bartoš, ii. 660, iii. 697, 1131; Czech variant: Erben,[1] 91. One of the manuscript variants is closer to the examples in Bartalus, but the remainder are closer to the example given here. Borrowed from the Slovakian (see p. 58, pars. 1–2). Compare with the three-line tune, Example 310.

4

188. Identical: Sz.N. 76.

191. Var.: Sz.N. 31, 32; Bartalus, i. 137, 140, iii. 16, 74, vi. 13, 26. A very widespread song, but known (except for one variant) only in region IV.

193. Has variants, known only in region III.

194. Var.: Bartalus, vi. 16. Might go into Class *A*.

196. Two variants, known only from district Csík. Probably borrowed from the Rumanian fund of Máramaros. Similar tunes: *Volksmusik der Rumänen von Maramureș*, Nos. 83, 84.

197. Slovakian and Czech variants: *Slovenské Spevy*, i. 242, 467; Erben, 306. Liszt has used one variant of this tune in his 7th Hungarian Rhapsody.

198. Var.: Színi, No. 40 (with minor third).

199. Match-making text.

200. Similar tune ($\boxed{3}$ $\boxed{1}$ $\boxed{7}$): Színi, No. 88.

201. Described as a dance tune. The structure is a kind of $A^5B^5A_vA$. Slovakian var.: 2 manuscript from district Nyitra; *Slovenské Spevy*, i. 32; Moravian var.: Sušil, 797 *b*; Bartoš, i. 188, iii. 859. Probably borrowed from the Slovakian.

202. Identical tune: Sz.N. 143. Here the *parlando-rubato*, which is exceptional, replaces the original *tempo giusto* ‖: ♩♩♩♩ | ♩♩♩♩ | ♩♩♩♩ | ♪♪♩ | ♩ :‖.

205. Slovakian 'rhythm-contraction' in lines 2 and 3 (see p. 58, pars. 1–2).

[1] K. J. Erben, *Nápěvy prostonárodních písní českých*, Praha, 1863.

Two manuscript Slovakian variants; Moravian and Czech var.: Sušil, 512; Erben, 750. Certainly borrowed from the Slovakian.

5

206. Structure ABCD and in sequences; cf. Examples 183 and 250. Slovakian var.: 1 manuscript; *Slovenské Spevy*, i. 68, ii. 490, iii. 48; Moravian var.: Sušil, 799 *f* (first on p. 665), 803 *r* (first on p. 680); Bartoš, i. 225, iii. 660.
207. Var.: Színi, 139; Bartalus, ii. 31; in both the structure of the strophe is heterometric; the second is probably the original form, and possibly an art song, from which the more rustic form of the example evolved.
208. So-called 'bridal dance'. Sung to wedding texts only. Moravian var.: Bartoš, ii. 145, iii. 36 *b*, 621.
209. Of this example there exist variants from a few western districts, and one from the Székely region. Appears to be an old art song, whose fixed text is likewise characteristic in this respect. The Székely variant consists of a half-tune only.
210. Similar tune (⌐6⌐ 6 ♭3): Bartalus, v. 38.

7

212. Var.: Bartalus, ii. 28 (the rhythm incorrectly given).

8

213. Var.: Sz.N. 28. Known from region IV only, but very widespread there.
214. Var.: Sz.N. 44.

9

215. Appears to be an old art song with fixed words. Variants in regions I and IV only.

10

216. A dance tune. The motions of the dancers comprise peculiar motions of the hands, among which—to the first quavers of the first and second bars of the third and fourth tune-lines—a threatening movement of the first finger. One Hungarian variant from Ujszász (district Pest). The third and fourth tune-lines in the example may have been originally fourteen-syllable, as they are in the variant from Ujszász. Therefore I have considered the tune as isometric. Three manuscript Slovakian variants; one Moravian: Bartoš, iii, p. cxxii; and one

Czech: Erben, 472. The Czechs, Moravians, and Slovakians call this tune and the corresponding dance 'strašiak' (i.e. the bug-bear).

C II

1

217. Var.: Bartalus, i. 2. Known from region IV only.

2

218. *a* is the authentic, *b* the plagal variant of the same tune. Slovakian var.: 3 manuscript; *Slovenské Spevy*, ii. 717; Moravian var.: Bartoš, iii. 704—all authentic.

220. Var.: Bartalus, vi. 117. There are two authentic variants from district Tolna. The fourth line shows the rhythm extension characteristic of the new style.

3

222. On account of its pentatonic turns, which recall the Székely tunes in the old style, this example ought perhaps to go into Class *A*. In determining the form, the syllables 'Csej-haj' in the third line were not taken into account. Originally, the fourth line too must have consisted of eight syllables:

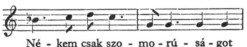

Né - kem csak szo - mo - rú - sá - got

wherefore the example is placed in sub-group II (with isometric strophe-structure). Of late years the song has spread throughout the country, and its lines have become eleven-syllable.

223. There are manuscript Slovakian variants, whose third line has the burden 'kiš and'alom' (for the Hungarian words 'kis angyalom', my little angel).

225. Variants *a* and *b* illustrate the change of a tune belonging to Class *C* into one belonging to Class *B* (*a*: AABC; *b*: AABA).

4

226. Wedding text. Var.: Bartalus, i. 35, given as 5 5 ⌊ı⌋ (and the rhythm being incorrectly noted). Many Slovakian and Moravian variants, probably of Hungarian origin: 5 manuscript Slovakian; *Slovenské Spevy*, i. 46; Sušil, 490, 782 *k* (last tune on p. 606), 803 *v* (first tune on p. 681); Bartoš, i. 131, ii. 177, 714, iii. 596, 1241.

227. Var.: Bartalus, vi. 44. Slovakian var.: 3 manuscript; *Slovenské Spevy*, ii. 348, 435, 461, 600, 761; Moravian var.: Bartoš, iii. 561; probably borrowed from the Hungarian.

5

228. Usually sung to the text 'Pápainé'.
230. Match-making text. One manuscript Slovakian var. (borrowed from the Hungarian).
231. In determining the form, the rhythm-extension at the end of the first two lines (♪♪♪♪ 𝅗𝅥 ⌣ ♪ 𝅘𝅥𝅭 𝅗𝅥) was not taken into account.
233. One manuscript Slovakian var. (borrowed from the Hungarian).
234. See Remark, p. 63.

C III

4

239. Both words and tune are of Slovakian origin. See note to second strophe of text, p. 165. Slovakian var.: 2 manuscript; *Slovenské Spevy*, i. 66, 243; Moravian: Bartoš, iii. 347.
241. Var.: Színi, 137, 138 (might also be considered as var. of Example 239).
242. Sung at the Easter traditional practices. On Easter Sunday boys go singing it near houses in which girls live. The words seem to belong to an old art song.
243. Wedding text (sung when the cart arrived at the house of the bride's parents, to carry her and her dowry to the bridegroom's house). Var.: Bartalus, i. 48, 71, v. 105. A very widespread tune, sung to various other words. Might go into Class *A* on account of its pentatonic structure. Slovakian var.: 5 manuscript; *Slovenské Spevy*, i. 44, 245, 258, iii. 84; Moravian var.: Bartoš, i. 25, 41, iii. 200; Peck, 30; Černík, 117. All these probably borrowed from the Hungarian.
244. May have been a dance tune. The scale is pure pentatonic, with the major third and major seventh that are characteristic of region I. The presence of both the F sharp and the F natural is correlative to the structure A^5B^5AB and the raising of the third. Might go into Class *A*. Compare with Example 261.
245. Var.: Bartalus, vii. 165 (from the collection of Ádám Horváth [1760–1820]; a half-tune). Slovakian var.: 2 manuscript; *Slovenské Spevy*, i. 333, 424, ii. 718; Moravian var.: Sušil, 791 *b*. Probably borrowed from the Hungarian.

6

246. A game-song.

211

249. Match-making text. One manuscript Slovakian var. from district Hont.

8

250. Tune of the 'Kalamajkó' dance—which, curiously, bears no relation to the Kolomeïka tunes of the Ruthenians. It was borrowed from the Czech fund, the Slovakian being the intermediary. Perhaps its origin should be sought even farther west. The Czechs sing it to the words 'Kalamajka, myk myk myk, Oženil se kominik', &c., with a few small variations (seven-syllable, isometric lines). See Erben, 231, and Bartoš, iii, p. cxxv, No. 53. Further Slovakian, Moravian, and Czech variants (with dissimilar words): three manuscript Slovakian; *Slovenské Spevy*, i. 602 *b*, ii. 14; Erben, 581; Sušil, 799 *f* (first tune on p. 665); Bartoš, ii. 391, 394, iii. 960, 1538. Structure ABCD and in sequences. That the tune is of Western origin is quite obvious. Compare with Examples 183 and 206.

252. Variants of the words occur among the Germans, the Slovakians, the Rumanians, and are surely to be found elsewhere too. Many such variants in the Hungarian fund.

254. Var.: Színi, No. 28; Bartalus, iii. 159. Known throughout the country. Perhaps borrowed from the Slovakian fund. Slovakian var.: 5 manuscript; *Slovenské Spevy*, ii. 444, iii. 185; Moravian: Bartoš, ii. 490, iii. 247, 308, 468.

255. Var.: Bartalus, i. 94 (with major scale).

256. Match-making text.

257. Game-song. Tune probably of German origin. Many Slovakian variants of the words.

259. Var.: Színi, 85, 134; Bartalus, ii. 7, 9, 130, v. 146, vii. 157; Kiss, p. 444, No. 1. 15 other variants are known. Very widespread. The words are either of the match-making order, or the well-known 'Zúg az erdő, zúg a mező', or variants of the words of variant *d*. Variants *a–e* constitute a most instructive instance of melody-transformation. Variant *a* is probably the oldest form, and was originally in *tempo giusto* rhythm: ‖: ♫♩ | ♫♩ | ♫ ♩ | ♫ ♩ :‖ . Thence may have evolved *b*, and from *b* again *c*, which has already adapted itself to the pentatonic structure of the old style. In *d* and *e* the evolution follows

another direction, as shown by the remarkable extension of lines 1 and 3. In *e* the main caesura is no longer ⑤ but ⑧. There are certain fluctuations in the scale: *e* and *e♭*, *a* and *a♭*; the tempo is more than twice as slow, and accordingly a corresponding rhythm has come into being. Slovakian variants of 259 *a*: *Slovenské Spevy*, ii. 233; of 259 *c*: ibid. i. 453; 5 other manuscript Slovakian variants, another in *Slovenské Spevy*, i. 437.

260. *b* is perhaps a match-making text.

II

261. On account of its pentatonic scale, might go into Class *A*. Compare with Example 244.

16

262. Match-making words.
265. Match-making words.
267. Match-making words.
268. Many similar songs in the Czech fund (e.g. Erben, 122, 140, 186, 710, 719), but these may have come there from German regions. The drinking-song-like text is certainly not rustic, and the urban classes must have helped in diffusing the song.

C IV

I

269. No Hungarian var. Rumanian var.: *Volksmusik der Rumänen von Maramureș*, Nos. 37 and 49. The tune was borrowed from the Rumanians, but had arisen among them under Hungarian influences. In determining the form, the fourth line also was considered as ♩ ♩ ♩ ♩ | ♪ ♩. ♩ | , i.e. seven-syllable.

270. Wedding text. The first strophe is sung on the same occasions as Example 243; the following three are sung when the bride arrives at the home of the bridegroom's parents. Var.: Bartalus, iv. 11. Around Kalotaszeg it is sung to the words given here, on nuptial occasions; elsewhere the tune is usually sung to the text 'Zöld Marci'.

271. No Hungarian variant. Rumanian variants: *Volksm. der Rum. von Mar.*, Nos. 110 *a*, *b*, and 134. Like the foregoing, arose among the Rumanians under Hungarian influences, and was borrowed from them.

3

272. One variant from Nagyszalonta. One manuscript Slovakian variant

from Ponik (district Zólyom), dating from 1915, in which the words are:

> A v tej našej zahradôčky
> Píška Janík na píšt'alky,
> Piroš a zezelen, hod' babám seretem ⎱ burden.
> Hod' igazán seretem. ⎰

The fourth tune-line is: [musical notation]. The burden, in corrupt Hungarian, of this variant shows that the song was borrowed from the Hungarian fund. And the burden of the Hungarian variant points out that the tune originated in an art song.

273. Cf. Example 114 and p. 69.

5

274. In determining the form, the fourth line was considered as seven-syllable (as with Example 269).

6

275. Var.: Bartalus, v. 75. The third and fourth lines of var. *b* contain rhythm extensions that are characteristic of Class *B*. Of *b* there exists a variant, double in length, whose structure is AABA, like Example 276 *a*. Cf. p. 69. Two manuscript Slovakian variants (borrowed from the Hungarian).

276. *b* is the plagal form of *a*. See remark to No. 275.

277. Var.: Sz.N. 148 (in *tempo giusto*, without the extension 'Ej haj'). The *parlando-rubato* interpretation of the example is exceptional. Slovakian var.: 4 manuscript; *Slovenské Spevy*, i. 299, 470, ii. 105, 140, iii. 214, 426, 470; Moravian: Bartoš, i. 157, ii. 17, 599, 643; Černík, 145 (borrowed from the Hungarian).

278. Slovakian variant, almost identical: *Slovenské Spevy*, iii. 251. Two other manuscript Slovakian variants.

7

280. Var.: Színi, No. 104. Two exceptionally interesting manuscript Rumanian variants, from districts Torda-Aranyos and Alsó-Fehér, which will be dealt with in the book on Rumanian folk-music. These are obviously borrowed from the Hungarian fund.

8

282. Said to be a 'bagpipe tune'. In determining the form, the seventh bar was not taken into account. Moravian and Czech variants (in non-dotted, invariable rhythm): Bartoš, ii. 644, iii. 232, 1568; Erben, 435.

284. Sung by soldiers in Beszterczebánya. Very widespread since 1915.
285. Originated, in all likelihood, in the second part of a well-known tune from the opera 'Hunyadi László', by Francis Erkel:

One variant of it stands closer to the model, and is to be found also in the Slovakian fund. Never sung to other words. The tune is very widespread.

286. Slovakian var.: 5 manuscript; *Slovenské Spevy*, ii. 311, iii. 217, 250, 386.
287. Var.: Bartalus, i. 37. In determining the form, the fourth line was considered as seven-syllable.
288. In determining the form, the fourth line was considered as seven-syllable.
289. This example and its two variants were found only in the Erdély country. The rhythm extensions of the line were not taken into account in determining the form: the count of syllables taken as basis was not 12, 7, 12, 9, but 8, 7, 8, 7—which was probably the original form.

11

290. One manuscript Ruthenian var. (borrowed from the Hungarians). Certainly originates in an isometric structure.
291. Var.: Sz.N. 98 (given as a 'Gipsy song'; the final note being curiously raised by a major third: ⌐♭6⌐ ⌐♭3⌐ ⌐4⌐, and the scale being Phrygian). Two Rumanian variants: *Volksm. der Rum. von Mar.*, No. 160, and the other manuscript from district Maros-Torda. There is also the following variant, with gipsy words, from Lissó (district Hont):

F. 1106 c. Tempo giusto, ♩ = 98. |5| 1914. B. |5|

¹ Ka-na gé-lyom ke-le szkri-daj Su-kar pa-tyiu me-szi ka-gyom haj dev-la,

burden

|1|

Du-var tri-val csu-mi-di-nyu Lesz-kra da-ko pa-le di-nyo haj dev - la.

burden

The origin of the tune is not determined. Probably it comes from an art song.

292. Var.: Bartalus, iv. 116. Found only in region IV. Its Rumanian variants, from district Maros-Torda, are known only as dance tunes, without words. Origin not determined.

293. Var.: Sz.N. 53. Despite its dance rhythm, is called by the Székely 'keserves' (which means, in Hungarian, a song of sadness).

294. A dance tune. Rumanian variants from district Maros-Torda occur as dance tunes without words. Origin not determined. The extension of lines 2 and 4 is usually carried out thus: ♩ ♩ ♩ ♩ | ♩ ♩ ♩ ♪ ‖ ·

tra la la la la la la

The extension as carried out in the example—in eight quavers and to repeated text-lines—is exceptional.

16

295. Sung only to variants of the words of the example.

297. Sung only to variants of the words of the example. The Slovaks and Rumanians have much longer variants of the words—variants consisting of 'homologous' strophes—which are sung to other tunes. In these variants the parts of the horse's corpse are enumerated, crude terms being freely used.

298. Match-making text. Var.: Bartalus, v. 192.

299. Var.: Bartalus, iv. 57. Cf. p. 69. The words b of var. c occur among the Slovakians, but in a longer form (comprising five homologous strophes) with a tune of similar strophe-structure. See *Slovenské Spevy*, i. 194 and iii. 62, 286.

300. Match-making text.

¹ The words are written according to Hungarian orthography.

302. Var.: Bartalus, iii. 146. Two manuscript Slovakian variants.
303. Form *c* is also sung to the following very well-known macaronic words (Hungarian-Rumanian):

> Tiéd rózsám, tiéd voltam, de már nem vagyok,
> Pintru csinye nu ma jade, meg sem is halok, &c.

There are 4 manuscript Slovakian variants of the tune.
304. Var.: in Káldy's 'Kurucz dalok',[1] the song whose words are 'Tyukodi pajtás'. Probably originates in an art song. Similar Slovakian tunes are known.

C VI

306. One manuscript Rumanian variant of the words (from district Alsó-Fehér) sung to another tune.

C VII

308. Match-making text. 4 manuscript Slovakian variants of the tune.
309. So far as I know, this is the only instance of this text to be found in the Hungarian fund; but there are more or less numerous variants of it in the Slovakian, the Czech, and practically all other European languages.
310. Var.: Színi, No. 18 (four lines: the first is repeated), No. 196; Bartalus, iii. 86 and 95 (this last quite incorrectly noted: it should be identical with Színi, 18).
311. Match-making text. Var.: Bartalus, i. 141 (in the minor). One manuscript Slovakian variant.
312. Var.: Bartalus, vii. 124.
313. See p. 77.
314. Match-making text.
315. Sung by a fifteen-year-old girl, who had learnt it from her grandmother.
316. Match-making text (?).
317. Var.: Bartalus, iii. 15 (in the form [V] [2], 8, 8, 12, v–5); vi. 89 (in the form [1] [5], 8, 8, 10, 1–9; rhythm incorrectly noted).
318. Var.: Bartalus, iv. 100. Sung especially to wedding texts, and only in the western part of region II. Slovakian and Moravian var.: 2 manuscript Slovakian; *Sborník*,[2] 7 *a*; *Slovenské Spevy*, i. 157, 335; ii. 321, 628; Sušil, 565; Peck, 90; Bartoš, iii. 951, 1215 *d*, 1357, 1571. Borrowed from the Slovakian.
319. Match-making text.

[1] Gyula Káldy, *Kurucz dalok XVII és XVIII század.*
[2] *Sborník Slovenských národních piesni*, published by the 'Matica Slovenská', Vienna, 1870 (contains 66 Slovakian tunes).

I, II, III. Three Tcheremiss tunes, phonograms of which were taken in 1906 by Mrs. Julia Wichman in the village of Yelassy (district of Kosmo-demiansk, government of Kazan, Russia). These were sung by Olga Stefanovna (20 years old), and are written down from the phonograms by Béla Bartók. Their scale is the pentatonic, characteristic of the old Hungarian style. The structure is A_4B_4AB (A_4 being a fourth below A), corresponding, so far as concerns essentials, with structure A^5B^5AB (A_4B_4 raised by an octave $= A^5B^5$). In order to emphasize the analogy, the first half of each tune is marked *octava*.

Translation of the words

I. I grew as grows a one-year-old seedling,
   And my hair was pledged to sacrifice before it had grown.
III. By the banks of the Jəŋgə grow water-melons.
   When you go to eat water-melons, wake us, call us.

The words of No. II are lacking.

A. I.

Muz. F. 1030 b); IV. Tekerőpatak (Csík), 1907.; B.

Parlando. ♩ = 68.

1.

Sir a kis ga-lam-bom, sí - rok én ma-gam is. Si-runk mind a ketten

i - gën ke - ser - ve-sën. A - nyám, é-dës a - nyám, mért ül-dö-zesz

en-gëm, Mért nem hagy-tad ezt a kis lë-ányt el - ven-nëm?

Muz. F. 1016 b); IV. Vacsárcsi (Csík), 1907.;B.

Parlando, ♪ = 192. *rit. - - - al - - -*

2.

Ke-mény kő-szik-lá - nak könnyebb megha-sad - ni, Mint két é - des szűv-nek

♪ = 160.

egy-más-tól meg - vál-ni. *M* Mi - kor két é - des szűv egy - más - tól meg-

vá-lik, Még az é-des méz es ke - se - rű - vé vá-lik.

Muz. F. 1272 a); IV. Gyergyószentmiklós (Csík), 1910.; K.

Parlando, ♩ = 76 - 72.

3.

Aj, Si-rass él-des a-nyám, mig e-lőt-ted já-rok, Mer az-tán si-rat-hatsz,

ha tő-led el - vá-lok. *Aj,* A jó is - ten tud-ja,

hol tör-tén ha-lá-lom, A jó is-ten tud-ja, hol tör-tén ha - lá - lom.

F. 1315 a); IV. Ehed (Maros-Torda), Nagy Ferencné (45), 1914.; B.

4.

Parlando, ♪=cca 126.

1. Nem ar-ről haj-nal-lik, a-mer-ről haj-nal-lott, I Nem ar-ről haj-nal-lik,
a-mer-ről haj-nal-lott, I Ma-gam sor-sa fe-lől szo-mo-rú hírt hal-lok,
Ma-gam sor-sa fe-lől szo-mo-rú hírt hal-lok.

Muz. F. 354 a); IV. Kadicsfalva (Udvarhely), Tibád Lajosné (75); V.

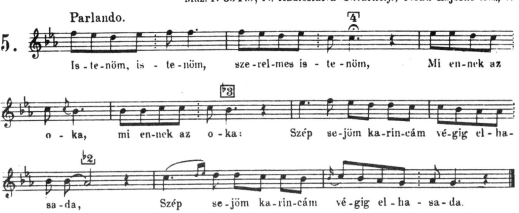

5.

Parlando.

Is-te-nöm, is-te-nöm, sze-rel-mes is-te-nöm, Mi en-nek az
o-ka, mi en-nek az o-ka: Szép se-jöm ka-rin-cám vé-gig el-ha-
sa-da, Szép se-jöm ka-rin-cám vé-gig el-ha-sa-da.

I. Felsőiregh (Tolna), Szabó Mihály (70), 1907.; B.

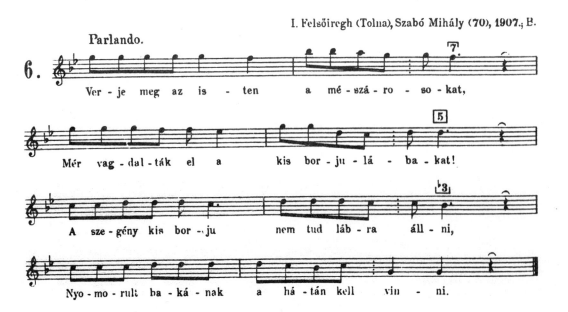

6.

Parlando.

Ver-je meg az is-ten a mé-szá-ro-so-kat,
Mér vag-dal-ták el a kis bor-ju-lá-ba-kat!
A sze-gény kis bor-ju nem tud láb-ra áll-ni,
Nyo-mo-rult ba-ká-nak a há-tán kell vin-ni.

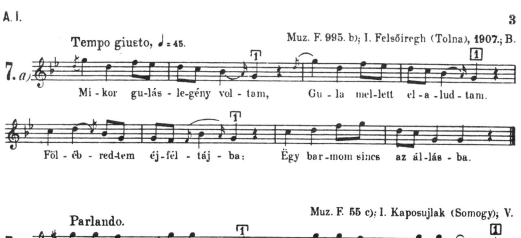

Tempo giusto, ♩ = 45.

Muz. F. 995. b); I. Felsőiregh (Tolna), **1907.**; B.

7. *a)*

Mi - kor gu-lás - le-gény vol - tam, Gu - la mel-lett el - a - lud - tam.

Föl - éb - red-tem éj-fél - táj - ba: Egy bar-mom sincs az ál-lás - ba.

Parlando.

Muz. F. 55 c); I. Kaposujlak (Somogy); V.

7. *b)*

Mi - kor gu-lás - boj-tár vol - tam, Nyáj-jam mel-lett el - a - lud - tam.

Föl - éb - .. red-tem é - fé - tá - ján: Egy bar - mom sincs az ál-lá - sán.

Parlando.

Muz. F. 258 a); II. Mezőkövesd (Borsod), Kovács Mátyás; V.

7. *c)*

1. Meg-állj paj-tás, hagy pa - na-szo - lom el sor - som, Mi-ként áll az

ál - la-po-tom: I-nyës-fi-nyës a put-li-kom, Har-mad-nap-ba sincs pró-fon-tom.

Parlando.

Muz. F. 1331 b); II. Ipolyság (Hont), 1910; B.

8.

1. El-ment Si - mon disz- nót lop-nyi, Nem jó hely-re ta-lált mennyi.

Ot-tan vár - ja egy pár fegy-ver: Ugy jár, kit az is-ten meg-ver.

Tempo giusto.

III. Vésztő (Békés), Kocsis Juhász Róza (15), **1917.**; B.

9.

1. Hal-lot-tá-tok - e már hí - rül Ka-szai Sa-nyi le-gény-sé - gül;

Bics-ká - val vág - ja ja nyár - fát, Hogy ne hall-ják do-bo-gá - sát.

Muz. F. 1635 a); II. Rafajnaujfalu (Bereg), Gajdos János (60), 1912.; B.

Parlando, ♩ = 80—90.

10.

1. Min-den em-ber sze-ren-csé-sen,   Csak én é-lek ke-ser-ve-sen;

Fe-jem le-haj-tom csen-de-sen,   Csak ugy si-rok ke-ser-ve-sen.

Muz. F. 1344 b); II. Ipolyság (Hont), 1910.; B.

Tempo giusto, ♩ = 148.

11. *a)*

Ar-ra gye-re, a mő-re én.   Maj mëg-tu-dod, hol la-kok én:

Csip-ke-bo-kor- ró-zsa mel-lett, — Gye-re ba-bám, mëg-ö-'-lel'-lek.

Muz. F. 1314; IV. Csíkmenaság (Csík), 1911.; L.

Tempo giusto.

11. *b)*

A cser-ol-dalt ösz-sze-jár-tam,   Se-hol pá-rom nem ta-

lál-tam. Ez a hat fo-rin-tos nó-ta,   Ki-nek tet-szik, jár-ja re-a.

Muz. F. 1518 a); IV. Gyergyócsomafalva (Csík), 1911.; M.

Parlando.

12.

Na-pom, na-pom fé-nyës na-pom,   Ho-mály-ban bo-rult csil-la-gom   *Hn*

Süss még ëgyszër vi-lá-go-san, *Hej* Ne süss min-díg ho-má-lyo-san.

F. 232 b); IV. Andrásfalva (Bukovina), Erős Kati (61), 1914.; K.

Tempo giusto, ♩ = 108.

13.

Ed-dig ven-dég jól mu-lat-tál;   Ha tet-sze-nék, el-in-dul-nál!

Sza-iadj gaz-da, kap-jál bot-ra,   A ven-dé-get in-dítsd út-ra.

14. Parlando, ♩ = 92.

Muz. F. 1040 a); IV. Gyergyóujfalu (Csík), 1907.; B.

1. Ha - ran-goz-nak ve-csër - nyé - re, Gye-re paj-tás az er - dő - re,

Az uj ut-nak te-te - jé - re, Az uj ut-nak te - te - jé - re.

15. Parlando.

l. Felsőiregh (Tolna), 1906.; B.

Er-dők, völ-gyek, szűk li - ge-tek, So-kat buj-dos - tam benne-tek. Buj-dos-tam én

az va-dak-kal, Sir-tam a kis ma-da - rak-kal.

16. Parlando, ♪ = 152.

Muz. F. 1015 c); IV. Vacsárcsi (Csík), 1907.; B.

Ha ki-in-dulsz Er-dély fe - lől, Ne nézz ró-zsám visz-sza - fe-lé:

Szi-ved-nek ne lë-gyën ne - héz, Hogy az i - de - gën föld-re mész.

17. Parlando.

Muz. F. 460 d); IV. Szentegyházasfalu (Udvarhely), Tankó Józsefné; V.

Meg - mond-tam én bus ger-li-ce: Ne rak' fész - ket az út - szél - re,

Mert az u - ton so-kan jár - nak, A fész - ked-ből el-va-dász-nak.

18. Tempo giusto, ♩ = 100.

Muz. F. 1332 b); ll. Ipolyság (Hont), 1910.; B.

Föl-mën-tem a szil-va-fá - ra, El - re-pedt a ga-tyám szá - ra.

Hu - szul b...... az ir-gal - mát, Maj mëg - varr-ja az én ba-bám.

Parlando, ♪ = 150.

Muz. F. 1028a); IV. Tekerőpatak (Csík), 1907.; B.

19.

Hej Gyu-la-i-né é-dës a-nyám! En - ged-je mëg azt az ë - gyet: Hogy
— kér-jem mëg Ká-dár Ka - tát, Job-bá-gyunknak szép lë - á-nyát.

Parlando.

II. Tura (Pest), 1906.; B.

20.

1. Szán-ta-ni kék, ta-vasz va-gyon, A szer-szá-mom széj-jel va-gyon,
A szer-szá-mom széj-jel va-gyon, E-kém szar-va Szar-va-son van.

Parlando, ♪ = 184.

Muz. F. 1014c); IV. Csíkrákos (Csík), 1907.; B.

21.

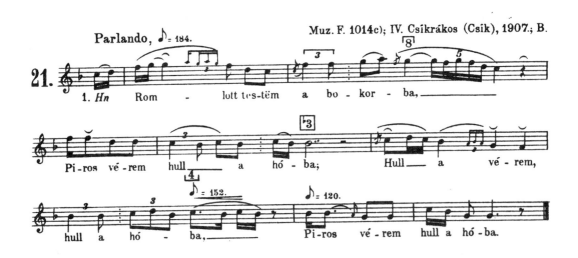

1. Hn Rom — lott tes-tëm a bo - kor - ba, —
Pi - ros vé - rem hull — a hó - ba; Hull — a vé - rem,
♪ = 152. ♪ = 120.
hull a hó - ba, — Pi - ros vé - rem hull a hó - ba.

Parlando, ♩ = cca 144.

Muz. F. 1016a); IV. Csíkvacsárcsi (Csík), 1907.; B.

22.

1. Mi-kor a nagy er-dőn ki-mész, Ar - ra kér-lek, visz-sza ne nézz;
Ne le-gyen szű-ved-nek ne - héz, Hogy az i - de - gën föld - re mész.

Parlando.

Muz. F. 1632 b); II. Rafajnaujfalu (Bereg), Demeter Károly (20), 1912.; B.

23.

A fe-ke-te ha-lom a-latt *De* Fe-hér Lász-ló lo-vat lo-pott. *De*

Lo-vat lo-pott szer-szá-mos-tul, Cif-ra nye-reg-kan-tá-ros-tul.

Muz. F. 943 a); II. Tura (Pest), Veszelka Mihályné (50), 1906.; B.

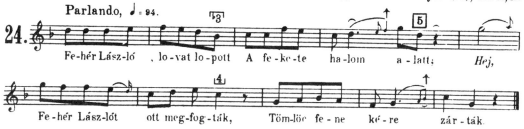

Parlando, ♪ = 94.

24.

Fe-hér Lász-ló, lo-vat lo-pott A fe-ke-te ha-lom a-latt; *Hej,*

Fe-hér Lász-lót ott meg-fog-ták, Töm-löc fe-ne ké-re zár-ták.

Muz. F. 402 d); IV. Lövéte (Udvarhely) Jánosi Anna; V.

Tempo giusto.

25.

Túl a vi-zön, a tön-gö-rön Ró-zsa te-röm a ken-dö-rön;

Min-dön szá-lon ket-tő-há-rom,— Van sze-re-tőm ti-zen-há-rom.

Muz. F. 1033 c); IV. Tekerőpatak (Csík), 1907.; B.

Parlando, ♪ = 180. allarg. - - - - al - - - - ♪ = 120.

26.

1. To-va më-nyën há-rom ár-va, Tö-lük kér-di a Szűz Már-ja:

-Ho-va mën-tëk há-rom ár-va? Ho-va mën-tëk há-rom ár-va?

Muz. F. 941 a); II. Tura (Pest), Versecky József (40), 1906.; B.

Parlando, ♪ = 73.

27.

1. Egy he-te-e vagy már há-rom. Mi-ó-ta a gaz-dám vá-rom?

A-mott jön már, a-mint lá-tom, Egy de-res-sző-rű sza-má-ron. 1) var.

Muz. F. 471 e); IV. Felsőboldogfalva (Udvarhely), Péter Ignác; V.

Tempo giusto.

28. 1. Ci-gány va-gyok,　rest a ne-vem.　Ha dol - go-zom,　fáj　a fe-jem.

-Ci-gány, ci-gány,　mért vagy ci-gány,　Mért jársz a ma - gyar lány　u - tán?

III. Vésztő (Békés), Ökrös Róza (18), 1918.; B.

Parlando.

29. 1. *Hej* Fe-hér Lász-ló　lo-vat lo-pott A fe - ke - te　ha-lom　a - latt,　*hej,*

Ha-tot fo-gott　su-ho-gó - ra,　Görc vá - ro - sa　cso-dá-já - ra.

Muz. F. 1633; II. Rafajnaujfalu (Bereg), Demeter Károly (20), 1912.; B.

Tempo giusto, ♩ = 126.

30. El-ment a pap al-mát　lop - ni,　El - fe - lej-tett zsá-kot　vin - ni;

Le - ve -tet-te a ga - tyá - ját,　Te - le -töm-te a két　szá - rát.

III. Ujszász (Pest), Dobóczi Bernátné (26), 1918.; B.

Parlando, ♩ = 75.

31. 1. Nem lop-tam én　é - le-tem - be,　Csak hat ti - nót Deb-re-cen - be;

Ha - za - haj-tot - tam a ti - nót, Mind a hat da - ru-sző-rű　volt.

Muz. F. 951 b); I. Dunapentele (Fehér), 1906.; B.

Parlando.

32. Fe-hír Lász-ló　lo - vat lo-pott A fe - kë - te　ha-lom　a - latt,

Min-dën nye-rëg - szer-szá - mos-tul,　Csi-kó-fé - kes kan-tá - ros-tul.

II.

Muz. F. 958 c); I. Balatonberény (Somogy), 1906.; B.

Parlando, ♪= 128.

33 *a).*

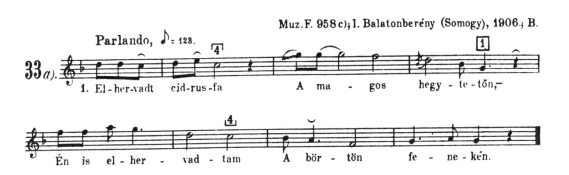

1. El-her-vadt cid-rus-fa   A ma - gos hegy - te -tőn,—

Én is el-her - vad - tam   A bör - tön fe - ne - kén.

Muz. F. 805 a); II. Nagymegyer (Komárom), 1910.; B.

Tempo giusto, ♩= 89.

33 *b).*

1. Ké - ret - ték né - né - met Szép ki - rály - fi - á - nak,

En - gem is ké - ret - tek Egy kó - dus fi - á - nak.

Muz. F. 55 b); I. Kaposujlak (Somogy); V.

Parlando.

33 *c).*

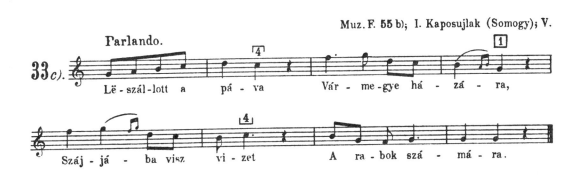

Lë - szál-lott a pá - va Vár - me-gye há - zá - ra,

Száj - já - ba visz vi - zet A ra - bok szá - má - ra.

III. Vésztő (Békés); Ökrös Róza (18), Simon Ferencné (33), 1918.; B.

Tempo giusto.

34 *a).*

1. An - go - li Bor - bá - la Kis szok - nyát va - ra - tott.

E - lül kur - táb - bo - dott, Há - tul hosz - szab - bo - dott.

39. Parlando.   I. Kánya (Tolna), 1907.; B.

Sze - ret - nék   szán - ta - ni,   Hat   ök - röt   haj - ta - ni,

Ha   a   ró - zsám   jön - ne   Az   e - két   tan - ta - ni.

40. Parlando.   Muz. F. 1132 a); I. Kórógy (Szlavónia); G.

1. Im - hol ke - re - ke - dik   Egy   fe - ke - te   föl - hő,

Ab - ban tol - lász - ko - dik   Sár - ga - lá - bú   hol - ló.

41. Parlando, ♩ = 66-56.   III. Ujszász (Pest), Dobóczi Bernátné (26), 1918.; B.

1. Meg - kö - töm lo - va - mot   Szo - mo - rú - fűz - fá - hoz,

Le - haj - tom fe - je - met   Két el - ső lá - bá - hoz.

42. Tempo giusto.   Muz. F. 2280 a); I. Szentgyörgyvölgye (Zala), Tóth Imre; V.

El - më - gyëk,   el - më - gyëk.   Visz - sza sëm   te - kin - tëk,

En - nek a   fa - lu - nak - - - - - -

43. Parlando, ♩ cca 184.   F. 253); IV. Kászonimpér (Csík), 1912.; K.

1. Egy ki - csi ma - dar - ka   Hoz - zám kez - de   jár - ni,

Vi - rá - gos   ker - tem - ben   Fész - ket kez - de   rak - ni.

III.

II. Nemesócsa (Komárom), Ferenczy János (84), 1913.; L.

44.

Le - fe - küd-tem csak a - lig, Nem e - gé - szen a fa - lig;

Jól meg - ö - lelj en - ge - met, Le ne es - sem mel - lő - led!

Muz. F. 1038 b); IV. Gyergyóujfalu (Csík), 1907.; B.

45.

Sar-jut e - szik az ök - röm, Ha jól - la-kik, bé - kö - töm;

Úgy me - nyek a ba - bám - hoz, Tu-dom, el - vár ma-gá - hoz.

Muz. F. 2325 b); IV. Diósad (Szilágy), 1914.; L.

46.

Té - len nem jó szán - ta - ni, Ne - héz e - két tar - ta - ni,

Jobb az ágy - ban ma - rad - ni, Me - nyecs-ké - vel jác - ca - ni.

Muz. F. 15 b); III. Szegvár (Csongrád), Szarvas Pál; V.

47.

Szép a le - ány i - de - ig, Ti - zen - nyolc esz - ten-de - ig;

De a le - gény mind-ad - dig, Míg mëg nëm há - za - so - dik.

Tempo giusto.

Muz. F. 1315 b); IV. Csíkszentdomokos (Csík), 1912.; L.

48.

A bú sir-jon a fa-gyon, Bá-nat üt-tes-sék a-gyon,

Ma ö-röm-nap-ja va-gyon, Mi es ör-vend-jünk a-zon.

Tempo giusto.

I. Felsőiregh (Tolna), 1906.; B.

49.

-El-mész ru-zsám? -El biz én! -Itt hagysz en-gem? -itt biz én!

-Ha te el-mész. én is el, Mind a ket-ten men-jünk el.

F. 173 d), IV. Hadikfalva (Bukovina), 1914.; K.

Tempo giusto, ♩ = 116.

50.

1. Vé-kony cér-na, ke-mény mag.- -Jaj de ke-vé' le-gény vagy!

Fű-nek-fá-nak a-dós vagy, Egy pénz-nek u-ra nem vagy.

II. Tura (Pest), Szilágyi János, 1906.; B.

Tempo giusto.

51.

Ker-tem a-latt se-lyem rét, Be-le-szo-kott két ök-rész. Hajtsd be bi-ró

az ök-rét, Va-sald meg az ök-ré-szét, va-sald meg az ök-ré-szét.

Muz. F. 1652 d); II. Fornos (Bereg), 1912.; B.

Tempo giusto, ♩ = 112.

52.

Ugy ég, a tűz, ha lo-bog,- Ugy é-lek én, ha lo-pok.

Lop-tam csi-kót, lo-pok is, Ha fel-a-kasz-ta-nak is.

Muz. F. 1644b); II. Derczen (Bereg), Orosz Ferenc (62), 1912.; B.

53.

Még az es - te jó vol - tál, Le - fe - küd-tél, a - lud - tál;

Ha - za jöt - tél vi - zes - sen, Csó - kot ad - tál szi - ves - sen.

Muz. F. 997c); I. Felsőiregh (Tolna), 1907.; B.

54 *(a).*

Ñ Duny-hám, pár - nám de haj-lik, Bej-jebb ba-bám a fa-lig;

Ö - lel - jük egy-mást haj - na-lig, Míg é - des a - nyánk a - lu - szik.

Muz. F. 985a); I. Felsőiregh (Tolna), 1907.; B.

54 *b).*

Tul - só so - ron, in - nend is Áld - jon meg az is - ten is,

Té - ged ró - zsám, en - gëm is, Még a - ki föl - ne - velt is.

IV.

Muz. F. 81 I.a); IV. Zentelke (Kolozs), Pálinkás Kulcsár Kata; V.

55.

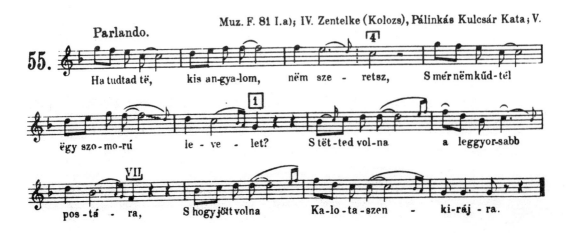

Ha tudtad të, kis an-gya-lom, nëm sze - retsz, S mér nëmkŭd-tél

ëgy szo - mo-rú le - ve - let? S tët - ted vol - na a leggyor-sabb

pos - tá - ra, S hogy jött volna Ka-lo-ta-szen - ki-ráj - ra.

Muz. F. 339 b); I. Kaposfüred (Somogy), Gyura László (50); V.

56. Parlando.

É - dös a - nyám, te - me - tő - ben e - redj ki, A leg - ár - vább
sir - hal - mot ott ke - resd ki. Â - ra bu - rujj, a - zon si - rasd
fi - a - dat, Â - ra ül - tesd ta - vasz - kor vi - rá - go - dat.

F. 1301a); IV. Jobbágytelke (Maros-Torda), Balog Györgyné (50), 1914.; B.

57. Tempo giusto, ♩ = 108.

El - men - tem a kút - ra vi - zet me - rít - ni, O - da - jött a
kis ger - li - ce csa - csog - ni; Kör - me kö - zött ho - zott egy kis
uj - sá - got, Hogy mind el - fog - ták az é - fi - ú - sá - got.

III. Gyulavári (Békés), 1906.; B.

58. Tempo giusto.

Asz hit - tem, hogy nem kel - lek ka - to - ná - nak, Gond - ját vi - se -
lem az é - des a - nyám - nak. De mán lá - tom, ka - to - ná - nak
kell len - ni, Fe - renc Jós - ka csá - kó - ját kell vi - sel - ni.

Muz. F. 1601 d);IV. Gyimesközéplokk (Csík), Ambrus Jozefa, 1912.; L.

Tempo giusto, ♩ = 108.

59.

Szá-raz fá-bul köny-nyű hi-dat csi-nál - ni, Jaj de ba-jos
szép sze-re-tőt ta-lál - ni! Ta-lál - tam én sze-re-tő - re,
de jó - ra, Ki el-vi-szen a bá-na-tos ha-jó - ra.

Muz. F. 1020 b); IV. Karczfalva (Csík), 1907.; E.

Tempo giusto, ♩ = 100.

60.

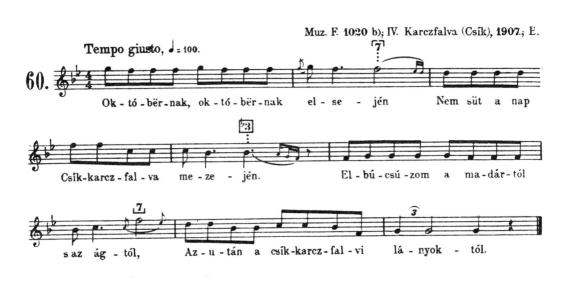

Ok-tó-bër-nak, ok-tó-bër-nak el-se - jén Nem süt a nap
Csík-karcz-fal-va me-ze - jén. El-bú-csú-zom a ma-dár-tól
s az ág - tól, Az-u-tán a csík-karcz-fal-vi lá-nyok - tól.

Muz. F. 810 a); IV. Magyargyerőmonostor (Kolozs), Imre Ilona, 1910.; B.

Tempo giusto, ♩ = 52.

61.

1. A Ti-szá - ból a Du-ná - ba foj a víz, — —Mi do-log az,
kis an-gya-lom, hogy te sírsz? —Hogy-ne sír - nëk, hogy-ne rí - nék
drá - ga kincs: Most a-kar - ta-lak sze-ret-ni, már el - mész.

Tempo giusto, ♩. = 76.

F. 1317 c); IV. Székelyvaja (Maros-Torda), 1914.; B.

62.

É - des a-nyám, be' szé - pen fel - ne-vel - tél. Mi - kor en-gem kar - ja-id-dal ren-get - tél. Ak-kó mond-tad, bé-vesz-nek ka - to - ná-nak, Fel - es - ket - nek egy szép ma - gyar hu-szár-nak.

IV. Körösfő (Kolozs), Péntek Gyugyi Györgyné (30), 1908.; B.

Parlando.

63.

Uj - ko - rá - ba meg-re -ped-jen a csizs - mám, Ha én já - rok több-bet a ba - bám u - tán! Ed - dig is csak a - zért jár-tam én o - da, Hogy a ba-bám kö-kény-sze - me csalt o - da.

Tempo giusto, ♩ = 96.

Muz. F. 1019 c); IV. Csíkjenőfalva (Csík), 1907.; B.

64.

De Mi - kor én - gem fér - hez ad - tak, Ti - zen - há - rom pen-delyt ad -tak, Tra la la la la la la la la la la De Ti - zen - há - rom pen-delyt ad - tak, tra - la - la.

IV. Csíkszenttamás (Csík) 1907.; B.

65.

Tempo giusto.

—É - des a - nyám, mi va-gyon a zse - bé - be? —Há - rom al - ma.

—Ad - jon e - gyet be - lő - le. Ugy sem e - szem so - ká - ig az

al - má - ját, Vi - se - lem a Fe - renc Jós - ka csá - kó - ját.

Muz. F. 926 a); III. Békésgyula (Békés), Borek András (40), 1906.; E.

Parlando, ♪ = cca 140.

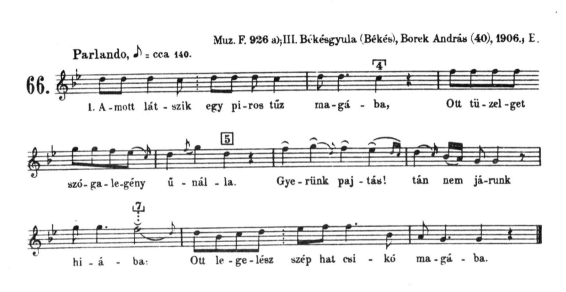

66.

1. A - mott lát - szik egy pi - ros tűz ma - gá - ba, Ott tü - zel - get

szó - ga - le - gény ű - nál - la. Gye - rünk paj - tás! tán nem já - runk

hi - á - ba: Ott le - ge - lész szép hat csi - kó ma - gá - ba.

Muz. F. 950 a); l. Baracs (Fejér), 1906.; B.

Tempo giusto, ♩ = 70.

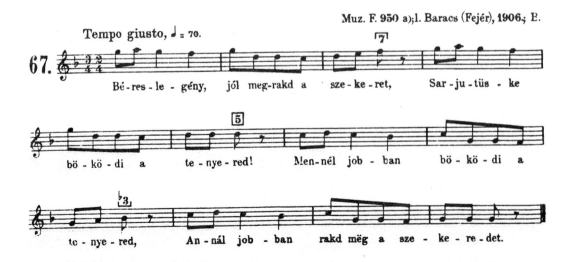

67.

Bé - res - le - gény, jól meg-rakd a sze - ke - ret, Sar - ju - tüs - ke

bö - kö - di a te - nye - red! Men-nél job - ban bö - kö - di a

te - nye - red, An - nál job - ban rakd mëg a sze - ke - re - det.

Muz. F. 2300 b); I. Felsőiregh (Tolna), Kolonics Mari (20), 1907.; B.

Parlando, ♩ = cca 102.

68.

1. Kon - do - ro - si szép csár - dás - né há - za e - lőtt

van egy szo - mo - ru - fűz - fa, Ar - ra kö - töm a lo - va - mat

jö - vő szom - bat haj - nal - ba. Üjj föl hát most kon - do - ro - si szép csár - dás - né

e-gyet - len egy é -des ked - ves Mar - csa ne - vű lë - á - nya a lo - vam - ra,

El - visz - lek az esz - ter - há - zi szám - a - dó - nak leg - el - ső ta - nyá - já - ra.

V.

Muz. F. 544 a); IV. Déva (Hunyad), Sebestény Józsefné.; V.

Parlando.

69.

Be - reg Ná - ni ve - res pán - ti - ká - ja Nem il - lik a

szép sá - rig *)ha - já - ba. — Tedd el, Ná - ni, a lá - dád fi -

á - ba, Majd jó lësz a le - á - nyod ha - já - ba.

*) sárga

Muz. F. 961 b); III. Doboz (Békés), 1906.; B.

70. Tempo giusto, ♪ = 104.

Hej, A-zér, hogy a sze-re-tőm el-hagyott, Én a-zér egy csöppet sem bú-su-lok.

A ró-zsa se nyi-lik ki ëc-ce-re, Lesz sze-re-tőm va-sár-nap es-té-re.

I. Felsőiregh (Tolna), 1907.; B.

71. a) Parlando.

Fe-ke-te föld ter-mi a jó bu-zát, Sü-rű er-dő ne-ve-li a bë-tyárt,

Sű-rű er-dő a bë-tyár la-ká-sa, Szép csár-dás-né gon-dot vi-sel rá-ja.

Muz. F. 341 c); I. Kaposfüred (Somogy), Kovács György; V.

71. b) Tempo giusto.

Fél-re tő-lem bu-bá-nat, bu-bá-nat, Kan-csót vá-gok

u-tá-nad, u-tá-nad, Szé-lös vi-lág csuf-já-ra,

csuf-já-ra, Mëg-fujt-lak ëgy po-hár-ba, po-hár-ba.

Muz. F. 1629 a); III. Gyanta (Bihar), Boros Péter (50), 1912.; B.

72. Tempo giusto, ♪ = 200.

Ket-ten men-tünk, hár-man jöt-tünk, tedd rá, Jaj de ha-mar so-kan let-

tünk, nyomd rá. Lehuzták a jegy-kö-tőt e-lő-le, Ugy takarták a gyer-me-ket be-le.

VI.

II. Menyhe (Nyitra), 1909.; K.

Tempo giusto.

73.

Ak-kor szép az er - dő, mi-kor zöld, Mi-kor a vad - ga -lamb ben - ne költ.

A vad-ga-lamb o - lyan, mint a lány, Ma-ga jár a szép le - gény u-tán.

Muz. F. 972 b); I. Felsőiregh (Tolna), Simon Mihály (50), 1907.; P.

74. a)

Az ü - rö - gi uc - ca si - ke -res,*) Pen-ne paj-tás szép lányt ne ke -ress,

Mer a - ki van ben-ne, mind gör-be, Ki-nek a szá - ja szé - le csem-pe. **)

*) = egyenes
**) = csorba, ferde

Muz. F. 341 b); I. Kaposfüred (Somogy), Kovács György; V.

Tempo giusto.

74. b)

Oh én é-dös pin - tös ü - ve-göm, Sü- ve-göm e - lőt - ted lë - vö-szöm.

A - hol szép lánt lá - tok, kö-szön-tök, Oj-jat i -szom, csak úgy nyö-ször-gök.

Muz. F. 984 c); I. Felsőiregh (Tolna), 1907.; B.

Parlando, ♩ = 57.

74. c)

Nem messzi van in - nen U - zo - ra, Csak egy ó - ra já - rás az út - ja,

Va - sas ko-csim, réz a szeg-je - i, Kis an-gya-lom csal - fa sze-me-i.

B. (6)

Muz. F. 2330 b); I. Őcsény (Tolna), 1913.; L.

75.
1. Jaj de be-teg va - gyok, Ta - lán meg is ha - lok,

Ta - lán bi-zony a sze-re-tőm é - des any-ja En-gem meg - át - ko - zott.

Muz. F. 776 c); IV. Ákosfalva (Maros-Torda), 1909.; B.

76.
1. Csü-tör -tö-kön es - te Ná-lad vol-tam les - be; Lát-tam, hogy pán-kót

sü-töt - tél, en - gem bé nem e - resz-tet - tél, Pe - dig é-hes vol - tam.

(7)

III. Apátfalva (Csanád), 1906.; B.

77.
Bi - ró Mar-csa li-bá - ja Be-le - ment a Ti-szá- ba; Ket-tőt

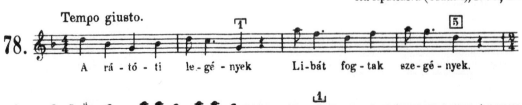

lé - pett u-tá - na: Ki-lát-szott a Bi-ró Mar-csa pi-ros al - só szok-nyá - ja.

III. Apátfalva (Csanád), 1906.; B.

78.
A rá-tó-ti le-gé - nyek Li-bát fog-tak sze-gé - nyek.

Nem jól fog-ták a nya-kát, a nya-kát, sej, a nya-kát: El-gá-gin-tot - ta ma-gát.

III. Ujszász (Pest), Dobóczi Bernátné (26), 1918; B.

83. Tempo giusto.

1. Vá-ra-di-né lá - nya Ma-ris - ka   Ki - ál-lott az ú - ca - sa-rok - ra.

—E-redj be te, sej, haj,   göndör-ha-jú   zsi-dó-lány, Mer meg-foga ren-dőr - ka-pi - tány.

(10)

III. Vésztő (Békés), 1906.; B.

84. Tempo giusto.

A gő-zös-nek pat-toga ke - re - ke,   Bar-na kis lány haj-lik ki be - lő - le;

A fá-tyo-lát   fuj-ja a szél,—   Lá-tod ba-bám, hogy meny-asz-szony let - tél.

Muz. F. 772b); III. Vésztő (Békés), Jakuts Róza (16), 1909.; B.

85. Tempo giusto, ♩ = 112.

1. Es-tevan már, csil-lag van az é - gen,   Var-ga Jul-csa me-zit-láb a jé - gen,

Saj-nál-ja a ci-pő-jit fel - húz - ni,   Gar-zó Pé - ter nem vesz több-bet né - ki.

Muz. F. 1004c); I. Felsőiregh (Tolna), Kolonics Mari (20), 1907.; B.

86. Tempo giusto, ♩ = 93.

I - de - lát - szik a te - me-tő szé - le,   Ab - ba nyug-szik

az én szö-mem fé - nye;   A ko-por-só ö - le - li he -

löt - tem, Mos tud - tam még, mi-len ár - va löt - tem.

I. Felsőiregh (Tolna), 1903.; B.

Tempo giusto.

87.

Az ü - rö - gi sű - rü er - dő a - latt
roz-ma-rin - got a - rat,
roz-ma-ring sze-dő-je,

Bar - na le - gény
Én va - gyok a
Bar - na le - gény i - gaz sze - re - tő - je.

Muz. F. 2237a); I. Resznek (Zala); V.

Tempo giusto.

88.

Reg-gel ko - rán ki - me-gyek a kút-ra,
zsaj-ta-rom az út - ra.
vár-me-gye haj-du - ja,

Le - te - szem a
Ar - ra ment a
Be - le - lé - pett, el - tö - rött a - lat - ta.

IV. Marosvásárhely (Maros - Torda), 1916.; B.

Parlando.

89.

1. Lem-berg a - latt van egy ma-gas er - dő,
Ab - banfek-szik száz-húsz - e - zer ba - ka:

Kö - ze - pi - be van egy gyász te - me - tő,
El - te - met - te gyá-szos Ga - li - ci - ja.

Muz. F. 144a); II Füzesabony (Heves), Kerekes István; V.

Parlando.

90.

Nem mesz-sze van i - de Kis-mar - gi - ta,
vi - ze kö - rül - foly - ta;
ko - po - nya - i csár - da,

Hor - to-bágy-nak
Kö - ze - pi - be
Ott i - szik egy nagy be-tyár bu - já - ba.

III. Apátfalva (Csanád), 1906.; B.

Tempo giusto.

91.

Ki - ön-tött a Ti - sza a part-já - ra,
jár a sár - ba,
a ke - zem - be,-

Kis pej lo - vam tér - dig
Sá-ros kan-tár - szá - ra
Gye-re kis an - gya - lom az ö - lem - be.

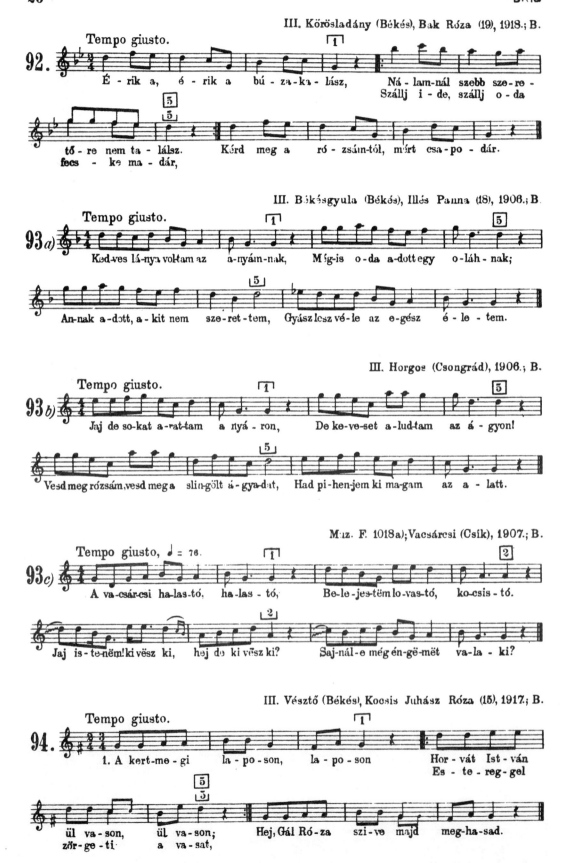

92. III. Körösladány (Békés), Bak Róza (19), 1918.; B.

Tempo giusto.

É - rik a,   é - rik a   bú - za - ka - lász,   Ná - lam-nál szebb sze - re -
Szállj i - de, szállj o - da

tő - re nem ta - lálsz.   Kérd meg a   ró - zsám-tól, mért csa - po - dár.
fecs - ke ma - dár,

93 a) III. Békésgyula (Békés), Illés Panna (18), 1906.; B.

Tempo giusto.

Ked-ves lá-nya voltam az   a-nyám-nak,   Míg-is o-da a-dott egy   o-láh - nak;

An-nak a-dott, a - kit nem   sze-ret-tem,   Gyász lesz vé-le az e-gész   é - le - tem.

93 b) III. Horgos (Csongrád), 1906.; B.

Tempo giusto.

Jaj de so-kat a-rat-tam   a nyá - ron,   De ke-ve-set a-lud-tam   az á - gyon!

Vesd meg rózsám,vesd meg a   slin-gölt á-gya-dat,   Had pi-hen-jem ki ma-gam   az a - latt.

93 c) Muz. F. 1018a);Vacsárcsi (Csik), 1907.; B.

Tempo giusto, ♩ = 76.

A va-csár-csi ha-las-tó,   ha-las - tó;   Be-le-jes-tëm lo-vas-tó,   ko-csis - tó.

Jaj is-te-nëm! ki vësz ki,   hej de ki vësz ki?   Saj-nál-e még én-gë-mët   va-la - ki?

94. III. Vésztő (Békés), Kocsis Juhász Róza (15), 1917.; B.

Tempo giusto.

1. A kert-me - gi   la - po - son,   la - po - son   Hor - vát Ist - ván
Es - te - reg - gel

ül va - son,   ül va - son;   Hej, Gál Ró - za   szi - ve majd   meg-ha-sad.
zör-ge - ti   a va - sat,

(11)

Muz. F. 927b); III. Békésgyula (Békés) Illés Panna (18), 1906.; B.

95. Tempo giusto, ♩ = 104.

Sej, fel-száll-lott a ka-kas a meggy - fá - ra, Ku-ko-ré-kol hajnal - ha-sad -
Hajnal ha-sad, fé-nyes csil-lag

tá - ra. Sej, én még most is a ba - bám-nál va - gyok.
ra - gyog,

III. Ujszász (Pest), 1918.; B.

96. Tempo giusto.

Ká - roly ki - rály bá - na-tá - ba, de i - ga - zán,
refr.

Ki - sé - tál a Du-na - part - ra, de i - ga - zán. Rá - bo - rúl a
refr.

ko - ro - ná - ra: Sej, ho-va lett a ka - to - ná - ja, de i - ga - zán.
refr.

II. Jánoshida (Szolnok), 1918.; B.

97. Tempo giusto.

1.Já-nos-hi - di vá-sár-té-ren, i - ca-te Legény vá - sár lesz a hé-ten,
refr.

i - ca-te; Ez-re-se - kér adnak e-gyet, Jaj de drá-ga, még-is vesznek, i-ca-te
refr. refr.

III. Békésgyula (Békés), 1906.; B.

98. Tempo giusto.

Ö-reg ba-ka af-fé-ról a szo-bá - ba, A ba-bá-ja si-rat-ja a kony-há - ba.

-Ne sirj ba-bám, kér-jed a jó te-rem-tőt, Ad-jon nó-ked egy remunda sze-re - tőt.

Muz. F. 983b); I. Felsőiregh (Tolna), 1907.; B.

Parlando, ♩ = 66.

99.

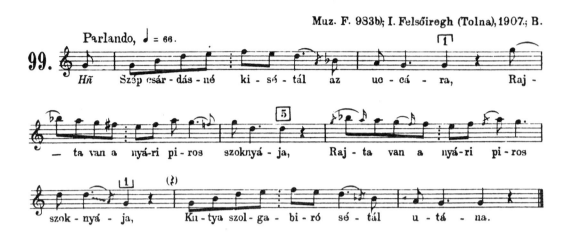

Hñ Szép csár - dás - né ki - sé - tál az uc - cá - ra, Raj -
ta van a nyá-ri pi-ros szoknyá - ja, Raj - ta van a nyá-ri pi-ros
szok - nyá - ja, Ku - tya szol-ga - bi - ró sé - tál u - tá - na.

III. Vésztő (Békés), Kocsis Juhász Róza (15), 1917.; B.

Tempo giusto.

100.

Megyen már a haj-nal-csil-lag lö - fe - lé, Az én ba - bám
mos me-gyen ha - za-fe - lé. Lá - bán van a la-gos-szá-rú
kis csizs - ma; Rá-sü - tött a haj - nal-csil-lag su - ga - ra.

Muz. F. 2328c); I. Őcsény (Tolna), 1913.; L.

Tempo giusto, ♩ = 72.

101.

Az ő - csé-nyi temp-lom pi-ros bá - do - gos,— Az én ked-ves
kis an - gya-lom de ma - gos. Ha ma - gos is, nem kell ar - ra
gon-dul - ni, Maj le - ha - jul, ha meg a - kar csó-kul - ni.

Muz. F. 935b); III. Vésztő (Békés), Szombati Zsuzsa (16), 1906.; B.

102. Tempo giusto, ♩ = 88.

Ká-sát et-tem, meg-é-get-tem a szá-mat;— Ki vi-se-li
gond-ját az én a-nyám-nak? Én már lá-tom, nëm vi-se-lem
sze-gény-nek, Ol-tal-má-ra bi-zom a jó is-ten-nek.

III. Jánoshida (Szolnok), 1918.; B.

103. Tempo giusto.

1. Da-ru-madár ut-nak in-dul hajnal-ba, Le-ve-let hoz i-de Já-nos-hi-dá-ra;
Az van ír-va a le-vél bel-se-jé-be: El kell menni hu-szon-ket-te-di-ké-re.

I. Bazsi (Zala), 1906.; B.

104. Tempo giusto.

Jaj de szé-les, jaj de hosz-szi az az út, |: A kin az a
ki-lenc be-tyár el-in-dult, :| Pá-pa-i-né ud-va-rá-ra be-for-dult.

Muz. F. 928a); III. Békésgyula (Békés), Illés Panna (18),1906.; B

105. Tempo giusto, ♩ = 90.

1. Már mi-kor én ti-zen-nyolc é-ves vol-tam, Már én ak-kor
há-za-sod-ni in-dul-tam. Ti-zen-két szép lá-nya volt egy
a-nyá-nak, Mind a ti-zen-ket-tőt kér-tem ma-gam-nak.

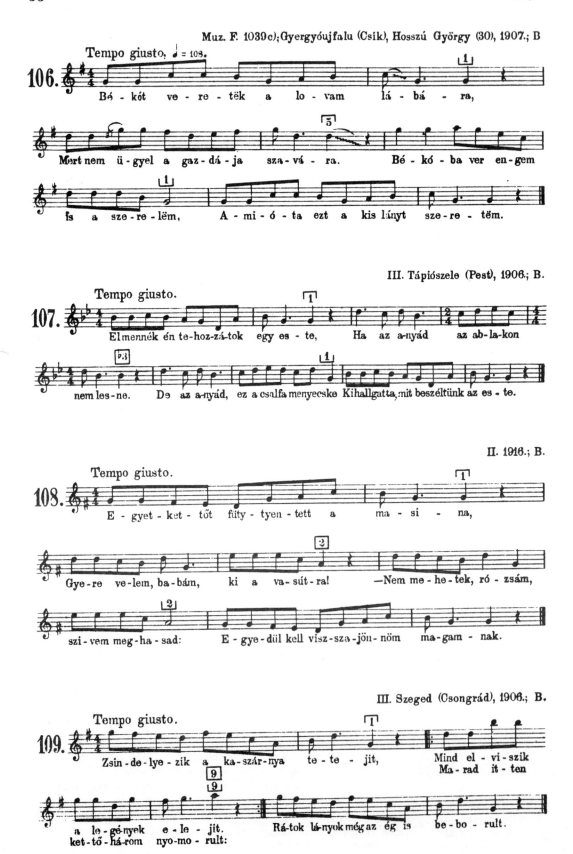

Muz. F. 1039c);Gyergyóujfalu (Csík), Hosszú György (30), 1907.; B

106. Tempo giusto, ♩ = 108.
Bé - kót ve - re - tëk a lo - vam lá - bá - ra,
Mert nem ü - gyel a gaz - dá - ja sza - vá - ra. Bé - kó - ba ver en - gem
is a sze - re - lëm, A - mi - ó - ta ezt a kis lányt sze - re - tëm.

III. Tápiószele (Pest), 1906.; B.

107. Tempo giusto.
El mennék én te-hoz-zá-tok egy es - te, Ha az a-nyád az ab-la-kon
nem les - ne. De az a-nyád, ez a csalfa menyecske Kihallgatta, mit beszéltünk az es - te.

II. 1916.; B.

108. Tempo giusto.
E - gyet - ket - tőt füty - tyen - tett a ma - si - na,
Gye - re ve - lem, ba - bám, ki a va - sút - ra! —Nem me - he - tek, ró - zsám,
szi - vem meg - ha - sad: E - gye - dül kell visz-sza-jön- nöm ma-gam - nak.

III. Szeged (Csongrád), 1906.; B.

109. Tempo giusto.
Zsin - de - lye - zik a ka-szár-nya te - te - jit, Mind el - vi - szik
                                                Ma - rad it - ten
a le - gé-nyek e - le - jit. Rá-tok lá-nyok még az ég is be-bo - rult.
ket - tő - há-rom nyo-mo - rult:

III. Körösladány (Békés), Kerekes Julia, (17), 1918.; B.

Tempo giusto.

110.

Ki - me-gyek a do-ber-dó-i harc-tér - re, Föl - te-kin-tek

a csil-la-gos nagy ég - re. Csil - la-gos ég, mer-re van a

ma-gyar ha-zám, Mer - re si-rat en-gem az é - des a - nyám?

III. Jánoshida (Szolnok), 1918.; B.

Tempo giusto.

111.

Ap - ró szë-me van a ku-ko - ri - cá - nak, Szép ter - me-te

van a ked-ves ba - bám - nak. Szép ter - me-tét el sem tu-dom

fe - lej - te - ni: Igy jár az, a - ki i - ga-zán tud sze-ret - ni.

II. Tura (Pest), Gólya Gábor, 1906.; B.

Tempo giusto.

112.

1. Stolac a -latt van egy magos sir-ha-lom, Abban nyugszik az én kedves pajtá-som.

Levág-ta a tö-rök szegénynek a jobb kar-ját, Ki-vel mindíg ö-lel - te a ba-bá-ját.

Muz. F. 960c); III. Vésztő (Békés), Szombati Zsuzsa (16), 1906.; B.

Tempo giusto. ♩ = 116.

113.

Túl a Tiszán juhász-legény vagyok én, Harminchárom birká-ra vi - gyá-zok én.

Gye-re babám, té-ritsd meg a bir-ka e - le-jét, Ne je-gye le a bo-dorka *) le-ve - lét.

*) = lóhere-fajta.

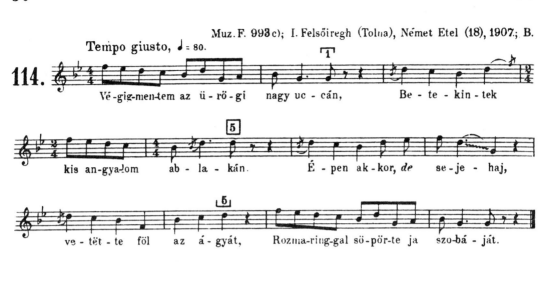

Muz. F. 993 c); I. Felsőiregh (Tolna), Német Etel (18), 1907.; B.

Tempo giusto, ♩ = 80.

114.

Vé-gig-men-tem az ü-rö-gi nagy uc-cán, Be-te-kin-tek

kis an-gya-lom ab-la-kán. É-pen ak-kor, *de* se-je-haj,

ve-tët-te föl az á-gyát, Rozma-ring-gal sö-pör-te ja szo-bá-ját.

Muz. F. 962 b); III. Doboz (Békés), Vas Zsófi (18), 1906.; B.

Tempo giusto. ♩ = 89.

115.

Ki-.do-bo-zi ke-rek er-dő de ma-gos, Kö-ze-pi-be bar-na kis lány

a-ra-nyos. Hogy-ha én az er-dő-nek a szél-ső fá-ja

le-het-nék, A ba-bám-nak vál-la-i-ra bo-rul-nék.

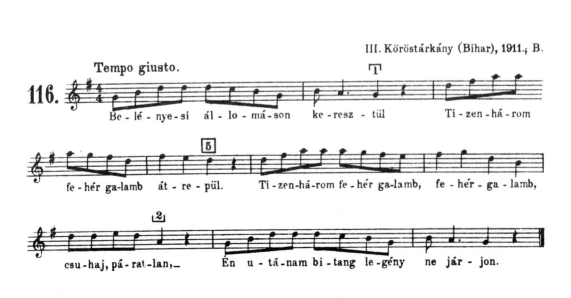

III. Köröstárkány (Bihar), 1911.; B.

Tempo giusto.

116.

Be-lé-nye-si ál-lo-má-son ke-resz-tül Ti-zen-há-rom

fe-hér ga-lamb át-re-pül. Ti-zen-há-rom fe-hér ga-lamb, fe-hér-ga-lamb,

csu-haj, pá-rat-lan,— Én u-tá-nam bi-tang le-gény ne jár-jon.

(12)

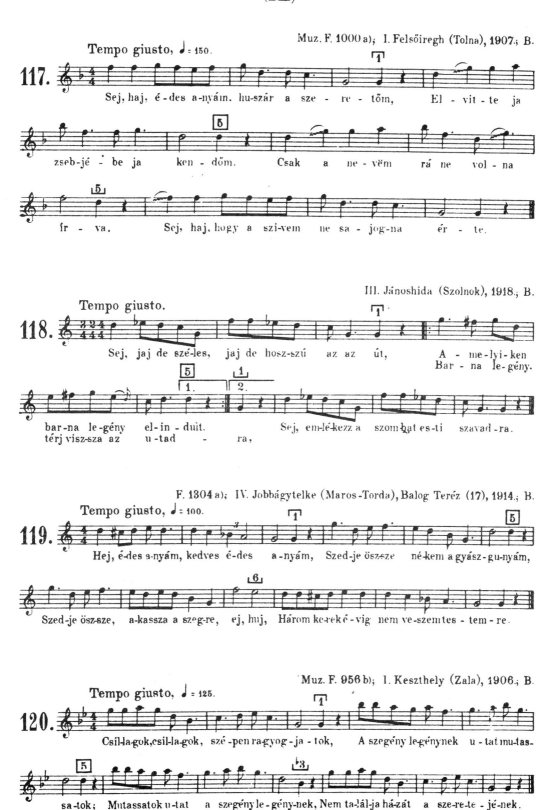

I. Keszthely (Zala), 1906.; B.

121. Tempo giusto.

En-nek a kis lány-nak rö-vid a szok-nyá-ja, Mond-tam az any-já-nak,
Asz mond-ta az any-ja,

varr-jon fod-rot rá-ja. A-ki-nek nem tet-szik, ne jár-jon u-tá-na.
nem varr fod-rot rá-ja,

(13)

III. Vésztő (Békés), Kocsis Juhász Róza (16), 1918.; B.

122. Tempo giusto.

Fe-ke-te cse-re-pes a mi há-zunk te-te-je, Vad-ga-lamb szá-lott a te-
Vad-ga-lamb, tur-bé-kold el

te-jé-be, Hogy a csár-dás tu-bi-cám sze-ret-e még i-ga-zán?
a nó-tám:

Muz. F. 172c); II. Adács (Heves), Kovács József; V.

123. Tempo giusto.

Sej, huj, vik-cos csiz-ma a lá-bo-mat szo-rít-ja,

Bar-na kis lány a szi-vem szo-mo-rít-ja. Ne szo-mo-rídd az én ár-va

szi-ve-met, Sej, huj, szen-ved-he-tek há-rom é-vig e-le-get.

Muz. F. 187a); II. Felsőtárkány (Heves), Kapocsi Teréz; V.

124. Tempo giusto.

Vé-gig men-tëm a tárkányi, sej, haj, fő-uc-cán, Be-te-kin-tet-tem a ba-bám ab-la-kán.

É-pen ak-kor ve-tët-te meg pap-la-nos á-gyát, Rozmaringgal sëp-rët-te ki pingált szo-bá-ját.

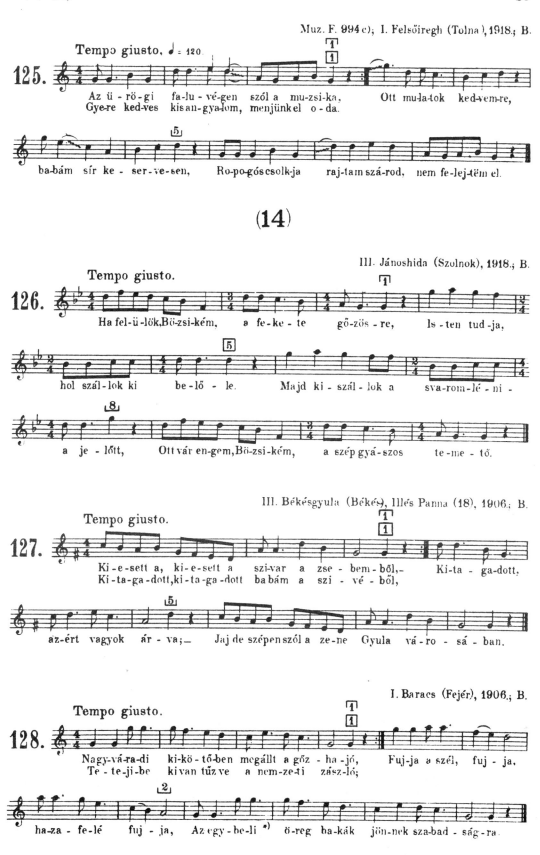

Muz. F. 994 c); I. Felsőiregh (Tolna), 1918.; B.

Tempo giusto. ♩ = 120.

125.

Az ü-rö-gi fa-lu-vé-gen szól a mu-zsi-ka, Ott mu-la-tok ked-vem-re,
Gye-re ked-ves kis an-gya-lom, menjünk el o - da.

ba-bám sír ke - ser-ve-sen, Ro-po-gós csolk-ja raj-tam szá-rod, nem fe-lej-tém el.

(14)

III. Jánoshida (Szolnok), 1918.; B.

Tempo giusto.

126.

Ha fel-ü-lök,Bö-zsi-kém, a fe-ke-te gő-zös-re, Is-ten tud-ja,

hol szál-lok ki be-lő-le. Majd ki-szál-lok a sva-rom-lé-ni-

a je-lőtt, Ott vár en-gem,Bö-zsi-kém, a szép gyá-szos te-me-tő.

III. Békésgyula (Békés), Illés Panna (18), 1906.; B.

Tempo giusto.

127.

Ki-e-sett a, ki-e-sett a szi-var a zse-bem-ből,— Ki-ta-ga-dott.
Ki-ta-ga-dott,ki-ta-ga-dott ba bám a szi-vé-ből,

az-ért vagyok ár-va;— Jaj de szépen szól a ze-ne Gyula vá-ro-sá-ban.

I. Baracs (Fejér), 1906.; B.

Tempo giusto.

128.

Nagy-vá-ra-di ki-kö-tő-ben megállt a gőz-ha-jó, Fuj-ja a szél, fuj-ja,
Te-te-ji-be ki van tűzve a nem-ze-ti zász-ló;

ha-za-fe-lé fuj-ja, Az egy-be-li *) ö-reg ba-kák jön-nek sza-bad-ság-ra.

*) 1901-beli.

III. Sámson (Hajdu) 1906.; B.

Tempo giusto.

129.

Csu-ha-ha, le-haj-lott a di-ó-fá-nak az á - ga,

Csu-ha-ha, rá-haj-lott a vi-zi-tá-ló szo-bá - ra. De sok é-des a-nya

sír-va jár el a-lat-ta: I-haj-la, hogy a fi-a há-rom é-vig ka-to-na.

Muz. F. 965a); III. Vésztő (Békés), Szombati Zsuzsa, (16), 1906.; B.

Tempo giusto, ♩ = 96.

130.

E - sik e - ső szép csen-de-sen. ta-vasz a-kar len - ni,

De sze-ret-nék a ba-bám kert-jé-be ró-zsa - bim-bó len - ni.

Nem le-he-tek én ró - zsa. el - her-vaszt Fe - renc Jós - ka

Bu - da-pes-ti há-rom-e - me-le-tes ma-gas ka-szár - nyá - ba.

III. Doboz (Békés), Hegedűs Zsófi (16), 1917.; B.

Tempo giusto, ♩ = 100.

131.

A gyu-la - i nagy pa-vil-lon fel van pánt-li - káz - va,
Az ab-la-ka, az aj-ta-ja sar - kig ki van nyit - va.

Ab - ba ül-nek a-zok az u-rak, a-kik en-gem be is so-roz-tak;

Be - so - roz-tak há-rom év - re. har - minc-hat hó - nap - ra.

(15)

IV. Mezőpanit (Maros-Torda), 1912.; L.

Tempo giusto.

132.

Bar-na kis lány le - ve-let ír,   rá-bo-rul az   asz-tal - ra,   O-da megy az

é-des any-ja,   kér-di tő-le: mi ba - ja?   –Ne kér-dez-ze   é - des a - nyám,

nincs sem-mi ba-jom,   Jól tud-ja, hogy ár-va va-gyok,   galambo-mat   si - ra - tom.

Muz. F. 310 b); II. Kistild (Bars), Varga Juli (19); V.

Tempo giusto.

133.

Már Kis - til - den,   már Kis - til-den   ré - gën lë - je - sëtt a   hó,–
Azt gon-dol - tam,   kis an - gya-lom,   vé - led lë - je - sëtt a   ló,

Ki - tö - rött a   jobb ke - zed,   mi - vel   ö - lelsz   en - gë - met;–

É - des ked-ves   kis an - gya-lom,   nëm lë - he-tëk   a   ti - ed.

I. Baracs (Fejér), 1906.; B.

Tempo giusto.

134.

Ha be-me-gyek,   ha be - me-gyek   a ba - ra-csi   csár-dá - ba,
Cif-ra-nye-lű   kis bics-ká-mat   vá-gom a ge - ren-dá - ba.

A - ki le -gény,   az   ve-gye ki,   a - ki bá - tor,   az   te-he - ti:

Még az éj - jel   zsan-dár-vér - rel   í-rom ki a   ne - ve - met.

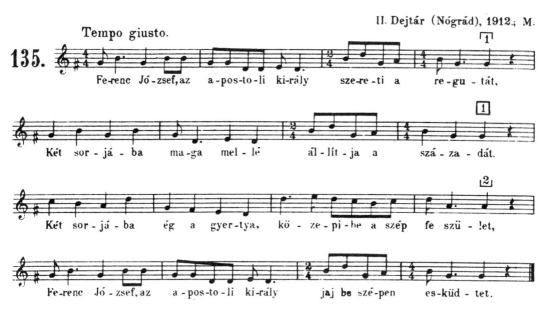

II. Dejtár (Nógrád), 1912.; M.

135. Tempo giusto.

Fe-renc Jó-zsef, az a-pos-to-li ki-rály sze-re-ti a re-gu-tát,

Két sor-já-ba ma-ga mel-lé ál-lít-ja a szá-za-dát.

Két sor-já-ba ég a gyer-tya, kö-ze-pi-be a szép fe-szü-let,

Fe-renc Jó-zsef, az a-pos-to-li ki-rály jaj be szé-pen es-küd-tet.

(16)

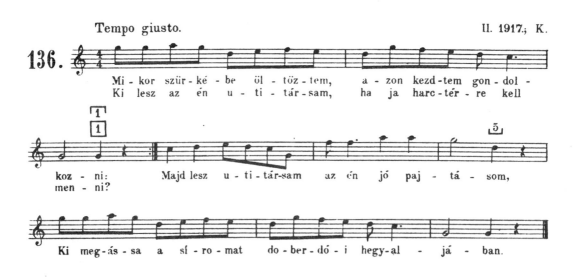

II. 1917.; K.

136. Tempo giusto.

Mi-kor szür-ké-be öl-töz-tem, a-zon kezd-tem gon-dol-
Ki lesz az én u-ti-tár-sam, ha ja harc-tér-re kell

koz-ni: Majd lesz u-ti-tár-sam az én jó paj-tá-som,
men-ni?

Ki meg-ás-sa a sí-ro-mat do-ber-dó-i hegy-al-já-ban.

Muz. F. 956 a); I. Keszthely (Zala), 1906.; B.

137. Tempo giusto, ♩ = 140.

Er-dő, er-dő, ke-rek er-dő, jaj de messzi-re el-lát-szik,

Kö-ze-pi-be, kö-ze-pi-be két szál roz-ma-ring vi-rág-zik.

E - gyik haj - lik a vál - lam - ra. má - sik a ba - bám - é - ra,

Rá - haj - tom a bús fe - je - met ba - bám ö - le - lő kar - já - ra.

138. Tempo giusto. III. Körösladány (Békés), Kerekes Julia (17), 1918.; B.

1. Mi-kor me-gyek Ro-má-ni - a fe - lé, még a fák is sír - nak,

Rez-gő nyár-fa hul-lat-ja le -ve-lét, az is en-gem si - rat. Si-rass, si-rass,

rez-gő nyár-fa, bo-rul - jál a ba-bám vál-lá-ra, Sugjad né-ki be-le a fü-lé-be:

fáj, fáj, fáj a szi-vem ér - te, ba-bám, fáj, fáj, fáj a szi-vem ér - te.

139. Muz. F. 966 b); III. Vésztő (Békés), Szombati Zsuzsa, (16), 1906.; B.
Tempo giusto. ♩ = 96 - 100.

Kis ker -..tem-ben, se-je hu-ja haj, egy ró-zsa-fát ül-tet - tem,

Es - te, reg - gel, i - haj csu-haj-ja, köny-nye-im-mel ön - töz - tem.

Meg-ár - tott a tö-vé - nek, se -je hu-ja, gyen-ge le -ve - le -jé - nek;_

Már én töb - bet, i - ca hej-re haj, nem hi-szek a le - gény - nek.

(17)

Muz. F. 639a); I. Resznek (Zala),; V.

140. Tempo giusto.

Gá-borgy-há-zi Te-lëk a-latt, an-gya-lom, ra-gyo-gú csil-la-gom,
refr.

De sok gya-log u-tak vannak, an-gya-lom, ra-gyo-gú csil-la-gom. Minden kis-lány
refr.

ëgy-gyet csi-nál, Sej, kja*) sze-re-tü-jé-hez jár, an-gya-lom, ra-gyo-gú csil-la-gom.
refr.

*) = ki a.

IV. Marosvásárhely (Maros-Torda), 1916.; B.

141. Tempo giusto.

Ez a kis lány, ez a bar-na kis lány re-zet ho-zott az es-te,
Réz-sar-kan-tyút, hej de réz-sar-kantyút csi-nál-ta-tott be-lő-le.

Aj de szé-pen csen-gett-pen-gett csü-tör-tök es-te,

Mi-kor azt a ré-gi jó ba-bá-ját aj-ta-ján be-en-ged-te.

(18)

Muz. F. 933 b); III. Békésgyula (Békés), Illés Panna (18), 1906.; B.

142. Tempo giusto, ♩ = 102.

Ha csak-u-gyan, csak-u-gyan, ha csak-u-gyan nem ta-lá-lok sze-re-tőt,

Fel-szán-ta-tom a csor-vá-si te-me-tőt. Ve-tek be-lé roz-ma-rin-got,

Az én ba-bám, a ba-bám, az én ba-bám más-sal é-li vi-lá-gát.

IV. Jobbágytelke (Maros - Torda), Balog Teréz (17), 1914.; B.

143. Tempo giusto.

Már mi - ná-lunk ba -bám, már mi - ná-lunk ba-bám az jött be szo -
Nem sze-dik a lá -nyok, nem sze-dik a lá -nyok megy-gyet a ko -

kás - ba, Fel - megy a le-gény meggy - fa te - te - jé - be,
sár - ba.

Le-ráz-za ja me gy-gyet te pejg' ba-bám szedjed ró - zsás kö-té - nyed - be

* = pedig

Muz. F. 998a); I. Felsőiregh (Tolna), 1907.; B.

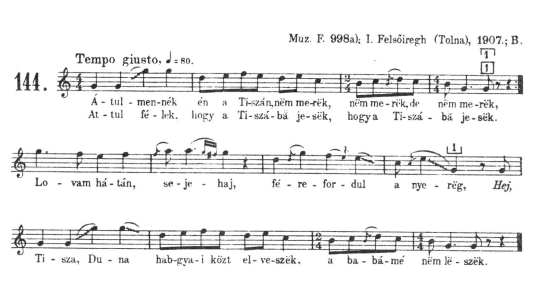

144. Tempo giusto, ♩ = 80.

Á - tul - men-nék én a Ti-szán, nëm me-rëk, nëm me - rëk, de nëm me-rëk,
At - tul fé - lek. hogy a Ti-szá-bä je-sëk, hogy a Ti-szá - bä je-sëk.

Lo - vam há-tán, se-je - haj, fé - re - for - dul a nye - rëg, *Hej,*

Ti - sza, Du - na hab-gya-i közt el-ve-szëk. a ba-bá-mé nëm lë - szëk.

III. Sámson (Hajdu), 1906.; B.

145. Tempo giusto.

Deb - re - ce - nyi nagy ka - szár - nya, csu-ha-ja, sár-gá-ra van
Há - rom é - vet, nyolc hó - na-pot, csu-ha-ja, én is el - töl -

me-szel - ve, Rá van ír - va csá - kóm - ra, csá - kóm mind a két ol -
tök ben - ne.

da-lá - ra: Há-rom hó-nap van még hát - ra, csu-ha-ja, ebb' a ko-misz ru-há - ba.

(19)

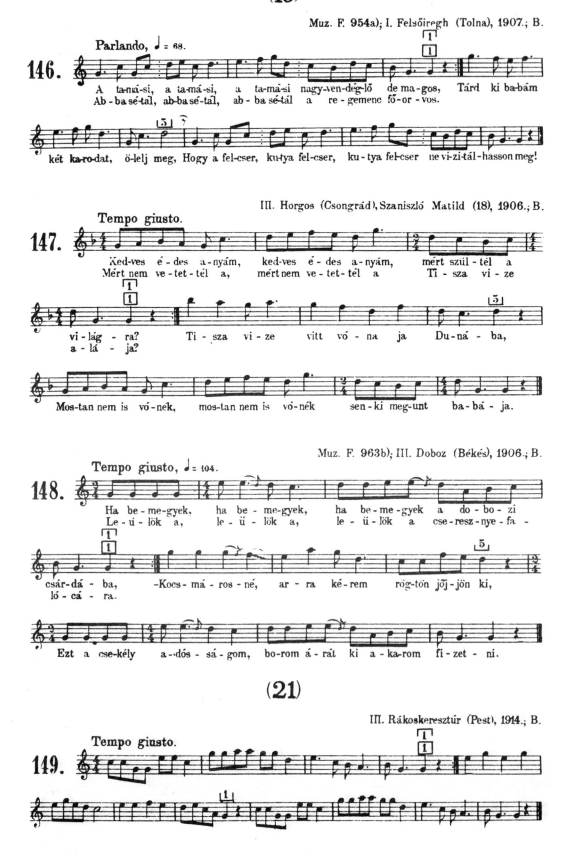

Muz. F. 954a); I. Felsőiregh (Tolna), 1907.; B.

Parlando, ♩ = 68.

146.

A ta-má-si, a ta-má-si, a ta-má-si nagy-ven-dég-lő de ma-gos, Tárd ki ba-bám
Ab - ba sé-tál, ab-ba sé-tál, ab - ba sé-tál a re - gemenc fő-or - vos.

két ka-ro-dat, ö-lelj meg, Hogy a fel-cser, ku-tya fel-cser, ku-tya fel-cser ne vi-zi-tál-hasson meg!

III. Horgos (Csongrád), Szaniszló Matild (18), 1906.; B.

Tempo giusto.

147.

Ked-ves é-des a-nyám, ked-ves é-des a-nyám, mért szül-tél a
Mért nem ve-tet-tél a, mért nem ve-tet-tél a Ti - sza vi-ze

vi-lág - ra? Ti - sza vi-ze vitt vó-na ja Du-ná-ba,
a - lá - ja?

Mos-tan nem is vó-nek, mos-tan nem is vó-nék sen-ki meg-unt ba-bá - ja.

Muz. F. 963b); III. Doboz (Békés), 1906.; B.

Tempo giusto, ♩ = 104.

148.

Ha be-me-gyek, ha be-me-gyek, ha be-me-gyek a do-bo-zi
Le-ü-lök a, le-ü-lök a, le-ü-lök a cse-resz-nye-fa-

csár-dá-ba, -Kocs-má-ros-né, ar-ra ké-rem rög-tön jöj-jön ki,
ló-cá - ra.

Ezt a cse-kély a-dós-sá-gom, bo-rom á-rát ki a-ka-rom fi-zet-ni.

(21)

III. Rákoskeresztúr (Pest), 1914.; B.

Tempo giusto.

149.

(22)

150.

Tempo giusto, ♩ = 100.

A ká-nya-i bi-ró há-za   de ma-gos,   kö-rös-kö-rül ki-lenc zsa-lu-
Ti-ze-di-ken ma-ga néz ki   a bi-ró: -No le-gé-nyek, meg-jött már a

gá-té-ros,   -En-gëm ba-bám ne si-rass,   ér-tem köny-nyet ne hul-lass,
be-hi-vó!

Be-ír-ták a ne-ve-met a na*y könyv-be,   a ta-má-si „Ko-ro-na"ven-dég-lő-be.

Tempo giusto.

151a)

Sze-gény   asz-szony   fi-a   va-gyok,   rom-ti-rá-ri
Min-den   kocs-má-ba tar-to-zok,   rom-ti-rá-ri

ra-ti ta-ti ta-ti-tom   ti-rá-rom.   Jaj is-te-nem, hogy ad-jam meg,
ra-ti ta-ti ta-ti-tom   ti-rá-rom.
1. refr.

rom-ti-rá-ri   ti-rá-rom,   Hogy a   ba-bám   ne tud-ja meg,
2. refr.

rom-ti-rá-ri   ra-ti ta-ti ta-ti-tom   ti-rá-rom.
3. refr.

Tempo giusto, ♩ = 88.

151b)

1. Já-nos bá-csi   he-ge-dű-je   Ej, ti-ráj-rom   ti-ráj-rom,
1. refr.

Ma-radt vó-na   az er-dő-be,   Ej, ti-ráj-rom ri-ti-ti-ti ri-ti-tom, ti-ráj-rom.
2. refr.

C. I. 1.

Muz. F. 1189c); I. Pankasz (Vas), Kardos Szidi; V.

Tempo giusto.

152.

1. Szán-tot-tam gyö-pöt, Ve-tët-tem gyön-gyöt, Haj-tot-tam á-gát, Szëd-tem vi - rá-gát.

2.

Muz. F. 2320b); I. Őcsény (Tolna), Nyul Rozália (53), 1913.; L.

Parlando.

153.

El-ment a zén ró-zsám I - de-gen or - szág-ba, Azt i-zen-te visz-sza, Men-jek el u - tá-na.

Muz. F. 301c); II. Pográny (Nyitra), Mészáros Ambrusné, V.

Parlando.

154.

So - ha - së lát - ta - lak, Nëm is ös - mer - te - lek,

Csak hi - red hal - lot - tam, Má mëg - sze - ret - te - lek. *Huj!*

Muz. F. 981a); I. Felsőnyék (Tolna), 1907.; B.

Parlando, ♪ = 92.

155.

1. Hi - rës bë - tyár va - gyok, Pat - kó az én ne - vëm,

Ti - zën - há - rom më-gye Rég ke - res - tet en - gëm.

Muz. F. 2303b); IV. Gyergyócsomafalva (Csík), 1907.; B.

Parlando.

156.

2. Csak azt szá - nom - bá - nom, Tő - led mëg këll vál - nom,

Sok_____ u - tán-nad va - ló Já - rá - sim saj - ná - lom.

Muz. F. 1012c);Csíkrákos (Csík), Péter Balázsné Szabó Tékla (35), 1907.; B.

157. Parlando, ♩ = cca 116.

1. Më-nyecs-ke, më-nyecs-ke, Te bar-na më-nyecs-ke,

Rég mëg-mond-tam né-ked, Ne mënj a cse-rés-be.

Muz. F. 2302a); IV. Gyergyócsomafalva (Csík), 1907.; B.

158. Parlando.

1. Dom-bon van a há-zam, *Hn* Szél-nek van for-dít-va,

Ej,— ke-rëk az ab-lak-ja, In-gem les-nek raj-ta.

2. Ej, ne bú-sulj, ne bán-kódj, *Hn* Ne is si-rán-koz-zál,

Mëg — se-gít a jó is-ten, Csak jól i-mád-koz-zál.

Muz. F. 796b);II. Nagymegyer (Komárom), Rácz József (60), 1910.; B.

159. Tempo giusto, ♩ = 77.

Hër-vadj, ró-zsám, hër-vadj, Mer az e-nyim nem vagy.

Ha az e-nyim vol-nál, Kü-lön-bet nyi-lon-nál.

Muz. F. 1345c); II. Ipolyság (Hont), 1910.; B.

160. Tempo giusto, ♩ = 144.

Ha-za, gaz-da, ha-za, Bé van a ló fog-va,

Héj vár-me-gye-há-zá-nál Szól a csen-gő raj-ta.

III. Ujszász (Pest), Kónyár Verka (12), 1918.; B.

Muz. F. 1002a); I. Felsőiregh (Tolna), 1907.; B.

Muz. F. 1644a); II. Derczen (Bereg), Orosz Ferenc (62), 1912.; B.

Muz. F. 1618c); III. Köröstárkány (Bihar), 1912.; B.

IV. Karczfalva (Csík), 1907.; B.

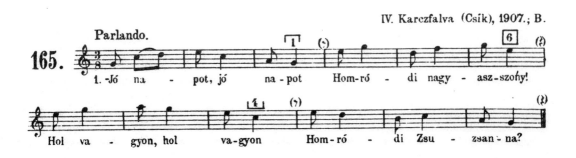

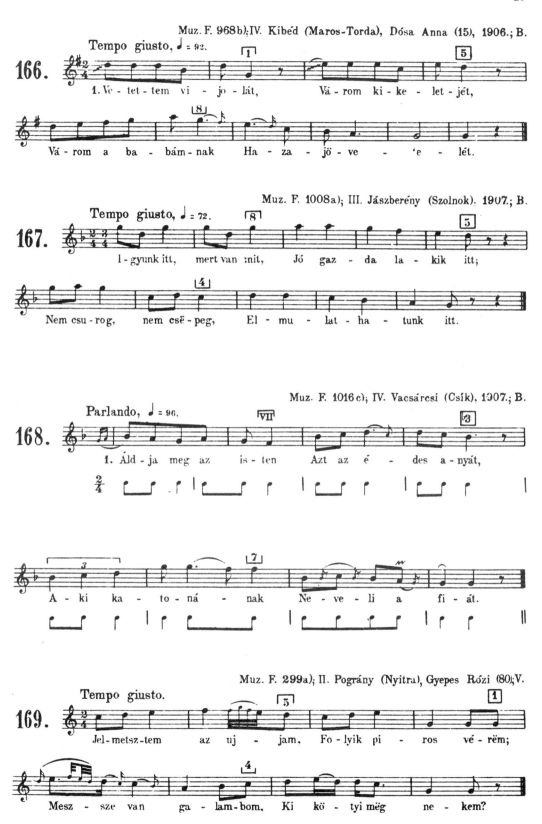

166. Tempo giusto, ♩ = 92.

Muz. F. 968b); IV. Kibéd (Maros-Torda), Dósa Anna (15), 1906.; B.

1. Ve - tet - tem vi - jo - lát, Vá - rom ki - ke - let - jét,

Vá - rom a ba - bám - nak Ha - za - jö - ve - 'e - lét.

167. Tempo giusto, ♩ = 72.

Muz. F. 1008a); III. Jászberény (Szolnok). 1907.; B.

I - gyunk itt, mert van mit, Jó gaz - da la - kik itt;

Nem csu - rog, nem csë - peg, El - mu - lat - ha - tunk itt.

168. Parlando, ♩ = 96.

Muz. F. 1016c); IV. Vacsárcsi (Csík), 1907.; B.

1. Áld - ja meg az is - ten Azt az é - des a - nyát,

2/4

A - ki ka - to - ná - nak Ne - ve - li a fi - át.

169. Tempo giusto.

Muz. F. 299a); II. Pográny (Nyitra), Gyepes Rózi (80); V.

Jel - metsz - tem az uj - jam, Fo - lyik pi - ros vé - rëm;

Mesz - sze van ga - lam - bom, Ki kö - tyi mëg ne - kem?

F. 1362a); III. Rákoskeresztúr (Pest), Burger Zsuzsa (16), 1915.; B.

Tempo giusto, ♩ = 84-100.

170.

a) Ül - tet - tem   i - bo - lyát.   Roz - ma - ring mi   vy - šou.,

Öz - vegy em - bert vár - tam.   Mlá - de - nec mi   pri - šou.

Muz. F. 815a), IV. Magyargyerőmonostor (Kolozs), Barta Erzsi (16), 1910.; P.

Tempo giusto, ♩ = 71-100.

171.

1. - Jár - jad pap a   tán - cot.   A - dok száz fo - rin - tot.

-Nem já - rom,   nem tu - dom.   Pap - nak tán - cot   jár - ni.
nem il - lik,   nem sza - bad

III. Ujszász (Pest), Dobóczi Bernátné (26), 1918.; B.

Tempo giusto.

172.

1. Egy - szer egy ki - rály - fi   Mit gon - dolt ma - gá - ba.

Hə hə hoñ.   ha ha ha,   Mit gon - dolt ma - gá - ba:
refr.

Muz. F. 952d); I. Felsőiregh (Tolna), 1916.; B.

Tempo giusto, ♩ = 50-60.

173.

1. Bé - res va - gyok.   bé - res,   Bé - res - nek sze - gőd - tem;

Sej, itt az   új - esz - ten - dő.   Jön a   sze - kér   ér - tem.

II. Nagymegyer (Komárom), 1910.; B.

Tempo giusto, ♩ = 108-120.

174.

1. Volt - e   o - lyan   ju - hász.   Volt - e   o - lyan   ju - hász,

Héj huj   ti - raj - lá - rom,   Héj huj   ti - raj - lá - rom,

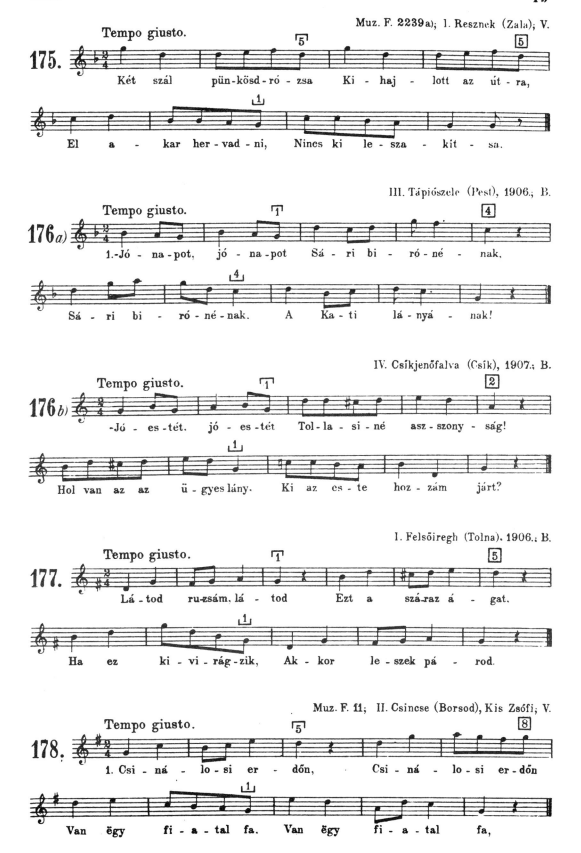

Muz. F. 2239a); 1. Resznek (Zala); V.

175. Tempo giusto.

Két szál pün-kösd-ró - zsa Ki - haj - lott az út - ra,

El a - kar her - vad - ni, Nincs ki le - sza - kít - sa.

III. Tápiószele (Pest), 1906.; B.

176a) Tempo giusto.

1.-Jó - na-pot, jó - na-pot Sá - ri bi - ró-né - nak,

Sá - ri bi - ró-né-nak. A Ka-ti lá-nyá - nak!

IV. Csíkjenőfalva (Csík), 1907.; B.

176b) Tempo giusto.

-Jó - es-tét, jó - es-tét Tol-la - si - né asz-szony - ság!

Hol van az az ü - gyes lány. Ki az es - te hoz - zám járt?

I. Felsőiregh (Tolna). 1906.; B.

177. Tempo giusto.

Lá - tod ru-zsám, lá - tod Ezt a szá-raz á - gat.

Ha ez ki - vi - rág-zik, Ak - kor le - szek pá - rod.

Muz. F. 11; II. Csincse (Borsod), Kis Zsófi; V.

178. Tempo giusto.

1. Csi - ná - lo - si er - dőn, Csi - ná - lo - si er - dőn

Van ëgy fi - a - tal fa. Van ëgy fi - a - tal fa,

3.

II. Nemesócsa (Komárom), 1913.; L.

Tempo giusto.

179.

1. Gu - ta ma - ga egy vá - ros. Van ab - ba egy mé - szá - ros;

Van két lo - va, jó há - mos, Ba - ga - ri - a szer - szá - mos.

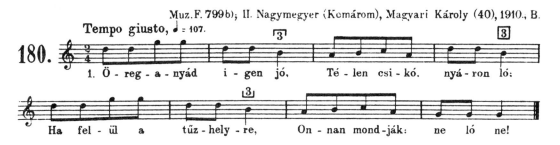

Muz. F. 799 b); II. Nagymegyer (Komárom), Magyari Károly (40), 1910., B.

Tempo giusto, ♩ = 107.

180.

1. Ö - reg - a - nyád i - gen jó, Té - len csi - kó, nyá - ron ló;

Ha fel - ül a tűz - hely - re, On - nan mond -ják: ne ló ne!

IV. Jobbágytelke (Maros-Torda), Boldizsárné (70), 1914.; B.

Tempo giusto.

181.

Ki - vi - rág - zott már a nád.– S ne-kem í - gért vót a - nyád.

Főd - be ve - szett a re - tek._ Más az, a - kit sze - re - tek.

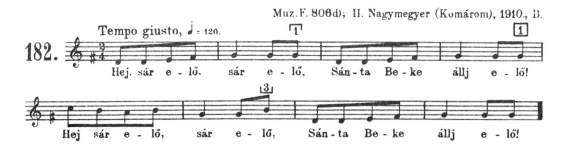

Muz. F. 806 d); II. Nagymegyer (Komárom), 1910.; B.

Tempo giusto, ♩ = 120.

182.

Hej. sár e - lő. sár e - lő, Sán - ta Be - ke állj e - lő!

Hej sár e - lő, sár e - lő, Sán - ta Be - ke állj e - lő!

Muz. F. 1173 b); I. Kisrákos (Vas), Marton Dániel (66); V.

Tempo giusto.

183.

Egy kis ker - tet ke - rí - ték, Ab - ba ró - zsát ül - te - ték;

Szom -széd asz - szon kis lá - nya Rá - ka - pott a ró - zsá - ra.

184. Tempo giusto.

II. Nagymegyer (Komárom), 1910.; B.

1. Borbély Bá-bi nagy beteg,
Nem e - he-ti a levest;
Vi-zet in - na, vi-ze sincs, Kút-ra küd-jön sen-ki sincs.

185. Tempo giusto.

Muz. F 58d); l. Pápa (Veszprém), Egerszegi János; V.

Pa-kony-er - dő gyász - ba van.
Ba-kony-er - dő gyász - ba van,

Ró - zsa Sán-dor ágy - ba van. Ró - zsa Sán-dor ágy - ba van.

4.

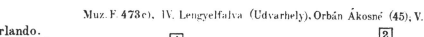

186. Parlando.

Muz. F. 473c), IV. Lengyelfalva (Udvarhely), Orbán Ákosné (45); V.

El - in - du - la há - rom ár-va, A há-rom kis csi - por-ká-val

Az er - dő - be ep - rőt szed-ni. Az er - dő -be ep - röt szed-ni.

187. Parlando. ♪= 200.

Muz. F. 959b); III. Doboz (Békés), 1906.; B.

1. Bé - kés vá - ros de szép helyt van, Mert a templom kö - ze-pén van;

Aj - ta - já - ba ró - zsa-csip-ke. Rá - szál-lott egy bús ger - li - ce.

188. Parlando, ♩= cca 104.

Muz. F. 1042b); IV. Gyergyóujfalu (Csík), 1907.; B.

1. I-de-je buj-do-sá - sim-nak, El-jött már ú - ta-zá - sim-nak, Sok

o - ka-i vadnak an-nak Az én el-buj - do-sá - simnak.

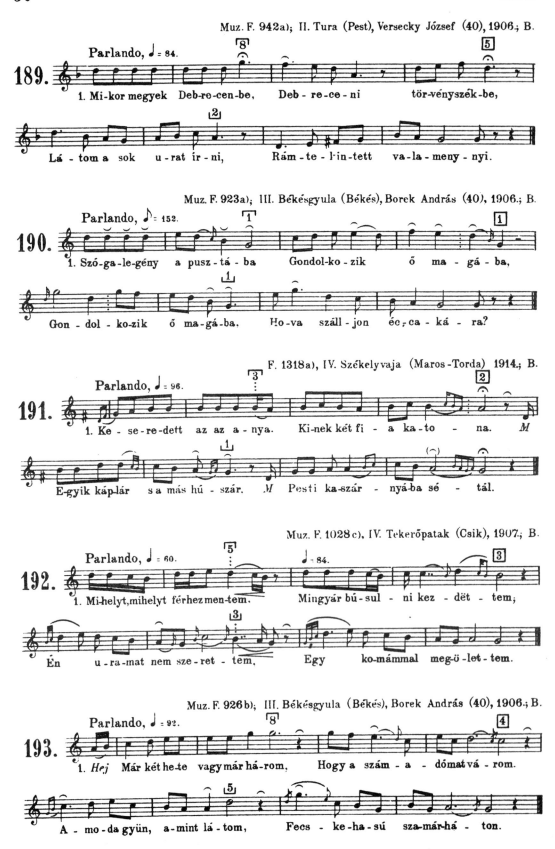

Muz. F. 942a); II. Tura (Pest), Versecky József (40), 1906.; B.

189. Parlando, ♩= 84.

1. Mi-kor megyek Deb-re-cen-be, Deb - re -ce - ni tör-vényszék-be,

Lá - tom a sok u - rat ír - ni, Rám - te - l-in-tett va - la - meny - nyi.

Muz. F. 923a); III. Békésgyula (Békés), Borek András (40), 1906.; B.

190. Parlando, ♪= 152.

1. Szó-ga-le-gény a pusz-tá - ba Gondol-ko - zik ő ma - gá - ba,

Gon - dol - ko-zik ő ma-gá-ba. Ho-va száll - jon éc-ca - ká - ra?

F. 1318a), IV. Székelyvaja (Maros -Torda) 1914.; B.

191. Parlando, ♩= 96.

1. Ke - se - re-dett az az a - nya. Ki-nek két fi - a ka-to - na. M

E-gyik káp-lár s a más hú - szár. M Pesti ka-szár - nyá-ba sé - tál.

Muz. F. 1028 c), IV. Tekerőpatak (Csik), 1907.; B.

192. Parlando, ♩ = 60.   ♩ = 84.

1. Mi-helyt,mihelyt férhez men-tem. Mingyár bú-sul - ni kez - dët - tem;

Én u - ra-mat nem sze-ret - tem, Egy ko-mámmal meg-ö -let-tem.

Muz. F. 926 b); III. Békésgyula (Békés), Borek András (40), 1906.; B.

193. Parlando, ♩ = 92.

1. *Hej* Már két he-te vagy már há-rom, Hogy a szám - a - dómat vá - rom.

A - mo-da gyün, a-mint lá - tom, Fecs - ke-ha-sú sza-már-há - ton.

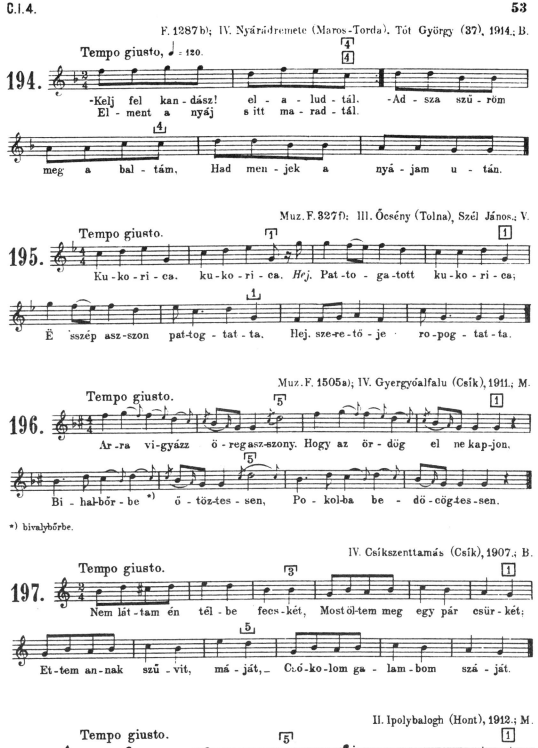

F. 1287b); IV. Nyárádremete (Maros-Torda). Tót György (37), 1914.; B.

Tempo giusto, ♩ = 120.

194.

-Kelj fel kan - dász!   el - a - lud - tál.   -Ad - sza szű - röm
El - ment a nyáj   s itt ma - rad - tál.

meg a bal - tám,   Had men - jek a   nyá - jam u - tán.

Muz.F.327f): III. Őcsény (Tolna), Szél János.; V.

Tempo giusto.

195.

Ku - ko - ri - ca.   ku - ko - ri - ca. *Hej.* Pat - to - ga - tott   ku - ko - ri - ca;

Ë ssszép asz - szon pat - tog - tat - ta.   Hej. sze - re - tő - je ro - pog - tat - ta.

Muz.F. 1505a); IV. Gyergyóalfalu (Csík), 1911.; M.

Tempo giusto.

196.

Ar - ra vi - gyázz ö - reg asz - szony. Hogy az ör - dög el ne kap - jon,

Bi - hal-bőr - be *) ö - töz-tes - sen,   Po - kol-ba be - dö - cög-tes - sen.

*) bivalybőrbe.

IV. Csíkszenttamás (Csík), 1907.; B.

Tempo giusto.

197.

Nem lát - tam én tél - be fecs - két, Most öl-tem meg egy pár csür - két;

Et - tem an - nak szű - vit,   má - ját, _ Csó - ko - lom ga - lam - bom szá - ját.

II. Ipolybalogh (Hont), 1912.; M.

Tempo giusto.

198.

Hajt - ják a fe - ke - te kecs - két, Ve - rik a bar - na me - nyecs - két.

Ha ve - rik is, meg - ér - dem - li.   Ki az u - rát nem sze - re - ti.

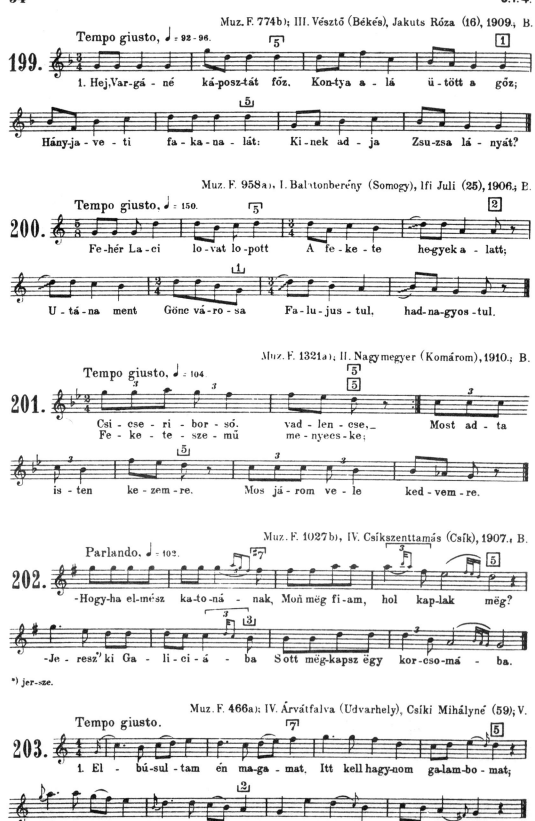

Muz. F. 774b); III. Vésztő (Békés), Jakuts Róza (16), 1909.; B.

199. Tempo giusto, ♩ = 92 - 96.

1. Hej, Var-gá - né ká-posz-tát főz. Kon-tya a - lá ü - tött a gőz;

Hány-ja - ve - ti fa - ka - na - lát: Ki - nek ad - ja Zsu-zsa lá - nyát?

Muz. F. 958a), I. Balatonberény (Somogy), Ifi Juli (25), 1906.; B.

200. Tempo giusto, ♩ = 150.

Fe -hér La -ci lo -vat lo -pott A fe - ke - te he-gyek a - latt;

U - tá - na ment Gönc vá -ro - sa Fa - lu - jus - tul, had-na-gyos -tul.

Muz. F. 1321a); II. Nagymegyer (Komárom), 1910.; B.

201. Tempo giusto, ♩ = 104.

Csi - cse - ri - bor - só. vad - len - cse,_ Most ad - ta
Fe - ke - te - sze - mű me - nyecs - ke;

is - ten ke - zem - re. Mos já - rom ve - le ked - vem - re.

Muz. F. 1027b), IV. Csíkszenttamás (Csík), 1907.; B.

202. Parlando, ♩ = 102.

-Hogy-ha el-mész ka-to-ná - nak, Mon mëg fi - am, hol kap-lak mëg?

-Je - resz*) ki Ga - li - ci - á - ba S ott mëg-kapsz ëgy kor-cso-má - ba.

*) jer-sze.

Muz. F. 466a); IV. Árvátfalva (Udvarhely), Csíki Mihályné (59); V.

203. Tempo giusto.

1. El - bú-sul -tam én ma-ga - mat. Itt kell hagy-nom ga-lam-bo - mat;

Már én a - kár - mer - re já - rok, Szép ró - zsá - ra nem ta-lá - lok.

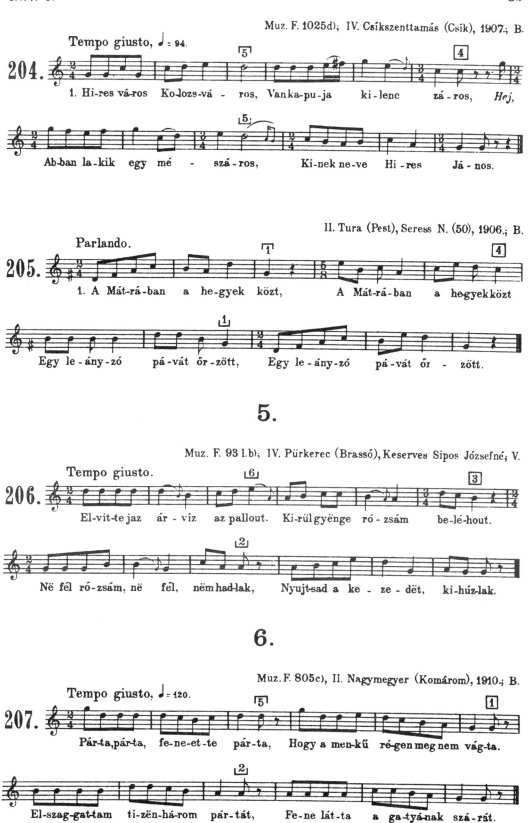

Muz. F. 1025d); IV. Csíkszenttamás (Csík), 1907.; B.

Tempo giusto, ♩ = 94.

204.

1. Hi-res vá-ros Ko-lozs-vá - ros, Van-ka-pu-ja ki-lenc zá-ros, *Hej,*

Ab-ban la-kik egy mé - szá-ros, Ki-nek ne-ve Hi-res Já - nos.

11. Tura (Pest), Seress N. (50), 1906.; B.

Parlando.

205.

1. A Mát-rá-ban a he-gyek közt, A Mát-rá-ban a he-gyek közt

Egy le - ány-zó pá-vát őr-zött, Egy le - ány-zó pá-vát őr - zött.

5.

Muz. F. 93 l.b); IV. Pürkerec (Brassó), Keserves Sipos Józsefné; V.

Tempo giusto.

206.

El-vit-te jaz ár - víz az pallout. Ki-rül gyënge ró - zsám be-lé-hout.

Në fél ró-zsám, në fél, nëm had-lak, Nyujt-sad a ke - ze - dët, ki-húz-lak.

6.

Muz. F. 805c), II. Nagymegyer (Komárom), 1910.; B.

Tempo giusto, ♩ = 120.

207.

Pár-ta, pár-ta, fe-ne-et-te pár-ta, Hogy a men-kű ré-gen meg nem vág-ta.

El-szag-gat-tam ti-zën-há-rom pár-tát, Fe-ne lát-ta a ga-tyá-nak szá-rát.

Muz. F. 804 b); II. Nagymegyer (Komárom), 1910.; B.

Tempo giusto. ♩=63.

208.

Hopp i - de tisz-tán szép pa - lútt dësz-kán, Ha lë - szek, lë - szek,
Nem lë - szek töb - bé nyo-szo - ló - lë - ány;

meny-asz-szony lë - szek, An - nak is pe - dig leg - szebb - je lë - szek.

Muz. F. 1253; Nyitraegerszeg (Nyitra), 1910.; K.

Tempo giusto. ♩=125-168.

209.

1. El - mënt a két jány vi - rá - got szëny-nyi. El - in - du -

lá - nak, kez - dé - nek mëny - nyi. Ë - gyik má - sik - nak

kez - di mon - da - nyi: -Vót-ë va - la - ki tí - gëd ki - ret - nyi?

Muz. F. 939a), I. Mikosszéplak (Vas), Hernic Anna (55), 1906.; B.

Parlando, ♪=cca 78.

210.

1. Le - tö - rött a pé - csi to-rony gomb - ja;_ E - redj ró - zsám,
Megszomjult a Rá-kop Jós-ka lo - va.

hoz-zál né - ki vi - zet. Rá - kop Jós - ka az Al-föld-re si - et.

Muz. F. 980 b); I. Felsőnyék (Tolna), 1907.; B.

Tempo giusto, ♩=46.

211.

1. Fe - hér hab-gya vagyon a Du - ná - nak,_ Kedves fi - ja
Ked-ves fi - ja voltam az a - nyám - nak,

voltam az a - nyám-nak, Még - is be-so - roz-tak ka-to - ná - nak.

7.

Muz. F. 2300a); I.Felsőiregh (Tolna), Kolonics Mari (20), 1907.; B.

212.

Parlando, ♪ = cca 144.

A szëgszár - di szől-lők al - ja ho-mo-kos. Ar - ra jár-nak
a - rany-, e - züst - gom-bo - sok. A - zok hajt-ják el a sár-ga
csi-kó - kat. A - zon vesz-nek a-rany, e - züst gom-bo - kat.

8.

Muz. F. 1021c); IV. Csíkjenőfalva (Csík), 1907; B.

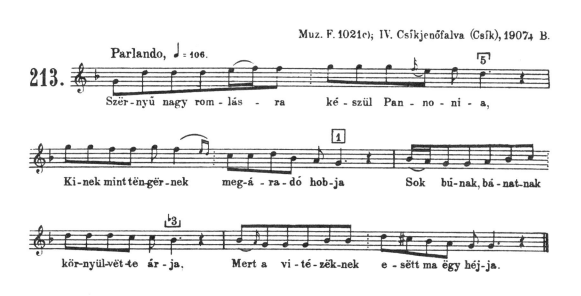

213.

Parlando, ♩ = 106.

Szër-nyű nagy rom - lás - ra ké - szül Pan - no - ni - a,
Ki-nek mint tën-gër - nek meg-á - ra-dó hob-ja Sok bú-nak, bá - nat-nak
kör-nyül-vët-te ár - ja. Mert a vi - té-zëk-nek e - sëtt ma ëgy héj-ja.

Muz. F. 1507; IV. Gyergyóalfalu (Csík), 1911; M.

214.

Parlando.

1. Ha fo-lyó-víz vó-nék, bá-na-tot nem tud-nék, Ha fo-lyó-víz vó-nék,

bá-n -tot nem tud-nék,   Hë - gyek. völgyek kö-zött   szép csën-de-sën foly-nék,

Hë - gyek, völ-gyek kö - zött   szép csën - de - sën foly-nék,

9.

Muz. F. 1036b); IV. Kilyénfalva (Csík), 1907.; B.

Parlando.

215.

1. Ó   én sze-gény   kis ma-dár,   mi-re ve-te - mëd - tem,

Mi-kor a szal - má-ban én   szë - met szë-de - get - tem!

Tőr -ben es -tek   lá - ba-im.____   o - da sza-bad - sá - gim,

Köt-ve vad-nak   szár - nya - im.____   o - da vi-gas - sá - gim.

10.

Muz. F. 993d); 1. Felsőiregh (Tolna), 1907.; B.

Tempo giusto. ♩ = 69.

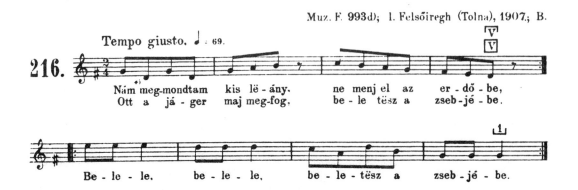

216.

Nám meg-mondtam   kis lë - ány,   ne menj el az   er - dő - be,
Ott a já - ger   maj meg-fog,   be - le tësz a   zseb-jé - be.

Be - le - le,   be - le - le,   be - le - tësz a   zseb - jé - be.

*) Lám.

II. 1.

Muz. F. 1029d); IV. Tekerőpatak (Csík), 1907.; B.

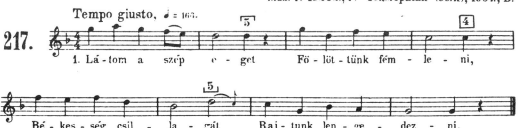

1. Lá-tom a szép e-get Fö-löt-tünk fém-le-ni,
Bé-kes-ség csil-la-gát Raj-tunk len-ge-dez-ni.

2.

II. Nagymegyer (Komárom), 1910.; B.

1.-Hej, ha-lá-szok, ha-lá-szok, Mit fo-gott a há-ló-tok?
-Nem fo-gott az e-gye-bet: Vö-rös-szár-nyú ke-sze-get.

Muz. F. 267b); Szegvár (Csongrád), Hérányi Pál; V.

1.- Héj, ha-lá-szok, ha-lá-szok, Mé-re mén az ha-jó-tok?
-Tö-rök-ka-ni-zsa fe-lé Vi-szi a viz le-fe-lé.

Muz. F. 313a); II. Derecske (Heves), Kovács András; V.

1. Most jö-vök én Gyu-lá-rul, A gyu-la-i vá-sár-rul;
Ott hal-lot-tam ezt a szót: -Nyisd ki ba-bám az aj-tót.

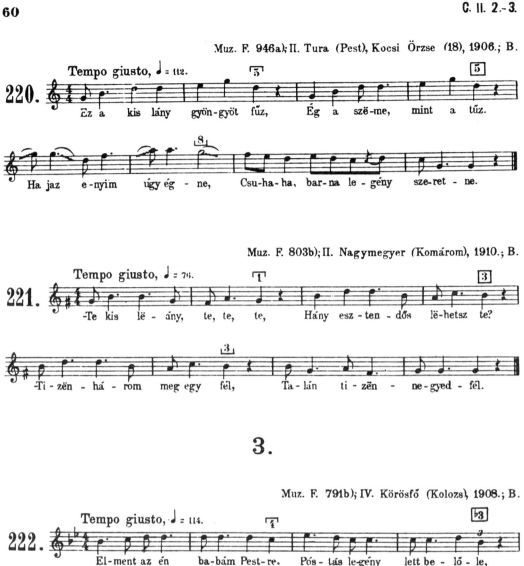

Muz. F. 946a); II. Tura (Pest), Kocsi Örzse (18), 1906.; B.

220. Tempo giusto, ♩ = 112.

Ez a kis lány gyön-gyöt fűz, Ég a szë-me, mint a tűz.

Ha jaz e-nyim úgy ég - ne, Csu-ha-ha, bar-na le - gény sze-ret - ne.

Muz. F. 803b); II. Nagymegyer (Komárom), 1910.; B.

221. Tempo giusto, ♩ = 76.

-Te kis lë - ány, te, te, te, Hány esz - ten - dős lë-hetsz te?

-Ti - zën - há - rom meg egy fél, Ta - lán ti - zën - ne-gyed - fél.

3.

Muz. F. 791b); IV. Körösfő (Kolozs), 1908.; B.

222. Tempo giusto, ♩ = 114.

El-ment az én ba-bám Pest-re, Pós - tás le-gény lett be - lő - le,

Csej, haj, minden-ki-nek kűd uj - sá - got, Ne-kem csak szo-mo-rú-sá-got, i-gaz a.

Muz. F. 1025b); IV. Csíkszenttamás (Csík), 1907.; B.

223. Tempo giusto, ♩ = 123.

Vé - gig mentem a rózsám ud-va-rán, Bé - te-kin-tëk a rózsám ab-la-kán.

Ró - zsa nyi - lik a cse - rép - be, Lát - talak, ró-zsám, a más ö - lé - be.

IV. Kibéd (Maros-Torda), Dósa Anna (15), 1906.; B.

224.

É-des volt az a-nyám te-je, Ke-se-rű a más ke-nye-re;

Úgy el-ma-rad-tam sze-gény-től, Mint a nyár-fa le-ve-lé-től.

Muz. F. 1639d); II. Rafajnaujfalu (Bereg), Demeter Juliánna (18), 1912.; B.

225 a)

Fel van a lo-vam nyer-gel-ve, Ma-gam ü-lök a te-te-jé-be.

E-nyím vagy te-hát drá-ga gyöngyvi-rág, El-me-gyek én te-hoz-zád.

Muz. F. 181 d); II. Eger (Heves), Varga András.; V.

225 b)

Le van a szi-vem lán-col-va, Nin-csen a-ki fel-ol-doz-za.

Ol-dozz fel hát gyö-nyö-rű vi-rág-szál, Ak-kor le-szek sza-bad ma-dár.

4.

Muz. F. 1852a); II. Fornos (Bereg), 1912.; B.

226.

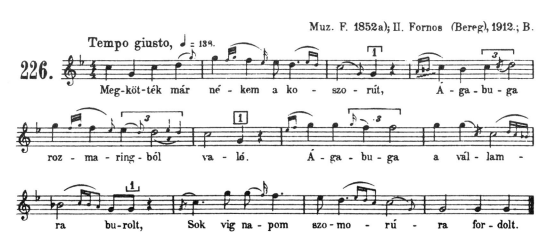

Meg-köt-ték már né-kem a ko-szo-rút, Á-ga-bu-ga

roz-ma-ring-ból va-ló. Á-ga-bu-ga a vál-lam-

ra bu-rolt, Sok vig na-pom szo-mo-rú-ra for-dolt.

Muz. F. 960b); III. Doboz (Békés), 1906.; B.

227.

Tempo giusto, ♩ = 116.

Sze-gény va-gyok, sze-gény-nek szü-let-tem, A ró-zsá-mat i-ga-zán

sze-ret-tem; Az í-ri-gyek el-ra-bol-ták tű-lem, Igy lett i-ga-zi ár-va be-lü-lem.

5.

Muz. F. 61a); I. Pápa (Veszprém), Kirili István; V.

228.

Tempo giusto.

Szé-na te-rëm, szé-na te-rëm a ré-ten, — Nem be-szél-tem a ba-bám-mal a hé-ten.

Ná-la van a zseb-ken-dőm a zseb-jé-ben, E-lől-ve-szi: ar-rul ju-tok e-szé-be.

Muz. F. 794c); II. Nagymegyer (Komárom), Rácz József (60), 1910.; B.

229.

Tempo giusto, ♩ = 113.

Kis pej lo-vam nëm sze-re-ti a za-bot, Kocs-má-ros-né ár-pá-já-ra rá-ka-pott. Mer az ár-pa nëm is o-lyan, mint a zab, — I-gaz kis lány nëm is kell az ma-gyar-nak.

III. Vésztő (Békés), Jakuts Róza (16), 1909.; B.

230.

Tempo giusto.

A Var-gá-ék ka-pu-ju-kon nin-csen zár, Ez a hí-res Gar-zó Pis-ta o-da jár.

Ka-pu-fá-hoz kö-tö-zi meg a lo-vát, Míg Jul-csá-val ki-be-szél-ge-ti ma-gát.

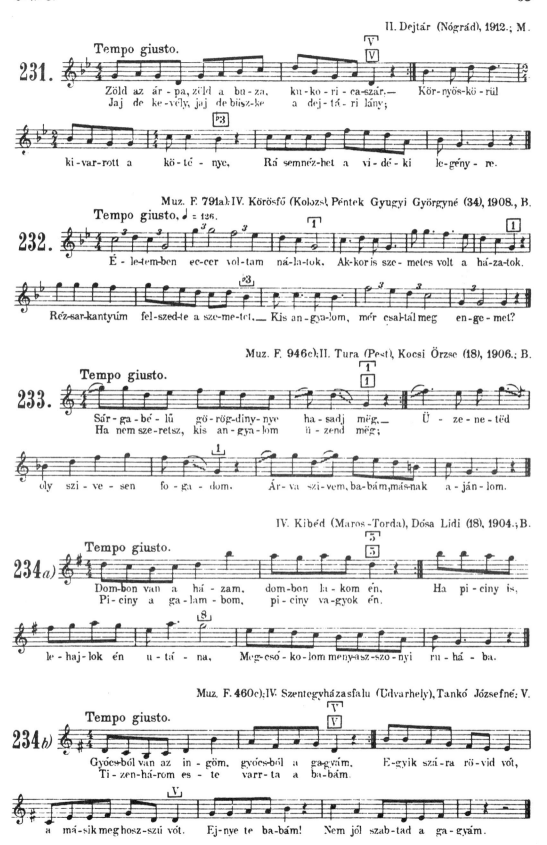

II. Dejtár (Nógrád), 1912.; M.

231. Tempo giusto.

Zöld az ár - pa, zöld a bu - za,   ku - ko - ri - ca-szár.—   Kör-nyös-kö - rül
Jaj de ke - vély, jaj de büsz-ke   a dej - tá - ri lány;

ki - var-rott a   kö - té - nye,   Rá semnéz-het a vi - dé - ki   le-gény - re.

Muz. F. 791a): IV. Körösfő (Kolozs), Péntek Gyugyi Györgyné (34), 1908., B.

232. Tempo giusto, ♩ = 126.

É - le-tem-ben ec-cer vol-tam ná-la-tok.   Ak-kor is sze - metes volt a há-za-tok.

Réz-sar-kantyúm fel-szed-te a sze-me-tct.— Kis an-gya-lom, mér csal-tál meg   en-ge - met?

Muz. F. 946c); II. Tura (Pest), Kocsi Örzse (18), 1906.; B.

233. Tempo giusto.

Sár - ga - bé - lű   gö - rög-diny-nye   ha - sadj még.—   Ü - ze - ne - tëd
Ha nem sze-retsz, kis an - gya - lom   ü - zend még;

oly szi - ve - sen   fo - ga - dom.   Ár - va szi - vem, ba-bám,más-nak   a - ján - lom.

IV. Kibéd (Maros - Torda), Dósa Lidi (18), 1904.; B.

234a) Tempo giusto.

Dom-bon van a há - zam,   dom-bon la - kom én,   Ha pi - ciny is,
Pi - ciny a ga - lam - bom,   pi - ciny va-gyok én.

le - haj-lok én   u - tá - na,   Meg-csó - ko-lom meny-asz-szo-nyi   ru - há - ba.

Muz. F. 460c); IV. Szentegyházasfalu (Udvarhely), Tankó Józsefné; V.

234b) Tempo giusto.

Gyócs-ból van az in - göm,   gyócs-ból a ga-gyám,   E-gyik szá - ra rö - vid vót,
Ti - zen-há-rom es - te   varr-ta a ba-bám.

a má-sik meg hosz-szú vót.   Ej-nye te ba-bám!   Nem jól szab-tad a ga-gyám.

III. 2.

Muz. F. 340d); I. Kaposfüred (Somogy), Kovács György; V.

235. Parlando.

Ez a bor nëm drá-ga: Hat kraj-cár az á - ra. *Hej,* Er-gye ró-zsám,

hozz ëgy mesz-szőt, had da-nol-jak mëg ëgy ver-söt, Az-u-tán el - më-gyünk.

3.

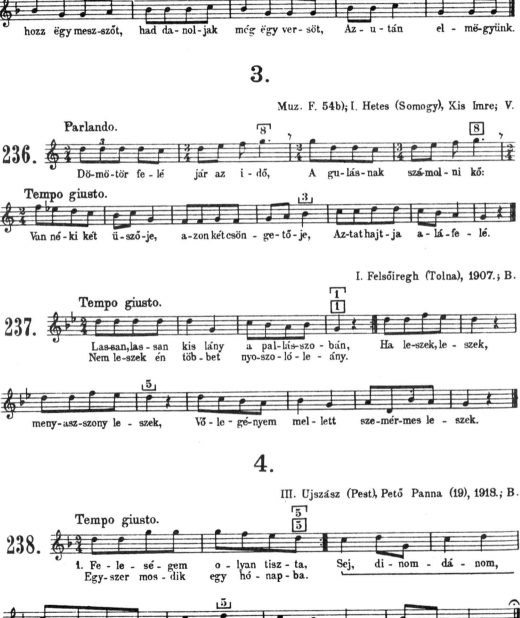

Muz. F. 54b); I. Hetes (Somogy), Kis Imre; V.

236. Parlando.

Dö-mö-tör fe - lé jár az i - dő, A gu-lás-nak szá-mol-ni kő:

Tempo giusto.

Van né-ki két ü-sző-je, a-zon két csön-ge-tő-je, Az-tat hajt-ja a-lá-fe-lé.

I. Felsőiregh (Tolna), 1907.; B.

237. Tempo giusto.

Las-san, las-san kis lány a pal-lás-szo-bán, Ha le-szek, le - szek,
Nem le-szek én töb-bet nyo-szo-ló-le-ány.

meny-asz-szony le - szek, Vő-le-gé-nyem mel-lett sze-mér-mes le - szek.

4.

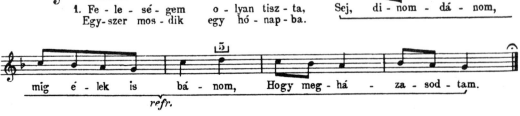

III. Ujszász (Pest), Pető Panna (19), 1918.; B.

238. Tempo giusto.

1. Fe-le-sé-gem o-lyan tisz-ta, Sej, di-nom-dá-nom,
Egy-szer mos-dik egy hó-nap-ba.

mig é-lek is bá-nom, Hogy meg-há - za-sod-tam.

refr.

I. Felsőiregh (Tolna), 1907.; B.

Parlando.

239.

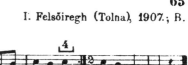

1.-Hol jár-tál Ruzsics-kám i-lyen ko - rán, -Zöld er-dő -ben jár-tam. É-des ró - zsám.
Hogy i-lyen har-ma-tos a ro - ko - lyád? zöld fü-vet a-rat-tam,

I. Felsőiregh (Tolna), 1907.; B.

Tempo giusto.

240.

Ne hagyj el an - gya - lom. meg - ö - reg - szem,
Lá - ba - im nem bir-nak, meg - be - teg - szem.

Tá - ma - dé - kom te le - gyél, Pa - na - szim-nak higy - jél.
ná - lam nél - kül ne le - gyél,

Muz. F. 1652c); II. Fornos (Bereg), 1912.; B.

Tempo giusto, ♩ = 112.

241.

1.-Ho - vá mégy te sző - ke kis lány? -Az er - dő - be
Szá - raz á - gér, süt - ni, főz - ni me - nyeg-ző - be.

Szá- raz ág el - lob - ban, a sze - re - lem job - ban, E - szem-ad - ta.

5.

II. Nagygút (Bereg), 1912.; B.

Parlando.

242.

1. Ma van hus-vét nap-ja, má-sod-éc-ca - ká - ja, Jól tud-já - tok,

Ki - nek el - ső nap-ján Jé - zus fel - tá - mad - ván Di-cső-ség - be.

Muz. F. 1636a); II. Rafajnaujfalu (Bereg), 1912.; B.

Tempo giusto, ♩ = 126.

243.

Zö - rög a ko - csi, pat - tog-tat Jan-csi, Ta-lán ér - tem jön-nek.

Jaj, é - des a - nyám, sze - rel - mes daj - kám, De ha - mar el - visz-nek.

Muz. F. 998c). I. Felsőiregh (Tolna), 1907.; B.

244. Tempo giusto. ♩ = 93.

Sző-lő - he-gyën kö-rösz-tül Megy a kis lány öcs-csös-tül. Du-ná - rul

fuj a szél: Ha Du-ná-rul fuj a szél, szegény embërt mindig ér. Du-ná - rul fuj a szél.

refr.

II. Nagymegyer (Komárom), 1910.; B.

245. Tempo giusto.

Héj, héj, mit tegyek, Po-zsony a - lá hogy menjek, Ott e-gye-dül éj - jek?

A sze-re-tőm el - ha-gyott, a szi-vi-bül ki-zá-rott Egy kis bo-lond - sá - gért.

6.

I. Felsőiregh (Tolna), 1907.; B.

246. Tempo giusto.

1.-Keresd meg a tűt, Én meg a gyű-szűt, Had varjam meg a babámnak A pergál ün-git.

Muz. F. 339c). I. Kaposfüred (Somogy), Gyura László (70); V.

247. Tempo giusto.

Én víg nëm vagyok, Szo-mo - rú vagyok. Apri kácse mále dutye. Ó jaj ne bugyre.

7.

Muz. F. 631a); I. Resznek (Zala); V.

248. Tempo giusto.

1. Az én lu-da - i-mak Tizënketten voltak. Ühüm, ej haj, Tizënketten voltak,

refr.

III. Vésztő (Békés), Jakuts Róza (16), 1909.; B.

249. Tempo giusto.

1. Es - te van már, nyóc ó - ra, Ég a vi - lág a bót - ba,

Sal - lá - rom. sal - lá - rom. Ég a vi - lág a bót - ba.

refr.

8.

I. Felsőiregh (Tolna), 1907.; B.

250. **Tempo giusto.**

1. Ka - la - maj - kó an - nak ne - ve, Ug - rán - do - zik, mint a fe - ne.

Hány - ja - ve - ti lá - ba - it, Nem saj - nál - ja i - na - it.

I. Felsőiregh (Tolna), 1907.; B.

251. **Tempo giusto.**

1. Hár-mat to-jott a fe - ke - te ká - nya,_ Engëm sze-ret a kend bar-na

lá - nya. Ki - ki - tyen - be, Ku - ku - tyon - ba. Gye-re ró - zsám a ko-csim - ba.

refr.

Muz. F. 979 d); I. Felsőiregh (Tolna), 1907.; B.

252. **Tempo giusto.**

1. -Adj el a-nyám, adj el, mer itt hal - lak. -*Hej*, Nëhagyj it-ten lá-nyom, férhöz ad-

lak. -Tyuh, had hall - jam, hogy kinek ád kend. Had halljam, hogy kinek ád kend.

9.

Muz. F. 794 d); II. Nagymegyer (Komárom), Rácz József (60), 1910.; B.

253. **Tempo giusto,** ♩ = 126.

-Hogy a csi - be, hogy? Hát az á - ra hogy? -Mit kér - de - zi,

mi az á - ra, Be - lé - vá - gom a mar - ká - ba!

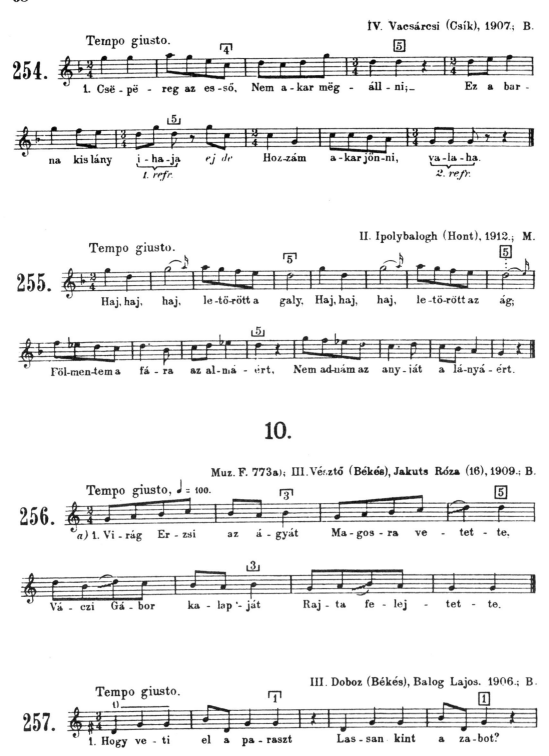

254.

Tempo giusto.

1. Csë - pë - reg az es -ső, Nem a -kar mëg - áll - ni;_ Ez a bar -

na kis lány i - ha -ja *ej de* Hoz-zám a -kar jön -ni, va -la - ha.
1. refr. *2. refr.*

II. Ipolybalogh (Hont), 1912.; M.

255.

Tempo giusto.

Haj, haj, haj, le -tö-rött a galy, Haj, haj, haj, le -tö-rött az ág;

Föl-men-tem a fá - ra az al-má - ért, Nem ad-nám az any -iát a lá-nyá - ért.

10.

Muz. F. 773a); III. Vésztő (Békés), Jakuts Róza (16), 1909.; B.

256.

Tempo giusto, ♩ = 100.

a) 1. Vi -rág Er - zsi az á - gyát Ma -gos -ra ve - tet - te,

Vá - czi Gá - bor ka - lap '- ját Raj - ta fe - lej - tet - te.

III. Doboz (Békés), Balog Lajos. 1906.; B.

257.

Tempo giusto.

1. Hogy ve - ti el a pa - raszt Las - san kint a za -bot?

Igy ve -ti el a pa-raszt Las-san-kint a za-bot. var.:

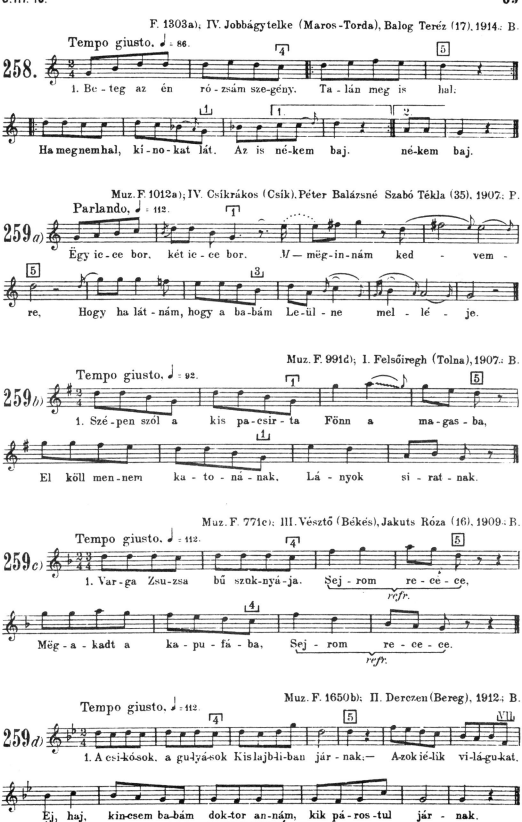

F. 1303a); IV. Jobbágytelke (Maros-Torda), Balog Teréz (17). 1914.: B.

Tempo giusto. ♩ = 86.

258.

1. Be - teg az én ró - zsám sze-gény. Ta - lán meg is hal:

Ha megnemhal, kí - no - kat lát. Az is né-kem baj. né-kem baj.

Muz. F. 1012a); IV. Csíkrákos (Csík). Péter Balázsné Szabó Tékla (35). 1907.: P.

Parlando, ♩ = 112.

259 a)

Ëgy ic - ce bor, két ic - ce bor. M — mëg-in-nám ked - vem -

re, Hogy ha lát - nám, hogy a ba-bám Le-ül - ne mel - lé - je.

Muz. F. 991d); I. Felsőiregh (Tolna), 1907.: B.

Tempo giusto. ♩ = 92.

259 b)

1. Szé-pen szól a kis pa-csir - ta Fönn a ma-gas - ba,

El köll men - nem ka - to - ná - nak, Lá - nyok si - rat - nak.

Muz. F. 771c); III. Vésztő (Békés), Jakuts Róza (16), 1909.: B.

Tempo giusto. ♩ = 112.

259 c)

1. Var - ga Zsu-zsa bű szok-nyá-ja. Sej - rom re - cë - ce,
refr.

Mëg - a - kadt a ka - pu - fá - ba, Sej - rom re - ce - ce.
refr.

Muz. F. 1650b); II. Derczen (Bereg), 1912.; B.

Tempo giusto. ♩ = 112.

259 d)

1. A csi-kó-sok, a gu-lyá-sok Kislajb-li-ban jár - nak;— A-zok ié-lik vi-lá-gu-kat.

Ej, haj, kin-csem ba-bám dok-tor an-nám, kik pá-ros-tul jár - nak.
refr.

Muz. F. 939b); I. Mikosszéplak (Vas), Hernic Anna (55), 1906.; B.

259 *e)* Poco rubato, ♪ = 82.

1. Zúg az er-dő, zug a me-ző, Nem tom,mi zu - gá - sa? Ta - lán bi-zony

Fáb-ján Pis-ta Sej. haj. bar-na ba-bám, az lo-vát ug-rat-ja.
refr.

Muz. F. 770a); III. Vésztő (Békés), Jakuts Róza (16), 1909.; B.

260 *a)* Tempo giusto, ♩ = 110.

1.-É - des ked-ves fe - le - sé-gem! -Mi baj, an-gya - lom?

-Mit ke - res itt a nyer-ges ló Az ud - va - ro - mon?

I. Felsőiregh (Tolna), 1906.; B.

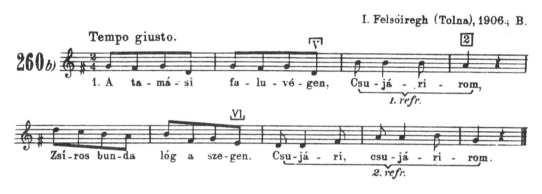

260 *b)* Tempo giusto.

1. A ta - má - si fa - lu - vé - gen, Csu - já - ri - rom,
1. refr.

Zsí-ros bun-da lóg a sze-gen. Csu-já - ri, csu-já - ri - rom.
2. refr.

11.

M. F. 1194b); I. Őriszentpéter (Vas), Németh Sándor (42); V.

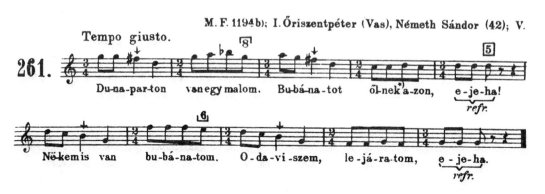

261. Tempo giusto.

Du-na-par-ton van egy malom. Bu-bá-na-tot öl-nek a-zon, e-je-ha!
refr.

Në-kem is van bu-bá-na-tom. O - da-vi-szem, le-já-ra-tom, e-je-ha.
refr.

*)örölnek

16.

262. Tempo giusto.

Muz. F. 301b); II. Pográny (Nyitra), Mészáros Ambrusné, V.

Nem lát - tam én mol-nár-csó-kot. De maj lá - tok most!

Héj, huj, Pin-des Le-nor, Majd ki-tet-szik most.
héj, huj, Fo-dor Jó-zsef,

263. Poco rubato, ♩ = 95.

Muz. F. 1033b), IV. Tekerőpatak (Csík), 1907.; B.

1. El - mënt u-ram a Put-ná-ra. Ha-za-jő hó - nap-u-tán-ra.

Ej, haj, ej, haj, Kor-co-vá-ré rip rop rop.

refr.

264. Tempo giusto, ♩ = 121.

Muz. F. 806b); II. Nagymegyer (Komárom), 1910.; B.

1. El - ve-szett a tar-ka tyú-kom. A-gyon csap-ta a szom-szé-dom,

Tojj, tojj, tojj, toj-jál már, Toj-jál i-de-ha-za már.

refr.

265. Tempo giusto.

III. Doboz (Békés), Virág Erzsi (13), 1917.; B.

a) 1. Vi-rá-gék-nál ég a vi-lág, Sü-tik má a rán-tott bé-kát,

Zi-me-zum, zi-me-zum, Re-ce-fi-ce bum bum bum. a)var.: Zi-me-zum, Re-ce-

refr.

Muz. F. 633c), I. Resznek (Zala), Németh Károlyné: V.

Tempo giusto.

266.

Er - re, ar - ra, a bo - ro - nya ié - lén Ki - nyíHott a

tu - li - pán a ka - la - pom szié - lén. Egy - két szál, há - rom

szál, Ál - nok vol - tál ba - bám, mëg - csal - tál.
refr.

Muz. F. 770b), III. Vésztő (Békés), Jakuts Róza (16), 1909.; B.

Tempo giusto, ♩ = 120.

267.

Et - tem szől - lőt, most é - rik, most é - rik, most é - rik,—
Vi - rág Er - zsit most ké - rik, most ké - rik, most ké - rik.

Ki - hö ment a le - ve - le? Gar - zó Pis - ta ke - zé -

be, Hej, ri - ca, ri - ca, ri - ca, hej Pis - ta te!

III. Békésgyula (Békés), Illés Panna (18), 1906.; B.

Tempo giusto.

268.

A zsi - dó - nak nincs Krisz-tu - sa, nincs is an - nak mennyben jus - sa,
Van né - ki egy rossz pa - pu - csa, av - val cso-szog a po - kol - ba.

Ic - ca i - gyunk rá - ja, ugy is el - jön a sír szá - ja,
Ott lesz fá-radt tes-tünk csen-des ha - zá - ja, ha ha.

IV. 1.

269. Tempo giusto.

IV. Körösfő (Kolozs). 1907.; B.

Ugy ég a tűz, ha lo - bog. _
Ugy é - lek én, ha lo - pok.

Se nem lo - pok, cse - ré - lek,

még-is i - ga - zán é - lek, I - haj, csu-haj, még-is i - ga - zán é - lek.

270. Tempo giusto, ♩ = 54.

Muz. F. 810b); IV. Magyargyerőmonostor (Kolozs), Sinkó Jánosné 1910.; B.

1. Jön - nek, jön - nek, majd el - visz - nek; . Hol a pár-tám,

hogy ké - szül-jek? Ö - kör - sze-kér a ka - pu - ba, a vő-le-gény

az aj - tó - ba, A meny - asz - szony az ab - lak - ba.

271. Tempo giusto, ♩ = 96.

Muz. F. 809a); IV. Magyargyerőmonostor (Kolozs), Barta Erzsi (17), 1910.; B.

Ugy el - megyek, meg - lás-sá-tok, So-ha hi - rem sem hall-já-tok.

Se hi-re-met se ne-ve-met, fe-lejt-se - tek el en - ge-met, Fe-lejt-se-tek el en - ge-met.

3.

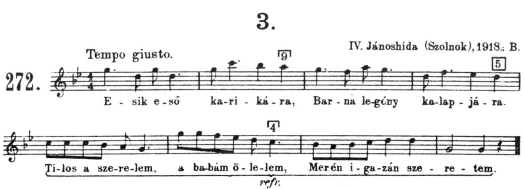

272. Tempo giusto.

IV. Jánoshida (Szolnok), 1918.; B.

E - sik e - ső ka-ri - ká - ra, Bar - na le-gény ka-lap - já - ra.

Ti-los a sze-re-lem, a ba-bám ö - le-lem, Merén i - ga-zán sze - re - tem.

refr:

Muz. F. 1017b); IV. Vacsárcsi (Csík), Takács Ferenc (20),1907.; B.

Tempo giusto, ♩ = 80.

273.

Har-ma-tos a ku-ko-ri-ca le-ve-le,— U-tol-já-ra jár-tam hozzád

az es - te. U - tol-já - ra, ej huj haj, fog - tam aj - tód

hú - zó - ját, Kis an-gya-lom, ki - vá-nok jó éj - ca - kát.

5.

Muz. F. 1530b), IV. Gyergyóujfalu (Csík), Nagy Máténé 1911.; M.

Tempo giusto.

274.

Hn De sok e - ső, de sok sár. de sok le-gény mëg-csalt már,

Tra da da da da da da. Ha még egy-szer ugy mëg-csal,

1. refr.

s mëg-át - ko-zom, hogy mëg-hal, Tra da da da da da da da tra da da.

2. refr.

6.

Muz. F. 288b); III. Kecskemét (Pest), Kelemen Jakab; V.

Tempo giusto.

275*a)*

1. El - sza-ladt a lo - vam Cid-rus - fa-er - dő - be,

Jel - sza-kadt a nyal - ka csizs-mám A ló-ke-re - sés - be.

275b)

Tempo giusto.

I. Baracs (Fejér), 1906.; B.

[7] [5]

1. A te - me - tő - ka - pu Mind a ket - tő nyit - va,

[1]

Bár-csak en - gem o - da te-met-né - nek, Sej, ab -ba a fe -ke-te föld - be!

276a)

Tempo giusto, ♩ = 124.

Muz. F. 948a); III. Vésztő (Békés), 1906.; B.

[1] [3]

1. El -vesz -tet -tem lo - vam Cit -rus -fa - er - dő - ben.

[3]

El - nyűt-tem már hat pár csiz - mát A nagy ke - re - sés - ben.

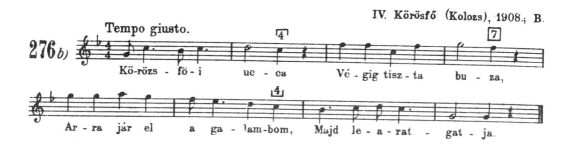

276b)

Tempo giusto.

IV. Körösfő (Kolozs), 1908.; B.

[4] [7]

Kö-rözs - fö - i uc - ca Vé - gig tisz - ta bu - za,

[4]

Ar - ra jár el a ga - lam-bom, Majd le - a - rat - gat - ja.

277.

Parlando, ♩ = 80.

Muz. F. 1030a), IV. Tekerőpatak (Csík), 1907.; B.

[VII] [5]

1. Mi-kor Ró-zsa Sán-dor Fel-ül a lo - vá - ra, Lo-bog raj-ta

[1]

gyócs-ga-tyá - ja, Ej, haj, u - szik a Du - ná - ba.

278.

Tempo giusto, ♩ = 126.

Muz. F. 927c); III. Békésgyula (Békés), Illés Panna (18), 1906.; B.

[5] [2]

1. Hosz - szú - far - kú fecs - ke,__ Szép bar - na me - nyecs - ke,

[VI]

Hogy tud - tál el - jut - ni er - re. Ez i - de -gen föld - re?

Muz. F. 72 b); IV. Zentelke (Kolozs), Kulcsár Kata; V.

Tempo giusto.

279.

Jól van dol-ga a mos-ta-ni hu-szár-nak, Mer a szé-na por-ci-ó-ba
Nëm këll szé-nát ka-száj-jon a lo-vá-nak,
van köt-ve, van köt-ve, de van köt-ve, Gye-re ró-zsám,tëdd a lo-vam e-lé-be.

7.

Muz. F. 978 b), I. Felsőiregh (Tolna), Vörös Ignác (50), 1907.; P.

Parlando, ♪ = cca 106.

280.

1. *N* Pej pa-ri-pám réz-pat-kó-ja de fé-nyës, *M*-
-ma-da-ra-si csár-dás lá-nya de ké-nyës! *N* Ké-nyës ci-pő-
je, kap-cá-ja, De sok pén-zö-met kós-tál-ja, hi-á-ba.

8.

Muz. F. 1003 e); l. Felsőiregh (Tolna), Kolonics Mari (20), 1907.; B.

Tempo giusto. ♩ = 144.

281.

1. Ki-haj-tot-tam én lu-da-mat, Ki-haj-tot-tam
én lu-da-mat A zöld pá-zsit-domb-ra, A zöld pá-zsit-domb-ra.

Muz. F. 803 c); Nagymegyer (Komárom), 1910.; B.

Tempo giusto, ♩ = 168.

282.

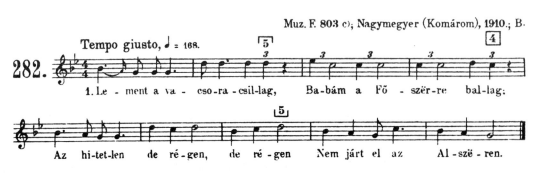

1. Le-ment a va-cso-ra-csil-lag, Ba-bám a Fő-szër-re bal-lag:
Az hi-tet-len de ré-gen, de ré-gen Nem járt el az Al-szë-ren.

9.

F. 1303 c); IV. Jobbágytelke (Maros-Torda), Balog Teréz (17), 1914.; B.

Pi - ros ku-ko - ri - ca szá - ra,— Há - za-so-dom nem-so - ká - ra.

I -ga-zán, csak-u-gyan, nem ta-ga-dom, A ba-bá-mat so-ha el sem ha-gyom.

10.

II. 1916.; P.

1. Su-gár - ma-gas, su-gár - ma-gas A nyár - fa te - te - je,

Hal -vány-sár - ga, de hal -vány-sár - ga An - nak a le - ve - le.

III. Sámson (Hajdu), 1906.; B.

1. Szé - pen szól a kis pa - csir - ta Fent a le-ve - gő - be,—

El köll men - ni ka-to - ná-nak Há - rom esz-ten - dő - re.

III. (Szolnok), 1918.; B.

1. Jász-kun - sá - gi gye-rek va-gyok, Jász-kun-sá - gon zü-let - tem,

Kis - ko-rom-tól nagy - ko-ro-mig Ben-ne fël - ne - ve-led - tem.

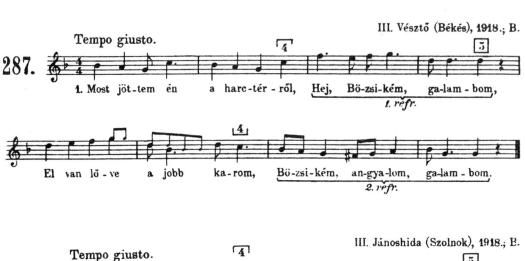

III. Vésztő (Békés), 1918.; B.

287. Tempo giusto.

1. Most jöt-tem én a harc-tér-ről, Hej, Bö-zsi-kém, ga-lam-bom,
1. réfr.

El van lő-ve a jobb ka-rom, Bö-zsi-kém, an-gya-lom, ga-lam-bom.
2. réfr.

III. Jánoshida (Szolnok), 1918.; B.

288. Tempo giusto.

1. Já-nos-hi-di vá-sár-té-ren Er-re gye-re ga-lam-bom.
1. réfr.

Le-gény-vá-sár lesz a hé-ten, Er-re gye-re, gye-re er-re, ga-lam-bom.
2. réfr.

IV. Ákosfalva (Maros-Torda), 1909.; B.

289. Tempo giusto.

Re-cse-gős a csiz-mám, a me-let te vet-tél, E-züst pat-kó a sar-kán,

Va-la-hány-szor lé-pek, any-nyi-szor re-cse-gi: Ked-ve-sem, so-ha-se sze-ret-tél.

11.

Muz. F. 1641 a); II. Derczen (Bereg), Biró Eszter, 1912.; B.

290. Tempo giusto, ♩ = 112.

Sár-ga ku-ko-ri-ca-szál Ka-pá-lat-lan, ka-pá-lat-lan ma-rad-tál.

Sző-ke le-gény, bar-na lány, Ö-le-let-len, csó-ko-lat-lan ma-rad-tál.

Parlando.

IV. Marosvásárhely (Maros-Torda), 1916.; B.

291.

Me-nyek az u-ton le-fe-lé, Sen-ki sem mond-ja: gye-re bé! an-gya-lom.
refr.

Mi-kor jöt-tem visz-sza-fe-lé, Ba-bám azt mond-ja: gye-re bé! an-gya-lom.
refr.

Tempo giusto.

Muz. F. 2320 b, IV. Diósad (Szilágy), Vég Gergely (68), 1914.; L.

292.

Ha tud-tad, hogy nem sze-ret-tél, Az ö-led-be mér ül-tet-tél, tyu-haj-ja?
refr.

Mér csó-kol-tad meg az én szám, Mér nem hagytál bé-két, ró-zsám, tyu-haj-ja?
refr.

Tempo giusto, ♩ = 54.

F. 1299 a.; IV. Jobbágytelke (Maros-Torda), Fülöp Jakabné (69), 1914.; B.

293.

1. Meg-ájj, meg-ájj, te küs ma-dár, Be-teg szü-vem mer riég hogy vár,

ja-jaj ja-ja-jaj, Be-teg va-gyok sze-rel-mem-be,
refr.

Eny-hítsd lel-kem ke-ser-vem-be, ja-jaj ja-ja-jaj.
refr.

Tempo giusto. ♩ = 113.

Muz. F. 1014 a); IV. Csíkrákos (Csík), 1907.; B.

294.

Azt a-kar-tam én meg-tud-ni, Sza-bad-e má-sét sze-ret-ni,

sza-bad-e má-sét sze-ret-ni? Tu-da-koz-tam, de nem sza-bad,

íg a szi-vem, gyász-ban ma-rad, íg a szi-vem, gyász-ban ma-rad.
tu-da-koz-tam, de nem sza-bad,

16.

Muz. F. 953a); I. Felsőiregh (Tolna), 1906.; B.

295 a)

Rubato, ♩ = cca 72.

1. Ti-szán-in-nen. Du-nán-túl, Túl a Ti-szán van egy csi-kós nyá-jas-túl.

Kis pej-lo-va ki van köt-vel, Szűr-kö-tél-lel pakróc nél-kül, gaz-dás - tul.

III. Doboz (Békés), 1906.; B.

295 b)

Tempo giusto.

Ti-szán - in - nen. Du-nán - túl Ott sü-tik a kis ma-la-cot

cser-fa - tű-zön, bikk-fa-nyár-son, Ti-szán - in - nen, Du-nán - túl,—

Gye - re ked - ves kis an - gya - lom az ágy - hoz.

Muz. F. 644d); I. Szombatfa (Zala); V.

296.

Tempo giusto.

Dësz - ka - ka - pu, ke - rí - tés, Az a - latt e - sik jó
Ö - lelj ba - bám, ö - lelj

ö - le - lés. So - ha - sëm ve - tëm a sze - med - re.
ked - ved - re,

III. Doboz (Békés), 1906.; B.

297.

Tempo giusto.

Meg-dög - lött a bi - ró lo - va, Jó lesz a bő-re du-dá-nak,
Meg-nyúz-ta ja bi - ró ma-ga.

A négy lá-ba pi - ku - lá-nak, a fe-je meg ko-cso-nyá-nak, csi-haj - la.

III. Ujszász (Pest), 1918.; B.

Tempo giusto.

298.

1. Kó-nyár Ver-ka ház - e - le - je Már-vány - kő - vel van ki - rak - va.

Jaj de cel - le - ri, cir - ko-mi, cel - le - ri Roz-ma-rin-gi vi - o - la.

refr.

Muz. F. 1002b); I. Felsőiregh (Tolna), 1907.; B.

Parlando, ♩ = 94.

299a)

Bú - za, bú - za, ke - rëk dü-lö bú - za, Le-ven-du-la kö-ze - pi-be,-
Föl - nyőtt ben-ne két szál le-ven-du - la.

gye-re ba-bám az ö-lem-be, Ugy-is tu-dom, ba - bám, nem szeretsz i - ga - zán.

Muz. F. 1001a); I. Felsőiregh (Tolna), 1907.; B.

Tempo giusto, ♩ = 82.

299b)

1. On-nand a - lul jön egy ván-dor - föcs - ke, Kör - me kö-zött

van egy le - ve - lecs - ke. Nin - csen, a - ki el-ol - vas-sa, *no de* nem is ma-gya -

rul van ir - va: Csár-dás kis an - gya - lom, el köll ma-sí - roz - nom.

F. 1504c); IV. Jobbágytelke (Maros-Torda), Balog Teréz (17), 1914.; B.

Tempo giusto. ♩ = 102.

299c)

a) Er - dő, er-dő, er - dő, maros-szé-ki ke-rek er - dő, Cukrot ad-nék
Ma-dár lak-ja asz - tat, madár lak-ja ti-zen - ket-tő.

an-nak a ma-dár-nak, da - lol-ja ki ne-vét a ba-bám-nak,- Csár-dás kis an - gya - lom,

1) var.:

ér-ted fáj a szivem na - gyon.

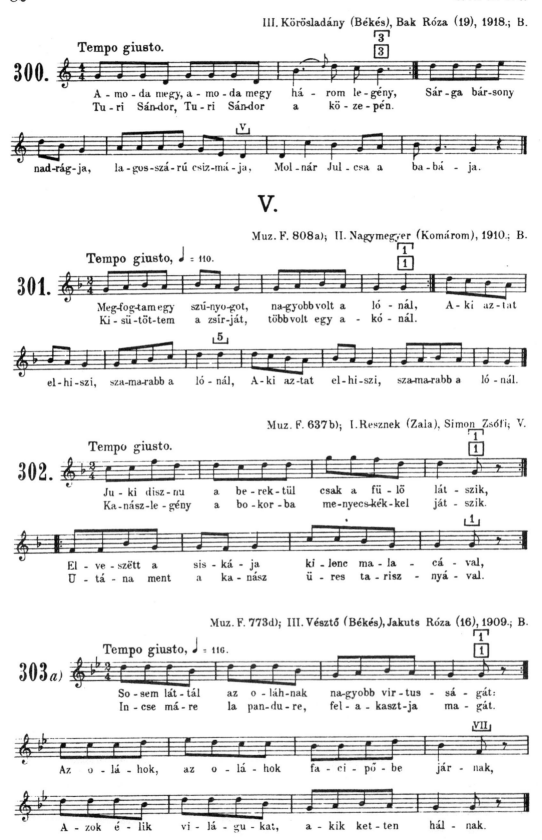

III. Körösladány (Békés), Bak Róza (19), 1918.; B.

Tempo giusto.

300.

A - mo - da megy, a - mo - da megy　há - rom le - gény,　Sár - ga bár-sony
Tu - ri Sán-dor, Tu - ri Sán-dor　a　kö - ze - pén.

nad-rág-ja,　la - gos-szá-rú csiz-má - ja,　Mol-nár Jul - csa a　ba - bá - ja.

V.

Muz. F. 808a); II. Nagymegyer (Komárom), 1910.; B.

Tempo giusto, ♩ = 110.

301.

Meg-fog-tam egy　szú-nyo-got,　na-gyobb volt a　ló - nál,　A - ki az-tat
Ki - sü-töt-tem　a zsír-ját,　több volt egy a - kó - nál.

el - hi-szi,　sza-ma-rabb a　ló - nál,　A - ki az-tat el-hi-szi,　sza-ma-rabb a　ló - nál.

Muz. F. 637b); I. Resznek (Zala), Simon Zsófi; V.

Tempo giusto.

302.

Ju - ki disz - nu　a be - rek - tül　csak a fü - lő　lát - szik,
Ka - nász-le - gény　a bo - kor - ba　me-nyecs-kék-kel　ját - szik.

El - ve - szött a　sis - ká - ja　ki - lenc ma - la - cá - val,
U - tá - na ment　a ka - nász　ü - res ta - risz - nyá - val.

Muz. F. 773d); III. Vésztő (Békés), Jakuts Róza (16), 1909.; B.

Tempo giusto, ♩ = 116.

303 a)

So - sem lát - tál　az o - láh-nak　na-gyobb vir - tus - sá - gát:
In - cse má - re　la pan-du - re,　fel - a - kaszt-ja　ma - gát.

Az o - lá - hok,　az o - lá - hok　fa - ci - pő - be　jár - nak,

A - zok é - lik　vi - lá - gu - kat,　a - kik ket - ten　hál - nak.

Muz. F. 976c); I. Felsőiregh (Tolna), 1907.; B.

Tempo giusto, ♩ = 84.

303 b)

N -Csó - ri ka-nász mit főz-tél? —Tü-dőt ká-posz - tá - val.

-Mi - vel rán-tot - tál be - le? -Ha - sa - sza - lon - ná - val.

-Hát az ö - reg e - szik - e? Tőtsd ne - ki tál - ba.

Ha nem e - szik be - lő - le, vágd a po - fá - já - ho!

Muz. F. 1620b); III. Köröstárkány (Bihar), 1912.; B.

Tempo giusto, ♩ = 108.

303 c)

Ti - éd vol - tam, ti - éd le - szek, de már nem va - gyok,

Azt is tu - dod sok - szor mond-tam, ér - ted meg - ha - lok.

De mi - vel - hogy nem sze - retsz, so - ha fel nem lelsz,

Még Ró - zsa - fát *) völ - gyé - ben ve - lem egy - be - kelsz.

*) = Jozsafát.

ll. Tura (Pest), 1906.; B.

Parlando.

304.

1. Kecs-ke -mét is ki - ál - lít - ja nyal-ka ver-bunk - ját, Gyer-tek i - de
Csár-da e - lőtt ki is tű - zi ve - res zász-ló - ját.

fi - a - ta-lok, tes-sik be - áll - nyi: Nyolc esz-ten-dő nem a vi-lág, le-het pró-bál - nyi.

Muz. F. 998b); I. Felsőiregh (Tolna), 1907.; B.

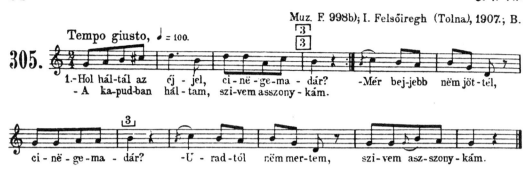

305.

Tempo giusto, ♩ = 100.

1.-Hol hál-tál az éj - jel, ci - në - ge-ma - dár? -Mér bej-jebb nëm jöt-tél,
- A ka-pud-ban hál - tam, szi-vem asszony - kám.

ci - në - ge-ma - dár? -U - rad-tól nëm mer-tem, szi - vem asz-szony-kám.

VI.

III. Doboz (Békés), 1906.; B.

306.

Tempo giusto.

1. Te - rí - ti egy lány a vász - nat Igy meg így, ip - pen így.

Muz. F. 1029c), IV. Tekerőpatak (Csik), 1907.; B.

307.

Tempo giusto, ♪ = 166.

1. Anna, An - na, Molnár An - na, Je-re vé - lem hosz-szú út-ra.

VII.

III. Ujszász (Pest), Dobóczi Bernátné (26), 1918.; B.

308.

Tempo giusto.

1. Fa-lu vé-gin van egy ház. Fa-lu vé-gin uj idrom fidrom Gá-li-ca szikszom van egy ház,
refr.

II. (Hont), 1917.; B.

309.

Tempo giusto.

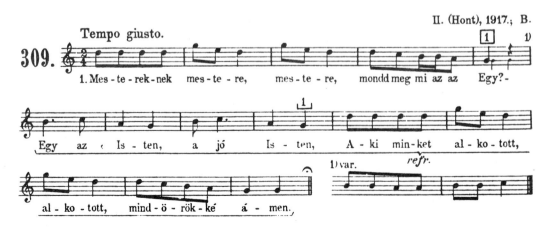

1. Mes - te - rek-nek mes - te - re, mes - te - re, mondd meg mi az az Egy?-

Egy az < Is - ten, a jó Is - ten, A - ki min-ket al - ko - tott,

1) var. *refr.*

al - ko - tott, mind - ö - rök - ké á - men.

310. Tempo giusto, ♩ = 100. [1] [6]
Muz. F. 773c); III. Vésztő (Békés), Jakuts Róza (16), 1909.; B.

a) 1. A kert-me-gi ká-posz-ta, *hm,*   Ká-posz-ta, ká-posz-ta Ki-borult az asz-tal-ra, *hm!*

311. Tempo giusto, ♩ = 132. [2]
Muz. F. 771b); III. Vésztő (Békés), Jakuts Róza (16), 1909.; B.

1. A Var - gá - ék   ab - lak - juk   Ró - zsá - bul   van

ki - rak - va, ki - rak - va,   Ki - rak - va, ki - rak - va, de   ki - rak - va.

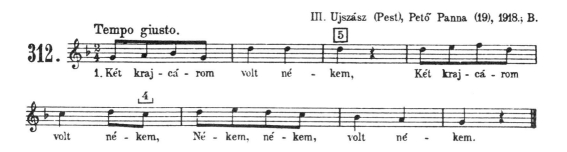

312. Tempo giusto. [5]
III. Ujszász (Pest), Petö Panna (19), 1918.; B.

1. Két kraj - cá - rom   volt   né - kem,   Két kraj - cá - rom

volt   né - kem,   Né - kem, né - kem,   volt   né - kem.

313. Tempo giusto. [8]
IV. Kibéd (Maros - Torda), Dósa Lidi (18), 1904.; B.

Pi - ros   al - ma   le - e - sett a sár - ba,   Ki fel - ve - szi,

nem ve - szi hi - á - ba,   Ki fel - ve - szi,   nem ve - szi hi - á - ba.

314. Tempo giusto, ♩ = 112. [8]
Muz. F. 773b); III. Vésztő (Békés), Jakuts Róza (16), 1909.; B.

1. Meg - é - rett a   meggy a   fán,   meggy a   fán,—

Fér - he ment a   Var - ga lány,   Ic - ca hej - re - hop.
refr.

Muz. F. 957c); 1. Keszthely (Zala), 1906.; B.

315.

Tempo giusto, ♩ = 92.

1. A ka - to - na a me - nyecs - két Er - dő - szél - be csa - lo - gat - ta, Er - dő - szél - be csa - lo - gat - ta.

Muz. F. 1210a); I. Zsida (Vas), Tibola Teréz (17); V.

316.

Tempo giusto.

Szán - tot - tam gyö - pöt, ve - tët - tem gyön - gyöt, Haj - tot - tam á - gát, szëd - tem vi - rá - gát, Ej, huj, ró - zsám, gye - re ve - lem. *refr.*

Muz. F. 923b); III. Békésgyula (Békés), Borek András (40), 1906.; B.

317.

Tempo giusto ♩ = 81.

1. E - ger fe - lé me - gyen egy út, Kin Klim - kó Er - zsi jel - in - dult, Klim - kó Er - zsi, Klim - kó Er - zsi jel - el - in - dult.

Muz. F. 804a); II. Nagymegyer (Komárom), 1910.; B.

318.

Tempo giusto, ♩ = 140.

a) Mëny - asz - szony, vő - le - gény, de szép mind a ket - tő, O - lyan mind a ket - tő, mint az a - rany - vesz - sző, *Hej.* mint az a - rany - vesz - sző.

III. Vésztő (Békés), Kocsis Juhász Róza (15), 1917.; B.

319.

Tempo giusto.

1. Sár - ga csi - kó, csen - gő raj - ta, Va - jon ho - va me - gyünk raj - ta? Hu - zse - dá - ré hu - zse - dom. *refr.*

320.

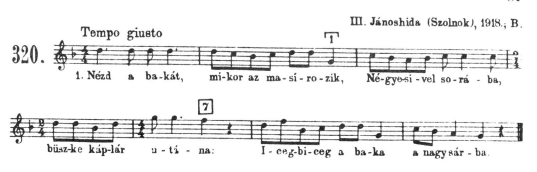

Tempo giusto

1. Nézd a ba-kát, mi-kor az ma-si-ro-zik, Né-gye-si-vel so-rá-ba,

büsz-ke káp-lár u-tá-na: I-ceg-bi-ceg a ba-ka a nagy sár-ba.

Appendix.

I.

Tempo giusto

Muz. F. 621c)

Ik i-äš saš-tər yà-nə̂ kä-pém ə̂-l'ə̂, Ik i-äš saš-tər yà-nə̂ kä-pém ə̂-l'ə̂,

Kuš-kə̂n-šo-tež-ok ú-βém puè-βə̂, Kuš-kə̂n-šo-tež-ok ú-βém puè-βə̂,

II.

Tempo giusto

Muz. F. 622a)

III.

Tempo giusto

Muz. F. 622b)

Jə̂ŋ-gə̂ ðə̂-reš ar-βù-zə̂ sàC-tšeš, Jə̂ŋ-gə̂ ðə̂-reš ar-βù-zə̂-sàC-tšeš,

Ar-βù-zə̂m yatš-kaš kè-mə-dà̂ yò-ðə̂m, Män-mǎ-žəm-ät šiš-tä-ren" gò-ðə̂-ðà

DATE DUE

MAR 1 0 1987 145263 2 08 5-95			